# SACRIFICE

## THE CHRONICLES OF SERVITUDE BOOK TWO

# J. S. BAILEY

OPEN WINDOW

Livonia, Michigan

# SACRIFICE

Published by Open Window
an imprint of BHC Press

Library of Congress Control Number:
2017938460

ISBN-13: 978-1-946848-09-3
ISBN-10: 1-946848-09-3

Visit the author at:
www.jsbaileywrites.com &
www.bhcpress.com

Also available in eBook


Book design by Blue Harvest Creative
www.blueharvestcreative.com

# ALSO BY J.S. BAILEY

## NOVELS

*Rage's Echo*

*The Land Beyond the Portal*

*Servant*
The Chronicles of Servitude, Book One

*Surrender*
The Chronicles of Servitude, Book Three

## NOVELLAS

*Solitude*
A Chronicles of Servitude Story

## SHORT STORY COLLECTIONS

*Ordinary Souls*

## MULTI-AUTHOR ANTHOLOGIES

*Through the Portal*

*Call of the Warrior*

*In Creeps the Night*

*A Winter's Romance*

*The Whispered Tales of Graves Grove*

*Tales by the Tree*

*In loving memory of Herman, Fred, and Rob.*

*Therefore, I urge you, brothers and sisters, in view of God's mercy, to offer your bodies as a living sacrifice, holy and pleasing to God—this is your true and proper worship.*

—Romans 12:1, New International Version

*This is my commandment: Love each other in the same way I have loved you. There is no greater love than to lay down one's life for one's friends.*

—John 15:12-13, New International Version

# 1

GRAHAM WILLARD sat on the edge of the cot in his cell, unable to stop shivering no matter how hard he tried to still his limbs. It wasn't even cold. If he had to guess, he would have said the temperature hovered around seventy degrees, give or take.

So it must have been nerves. He could feel them fraying like the edges of an old cloth. He hadn't entered the world just to be shut away like an animal in the end, yet that's what had happened. If they didn't kill him for what he'd done, he could sit here rotting for the next two decades. One of his grandfathers had lived to be ninety-eight, and Graham was only seventy-five now.

Twenty-three years was far too long to stay here. If Graham wasn't so afraid of what might come after, he would kill himself just to put an end to things.

Ever since he'd arrived in this abode of wasted lives, conflicting thoughts flitted through his mind. For the past year he'd been consumed with plotting Randy Bellison's demise, and finally killing the young man had brought him great satisfaction, but only for a moment.

*But did he die, or did he survive? I can't remember...*

Graham felt a strange hollowness inside of him. He'd loved Randy like a grandson but had to kill him anyway because—

Because why?

Because Graham would be at peace when Randy died.

*But why? Why did I think I would be at peace? Why did I ever think that Randy needed to die?*

He examined these thoughts from every angle and didn't like the conclusion he drew from them. Randy was a good man. A pious man. A man who would have given his own life to save Graham if things had ever come to that. Any person who sought to kill such a man had to harbor great evil in his soul.

"I am not evil," he said aloud.

Graham had killed many people, true, but he hadn't hated them or wished them undue harm. He had used them to understand death better and grant them release from a world of illness and pain. Surely acts such as those couldn't be considered sins. They should have made him a saint.

An inmate in a cell further down the block let out a cry in his sleep. Graham wondered what had brought the man here and if he remained sinless as well.

A sudden memory entered Graham's mind: his daughters Kimberly and Stephanie playing in the yard of the old house near Hillsdale that he and his wife Lisa had finally sold once the girls were gone. There had been a swing set and a mound of sand they pretended was an ocean, and Stephanie would sometimes get the swing going high and then jump off to land in the imaginary water. Kimberly would then run into the house screaming that Stephanie was being dangerous again and to please make her stop before she killed herself.

He wished he could see his daughters now. He hadn't laid eyes upon Stephanie in more than twenty years because Lisa had thrown her out of the house for sleeping with a young man from church, and he hadn't seen Kimberly since before trying to kill Randy the first time.

He pictured Kimberly now: heavyset, with blondish hair and rosy cheeks, and then her face morphed into Lisa's face, and Lisa, dear Lisa who'd ended up cheating on him for no logical reason at all, was crying. *Graham, I'm so sorry, I never meant for things to go that far with him, it was just supposed to be drinks and dinner and nothing more than that, please forgive me, please, please...*

And then from somewhere deep inside a new memory rose from the murk, and Graham saw himself as a young boy running through a golden field in the valley behind his grandparents' house, just running and running, and he felt so free, and nothing terrible would ever happen to him because life was a beautiful thing without sorrow.

The sound of light footsteps coming his way brought Graham crash-landing back into the present, where Lisa was dead, his daughters aloof, and the golden fields of his childhood interred beneath a housing development.

He held his breath. Something in his gut told him this wasn't a guard.

The footfalls ceased when a man dressed in civilian clothing appeared outside the cell. "Graham Willard," he said with a note of amusement in his voice. "It's good to see you."

Graham's mouth hung open in disbelief at the figure staring in at him. "Nate?"

The man dipped his head, remaining mostly in shadow. "It's been a long time."

Graham got to his feet and approached the bars, looking the man up and down to make sure his eyes didn't deceive him. "I don't understand. How did this happen?"

"A miracle from my father," Nate said, his face twisting into a smile.

"Your father?"

"Yes, the one who speaks into my soul. I'm sure you know his name."

Now Graham did feel a chill wash over him. "You're speaking of our Maker?"

Nate gave a light laugh. "Don't be so dense."

"What other father could have done this to you, then?" But before Nate could reply, Graham understood. "Surely you don't mean the Father of Lies."

A smile. "It's funny you should call him that. He has yet to lie to me."

Graham's mind spun like a top. All those conversations they'd had—could Nate have been deceiving him the entire time? "You told me you're a devout man," he said.

"I am."

Nausea crept into Graham's gut at Nate's implication. "You did deceive me."

"Oh, but it's been so *fun*. You've become a rather useful tool in my hands. Just look at the things you've done since we met. Finding those poor sick people and slaughtering them like sheep."

Nate couldn't have known about that. Graham had never told him. "I was doing that before we met," he said.

"Were you?"

Graham's hands tightened into fists. "Do you think I don't know what I've been doing all these years?"

"Yes, I do think that. The mind is an impressionable thing, Mr. Willard. It's amazing what fantasies it can cook up without even being aware of it."

"What I've done is no fantasy. I've brought peace to dozens of people. Dozens!"

"Starting with the drunk and then your grandmother."

"I never told you that." *Had he?*

Nate shrugged.

"And all the others?"

"Some you killed. Some you didn't. I'll bet you can't even tell the difference."

Graham glared at him. "You're just trying to mess with me."

"Am I?"

"Why are you here?"

"Because I'm finished with you. You're used up. Can't you feel it inside?"

Nate's words filled him with alarm.

Nate went on. "It's time for us to part ways, my dear friend. I admit I've enjoyed working with you. It's a pity I can't use you further."

A spike of agony drove itself through Graham's head the moment Nate turned and retreated in the direction from which he'd come, and he collapsed to the floor with a tear running down his cheek.

# 2

JACK WILLARD sat at the bar counter rolling a quarter across his knuckles, glaring at the bubbles in the glass of Bud Light in front of him.

His internal burners had set his anger to a low simmer.

"You all right there, Johnny Boy?" Chuck, the bartender, asked as he mopped up a spill with a rag that might have been yellow in a former life.

Jack jerked his head up. "It's none of *your* business if I am or not."

Chuck stuck out his bottom lip and gave a halfhearted shrug. "Sorry. You look like you've got a lot on your mind this evening."

*And you look like you're asking for a black eye.* He'd never liked Chuck. The man couldn't mind his own business if his life depended on it. Jack put on a placating smile. "Don't we all?"

Chuck gave a sharp bark of a laugh. "Not me. All's on my mind is a good beer and a good babe. You let me know if you need anything else."

Jack continued brooding. He was a wanted man who hadn't been back to his apartment in days because police watched it day and night. His grandfather was in prison awaiting sentencing, and before good old Grandpa got carted away by a bunch of uniformed pigs, he'd said that he'd murdered his dying grandmother by helping her overdose on pills.

Jack set the quarter aside and took a slow gulp of the amber liquid that was supposed to help him relax. The woman Graham had killed would have been Jack's great-great grandmother. He wondered what her name was. What she'd been like before she fell asleep forever at Graham Willard's hand.

What bothered Jack more than anything was that hearing about the woman's murder *did* bother him. It didn't make sense. Graham had murdered scores of people over the years and Jack admired him for it. Too often people feared doing what they wanted because they would be punished if caught. Not Graham. Jack's grandfather had been a bold, sly dog who'd found his calling and gone after it without reservation.

But he'd killed his own *grandmother*. Why, if that woman had never existed at all, Jack never would have been born, either, and that was a tragedy Jack wasn't willing to contemplate.

Jack drank more of the beer, ordered another, and then picked up the quarter and started rolling it across his knuckles again.

A lanky, fortyish woman with limp, black hair that hadn't been washed for at least a week staggered up to the bar and occupied the stool next to Jack's. With the way she moved, she'd been drinking already that evening, most likely at a different bar since Jack hadn't seen her when he came in. Wet stains were evident on her blouse and torn jeans—she must have sloshed a drink on herself prior to her arrival.

"That's a neat little trick," she said, eyeing the quarter as it traveled from Jack's thumb toward his pinky and repeated the process. "How do you do that?"

Jack wasn't particularly in the mood for talking to anyone, but he put on a smile and looked the woman in the eye. No makeup adorned her pale face. "It's a piece of cake," he said, bringing the quarter to a halt between his thumb and forefinger. "All you've got to do is—"

"What'll it be, ma'am?" The nosy barkeep was back and giving the woman a lascivious look Jack didn't feel she deserved.

The woman tore her eyes away from Jack's quarter. "I'll have a Miller Lite." She slid two disintegrating five-dollar bills across the counter with a hand that trembled when she moved it. "You keep the change."

Jack composed his face to hide his amusement. *Too drunk to count money, too.*

When a tall glass of beer had been filled from the tap and set in front of her along with a receipt, she returned her attention to Jack. "Sorry, honey. You were saying?"

"Quarter rolling is easy. Look." He stuck the quarter between his thumb and index finger. "You flip it over the top until it's here." The quarter now rested on its edge between his index and middle fingers. "You do that all the way to the end. Then you pass it under your hand from your pinky back to your thumb and do it all over again. You have to do it a lot if you want to be fast."

The woman tilted back her glass and licked her lips when she'd set it back down. "I don't know," she said, uncertain. "It looks tricky."

*Only because you haven't tried doing it, you old bag.* Jack knew her type. This was a woman who'd always wanted everything handed to her. If something looked too difficult to get right the first go around, then it couldn't be done. She was probably one of those mooches who couldn't keep a job and lived off of good old Uncle Sam, the world's largest enabler. "Only at first," he said. "Like I said, it takes practice."

"I've never been much of one for practicing things." She smiled, but there was no joy in it.

"So...are you from around here?" He set the quarter down to see if she'd try to pocket it when he wasn't looking.

"Oh, no," she said. "I'm from Ohio. I've been in Michigan for a long time, though."

"That's a long way from here."

"Yeah, well, it needed to be done. Coming here, I mean. My name's Adrian, by the way. Adrian Pollard."

Jack wasn't about to give her his real name, so he supplied her with a false one. "And I'm John Yockey. It's nice to meet you."

Technically, his name should have been John Yockey. Though he'd never met his father (his mother had conceived him at a wild party one summer in Sacramento), Stephanie Willard had told him the man's name was William Joseph Yockey III. Jack was surprised she'd been lucid enough to remember it. At one time Jack had searched for the man and had some of his contacts look him up only to learn that Mr. Yockey sold insurance in Eureka and raised orchids as a hobby.

Like he was going to sit down with good old Dad and talk about flowers. It was surprising that someone who sounded so boring could have fathered someone like *him*.

Adrian's cheeks flushed. "A young man with manners," she said. "Wonders never cease." She continued draining her glass.

"My mother always told me that manners are the lubricant of society," Jack said, wearing a smirk. "So what brings you to Oregon?"

"Hold on a minute." Adrian's glass was empty so she called for another. Chuck informed her it would be on the house.

With her new glass in hand, she said, "I'm looking for my son."

For the first time since she'd arrived at the bar, Jack was genuinely interested in their conversation. "Oh?"

Adrian's expression darkened. "I was so young. So *stupid*."

"Mother also said we can't ever mature unless we make mistakes and learn from them." Stephanie Willard had strived to pound a sense of morality into him, even after she'd pretty much failed at it herself.

The woman gave a halting laugh. "I learned from mine a little too late. I just hope I can fix what I broke."

"Where does your son come into this?"

"He's one of the things I broke."

"You beat him?"

She shook her head. "I did a whole lot worse than that. I abandoned him."

Jack had no words. His own mother had been looser than an unscrewed light bulb, but at least she'd had the sense to take care of him and his half sister Chloe, who had been conceived when Stephanie couldn't make rent on the apartment one month and slept with the landlord as payment.

Adrian went on. "His daddy and I were together two years when I got pregnant. I loved how I could feel our baby kicking around in there and I knew I'd be the best mother in the world. I was going to name him after my dad who died when I was just a little thing." She paused to tuck a strand of greasy hair behind her ear. "He was tiny when he was born—just five pounds—but other than that, he was healthy as a horse. That's what the doctor told me. I said I didn't think horses were supposed to be that small and the doctor just laughed. So we went home, me and Ken and our new little boy. And then..." She blinked, and Jack saw that her gray-blue eyes had filled with tears.

Jack held his breath.

"I left them when my little baby was just a week old. And you want to know why?"

"Why?" Jack asked quietly.

"Because I was *stupid*!"

At this point several heads swiveled their direction. Jack saw some of the regulars snickering like this was the most entertaining thing they'd seen all week.

Adrian wasn't finished. "I did it in the middle of the night, too, so Ken wouldn't know I'd gone. That was the worst part because I really did love him. But I couldn't stay. I didn't know a thing about raising kids. So I left."

Jack's anger simmered again. If the woman couldn't take the time to learn to flip a stinking quarter across her knuckles, then it only made sense that she wouldn't bother learning how to take care of her own kid, either.

Adrian continued. "I had three other babies after that. One with a guy in Dayton, Ohio. Two more in Michigan. They've all got different daddies."

"And you left all of them?"

She nodded.

The tiniest shred of sympathy he'd felt for the forty-year-old wreck of a woman sitting next to him evaporated on the spot. He remembered watching *The Price is Right* with his mother when he was a small boy. At the end of each show Bob Barker would remind viewers to get their pets spayed or neutered. Well, it wasn't just pets that needed to be fixed. All the Adrian Pollards of the world needed to be fixed too so they wouldn't keep passing sheer idiocy on to future generations.

"So *why* are you in Oregon?" he asked in a voice that came out sounding dangerously soft.

Adrian took no notice of his change in mood. "Because after all these years I finally grew up. My son's out here somewhere. I intend to find him."

What a heartwarming reunion that was bound to be. Jack wondered if her son was one of the other urchins that had crawled into the bar that evening. "Do you have his address?"

"I sure do. I just haven't worked up the courage to go see him."

*I can't imagine why.* "What will you say when you do see him?"

She swallowed and looked away. "I'll tell him I'm sorry."

Yeah, right. People like her didn't have a sorry bone in their bodies. "So what's this fine young man's name?"

"We named him Robert Roland." Adrian's eyes welled up with tears. "His stepmother says they call him Bobby."

# 3

MIDNIGHT JUST changed over to morning when, in high
spirits, Bobby Roland pulled up in front of his new rental house on
Oakland Avenue in Autumn Ridge, Oregon. He'd experienced no
premonitions for days, his Nissan sported a new set of tires (Jack
Willard slashed the old ones beyond repair), and the new house
had the lowest monthly rent of any place he'd lived in, and it wasn't
even a dump.

In fact, it was the sort of house that Charlotte, his stepmother
back in Ohio, would have called "cute"—one story, brown siding, a small covered porch with one step leading up to the door.
Bobby had even gone to Walmart's garden center the day before
and bought a couple of terracotta pots and some bagged dirt and
planted orange and purple impatiens to liven the place up a bit.
Currently the pots sat on either end of the porch like a pair of flam-
boyant sentinels.

A cloud of moths swarmed around the porch light as he
approached the door, key in hand. He'd spent the past five hours
vacuuming, dusting, and sanitizing every surface inside St. Paul's

Catholic Church, and he couldn't wait to shower and slip into a pair of boxers so he could lounge around drinking Sprite and picking out new tunes on his guitar until he got tired and went to bed around three.

He swung the screen door open and jerked backward.

A white envelope was taped to the inner door at the height of his face. Someone had drawn a red smiley face on it—hopefully in paint and not blood.

*It's okay,* the Spirit inside of him murmured. *You may open it.*

Bobby's skin crawled as he touched a finger to the smiley face on the envelope. He had the uncanny sensation that someone hiding in the shadows was spying on him to see what he would do. He swept his gaze across the dark yard, where the outline of a large maple was silhouetted against the light from a neighbor's post lamp. Seeing no one, he faced the door again and carefully peeled the tape off the wood so it wouldn't damage the paint. He flipped the envelope over and pulled up the flap.

At least two sheets of inkjet paper nestled within. He reached to pull them out when the weight of immense terror crashed down upon him, bringing him to his knees.

A genderless voice spoke with a sneer inside his mind as his vision went black. *You deserve this,* Servant.

"Who are you?" he croaked, even though he knew the answer.

*We didn't want you, and now you're going to pay.*

Bobby's vision cleared as quickly as it had gone dark. He was still kneeling on the porch. The light above him continued to glow with yellow indifference, and one of the moths bashing itself against the light fixture took a sudden dive into Bobby's face. He flailed, dropped the envelope, and blushed profusely as he stood up on wobbly legs.

He doubted there had been a Servant this jumpy in the entire history of Servants.

Many entities who longed to harass him would be watching him now that he'd taken on this position. Until now, the past few days had been harassment-free. Phil Mason had cautioned him not to let his guard down—ever. The demons, Phil said, would want to lull Bobby into a false sense of security so he'd be an easier target.

Bobby wasn't about to grant them the pleasure of trying to torment him. "You can't hurt me," he said into the night before unlocking the door. And based on the events of the previous week, he had reason to believe they couldn't as long as he prayed.

Inside, Bobby threw on the overhead light and sat down in the kitchen at a cheap card table he'd purchased after he learned the new house didn't have a built-in island like the old one. Hoping but doubting the envelope contained a friendly note left by a neighbor he had yet to meet, he slid out the papers and unfolded them.

And felt his stomach flip.

One showed a photograph that shouldn't have been printed on such thin paper because the ink had made it ripple. The other was a note, and Bobby hoped to God it hadn't been left by a neighbor since someone had clipped letters of various fonts, colors, and sizes out of a newspaper and glued them onto the sheet ransom-note-style to spell the sentence *I know something you don't.*

So simple. So succinct.

And so recent, because the glue adhering the letters to the paper hadn't dried.

The note had to be some weirdo's idea of a joke. Welcome to the neighborhood, Mr. Roland. Don't mind the serial killers.

The thing that made it seem less like a joke—aside from the demonic voice that had tried to frighten him—was the photograph on the other paper. The image had captured a gaunt, dark-haired woman midstride in front of a log cabin that had small, square windows open high up on the walls. She wore a faded turquoise blouse and tan shorts that stopped just above her knobby knees, and a giant tote bag was slung over her shoulder. Her haunting gaze was fixed on a point somewhere beyond and to the left of whoever had taken the picture.

Was this supposed to be someone he knew? Bobby squinted, tilted the picture to different angles, and held it at a distance from his face. Nope. He'd never seen her before. He was sure of it.

The envelope with its sinister red smile might have been taped to his door by mistake. He'd only lived here a few days. The note may have been intended for a previous tenant.

His new landlord, a squat black man named Kent Lawson, had mentioned that the house sat empty for a week before Bobby moved in. It was possible someone didn't know the former renters had moved.

Bobby crossed the kitchen and grabbed a Sprite out of the refrigerator, then sipped on it while he decided on a course of action. One: he could ignore the whole matter and move on with his life, but he had never been one for ignoring things so that was out of the question.

Two: he could go outside and try to find whoever left the envelope.

Gritting his teeth, Bobby turned off the kitchen light, opened the back door just a sliver, and held an eye to the opening. He could barely make out the tall fence at the back of the yard. Nothing out there moved.

*A false sense of security...*

If something invisible started chucking rocks at him he would probably run and barricade himself in the bathroom with a Bible and the bottle of holy water he'd acquired at church, but when stillness continued to reign, he crept out into the night with all senses on full alert.

A quick search of the postage-stamp-sized yard revealed nothing.

To be honest, he hadn't expected much different.

He stomped back into the kitchen and switched the light on. "Could you please give me some advice?"

The image of his new landlord's face filled his head. Kent Lawson was sixty years old and had about as much hair as a cue ball. He told Bobby he'd once been in the Marines, though Bobby had difficulty picturing it since no Marine would have been permitted to weigh as much as Kent.

Should he call Kent now? The note and photograph didn't exactly constitute an emergency, and Kent and his wife might not take kindly to being awakened at this hour over something that could very well wait until morning.

"Heck with it." Bobby wasn't going to be able to sleep until he'd learned something. He slid his phone out of his pocket and dialed Kent's number.

Kent picked up on the second ring, sounding surprisingly awake. "Lawson speaking. Who's this?"

"Kent, it's Bobby, your new renter. Sorry to bother you so late."

The man's tone changed in an instant. "What's the matter? Did something happen to my house?"

Bobby half expected to hear windows shatter as bad guys forced their way in with clubs and guns, but all remained still. "Not exactly. I probably shouldn't have called."

"No, that's fine. Marge and I've been up watching old movies on AMC. What kind of bee is trapped in your bonnet?"

Bobby wasn't about to tell him about the items in the envelope. "I was wondering about the people who lived here right before me. What are their names?"

"Looking to write them a letter calling them fools for moving out of a showplace like that?"

Bobby tried to sound upbeat even though the sensation of dread continued to swell within him. "Sure."

The phone line was filled with the sound of Kent's hearty laugh. "Got a pen? Their names are Jenny and Myron Asher, and they didn't leave me a forwarding address so I'm afraid you're out of luck if you're looking for some new pen pals."

Bobby committed the names to memory. "Does Jenny have dark brown hair?" he asked as he returned his attention to the slender woman in the photograph. Her eyes were haunted pools in her white face.

"Afraid not. Her hair's as red as Lucille Ball's. She's kind of pudgy, too, but not as pudgy as me." He chuckled. "So what else do you want to know? Eye color? Dates of birth? Social security numbers?"

"Actually, I wondered where they worked."

"The Home Depot. They might still be there for all I know."

"Were they ever involved in anything shady?"

"I never saw the cops over there, if that's what you mean. They seemed like nice folks."

"Why'd they move out?"

"Because they knew a nosy kid would need a place to live sooner or later. How should I know? I don't pry into people's business, unlike you, apparently."

It didn't look like Kent had any useful information after all. At least Bobby couldn't say he hadn't tried. "I think my prying is done for now. Enjoy the rest of your movie."

Bobby laid the phone down when he ended the call. He doubted the Ashers had anything to do with the envelope and its contents. That meant whoever left it either had the wrong house or really did intend for it to fall into Bobby's hands.

The Spirit that dwelled inside of him now that Bobby had taken on the mantle of Servitude—a position granting him the ability to cast evil spirits out of the possessed—remained silent. Phil said that while Bobby would always be able to sense God's Spirit during his years as the Servant, it wouldn't always provide him with the answers he desired.

It would have been nice, though.

Knowing he would never be able to concentrate on playing his guitar at this point, Bobby wished he had someone human to talk to. Problem was, Phil Mason and his wife Allison would undoubtedly be asleep, Randy Bellison was recovering at home from a violent altercation with his old mentor, Lupe Sanchez had gone through so much turmoil that Bobby wasn't about to burden her with anything else, and Carly Jovingo...

His face flushed. Even though Carly had been friendly to him for the past week, he couldn't forget the silly argument they'd had on the day they met. Phil had brought a bewildered Bobby to the Servants' safe house to talk to Randy, and Bobby, knowing nothing of the Servants at that time, accused Carly and Randy of being part of a religious cult.

Carly, who counseled many of the victims Randy healed, hadn't taken kindly to that.

She seemed to have forgiven Bobby for being a jerk, though. The day after Bobby took Randy's place as the Servant Carly gave Bobby her cell phone and home numbers and told him to call her whenever he wanted. After all, she said, Bobby was now technically her boss, which made him far more uncomfortable than it probably should have.

He entered her number into his phone and hit send before he could convince himself to wait until morning.

While he waited for her to pick up, he gazed at the rippled picture. "Who are you?" he asked the woman by the cabin. "And why did somebody put you on my door?"

Carly's voice startled him. "Hey." A muffled note in that single word made it sound like she'd been crying.

Bobby swallowed, unsure of what to say now that Carly was on the line and clearly not in a great mood. "Hey," he replied, silently cursing himself for his lack of eloquence. "Are you all right?"

She sniffled. "Are you?"

He wanted to ask what was wrong but feared he'd accidentally alienate her as he had when they met. "I have a mystery on my hands."

"A mystery?"

"Yeah, but if it's a bad time, I can tell you about it in the morning."

"Technically speaking, it is morning."

"I meant the part of morning that can't be confused with night."

More sniffling. "I'm awake now, Bobby. If something's bothering you, tell me."

Here went nothing. "Someone left a funny note on my door. I wondered if you might know who sent it."

"Was it Roger? That sounds like something he might do."

"I'm about a million percent sure it wasn't him." Roger Stilgoe, like Randy and Phil, was formerly a Servant. Bobby met him a few days previously when a meeting of all the former Servants minus Randy was called together to discuss the training Bobby would have to undergo before he faced his first victim.

Round-faced Roger was in his fifties and had salt-and-pepper hair and a perpetual twinkle in his eyes that made it look as though

something constantly amused him. Bobby could picture him playing lighthearted jokes on his friends, but the note left in the envelope seemed too sinister to have come from him.

"But you said it was funny."

"I meant weird funny. They left a picture of some woman, too.
I wondered if any of you might know who she is."

"What's she look like?"

"Tall, skinny, dark brown hair. She might be in her forties."

"That could be a zillion different people. Want me to come
over and take a look?"

"Carly, it's after *midnight*."

"So? You called me. Besides, I can't sleep."

"But—"

"You can't throw this on me and expect me not to do something. I'll be there in a jiffy."

Before Bobby could continue to object, the line went dead.

He put his head in his hands. "Crap."

———◆———

A TIMID knock sounded on Bobby's door ten minutes later.
Before unlatching the deadbolt, Bobby peered through the peephole. His stomach fluttered when he saw Carly waiting for him to
let her in.

Carly had tied her auburn hair back in a sloppy ponytail and
put on flannel pajama shorts and a white tank top. In addition to
her purse, she carried a bag of chips and a six-pack of Sprite in glass
bottles—a peace offering if he had ever seen one.

Bobby pulled the door open, fully aware that he had yet to
take the shower he'd desired prior to finding the envelope. Dirt he'd
picked up from somewhere inside the church smudged his gray
t-shirt, and he was fairly sure he smelled like something that was
supposed to live in a barn.

Carly's eyes were puffy and bloodshot.

"You look nice," he blurted when he realized he might have
been staring just a little bit too long.

"You're full of crap." Carly stepped past him and went through the living room into the kitchen.

Bobby closed and re-bolted the door. "Do you want to *not* look nice?"

She was already digging around in a drawer, probably looking for a bottle opener—she had helped him unpack and organize when he'd made the big move from the bungalow over on Fir Street, so she probably knew where his things were better than he did. "I'm here to help solve a mystery, not to look pretty. Or was that just a ruse to get me to come out here?"

"Coming here was your idea. Don't you ever sleep?"

Carly held up the bottle opener in triumph and slid the drawer shut. "I sleep plenty. One little night of insomnia isn't going to hurt anything. Have some chips." She proceeded to pry the lid off of one of the Sprite bottles and eyed Bobby's can of the same drink with disgust. "So this is the great mystery." She picked up the papers after setting aside her drink, and her expression faltered. "I can see why this might have caused you some concern."

Bobby's heart sank. He'd hoped she would recognize the woman. "Don't you know who she is?"

"Nope. But this cabin looks like one of the shower houses at Mountain Lake State Park."

"Where's that?"

"About thirty miles east of here, in the middle of nowhere. I went with some girlfriends last summer. Are you going to have some chips or not?"

He wasn't hungry, but to appease her he tore open the bag and popped a barbecue-flavored crisp into his mouth. "That doesn't help me figure out who she is or why she was on my door."

"No, it doesn't."

Bobby didn't bother masking his disappointment. "I just don't get it."

"Me neither." Carly withdrew a single chip from the bag and chewed it slowly, deep in thought. "You could take these to the police."

"What are they going to do? Leaving papers on my door isn't a crime."

"Hmm." Carly bit her lip. "Whoever did this clearly wants to taunt you about something."

"Yeah. Something I don't know a thing about. Maybe this just means I'm stupid."

"Don't say that about yourself." Carly sat down in one of the folding camp chairs Bobby had brought with him from when he'd lived in Utah and put her head in her hands. Her eyes reddened as if she were desperately trying to hold in more tears.

Not wanting to come across as a total dunce, Bobby said, "I know it's not any of my business, but—"

Her lips formed a faint smile, and a single tear glistened on her eyelashes. "I'm fine. I really am."

"You're a counselor. Shouldn't you let other people counsel you if something's wrong?"

"I don't think you can counsel me, Bobby, but thanks for asking. So what are you going to do about Mystery Woman?"

So much for wanting to find out what was bothering her. "Nothing, I guess, unless the person who dropped this off is going to come back with an explanation."

Carly picked up the picture again. "She looks lost."

"I know." Bobby rubbed at his chin. "Do you think she knew someone was taking her picture?"

"I'm not *that* good at reading people."

Bobby racked his mind for ideas and came up with zip.

Then it hit him. "Someone's stalking her."

Carly gave a thoughtful nod. "I can see that. But if you don't know her, why would someone leave this here?"

"That seems to be the central question."

As Bobby reached for his can of Sprite to finish it off and start on one of the bottles, the too-familiar jolt of terror signifying an oncoming premonition filled his veins.

Carly, detecting his abrupt change in mood, said, "What is it?"

Bobby was already moving out of the kitchen as he processed what the premonition was telling him. "Someone's outside. They need me to help them." *Hurry, hurry, hurry!* a voice from within shouted at him.

He fumbled with the locks and flung the door open, his heart beating so fast that dizziness threatened to overcome him. He raced outside through the swarm of moths and into the driveway, blinking so his eyes would adjust to his darker surroundings, then looked up and down the street to try to find the person who needed him.

Carly was right on his heels. "Is this one of your premonitions?"

He didn't answer. He swiveled his head to the right, where a street lamp illuminated a four-way stop, then to the left, where most of the houses sat in the unbroken shadows of night.

A human form that he couldn't quite make out stood in darkness on the other side of the street about six houses down from his. Not knowing if he or she was to be the victim or the perpetrator, Bobby set off in a jog to prevent whatever it was that needed preventing.

A flash of headlights coming from behind made Bobby halt and glance back. A white work van had just turned onto Oakland Avenue from another street and passed Bobby in a matter of seconds.

It stopped next to the person standing on the opposite sidewalk, blocking him or her from view.

Faint voices carried through the night. Then a high-pitched scream that was quickly muffled and silenced froze the blood in Bobby's veins. By the time he convinced his feet to start moving again, the van accelerated and disappeared from view.

The figure he had seen was gone.

Carly caught up to him, panting and holding her side. "What happened?"

Bobby stared helplessly after the van. He didn't have time to run back inside, find his keys, and hop into his Nissan, which Carly had inconveniently blocked in with her car.

"Bobby?"

His breath hitched in his chest as the full weight of dread slammed back into him. "I should have run faster. Then I might have stopped them."

"What are you talking about?"

"I'm too slow, that's what!" Tears stung his eyes. "Phil told me I need to get into shape. Now I know why."

"Are you going to keep speaking in riddles? What did you see?"

Bobby started back toward the house, his head now pounding. "Someone in that van just swiped someone off the sidewalk, and I wasn't fast enough to stop them."

# 4

A SINGLE police cruiser glided into Bobby's driveway at 12:30 am without the clangor of sirens or lights.

Two uniformed officers—a man and a woman—climbed out and approached Bobby's porch, where he and Carly had chosen to wait with the open bag of chips sitting between them.

Bobby rose, brushing chip crumbs from his hands.

"Mr. Roland?" asked the male officer, a fortyish man who looked capable of bench pressing a car. His nametag identified him as D. Dodgson.

"That's me." Bobby glanced over at Carly, who was on the verge of crying again. He didn't know if the source of her sorrow was the apparent kidnapping, the unnamed thing that had upset her prior to his calling her on the phone, or both.

"I understand there was some kind of disturbance here."

"Well, not here exactly. It was down the street."

The female officer—F. Jergens—was already jotting down notes, her mouth set in a firm line. "Could you please describe what happened?"

Bobby had already fabricated a plausible cover story so he wouldn't have to explain anything about his premonitions. "I was walking Carly out to her car when a van stopped down the street. I thought I saw someone standing on the sidewalk before that."

"Approximately what time was this?"

"About 12:20. The van stopped next to them and we heard screaming, and when the van pulled away nobody was there anymore. We thought someone must have opened the passenger side of the van and pulled the other person into it."

"Can you describe the vehicle?"

Bobby strained to think. He'd been so caught up in the moment that he recalled few details. "It was a white work van that didn't have windows in the back."

"It was a Trautmann Electric Company van," Carly said. "I saw the logo when it went by."

The two officers exchanged a glance. "I'll be darned," Jergens muttered as she scribbled down the name.

"Wait a minute," Dodgson said, his eyes widening in surprise. "You're the Jovingo girl, aren't you?"

Carly gave a wordless nod.

Bobby didn't dare ask what had brought on this sudden exchange.

"Sweet Jesus," the man murmured. "I'm so sorry."

Carly cast her gaze down at her feet. "Thanks."

Officer Dodgson seemed to forget that he was in the middle of conducting an investigation, for his face became incensed. "I couldn't believe they let her out early. Good behavior, they said. Well, what did they expect? She couldn't get hold of a gun while she was locked up."

Bobby looked to Carly for an explanation, but she wouldn't look at him.

Officer Jergens lightly cleared her throat and eyed her partner with some disdain. "Could we please get back on track?"

Dodgson sighed and became all business once more. "Okay," he said to Bobby. "Show us where you saw this happen."

Bobby pointed at one of the houses on the other side of the street. "It was over there in front of that big brick house. Do you want me to go over there?"

Officer Jergens smiled. "That won't be necessary. If we have any more questions, we'll be back. Enjoy the rest of your evening."

Bobby took that as his cue to go back inside. He and Carly watched from the front window as the cruiser backed out of the driveway and approached the place where the person had vanished. Soon flashlight beams swept the ground as the officers examined the scene. Next they would probably knock on a few doors to see if any of the neighbors had witnessed the kidnapping.

"Who do you think that was out there?" Carly asked.

Bobby thought about the dark-haired woman in the photograph. "Hopefully nobody we know."

⸎

HE AND Carly stayed up for a while longer bouncing ideas off of each other, and when they continued to get nowhere with their speculations, Carly announced she was going home to try to get some sleep.

She left the Sprite bottles and partially-eaten bag of chips behind.

Bobby had refrained from asking her about Officer Dodgson's strange comments because he knew he'd likely get more information out of a brick wall. He didn't need to be a genius to know that what had upset Carly was the same thing that had upset the officer.

Having three mysteries to ponder now—the note, the apparent kidnapping, and the source of Carly's distress—Bobby stripped out of his clothes and let hot water blast him clean in the shower for ten blissful minutes. He toweled off, put on a clean pair of boxers, and sat on the edge of his bed with his baby blue Fender Stratocaster. He fingered an A minor chord and picked the first notes of "Stairway to Heaven," but his eyelids grew heavier and after a few measures he set the guitar aside and turned off the light.

Despite his fatigue, sleep remained elusive for him as well.

"Who is she?" he asked the ceiling. "Can you at least tell me that?"

Eventually his mind conjured images that were only half-dreams, as he still had the sense he lay in bed. The dark-haired woman stood wild-eyed at the end of the bed with her hands clasped together in front of her. "Who am I, Bobby?" she asked in Carly's voice. "Who am I? Can you tell me who I am? Who am I? Who am I? Who am I?"

A scuffling noise outside made him jerk awake before he could tell her he didn't know. He lay still, waiting for the sound to repeat itself, but all remained quiet.

Unlike in his old bungalow, his bedroom here sat at the front of the house. He rose, peeked out through the blinds, and saw a car of indeterminate color and make slowly drive by.

The sound had probably been nothing.

*A false sense of security...*

He walked out into the living room anyway and opened the front door.

Another envelope—complete with red smiley face—was taped in the same place where the other one had been. He tore it off, took it to the kitchen, and withdrew another ransom-note-style message:

*Missed her by that much.*

———————◆———————

**BOBBY ATE** his breakfast bagel at the card table in the kitchen with the two notes and the photograph laid out in front of him, wondering if detectives usually felt this frustrated when trying to piece together clues to solve a mystery.

Upon rising at eight o'clock, he'd gone outside and scoured the tiny lot again to see if the nameless Bringer of Notes had left any indication of who he or she might be. Although Bobby had the lanky build of the constantly-eating Norville "Shaggy" Rogers, this was not an episode of Scooby-Doo. Criminals just didn't leave trails of footprints behind that would lead to their capture, and they were (usually) smart enough not to leave personal items lying around that could be traced back to them.

He could just forget about the woman and the notes, of course. God knew he'd have enough on his plate already working up the courage to face the possessed. But last week when he met Randy, who devoted his entire life to aiding those in need, Bobby realized something: while Bobby had always tried to save people whenever a premonition told him someone was in danger, he had never made an active effort to help others.

He would no longer be so laid back in regard to his fellow humans, and not just because he was now the Servant.

It was a fact that was still difficult for Bobby to fully accept. He had often been angry with God for scores of reasons he didn't want to think about at the moment, and now he was gifted with the ability to sense God's Spirit—a sensation that reminded him of what it might feel like if a coach or mentor was hanging out nearby at all hours of the day ready to dish out encouragement and advice.

It was interesting, to say the least.

Bobby paused in his pondering to sip at his coffee, then refocused his attention on the second note to try to glean further meaning from it.

*Missed her by that much.*

Missed who? The woman in the photograph? Perhaps Bobby was making connections where none existed, but it seemed like the person who'd left the notes must have observed the kidnapping, which would indicate that he or she had helped orchestrate it.

It also meant that the dark-haired woman and the figure standing in shadow on the other side of the street were one and the same.

Wondering if word of the kidnapping would appear on the news, he went to the living room and switched on the television.

"Is Autumn Ridge the new vehicle theft capital of Southwest Oregon?" a news anchor was saying as soon as the picture came up. "Some residents think so. Since January of this year, more than a hundred cars, trucks, and vans have vanished from their owners' driveways, never to be seen again. Law enforcement has been working to uncover a possible theft ring."

The screen changed and showed a picture of a Trautmann Electric Company van.

"Local businessman Bill Trautmann has not been immune to this string of thefts. Just last night he reported one of his company vans missing from his lot. He told us at Channel 8 News that he will not press charges if the van is quietly returned undamaged.

"Police advise residents to keep their cars locked at all times and to keep an eye out for suspicious activity." The anchor ended by providing a number for people to call if they had any information about the thieves.

"Huh." Bobby went to the window and breathed a sigh of relief when he saw that his Nissan had been spared.

He switched off the TV when the news ended and went back to the kitchen, disappointed that nothing had been mentioned about an abduction. He wished he knew Mystery Woman's name. It would feel nicer to think of her as someone with an identity.

*What can I do to help her?*

He stared at the picture on the table and at the cabin-like building in the background. The woman stood partly in shadow, and the quality of the light made it appear the picture had been taken sometime during the morning.

What was it Carly had said? That's right. The building looked like one of the shower houses at a state park she'd visited, but Bobby couldn't remember its name.

He called Carly's cell phone, and she picked up in a breathless voice. "Hello?"

"Carly? This is Bobby."

"I told you I'm fine."

"No, it's not that. Are you busy this morning?"

"I'm unemployed and live with my parents. You tell me."

"Then I hope you're up for a road trip."

# 5

JACK FELT immeasurably better about himself than he had at the bar the other night as he sauntered into the office of his employer, Troy Hunkler. His moods always tended to improve whenever he'd found a new way to make someone's life hell, especially when it involved getting back at that person for doing the same to him. Some might have considered that a personality flaw, but Jack had never found a problem with it. It was an engrained facet of his very being. He couldn't change the way he felt even if he wanted to.

The base of operations was vastly better than the one Troy worked from when Jack first got the job. The old one occupied a dank, windowless basement that constantly smelled of Lysol. This one sat on the top floor of an old building and had broad windows, comfortable furniture, and a wine rack along one wall.

Hunkler Enterprises was moving up in the world, and Jack was moving right up with it.

And to think his old teachers were convinced he'd never amount to anything. He half-wished they could see him now.

Troy was speaking heatedly into his iPhone when Jack entered. "I don't care if Vincent wants to see his family!" he snapped, his face red. "He agreed to cut off all contact with them when he started working for me." A pause. "If he keeps whining, tell him I'll be over to set him straight." He ended the call with the stab of a finger and laid the phone down on top of the desk. Troy's face resumed its normal color, and he smiled. "Jack, you're early."

"Of course I am."

Troy laughed. He was shrewd enough to never be swayed by the powers of persuasion Jack executed so well over other members of their species. Forty, with a patch of blond hair, Troy had once been into boxing and had two cauliflower ears to prove it. If Jack ever wanted to try anything funny in Troy's presence, he would likely end up with two black eyes and a shattered nose.

Or worse. Most likely worse.

"Sit down." Troy gestured at the empty seat. "We've got a lot to talk about."

That could either be a good thing or a bad thing. "Does this have something to do with Vincent?"

Troy rolled his eyes. "I never knew a grown man could be such a sissy. It's like he was supposed to be born a girl but his DNA got all screwed up and spat him out like this instead."

"If he gives you too much trouble, I can kill him," Jack said, only half-seriously. Vincent was too important to die.

"I'd agree to that in a heartbeat if I had someone else like him lined up to take his place. Without his *ability*, half our enterprise goes right down the drain."

Jack nodded. Until he'd tracked down Graham and learned about the Servants, he had no idea that other people like Vincent existed. "Is anyone looking for a new one just in case?"

"I've had Orin snooping around in Internet chat rooms for leads, and Theo went down to L.A. to ask around in psychic shops and places like that. But what's it matter to you? Vincent isn't even the reason you're here."

"Good. Vincent isn't my problem."

"Nor should he be." Troy rose, went to the wine rack, withdrew a bottle of merlot, and poured it into two glasses sitting on a sideboard. He brought them back to the desk and offered one to Jack, who took it without objection even though he would have preferred to drink bleach. "You're a very good employee, Jack."

Jack sampled the wine with the tip of his tongue and did his best to maintain a straight face. "I try to be."

"I often wonder what your motivation is. What keeps you going when others have opted to quit."

*This isn't like Troy. He's up to something.* "I enjoy the work." *And the control.* Working for Troy gave Jack a certain level of autonomy he wouldn't have had elsewhere. He didn't have to abide by a dress code. He didn't have to clock in and leave at a certain time each day. The world was Jack's domain, and as long as he did what was expected of him, he maintained his standing in the company.

Troy was giving him such an odd look that Jack wondered if he'd accidentally uttered his thoughts aloud. "But *why* do you enjoy it?"

"It's who I am."

"Is it?"

"You know I get bored. Working for you keeps things interesting."

Troy's eyes grew cold. "Your contributions to this enterprise have taken a nosedive ever since you found your grandfather and started gallivanting around the county with him, and with Trish Gunson dead—again thanks to you—our income has taken a plunge. We can't expand unless you keep bringing in fresh merchandise. Do you understand?"

"I do." Hunkler Enterprises encompassed three distinct businesses, none of which Jack had ever told his grandfather about because he suspected that Graham, despite his own iniquities, would not have taken the news well.

One side of the business involved working with buyers from all over the Pacific Northwest. Jack's work was simple: arrange for the capture of as many young and ignorant human beings as possible, who would then be sold to the highest bidder.

It wasn't Jack's job to know what happened to those people afterward.

The second business was known only to those with whom Troy had some level of trust. Its darker nature had enthralled Jack when he first learned about it—and to think it had only come about because of sissy-boy Vincent's peculiar gift!

The third side of Troy's business—logging—was the one the public got to see. Jack had never been part of that division. The employees who gleefully obliterated Oregon's forests didn't even know that the other two divisions existed.

"Then I have a proposal to make," Troy said, bringing Jack back to the present. "Show me you'll continue to be a worthy part of this company, and I'll promote you. Fail me, and you're gone."

In this instance, "gone" could very well mean "dead" since Jack knew too much about Troy's business.

A spark of anger flared up within Jack but he quelled it. "What do I have to do?"

That smile again. "Bring me five."

"Five?"

"By next Saturday. That gives you eight days."

"Don't you mean you want four? I already got one this week."

"No."

Jack didn't bother masking his irritation. "Are you nuts? It's hard enough for me to get two in one week. This is freaking *Hillsdale*. You want more, send me up to Portland."

Troy's cold eyes studied him. "You know Portland is Lyman's territory. I send you up there and he finds out, he'll rat us all out before you'll know what hit you. If you're willing to move—assuming that you achieve your promotion—I'd much rather send you back to Sacramento. I'm sure you won't mind so much now that your grandfather's gone."

"What do you mean, gone?" Jack sat up straighter in his chair. "He's just in lockup."

A muscle twitched in Troy's cheek. "I take it you have yet to hear the news."

Jack's insides squirmed. "I rarely watch that stuff."

"It wasn't *on* the news. I heard it through some of my contacts at the prison. Graham Willard suffered a brain aneurysm the other night and they don't think he's going to recover. The old man's a vegetable. As good as dead."

Jack didn't want to believe it. "How do you know your contacts weren't misinformed?"

"They never are." Troy folded his hands together. "But it seems we've strayed a bit. Get me five more by next Saturday, Jack. I wouldn't want to be in your place if you fail."

# 6

CARLY ARRIVED at Bobby's house in her red Chevy Aveo. She unfolded herself from the car just as Bobby walked out the door with a PlayMate cooler full of Sprite in hand. Her auburn hair was brushed out and tied back once more, she wore the same orange sleeveless blouse she'd had on the day they met, and a giant pair of red-framed sunglasses hid the upper part of her face.

"Did you bring the picture?" she asked.

"Trust me, that's about the last thing I'd forget right now."

He made a move to get in his Nissan, but Carly said, "Hold it, Roland. I said on the phone I'd drive."

"But this trip was my idea."

"And driving you there was mine. What's the matter? Do you feel emasculated if a chick is behind the wheel instead of you?" She shoved her sunglasses onto her forehead and grinned.

As far as Bobby could tell, she had yet to shed a tear today. "It's called being a gentleman," he said.

"Lord, now you're acting like Randy. Get in and let's go."

Bobby obeyed and set the cooler on the floor between his feet, eager to be on the road. Sitting around the house waiting for Carly to show up had increased his anxiety for the woman in the photograph, as if delaying learning more about her would place her in even greater danger.

Once Autumn Ridge lay behind them, Carly said, "Why do you want to find this woman so badly?"

Bobby looked at her in surprise. "Why wouldn't I?"

"I'm just curious."

Bobby stared straight ahead through the windshield. Homes grew sparser and were being replaced by woods and patches of farmland. "Who else is going to do it?"

"The police?"

"The police barely have anything to go on. Besides, Randy doesn't trust the police. Why should I?"

Carly's expression soured. "Randy has every reason in the world not to trust a cop. I mean, look what his dad did to him. If I were him, I wouldn't trust one, either."

Bobby whipped his head to the side and gaped at her. "What did you say?"

Color rose in her cheeks. "Crap. I figured he'd told you."

"But he did." The day Randy was shot, Randy told Bobby about a child he'd known who was molested by his policeman father. The abuse went on for years even though the child reported him to the other cops, but nobody believed him until a neighbor accidentally witnessed the abuse and reported it. "He said it happened to someone else. I wondered if he was talking about himself but figured I was wrong." He paused, thinking of Randy's tired face and the bags that lined his prematurely-aged eyes. "Jesus," he whispered. Then, "Sorry."

"In this case," Carly said, "I don't think saying Jesus' name should be considered using it in vain."

"What happened to Randy's parents after he was taken away from them?"

"It isn't a very nice story."

"I kind of got that already."

Carly sighed. "I only know what I've been told. I was practically still a baby when all this went down, and none of our family even knew Randy yet so I might not have all the details right."

"Well, what *do* you know?"

"Parker Bellison, the scumbag who did it, was murdered in prison a few months after he got put away."

"Geez."

"And then Barbara, Randy's mother, slashed her wrists because she was so upset her husband was gone."

Bobby was starting to wish he hadn't asked. "She wasn't upset that her own kid was abused and stuck in foster care?"

"As far as I know, no. Some people are like that. They just don't care."

"See?" Bobby said, jumping at the opportunity to change the course of the conversation to something more positive. "That's why I want to figure out who this woman is and try to find her. Everyone needs someone to care about them."

"But why do *you* care?"

He opened his mouth to reply but paused. It was true he wanted to make a greater effort to help people, but he had the idea that if the woman's kidnapping had happened prior to meeting Randy, he still would have done his best to track the woman down.

"I just do," he said. "I wasn't always that way, though. I used to kind of be a jerk."

"A jerk can still care about people, you know. Case in point? My father."

They stopped for gas in a rural town with the unlikely name of Bird, and while Carly stood outside chatting with the attendant who filled the tank, Bobby withdrew the now-wrinkled picture from his pocket.

Why did he really care about finding the woman? She was a stranger, and for all he knew she might be as depraved as Randy's parents or as arrogant as Bobby's old boss at the Stop-N-Eat.

He wouldn't be able to judge her character unless they met. If she turned out to be cruel, that wasn't his problem. At least he would have done his part in bringing her to safety.

The Spirit murmured, *She needs you.*

Goosebumps lifted the hairs on his arms. "Can you at least tell me her name?"

No response.

Bobby stuffed the picture away when the attendant hung up the nozzle.

"Who calls their town Bird?" he asked when Carly got back behind the wheel.

"I don't know. Further north there's a town called Boring." She eased back onto the road and continued east, where the straight blacktop devolved into curves that Carly took too fast.

"My hometown should have been called Boring," Bobby said, "but they named it Eleanor instead."

"That's a pretty name."

"It isn't a pretty place. Half the town is addicted to heroin, and it's on the Ohio River, so when you aren't fortifying your house against a flood all you can do is stare at Kentucky all day."

"Is Kentucky boring, too?"

"Pretty much."

The Aveo's tires squealed as Carly rounded another curve in excess of the speed limit. Bobby gripped his knees and prayed he wouldn't wet himself if the car flipped. "Are we there yet?"

"Are you serious or just trying to annoy me?"

"Do you drive like this all the time or are you just trying to kill me?"

She eased off the accelerator as they moved into another curve. "Sorry."

After a while a brown sign that whizzed by on Bobby's right announced that the Mountain Lake Campground was two miles ahead.

*Thank you, God.*

The road leading back to the campground came into view on their left. Bobby was grateful when Carly slowed down sufficiently to make the turn. He sat up straighter in his seat and watched as they passed a secondary turnoff that led to a trailhead.

"You ever do much hiking?" Carly asked.

"No. Only a couple times when I was a kid. In Kentucky, actually."

"I thought you said Kentucky was boring."

"I'm not much of a hiker. Sometimes I pass out. Phil says it's because I need to exercise more." Which to Bobby seemed counterintuitive, but he wasn't about to argue with a nurse on health-related topics.

"That's too bad," she said as they approached the park office which, like the shower house in the picture, looked like a log cabin. "Hiking can be a lot of fun if you're with the right people. Now hand me that picture."

Bobby passed her the wrinkled image, wishing he'd thought to make copies before heading out here.

They drew to a stop alongside the office. A glass-covered bulletin board mounted on the outside wall at vehicle height displayed flyers pertaining to fire ordinances and upcoming park activities and a hand-sketched map of all the campsites. Bobby wished the map showed where Mystery Woman had stayed.

The office window slid open just as Carly was lowering hers. "What can I do for you today, ma'am?" a cheery woman wearing a khaki park uniform asked when she appeared in the opening.

"We're looking for someone," Carly said without preamble. "And we think she was staying here."

She passed the picture out the window and into the woman's hand. The woman took it and frowned, then passed it back. "We get a lot of campers so I don't remember this lady in particular, but if it helps, that building behind her is Shower House A. You can see it just down the way there." She leaned out the window and pointed, and perhaps a tenth of a mile away Bobby could see the cabin from the picture sitting to the left of the campground road among scattered tents and popup campers.

"Can we drive on back and see if she's still here?" Carly asked. "We don't plan on camping. We just want to talk to her."

Bobby lifted his eyebrows but said nothing so the park employee's suspicions wouldn't be raised.

The woman glanced behind her, and in a lowered voice said, "Technically I'm supposed to make you pay a visitor's fee, so try to make it quick, okay?"

"Don't you worry. We'll be out of here before you can blink." Carly rolled up the window and moved the car forward at a crawl.

"You know she's not here anymore," Bobby said, agitation forming in his gut.

"We can still ask some of the other campers about her. They might have seen something fishy going on."

Bobby shrugged, having no argument against that. "Okay."

Carly pulled into an empty campsite next to the shower house, and they both climbed out. Bobby held up the picture and looked from it to the shower house door. "Whoever took the picture would have been standing about where I am, unless they had the camera zoomed in." He squinted at the image again. "And the shadows are different. I think it might have been taken earlier in the morning than it is now."

"Too bad we don't know what day it was." Carly turned and walked toward a blue and white tent erected three sites down from them.

Bobby straightened his shoulders and followed.

A bearded man sat on a campstool next to the fire barrel prodding at its smoldering contents with a stick. "Hi," Carly said to him. "We were wondering if you might have seen the woman in this picture."

Bobby hurried up beside her and passed the picture into the man's hand, feeling about as awkward as a Jehovah's Witness on his first door-to-door route of evangelization.

"What is this?" the man asked. "Some sort of investigation? I don't want no part of it."

"We think she was staying near here," Carly said, undeterred.

Scowling, the camper examined the paper half a second before shoving it away. "I didn't see nothin'. You'll have to ask someone else." He returned his attention to the fire he was attempting to kindle.

Bobby glanced at Carly, shrugged, and together they proceeded to the next occupied campsite and repeated their question to the couple staying there.

They didn't strike gold until they reached the fourth site, where a plump, sixtyish man who had a white beard rivaling that of Santa Claus sat at a picnic table untangling fishing line. A plastic tackle box lay open on the table beside him.

His eyes lit up when he saw the picture. "I sure did see her. Maybe two mornings ago? I was coming back from the toilet and saw her emptying out her car into the fire barrel at that spot over there." He pointed at the Aveo. "She seemed awful excited about something, but I couldn't figure out what was so special about getting rid of trash. Odd thing was, she didn't have a tent or anything. I think she spent the night in her car."

Bobby's pulse thudded out a rapid beat behind his ribs. "Was someone with her?"

"Yeah. Blond guy, average height. I didn't get a good look at him."

"Did he have a car, too?" Bobby asked.

"Yeah, but I don't remember what it was. Might have been black, though."

"Thank you," Carly said, giving the man the sweetest smile Bobby had ever seen her use. "You've been very helpful."

"Yeah," Bobby said, his thoughts whirling. "Thanks."

They returned to the Aveo.

"I'm going to see if her garbage is still here," Bobby said, starting down a short slope to where that site's picnic table sat yards away from the rusty fire barrel.

Carly came with him. "How will you know it's hers?"

"I won't, but it's all we have to go on right now." Bobby sat on his haunches beside the ring, knowing the other campers probably thought he'd flipped his lid.

The pit was full of garbage consisting in large part of McDonald's wrappers and empty Mountain Dew bottles. Bobby picked up a large stick lying in the grass beside the pit and prodded at the mound of waste to see what might be underneath it.

"Oh for goodness sake," Carly said, and dug her hands into the mound.

Bobby set the stick aside and did the same.

Beneath the wrappers and bottles was a mound of wrinkled receipts from gas stations and restaurants from as far away as Indiana and as close as Autumn Ridge.

"Looks like someone came an awfully long way to get here," Carly said, arranging the receipts on the ground by date. "Look, the earliest receipt is from a gas station in Ann Arbor, Michigan."

Bobby was in the middle of examining a receipt from a place in Hillsdale called The Pink Rooster. "I don't know anyone in Michigan." He handed it to Carly and pulled out another from the same place that was dated the next day. "What's The Pink Rooster? A restaurant?"

She wrinkled her nose. "It's a bar. I've heard things about it."

Her tone made his stomach squirm. "What sort of things?"

"The place is crap. My friend Amber's ex-boyfriend took her there while they were still dating and she said when she finished her beer she found a burnt match lying in the bottom of her glass, and they wouldn't even give her a refund!"

"You have friends?"

Spots of pink appeared on Carly's cheeks. "Just because I hang around with Randy and the gang doesn't mean I don't have other friends, too. Amber and our friends Carmen and Julia have known each other since grade school." Sadness filled her eyes. "Though I do admit there's been a bit of a rift between me and them lately. I can't tell them about the Servants, and they think I'm a bum for not having a paying job or going to college."

"Are you going to go to college?"

She shrugged. "I've thought about studying to be a social worker. I'll do that someday, but right now my job is with you. *Anyway*, back to The Pink Rooster. My cousin Brandon works for the health department, and The Pink Rooster always ends up having a ton of violations."

"Then how is it still open?"

"They do clean up every once in a while, and their stuff is cheap. It draws customers like a landfill draws rats, no offense to Mystery Woman here."

"We need to go there," Bobby said, straightening. "If this is her garbage, then she's been there more than once. And I'm not about to start asking around about her in Ann Arbor."

Carly brushed her hands against her pants. "Maybe you can go there, but I'm skipping out on that one. I have an image to keep."

# 7

IT HAD taken Adrian Pollard years to realize her life consisted of one long chain of mistakes, one leading to another then another like a falling line of dominoes.

Looking back, she saw that her fear of parenting the children she'd carried had stemmed from a self-absorption buried so deep within her she didn't even know it existed.

She'd always considered herself a kind woman—she didn't gossip or pick fights, she didn't lie or steal—but the other, darker Adrian hidden beneath the surface had total reign over all.

This realization came one day when Adrian had the news on at the house she shared with her now-estranged husband, Yuri Polusmiak (never would she use *that* surname again). The anchor reported on a story about a woman who allowed herself to be murdered by a violent burglar so her young child would have time to escape and call for help. The woman's brokenhearted husband, who hadn't been home during the burglary, praised her self-sacrifice because their daughter had survived the ordeal without a scratch.

The story rendered Adrian more than speechless. Never before in all her years had the idea of a mother losing her life for her child crossed her mind. She'd thought the anchor would go into additional details about the woman and her child but he moved on to lesser stories about a celebrity's million-dollar wedding and an unfortunate hike in energy prices.

Adrian left the room unnerved and located the story on the Internet. The woman's name had been Krista Boone. She was a stay at home mother who often volunteered at the school where her daughter, Lila, attended kindergarten. The entire community where the woman lived had gone into mourning. A few kind souls started a fund for the Boone family to cover funeral expenses because while they had been a happy family, they had not been rich.

Adrian took one look at the four-carat diamond mounted in white gold on her left ring finger, then at the designer bathrobe draped over her thin frame, feeling somewhat lower than the dirt she and the cleaning staff never allowed to cross the threshold of the house.

She grew increasingly withdrawn over the next several days as she pondered the disparity between her own life and that of the late Krista Boone. Yuri, her husband of five years, demanded to know what her problem was since she could barely bring herself to crawl out of bed and cook for him, but she had not yet formulated her thoughts and feelings into words that could easily be conveyed.

He'd taken her silence for insolence and punched her so hard he blackened her eye. Sobbing, on her knees, Adrian had blubbered out the story she saw on the news and how she felt she'd made a grave error by not bothering to raise any of her children.

Yuri, who despised all children and had even paid for Adrian to have a tubal ligation the week after they were wed, laughed at her and asked if she was stupid.

Stupid was an understatement that did not fully describe the irresponsibility of her actions. She'd given birth to four children—two boys and two girls—and left them all when they were less than a month old, partly from fear. Or was it mostly fear? Parenting would have required her life to change, and change had always frightened her.

Would she have chosen to die for her children? Never.

Days passed, and Adrian's despondency showed no signs of lifting. Yuri mocked her, telling her she needed to get over herself and forget about her children since she'd never had anything to do with them in the first place.

His words and increasing hostility deepened her awareness of her extensive failures. During the years they'd been together, he'd often knocked her around if she didn't do things precisely how he requested. She'd taken it all without complaint. After all, he was her husband and provider. He paid for her nice clothes and her favorite wines and beer and gave her everything she ever asked for. Sometimes she didn't show enough gratitude, so she more than deserved the punishments he periodically bestowed upon her.

Except for this. Regretting her past decisions didn't disrespect Yuri in any way she could see.

Over dinner one evening she casually brought up the topic of her children again. "Yuri," she said, mindlessly twirling her fork through the pasta on her plate, "I really do think it's appropriate that I call on each of them so they know I'm sorry for treating them like I did."

That sent Yuri over the edge. "You know what'll happen if you go knocking on their doors at this point?" he'd screamed as a vein throbbed in his temple. "They'll find out I've got money, and they'll want to bleed me dry like a bunch of little leeches. Is that what you want to do to me? Make me go broke over a few little whelps whose only connection to me is that they came out of that hole between your legs?"

Adrian bowed her head to avoid meeting his gaze. "You're right. I was wrong to think I should see them. I'm sorry, Yuri. I'm so, so sorry."

He seemed to accept her apology for the time being, but he kept his gaze fixed on her for the rest of their meal like some wild beast monitoring its prey.

That night Adrian slipped two sleeping pills into one of his drinks. Once he was out like a hibernating bear, she gathered up as much cash she could find around the house, packed a travel bag, and left on foot.

She paused once to glance back at her home, knowing she wouldn't see it again. Tonight the three floors and sprawling north and south wings looked more like a cold fortress than a place where a family might live.

Strangely, leaving Yuri was harder than leaving any of her children or their fathers. With Yuri she'd lived with riches and comfort, and she was reluctant to let those things go. Did that make her a bad person? Of course it did.

She walked for an hour before calling a cab that took her to a used car lot, then waited by the entrance until it opened in the morning. She bought a disintegrating Ford Escort for $300, picked up some clothes at the thrift store next door, and got out of town before Yuri could find her.

It took Adrian several weeks to track down her three youngest children, and her reunions with each of them were anything but heartwarming. There had been tears. Screaming. Cold indifference, which somehow was worse than anything else.

Not that she'd expected much different.

When she learned that her oldest child had moved to the west coast, she'd almost thrown in the towel, but her conscience wouldn't let it go. The fact that he was her firstborn seemed to make it even more important that she speak with him, if only for a minute or two—however long it took for her to say what needed to be said.

So she set out on what would prove to be the longest road trip of her life. About midway through Iowa the Escort's exhaust started making an unpleasant rattling noise that made her think the whole bottom was going to fall out of it. Then a couple states after that the brakes began grinding whenever she applied them. If she didn't know any better, she'd have said the Escort was trying to self-destruct like one of those spaceships in the movies.

All of this went through her head as she stood waiting on a sidewalk in the darkness, arms hugged against her chest. Squares of pale light shined from the fronts of silent houses, and further down, a yellow porch light cast its glow over a narrow front yard.

*Things are going to be better now,* she thought as she continued to wait for the people who might give her a job. *So much better.*

The front door of the house with the porch light flew open and one, then two figures bounded out. Adrian squinted to see better but a sudden flash of headlights blinded her and then—

———◆———

**THE FIRST** things Adrian became aware of when she awoke were blinding pain in her head and overwhelming nausea in her gut. *I've been in an accident,* she thought, though she could remember no such event. Perhaps she'd hit her head so hard that she was experiencing temporary amnesia.

Something cold and damp touched her head, and her eyes flew open. A fiftyish brown-skinned woman standing beside her held a wet cloth that dripped onto Adrian's shirt.

Adrian scrambled to sit up. Instead of a hospital, she found herself in a windowless room with concrete walls lit by three bulbs in pull-chain fixtures on the ceiling.

She tried to think, but it only deepened her pain. How had she arrived in this place? The last thing she could remember clearly was driving past the green and white Welcome to Oregon sign beside Interstate 84. Other things must have happened between then and now—the dull shadows of them flitted back and forth in her mind, and like dust motes, the more she tried to grasp them the further they drifted away.

Two other women sat on cots nearby, quietly weeping. One was Asian—Chinese, maybe?—and the other was white like Adrian.

"Where am I?" Adrian asked in a cold voice.

The brown-skinned woman pursed her lips and said something in Spanish, but it had been so long since Adrian studied it in school that she couldn't understand.

"Doesn't anyone here speak English?" She glanced over at the white woman, who had blonde hair and looked young enough to be Adrian's daughter. "Hey. You on the cot. Can you hear me?"

She gave no acknowledgment that Adrian had made a sound.

The woman with the dripping cloth backed away, her posture and expression oozing smugness. She wore nice clothes in contrast to the other women, whose outfits were torn and stained with grime.

A bucket topped with a toilet seat occupied the back corner of the room. A half-used roll of paper sat on the floor beside it.

The walls closed in around her. Adrian rose on trembling legs and seized the Spanish-speaking woman by the shoulders. "Where are we? Why can't you tell me where I am?"

The woman pulled away and slapped Adrian hard across the cheek.

Their two companions glanced up but said nothing.

Tears stinging Adrian's eyes, she said, "I know you can understand me. I demand to know what's going on."

The woman slid a phone out of her pocket, dialed a number, and spoke rapidly into it for ten seconds. Then she moved toward a smooth metal door that didn't have a knob and waited.

A minute later the door swung open and a beefy man holding a gun stepped into the room, raked his eyes over its occupants, and then let the woman out into the hallway that lay beyond it.

He gave a nod and followed her out. The door swung shut so hard that Adrian felt the floor vibrate.

The blonde woman lifted her head. "It sure sucks to be you right now, doesn't it?"

Adrian's heart skipped a beat. "You *can* understand me."

"Yeah, but she can't." She gestured at the Asian woman, who gazed longingly at the closed door. "They don't like it if you talk too much. Your best bet is to stay calm and just accept whatever happens because freaking out isn't going to fix anything."

"But where are we? Why are we here?"

"Haven't you guessed?" The woman gave her a sardonic smile. "We're for sale."

# 8

PHIL MASON, Randy Bellison's predecessor as the Servant, stood at the window with his back to the living room, thinking about too many things, one of them being the fact that he would essentially have to train a terrified weakling to be an exorcist. With Randy it had been easy. Randy had known ahead of time what he was getting himself into.

Bobby didn't.

And that was only one problem. The tip of the iceberg, so to speak.

When Phil and Allison first wed, the humble dwelling in which they lived was a refuge where he could leave his woes on the doorstep and not be bothered by them again until he left. Lately Phil had been unable to switch off his worries, and they crept inside the house like malevolent spirits and turned the calm atmosphere into one that was slowly poisoning the home's inhabitants.

It didn't help that his hours at the doctor's office where he worked had just been cut in half. That announcement had come just this past Monday, and he and Allison hadn't yet settled on a solution for their upcoming financial crisis.

In addition to that, Phil's thoughts kept drifting to the stack of papers sitting on the desk in his home office, or, rather, what he'd learned about the information printed upon them.

And still, that wasn't the extent of his problems.

Allison came up behind him and massaged his shoulders. Ashley, their five-year-old daughter, was in her room playing with dolls. "What is it?" Allison asked.

A fraction of the tension went out of his body at her touch. He couldn't tell her everything, of course—at least not until he'd checked a few more facts in regard to the papers on his desk.

He began with the safest thing that came to mind. "I was thinking about Bobby. About how he's so..."

"Unprepared?"

"Exactly."

"Everyone has to start somewhere. Is that really all that's bothering you right now?"

"Frankie's run off again."

She gave a soft laugh. "You sound surprised."

"And it seems he's taken Janet with him."

"Now *I'm* surprised. Any idea what he's up to?"

"I haven't got a clue."

Frankie Jovingo had been the Servant from 1987 to 1992—long before Phil entered the fold in the spring of 2002. Unlike Randy's gift of Tongues and Phil's gift of Healing, Frankie was blessed with the gift of Evangelism. When Frankie hadn't been cleansing the possessed, he went from town to town spreading the gospel from Seattle to San Diego. Due to his gift, people actually listened to what Frankie had to say.

Frankie never boasted the number of people who had been saved as a result of his works, though Phil suspected they may have numbered in the hundreds. "I take no credit for changing people's hearts," Frankie had once said when Randy pestered him one evening over drinks and cards. "It was all God's work. I was just a vessel."

"Do you think he went up to Portland again?" Allison asked.

"Lord, I hope not."

Frankie no longer held a crowd's attention as he once could, much in the way that Phil's ability to heal people had waned over the years. The summer before last Frankie got it into his head to proclaim the word of God in the streets of Portland, which like many cities was not known for its piety. Frankie claimed that an undisclosed number of people were saved through his efforts, though not without cost: a group of young men who didn't like what Frankie said ganged up on him and would have beaten him to death if the police hadn't intervened.

In the end Frankie was arrested for disturbing the peace by the same cops who saved him and spent one night in jail. The young men who'd beaten him were verbally chastened and sent on their way with no further punishment. For the next week Frankie wore his black eye, bruised ribs, and new arrest record like badges of martyrdom. "There is no greater pleasure," he'd said, wearing a look of utmost radiance, "than suffering for Christ."

Phil shook his head at the memory. "If he tries a stunt like that again, someone's going to kill him."

Allison laughed. "But he'd love that. Saint Frankie the Evangelist. They could start naming churches after him."

The thought of a place of worship bearing Frankie's name was enough to give Phil an ulcer.

He returned his attention to the street.

Allison quit rubbing his shoulders and gave him a piercing stare. "Phil Mason, is there something else bothering you?"

"That black car has been parked across the street for a long time now."

"So they're visiting someone."

The car's windows were tinted so Phil couldn't see into it. "I haven't seen anyone climb out."

"Maybe they broke down and are waiting for a tow truck."

The tension that Allison had so recently massaged out of him came back with reinforcements. "They never found Jack Willard."

Allison tossed her blonde hair over her shoulder and put her hands on her hips. "Any self-respecting scum like him would have scampered days ago. Quit worrying."

"On the news they said he was arrested three years ago on charges of assault. He beat a man so badly the guy had to have reconstructive surgery on his face. If he comes here and tries something, I...I..."

Allison held a finger to his lips. "Will worrying add one moment to your life?"

"Allison, I'm being realistic. People do bad things."

"People do good things, too. You should know."

Phil had nothing to say about that. Being lax invited trouble. Jesus may have said to turn the other cheek, but Phil wasn't about to sit idly by while the man who'd shot Randy in the leg walked free.

As he thought this, the driver side door of the black car opened and a teenage girl talking on a phone climbed out. She checked something on a slip of paper, stared at the row of houses on that side of the street, walked up to the door of one of them, and knocked.

"I'll tell you what," Allison said with a smile. "I'll go ahead and get some lunch started and you can take some to Randy. Okay?"

Phil could feel a headache coming on, and he kneaded his eyelids. He'd planned on going over to Randy's anyway to show him the papers. "That sounds great."

When Allison disappeared into the kitchen, Phil sighed. Allison was probably right. He shouldn't worry. After all, the black car that had caused him concern turned out to be nothing. Maybe that meant Bobby and Frankie would be okay, too.

# 9

BOBBY COULDN'T suppress the dread that assaulted him on the ride back to his house, knowing it meant he had to hurry and find the woman before it was too late.

He let himself inside, deciding he'd look up The Pink Rooster in the phonebook and ask for their hours of operation so he wouldn't end up sitting in their parking lot all day waiting for them to open.

The bar might be a dead end, but it was the only lead he had.

He started toward the kitchen and froze.

A man with a thick mop of reddish-brown hair, dark eyes, and a beaming smile lounged at the card table. Bobby had never seen him before.

"Who are you?" Bobby squeaked as he tightened his grip on the handle of the PlayMate cooler he'd carried in from the Aveo. If the guy tried to come after him, Bobby could swing it at his head and maybe knock him out.

The man stood and held his palms out as if to show he meant no ill will. "A friend."

Bobby took two tentative steps closer to the kitchen. "My friends wouldn't barge in uninvited." Bobby was sure the doors had been locked when he and Carly left. This man must have broken in through a back window.

Bobby's unwanted visitor gave a casual shrug. "Nevertheless, I'm still your friend."

"Do you have a name?"

"Of course: I'm Thane. And you, my friend, are Bobby Roland."

Bobby raced to think of any Thanes he may have encountered during the past year but drew a blank. And although he was getting some mighty strange vibes from the visitor, none of them were bad enough that he felt the need to run and call Officers Dodgson and Jergens back to the scene.

Then it hit him. "You left the notes and picture on my door."

"I'm afraid you're mistaken. It wasn't me."

Bobby's heart sank. "Then you know about the notes?"

"Only because you do."

"You're saying you can read my mind?"

Thane's smile broadened.

This conversation was getting weirder by the second. "Seriously. Who are you and why are you here?"

Amusement flickered in Thane's dark eyes. "I already told you who I am. And I'm here because you need help."

"I'm pretty sure I can manage things just fine by myself."

"If you think you're fine on your own, you never would have joined forces with Randy Bellison and his friends."

Bobby gaped at him. "You know about that."

"I know many things."

"Okay," Bobby said, aware that the Spirit was telling him to not try anything rash. "If you know so much, what am I thinking?" He envisioned his stepmother and held the image of her in his mind's eye.

"I see a woman," Thane said. "She's in her forties, has dark brown hair in a braid, and is wearing black yoga pants and a fluorescent pink tank top. Quite attractive, really. Her name is Charlotte

Roland, and she's raised you since you were a small child. You don't need to tell me I'm right."

Bobby wasn't sure what to do or say. "You're—you're like Caleb," he managed after long seconds of awkward silence. Caleb, his old roommate, had vanished without warning the week before. Bobby had pieced together some clues that made him realize Caleb was far more than the unassuming college student he'd seemed.

"Did Caleb know your innermost thoughts?"

"I don't know. If he did, he never mentioned them."

"I wonder why."

"It would have been rude," Bobby blurted, his face hot. "Sorry."

Thane didn't appear to have taken offense. "It's only natural for you to be wary of someone like me. After all, we don't really know each other and have yet to gain each other's trust."

"Digging around in my head won't earn you mine."

Thane shrugged. "Fair enough. But back to your problem. You wish to find the woman whose picture was taped to your door."

"That's right. What's her name?"

"I can't say."

"Let me guess: I don't know her name so you don't, either."

"Bingo."

"I take it you can't tell me who made the notes for the same reason."

"You're becoming more astute by the second."

Bobby set the cooler down and crossed his arms. "What help is it if you can't tell me who these people are? What's in it for you, besides?"

Thane's eyebrows rose. "You're asking me why I've bothered to help when *you're* the one willing to drive all over the county to find a woman you don't know just because you think she's in danger?"

"Okay, forget I asked that. But I still want to know how you can help me."

"I can give you advice, and we can bounce ideas off of each other. As they say, two heads are better than one."

"I'm all ears."

Thane tilted his head again. "What did you learn about the woman while you were at the campground?"

"Assuming those were her receipts, she came a long way to get here. And some blond guy was with her."

"Do you know any blond guys?"

"Yeah." Bobby counted them off on his fingers. "The guy who brought mail to the bungalow, my old boss, the dude who works at the bagel shop, Phil Mason..." He paused. "Phil couldn't have been at the campground. He works four or five days a week." *Well, he did before he got his hours cut the other day.*

"He could have been there early in the morning."

"I don't believe it. Phil isn't that type of person." Though Phil and Bobby had initially gotten off on the wrong foot, Bobby wasn't about to believe that Phil met a strange out-of-state woman for a romantic rendezvous at a local state park. He had a wife and kid, *and* he'd been a Servant.

*Graham Willard was a Servant, too.*

Well, Graham was an oddity. Not every Servant could have ended up evil. That would defeat the purpose of the program.

"Suit yourself, then," Thane said with a smile.

"When I go to the bar, I'm going to ask if anyone's seen the woman. I can ask if they saw a blond guy with her."

"That's a logical place to start."

"It's all I've got."

"You'll do anything to save her?"

Bobby narrowed his eyes. "Within reason."

"Sometimes you have to do things that make you uncomfortable in order to get what you want."

Bobby's thoughts jumped to the day he'd gone to the property where Graham had lured Randy. He'd snuck through the woods, expecting certain doom, yet he kept his head enough to call the authorities in time for Randy's life to be saved.

Nothing about that day qualified as "comfortable."

Grimacing, Bobby said, "Yeah, I guess sometimes you do."

"Exactly." Thane smiled. "I'm afraid I have to go for now. If you need anything, don't hesitate to call."

"How do I—"

Thane blinked out of existence as if he'd never been there.

Bobby swayed where he stood. No, Thane wasn't like Caleb. Both had made unexpected departures from his life, but at least Caleb hadn't done it in front of Bobby's astonished face.

It occurred to him that if this same thing had happened before he became the Servant, he would have fled the house in terror. Interesting, how the bizarre had become as commonplace as air.

Now that Thane was gone, Bobby felt as though he'd just awakened from a dream. He shook his head. What had he been about to do when he discovered he wasn't alone? Get the phone-book. Of course.

***

A RECORDING told him The Pink Rooster didn't open until one, so Bobby took a detour to Randy's house to pay him a visit.

A sour-faced Phil Mason answered Bobby's knock. As usual, the bespectacled thirty-eight-year-old wore a nondescript polo shirt and khaki slacks, which were evidently his casual clothes since he wore scrubs at work. "Well if it isn't the bad penny again."

Bobby walked past the short man into the living room. "You can't get rid of me now."

"It's a shame." A muscle twitched in Phil's cheek, and he made a furtive glance behind him before turning his attention back to Bobby. "I'm actually glad you came. I was about to call you."

Bobby sensed Phil's unease. "What's this about?"

"We'll discuss it once Randy's more coherent."

Bobby saw that Randy, who had been discharged from the hospital two days ago, rested on one of the IKEA couches with his upper half propped up by about five pillows. Ever a fan of black t-shirts, the one Randy wore today had a picture of a skull wearing sunglasses printed on it.

Despite Randy's pallor and the fact that he lay as though dead, the living room held a much warmer ambience than when Bobby first set foot in it last week because he, Phil, and Lupe had removed the plywood from the windows the day before Randy came home. In his paranoia, Randy had covered the windows to make the house look unoccupied in case Graham showed up looking for him. The sunlight shining through the windows now made the coral walls glow.

Bobby lowered his voice. "Is he asleep?"

Randy's eyes fluttered open before Phil could reply. "Roberto, my love! You're here!"

"His painkillers have been making him loopy," Phil said with a smirk.

Randy sat up straighter so it seemed that the skull on his shirt was staring at Bobby from behind its shades. His shaggy, coffee-colored hair hadn't been combed, stubble covered his chin, and the bags under his eyes were more pronounced than Bobby had ever seen them, but other than that Randy looked at peace.

He still appeared much older than his twenty-six years.

"How's it going?" Bobby drifted over to Randy's side. He hadn't spoken with him since his release.

Randy shifted and winced. "Just swell. How do you like my nurse? I told him he'd look much cuter if he put on one of those sexy nurse costumes but he said he'd put arsenic in my next meal if I said that again."

Phil rolled his eyes. "All right. It's time we got down to business." At that moment, Phil's cell phone let out a ring. He withdrew it from his pocket, stared at the screen, and frowned. "Hold that thought. I'm taking this outside."

When Phil went out to the concrete porch and closed the door behind him, Randy grinned.

"Let me guess," Bobby said. "The painkillers haven't really done a thing."

"Oh, they've done plenty. I completely understand why people end up addicted to the stuff."

"Why the crazy act?"

"Because it's fun driving Phil nuts. He deserves to have his feathers ruffled once in a while. It's good for his health."

Bobby found himself grinning, too. "It's good to see you here."

"As opposed to a casket? Can't help but agree." A wistful look entered Randy's eyes, and he became more serious. "And thank you for taking my place."

Bobby nodded, a knot of emotion dampening his ability to speak.

"So what do you think about your new job?"

Bobby had to search for the right words. "It's different from what I expected. At first I felt all light inside, like I could jump up and fly."

"But it wore off, didn't it?"

*Unfortunately.* "Phil said that the beginning was the honeymoon stage and that now is the beginning of the rest of the marriage. It's weird calling it a marriage, though."

"You'll get used to it soon enough, among other things."

Bobby gave an involuntary shiver. "I haven't run into anyone who's possessed yet. Phil said I'll have to be on the lookout for them these next few weeks to get an idea of what I'll be up against." Phil told him it wouldn't be easy the first few times Bobby ran into such a person. But then again, Bobby couldn't ever remember his life being easy, so maybe confronting demons on a regular basis wouldn't be so bad.

Randy's expression sobered. "That reminds me. There's something I should tell you."

Bobby's insides began to churn. "Yeah?"

"When I was in the hospital, I had this crazy dream that something was after you."

Bobby made an involuntary glance out the window. "Aren't things supposed to be after me now?"

"Like I said, it was just a dream. But it shouldn't hurt to be careful."

*I thought I already was careful,* he thought, but he said, "Okay. Do you know what Phil wants to talk to us about?"

"I haven't got a clue."

Phil came back inside, his face white, and disappeared into the kitchen without a word to either of them. Bobby heard the fridge open and close, followed by the sound of a drink can cracking open.

That couldn't be good.

"Anyway," Randy continued, "I want you to be as vigilant as possible."

His words made Bobby nervous. He'd always thought he *was* vigilant, but maybe it wasn't enough. "Won't God warn me if someone's coming after me?"

"The Spirit gives us guidance, not play-by-play instructions. Haven't you noticed?"

"I get messages from time to time. Like little urges. I don't know how else to describe it."

"The still, small voice that isn't so small," Randy said. "I can still hear faint whispers of it, but nothing like before."

"You know," Bobby said, "if anyone tries to kill me, I'll have one of my premonitions first."

Randy raised his eyebrows. "Will you?"

"I don't see why not."

"It seems to me you're only forewarned when other people are in danger. Not you."

Bobby wanted to object but kept his mouth shut. He'd known something bad would happen at the restaurant he used to work at, but he hadn't been there alone—Chrissy, a coworker, had been clocked in, too. And Bobby had been with Randy and Phil when he'd had the premonition that they would be killed if they stayed at Randy's house.

"It's not just other people," Bobby said, a new realization sinking into him. "It's other people I've met." He bit his lip. "But that doesn't explain the one I had last night." He recounted what had happened on Oakland Avenue in the wee morning hours and even showed Randy the items left on his door. While he talked, Phil entered the room holding a can of beer, his expression tight. "So because I had the premonition that someone would be hurt, and because I know it has to have been this woman, I know I have to go find her," Bobby finished.

"Don't you think it's a little too soon for you to be putting yourself in danger?" Phil asked.

"I'm not planning on driving a demon out of anyone. I just want to find her."

"Someone wants you to go after her. Can't you see? She's bait."

"Like Lupe was bait for Randy."

"That's why I don't like this."

"If God didn't want me to go after her, he wouldn't have told me to run outside and witness her kidnapping."

"You don't even know for certain that's who it was." Phil's frown deepened. "You said it was so dark you couldn't see what they looked like."

"I just have this feeling."

"The Spirit warns you about people you know. You don't know this woman. Therefore your premonition wasn't from God."

"Maybe Bobby does know her and he just doesn't remember," Randy said.

*I doubt it.* "Or maybe I was upgraded to Premonitions 2.0."

Exasperation shone in Phil's eyes. "If that were the case, you would have been forewarned early enough that you would have been able to stop the abduction."

Bobby frowned as he thought about the demonic voice that had greeted him upon his return home last night. "Maybe a demon was suppressing it."

Phil paused to take a sip of his beer. "I don't like this at all. I didn't face my first task until I'd been the Servant for two months, and it was about the same for Randy. You need to be better prepared before you take anything on."

Phil obviously wasn't getting it. "I told you, I'm not driving out demons. I'm tracking this woman down and getting her away from whatever creep pulled her into that van."

"Do you at least understand why I have misgivings about this?"

"Sure. You don't want me to get killed."

Phil moved to a chair. "Sit down and let me tell you a story so you might understand a bit better."

Bobby took the other couch. "Let me guess. Once upon a time, there was a Servant."

"His name was Hans Mueller."

"Wow, I'm really good at this."

"Just shut your mouth and listen. Hans was born in present-day Germany."

"There were Servants in Europe?"

"Yes, and before that they were in Asia Minor and the Holy Land. Hans died on June 28, 1914 when a demoniac stabbed him in the heart. He had no replacement."

Bobby had been told that when a Servant died without a replacement, evil would reign free for the next eighteen years. "Okay. So then what happened?"

Phil and Randy exchanged glances. "You don't know what happened that day?" Randy asked.

"Aside from this Hans guy getting stabbed? No."

"You have no idea what happened on June 28, 1914."

Bobby had never paid particular attention to his history lessons since he never felt that the troubles of long ago had any bearing on his own life. "I'm guessing it wasn't something good."

They both gave him hopeless looks. "That may have just been the understatement of the millennium," Phil said. "Bobby, that was the day Archduke Franz Ferdinand of Austria-Hungary and his wife were publicly assassinated by a Bosnian Serb."

Bobby didn't think he should mention that the only Franz Ferdinand he'd heard of was a Scottish indie rock band he used to listen to. "That doesn't sound like evil reigning free. That sounds like every day on the news."

"One month after the assassination," Phil went on, "Austria-Hungary declared war on Serbia. Austria and its allies became known as the Central Powers, and Serbia aligned itself with Russia, France, and the U.K., who became the Allied Forces. Is this ringing any bells yet?"

It did. A bead of sweat rolled down the back of Bobby's neck. "You're talking about World War I."

Phil bowed his head. "Do I need to go on?"

Bobby swallowed. "So you're saying the whole war happened because this Hans guy got stabbed?" He looked to Randy for clarification.

"We wouldn't say it happened *because* of it," Randy said, "considering it's unlikely that Hans had anything to do with the assassin himself."

"Also," Phil was quick to add, "it's very likely that the war would have eventually begun anyway. However, we doubt that it would have been so catastrophic if Hans had lived. His death caused some kind of disruption that led to unspeakable violence that continued even after the eighteen years were up."

"What kind of disruption?"

"Well...instead of focusing much of their energy on destroying the Servant, the demons focused it elsewhere since the Servant was dead. This is why we can't lose you."

"But what if I get hit by a car or something?"

"Stay out of the street."

Bobby wished Phil hadn't brought any of this up. His duties would place enough pressure on him. He didn't need the rest of the world's weight piled on top of that. "So how did the Servants get out of that mess? One of you said something about the first male child born after the fact..."

"Yes. In the same moment Hans died, a baby named Frank Jovingo was born in a cabin near Eugene, Oregon."

"You mean the old guy I met at your house the other day?" Phil had gathered together the remaining former Servants—Bobby's new support group—and together all of them went over what Bobby would have to do in preparation of his first exorcism. The aforementioned Frank, grandfather of Frankie and great-grandfather of Carly, had sat in an armchair off to one side and slept through half the meeting.

"I'm sure he'd be thrilled to hear you refer to him that way. Hans Mueller's surviving predecessors had to find Frank so he could become the Servant when he turned eighteen."

"How'd they do that?"

"They let the Spirit guide them, of course. The predecessors were led west over the ocean, came to America, and crossed the whole continent before they found him."

"And the rest is history," Randy said.

The three of them fell into silence. Phil's dour expression did not lighten. "I hate to be the bringer of bad news," he finally said, "but that was Kimberly on the phone."

Bobby tensed. Graham had a daughter named Kimberly, though he had never met her.

"What happened?" Randy asked, his eyes wide.

Phil drew in a deep breath. "Graham had a brain aneurysm a few nights ago. Kimberly is friends with the warden's wife, and she just found out from them this morning."

Bobby felt cold. "Graham's dead?"

"Not quite. All Kimberly knows is that he's in a hospital somewhere, that he's guarded round the clock, and that he's not allowed any visitors. She said she'll keep me posted when she learns anything more."

The Spirit stirred within him. *He is in my hands now. Do not worry about him.*

"And while we're on the topic of Graham," Phil said, "I learned something unfortunate about him, myself." He reached for his black zippered tote bag, which sat on the floor by the chair. As he unzipped it and pulled out a sheaf of papers, he said, "Randy, I don't know if anyone told you this or not, but Lupe swiped a notebook out of Graham's basement. Before we handed it over to the police, I took pictures of all the pages and printed them out a few days ago." He waved the papers in the air for emphasis. Bobby could see handwriting on them but wasn't close enough to make out the words.

Randy's mouth drew into a straight line. "What kind of notebook?"

"One where he recorded information about all the people he's killed—or so I thought. This morning my curiosity got the better of me and I did a search for every name in the book." A shadow passed over Phil's eyes. "I just wanted to see how many of those people had been listed as missing. Call it morbid curiosity. And imagine my surprise when for the first nine years of entries, every single name appeared in the obituary section of the Cascade Chronicle."

Bobby looked at Randy, who was staring at Phil with wide eyes. "I don't get it," Bobby said.

"It's simple. Those people died of natural causes, their loved ones posted obituaries in the paper, Graham read the paper, and decided to claim their deaths as his own kills. Only in 2009 did the names in here—" Phil shook the stack of papers again— "start matching up with missing persons reports."

Phil fell silent, but Bobby had the sense that he wasn't finished. Apparently so did Randy. "What else?" he asked.

Phil pulled a few sheets from the bottom of the stack and held them up. "I did a real estate search for that David Upton alias he was using. He bought four houses under that name all in the same year."

"Let me guess," Bobby said. "2009?"

"Yes."

"That's the year I became the Servant," Randy said, his face ashen.

"I noticed that, too."

More silence. Randy broke it by saying, "He used to hang out with Bill Trautmann and Orville Hunley all the time. I wonder if they'd know anything about this."

Bobby gaped at him. "Did you say Bill Trautmann?"

"Sure did. He and Graham go way back. You've probably seen some of Bill's vans around town. He must have about a thousand of them."

"That must be where I've heard of him, then." Bobby hadn't mentioned the clip he saw on the news or the fact that the kidnapping van bore the Trautmann logo. "I'm really sorry about Graham. Is there anything I can do?"

"Pray for his soul," Randy said. "Before it's too late."

———◆———

PHIL WALKED Bobby out to his car. "So what's on today's agenda?" Phil asked, making a poor attempt at sounding cheerful.

"I figured an afternoon trip to Hillsdale might be nice. You know, get out, get some fresh air, see the sights, that kind of thing."

"Have you been keeping your eyes peeled?"

"Yeah. If I've run into anyone who's possessed, they've hidden it well."

Phil gave him a faint smile. "It isn't something one can hide. Your first encounter with one of the fallen won't come easy for you."

"So you've said. No pressure, right?"

"You have to keep your head. Pray at all times. If you trust in God, they will not hurt you."

"They killed Hans what's-his-name."

"We don't know what was going through the man's head when he was killed." Phil put a hand on Bobby's shoulder and squeezed it, an unexpected gesture from one generally so irritable. "Please be careful about this woman you want to find. You may not believe it, but I really don't mind having such a bad penny lying around now that I know he isn't out to do us in."

Phil retreated to the house, and Bobby had the sudden mental image of Phil embracing Mystery Woman in a long, passionate kiss.

*Quit that.* There was no way Phil could have been the man who met Mystery Woman at the state park. The man who'd seen her said the blond man was of average build, a description Phil might achieve if he happened to be wearing platform shoes.

Bobby shook his head. He had no time to entertain sick fantasies. He had work to do.

# 10

FOR LUNCH Carly fixed a bowl of ramen noodles and took it and a glass bottle of Mexican Coke out to the back patio.

Janet, her mother, designed the patio herself. She'd selected the sand-colored stones from the hardware store, hauled them here in the back of the pickup truck, leveled out the ground, and arranged the stones in a pattern flowing out into the backyard and around the old maples. Here and there Janet built raised beds from a grayer stone that rose out of the patio like islands, and in these she had planted blood red roses, bright impatiens, ferns, and lilies that made the property explode with color.

A ten-foot-tall privacy fence surrounded their yard like a wooden fortress. The only way a neighbor would be able to see the Jovingos' lovingly-tended domain was if they leaned a ladder against the other side of the fence and climbed it.

Janet loved it that way, and Carly supposed she liked it too, though it made her feel somewhat like she was sitting in a lidless box whenever she went outside.

Carly planted her rear on a stone bench sitting six feet back from a gray angel statue and set the Coke down beside her.

The statue and the rest of the patio had been installed eight years before. The whole project had been Janet's personal form of therapy, and even now Carly took some comfort in sitting here among the flowers and the trees.

She'd considered bringing a book outside with her to pass the time while she ate. Since she'd become one of the counselors at the safe house, she'd read through her parents' entire collection of books and had recently begun what she dubbed The Conquest of the Stacks at the Autumn Ridge Public Library.

Being the counselor gave Carly a great deal of free time—perhaps too much of it since she had exactly zero people to counsel at the moment. If she'd been in a better mood she'd have continued reading Dante's *Inferno*, but she couldn't get a certain woman's face out of her head.

*Dark curls. Pale skin. Cold, wicked eyes: the face of Cassandra, the monster.*

She twirled her fork around and around in the noodles and stuffed it into her mouth. When she finished chewing, she said, "I need to just let it go, don't I?"

The concrete angel didn't respond.

Carly thought she *had* let it go. It happened so long ago, and yes, the pain had been terrible, but eventually it grew duller until finally it became nothing more than a faint heartache over what was lost and what might have been.

As a child Carly hadn't known that her father once drove demons out of the possessed. All she knew was that he had a close group of friends from church who helped counsel troubled souls. When she turned eighteen she told her parents that she wanted to help people just as members of their church had helped her heal from her pain, and the rest was history.

Those who'd been possessed had lost something of their innocence just as Carly had lost hers thanks to Cassandra, whose life choices had turned Carly into an only child. They were often shell-shocked and somewhat doubtful that life would be the same again.

It wouldn't be the same, she told them. It would be different but better because now they had the tools they needed to protect themselves against future attack. Their triumph over evil had strengthened them like metal forged in a blacksmith's fire.

And Carly herself had felt just fine about her life until she saw Cassandra in the grocery store buying a bottle of wine the size of a propane tank. Cassandra had seen her. Somehow recognized her after so many years, and smiled.

Carly nearly lost it then. She thought she'd forgiven the woman, but the sight of her triggered so many flashbacks of that terrible day that Carly left her shopping basket on a random shelf and fled the store before she broke down in front of all the other shoppers.

She was grateful for the current break in her duties. Joanna, the safe house's most recent resident, had gone home, and Bobby wouldn't be sending anyone over for her to counsel for a while yet. She felt so distraught that she didn't think she would have been able to successfully help anyone. After all, who in their right mind would follow the advice of a counselor who couldn't stop crying over a tragedy from almost a decade ago?

The fact that she felt like this at all meant that Carly had some serious mental issues to address.

She took a swig of Coke. "I'm fine," she said to the statue. "I'm really fine. She can only hurt me if I let her."

Some undefined anomaly in her surroundings made her jerk her head up. She scanned the yard beyond the patio trying to figure out what had caught her attention and gave a start when she laid her eyes upon a human face peering over the top of the privacy fence at the back of the yard.

She remained immobile while she ran a mental assessment of the face. Male. Mid to late thirties. Reddish-brown hair about the same color as hers. A beaming smile.

Carly could say with all honesty she had never seen him before.

Irritated that someone would be so rude, she stood up and crossed the yard. "Hey! Get down from there!"

The man winked but didn't budge.

Her mother would freak if she knew some guy was spying on her.

He ducked below the top of the fence as soon as Carly reached its base. "What do you think you're doing? They call it a privacy fence for a reason."

No response. Carly rapped on the wood with her bony fist. "Are you going to answer me or not?"

No sound came from beyond the fence, not even retreating footsteps. That meant he was still standing on the other side, just feet away from her.

"If you look over the fence again," she growled, "I'll report you to the police."

She turned to go back to her lunch and nearly lost control of her bladder when she saw the same smiling face peering over the back of the bench she had so recently vacated. The man winked at her again and grinned.

Then he disappeared.

She approached the bench with caution and peered around the back to see if he'd just hunched down at a superhuman speed.

He wasn't there.

Feeling prickles on the back of her neck, she turned and found him staring over the top of the fence again.

Without thinking, Carly grabbed up her bowl and her Coke and took them inside the house, then checked all the doors to make sure they were locked.

She half-expected to find Peeping Tom in the house but she appeared to be alone.

Her parents had left town the day before for a reason they wouldn't disclose to her and didn't expect to be home for another day or two. Carly figured that her father had gotten another one of his flights of fancy and dragged her mother off to Portland or Salem or someplace to start preaching to the masses again.

If she called and told them about the teleporting face, they would think she'd lost her mind—and maybe she had.

She dialed her father's cell phone number anyway and prayed he would answer.

FRANKIE JOVINGO kept his hands on the wheel precisely at ten o'clock and two o'clock, his eyes locked on the interstate spread before him like an unfurling gray ribbon. The glimmering Snake River came into view again on the left. To the right were some low hills dotted with bushes and not much else.

There weren't any trees. Frankie was starting to think they couldn't grow here. If he didn't know any better, he would have thought he'd gone back in time to the days before settlers colonized this half of the continent. It was *barren* out here. Why anyone would choose to live in this part of the country was beyond him.

"Kevin certainly picked a desolate place to hide from us," he said as they passed a buzzard picking through what used to be an animal on the shoulder of the road.

Even though he wasn't looking at her, he knew Janet was rolling her eyes. "Frankie, I've told you a thousand times. He isn't hiding. He just wants to have his own space."

"What reason should he have for that? I never did him wrong." He glanced to the side and saw his wife pursing her lips. "You're thinking about what I said to him before he left."

"You called him a coward, Frankie."

"Because he was." Frankie tilted his head from side to side to work out a kink in his neck and stopped when he felt a satisfying click. Kevin Lyle, Frankie's successor, had been a thin man of twenty-two when Frankie passed the mantle of Servitude on to him. He'd seemed ready enough for the job in the beginning—but then things changed.

"He did his part," Janet said. "And that's all that should matter."

The river veered away from the road and was replaced by a patchy expanse of vegetation that looked dead—or maybe grass out here was supposed to be that lifeless brown color. For as far as Frankie could see in each direction, the only sign of civilization was the road on which they traveled. Having spent his entire life within a hundred-odd miles of the Pacific Coast, he'd had no idea that any part of the United States could be this empty of humanity.

Yet somewhere out here was Kevin Lyle, whom the remaining former Servants desperately needed.

Frankie's cell phone rang in the cup holder between the seats. "You answer that," he said.

Janet checked the screen. "It's Carly." She held the phone to her ear. "Hey, sweetie. Is everything okay?" A long pause. "We haven't quite gotten to where we're going yet. No, we haven't decided to drive to Timbuktu. We only drove six hours yesterday. That's right." Another pause. "Well...I suppose we can make the return trip all at once if your father's willing. Yes, I'll tell him. Love you too, Carly. Goodbye."

A weight settled in the pit of Frankie's stomach. "Did something happen?"

Janet's shoulders slumped. "She said she's just feeling lonely and hopes we come home soon. I don't think it was fair to keep her in the dark."

Frankie felt a slight pang of regret. "If I'd told her, then she would have told everyone else and then they'd all question my judgment. Again." He sighed. "She can't hang out with her friends until we get back?"

Janet pursed her lips again. "Amber got a job in Seattle a couple of months ago. Remember? And Julia and Carmen are in Costa Rica for a summer mission trip."

Part of Frankie hated the thought of Carly sitting in their home all by herself. She may have been a grown woman now, but she would always be his little girl. Any time Carly was sad or upset, Frankie wished she was still of an age where he could set her in his lap and sing her songs or read her silly stories until her tears changed to laughter.

But those days were gone. Like smoke blown away by the wind.

Interstate 86 ended miles later at the edge of a town called Pocatello, and they sped into the northbound lanes of Interstate 15. "We're almost there."

"I hope so," she murmured.

*You asked for this,* he thought. It hadn't been Frankie's intention to bring Janet with him, but she'd persisted, saying she needed to make sure he stayed safe.

Frankie hadn't let the arrest in Portland bother him, but she'd never gotten over the ordeal. Being arrested was just one of those unpleasant things that happened from time to time, like flat tires and root canals. When you just went with the flow and remembered that your troubles were tiny blips in the grand scheme of things, you were a much happier person.

He and Janet couldn't have been more different.

They were driving through another sea of brown. Frankie squinted to look for their exit. "There it is," he said when one of the normally-ubiquitous green road signs came into view.

He drove onto the ramp and merged onto a two-lane country road. The directions he'd found online told him that Kevin's home lay just four miles east of here.

He hoped his old successor was there.

"I don't see any houses," Janet said after they'd traveled a mile or so down the road. More low, brown hills came into view. A spindly cell tower had been constructed on top of one of them.

"The directions said this is the way to go."

She gave a curt shrug and fell silent. Frankie wasn't going to admit that he was starting to have some misgivings about this, too. Neither he nor Janet owned phones that had internet access. If the directions he'd gotten were wrong, he would have to turn back and find a public library in Pocatello so he could use the computer and recheck the information he found about Kevin's whereabouts.

When he was about to turn around in the middle of the road and do just that, he spotted a crooked black mailbox emblazoned with the number of Kevin's address sitting at the end of a gravel lane so long it seemed to disappear in the distance.

He swung the car off the pavement. "This must be his driveway."

A couple gray silos and a Quonset hut appeared on the right after several minutes of bumping and jolting down the lane. Ahead of them was a cream and brown double-wide house trailer with a satellite dish mounted out front. One large tree in the yard stood starkly green against the drab landscape.

A spotted mutt ran out to greet them when they pulled up next to a red pickup truck parked in front of the trailer. Janet recoiled and her expression tightened.

"Don't worry," he said to her. "I'll have Kevin tie him before you get out."

She gave a wordless nod.

Frankie climbed out of the car, straightened his shoulders, and strode up three wooden steps to the door. The muffled voice of a sportscaster coming through the thin walls told him a radio was blaring inside.

He rapped on the door three times and waited. He could imagine Kevin halting in the middle of whatever he was doing, jerking his head toward the door, and racing through some kind of mental catalog to figure out who in the world could be calling on him.

Frankie stepped aside when he sensed movement from beyond the door. The inner door swung open and a man he barely recognized appeared behind the screen that separated them.

"Can I help...?" The words died on the man's lips. "*Frankie?*"

"The very same," Frankie said. "It's been a long time."

"N-nineteen years, I think." Kevin opened the screen door and ran a shaking hand through his sparse hair. It used to be full and blond, but now it had thinned and turned the color of dried brush. He'd developed a paunch around his middle in the past nineteen years, too. He wore faded bib overalls over a faded work shirt, which matched his faded boots.

The dog came up behind Frankie and was now barking as if to alert Kevin that an intruder had entered the premises. "I don't mean to be rude," Frankie said, even though showing up unannounced like this might have been considered such, "but could you tie up your dog? Janet doesn't like—"

"Oh, I remember," Kevin blurted. "She had that Doberman attack her when she was a kid. Sure, I'll put him around back for you. Chet!" He whistled and stepped past Frankie. "C'mon, boy. Let's go give the lady some peace."

Chet was more than happy to oblige. Tail wagging, he followed Kevin around the corner of the trailer.

Kevin returned a minute later and dragged a hand over his sweaty forehead. "Sorry about that. If I'd known you two were coming, I'd have had him tied already. So what brings you to Idaho?"

Frankie beckoned to Janet. "Bad news. We should talk about this inside."

Kevin's face paled. "Did somebody die?"

"Not yet," Frankie said. "That's why we need you."

# 11

FRANKIE AND Janet took seats at a round table in Kevin's kitchen. Kevin poured three glasses of tea and offered them Fig Newtons before sitting down.

"So how is everyone?" Kevin asked once they were settled. "How's my boy Gary doing? I bet he's married now and has a brood of kids who look just like him."

Frankie exchanged a dark look with Janet, whose lips formed a thin line. Gary Humphrey was Kevin's successor. "Gary was killed in a car accident seventeen years ago," Frankie said, feeling an uncharacteristic twinge of sorrow as he remembered the day it happened. "It was one of those freak things. He had the windows rolled down and they think a bee or spider got inside and caused him to panic. He went off the road into a utility pole."

Frankie could hear the breath leaving Kevin's chest. "Oh no." Kevin's Adam's apple bobbed up and down. "Did he have a...a..."

"Replacement? Yes. He chose Martin Hampstead shortly before he died."

Kevin's mood lightened a little. "I remember him! He went to that Methodist church down the street from St. Paul's. Always cracking jokes, that one was. Never knew he'd end up being chosen. Is he doing all right?"

Frankie had known their conversation would take a turn like this since Kevin had been out of the loop for so long. "I'm sure he's doing quite a bit better than we are. He was murdered in 2002."

Kevin's face was now utterly devoid of color. "Murdered?"

"He was helping a woman and her ex didn't like it, so he shot Martin in the chest. I've been told his death was instant."

Kevin bowed his head, and his shoulders shook. "I just can't believe they're *both* gone. And so young! I mean, I..."

"They're not *gone*, Kevin. Did you forget who called us to be Servants? Do you think the death of our bodies is the very end? You know it's not! Or have you chosen to forget everything you knew back home?"

Kevin's pouchy face was damp with tears. "No, Frankie. You don't understand. I came out here because it's so quiet. Nothing ever bothers me out here. I didn't think I'd find peace again, but I did. This is where God wants me to be."

"Can you still heal?"

The question took the former Servant by surprise. "Pardon?"

"I said, can you still heal?"

Kevin frowned. "Of course I can still heal. Why wouldn't I?"

"Prove it."

"I don't understand. You don't believe me?"

"When was the last time you did it?"

"I don't know. Maybe last month? Chet cut his paw on a rock when we were walking through the creek at the back of my property. All I had to do was touch him and he was just fine. He's a good dog."

Janet squirmed in her chair and gazed into her tea. She had never allowed Frankie or Carly to have any pets that weren't fish. The idea that a dog might be good was wholly foreign to her.

"So we'll practice and see if your ability still works on humans." Frankie eyed a knife block sitting on Kevin's cluttered counter. "Excuse me." He rose from the table and selected the largest knife he could find. Kevin needed to get over his cowardice. This might help.

Janet gasped when Frankie returned to the table with the knife. "Frankie Jovingo, what in the world are you doing?"

Frankie twisted his left arm so his palm faced upward. He pressed the tip of the knife to the skin of his wrist and made a light incision about two inches long. It stung when the top layer of skin separated from itself, but the pain would pass soon enough. "There," he said. "Heal it."

Kevin looked ill even though the quantity of blood seeping from the cut couldn't have filled a thimble. "You're crazy," he said, and brought the fingers of his right hand to rest on the cut.

Warmth penetrated his skin, and the pain vanished.

"That's what they keep telling me," Frankie said as Kevin took his hand away. Frankie pulled a napkin out of the holder sitting in the center of the table and wiped away the blood. He held his arm closer to his face. His skin was unbroken—there wasn't even a scar.

Kevin rose on shaking legs and went to the sink to wash his hands. "I had nightmares," he said in a strained voice. "Horrible ones. Since I've lived here, they've mostly gone away."

"You didn't need to have nightmares," Frankie said. "God is on your side. With him, there's nothing to fear."

"I'm not you, Frankie." Kevin dried his hands on a dish towel and resumed his seat, looking forlorn.

Janet looked to Kevin. "I'm sorry he's treating you like this. I told him to leave you alone but he insisted on finding you, so I came along to keep him in line."

To Frankie's surprise, Kevin's face broke into a smile. "Keep Frankie in line? That'll be the day. I remember what it was like. Roger would just about have a heart attack whenever you'd skip town without notice. Graham always thought that was so funny." His expression sobered. "Please tell me Roger and Graham are still doing okay."

Frankie cleared his throat. "Roger is quite well, though I do keep advising him that he should probably lose some weight. Graham, however, is not." He proceeded to tell Kevin about all that transpired during the past year in regard to Graham's plot against Randy, whom Kevin had never met.

"So if this Randy survived and was replaced by a new guy," Kevin said when Frankie finished, "then what in the world do you need me for?"

Frankie straightened his shoulders. "An angel told me to find you."

"An angel."

"Do you doubt me?"

"You're making it up."

Frankie had expected Kevin to doubt him. Many would. "He clearly thinks your ability will be of use to us."

Kevin's bottom lip trembled. "Do you want to know what I dreamed about before I left?"

"I don't need to know. We do ask that you consider returning with us. I don't know what disaster awaits, but I do know it must be bad enough that God sent one of his messengers to intervene."

"Did this messenger have a name?"

"Yes. Caleb."

Kevin looked like he'd just been slapped. "You're sure?"

"Why?"

Kevin cleared his throat. "He and I may have been somewhat acquainted at one point. Back when I was the Servant, you know. He told me...never mind."

*Interesting.* Frankie's own grandfather had mentioned receiving help from an entity named Caleb, as well, which had lent some credibility to the message Frankie had received.

"I don't want to go back," Kevin said.

"I didn't think you would."

"Then why did you come?"

Frankie leaned forward. "Because I didn't feel it would be proper to disobey such an urgent request."

Silence. Then, "No offense, but I don't want to deal with you people again. I've been a happy man since I came out here. I've got my land, I've got my dog, and I've got my God, and I don't need anything or anyone else."

"If you truly feel you're right in the eyes of God, come with us. If someone dies because you're too stubborn to come out of your little hermit hole, *you* will take the blame for it."

Tears filled Kevin's eyes. "Oh Lord. Oh geez. Oh Lord." His breaths became shallow, and he grabbed onto the edge of the table. "Lord, what am I going to *do*?"

"That's your decision to make."

"Oh geez." Kevin shook his head. "Word for word, what did Caleb tell you?"

"He said, 'Find Kevin Lyle and tell him to return to Oregon.' I asked him why and he said, 'Because someone important will need him.'"

Kevin dragged a hand over his tired face. "Lord have mercy. Let me think this over."

# 12

BOBBY'S MIND wandered as he headed north on Interstate 5, the directions to The Pink Rooster displayed in his mind's eye.

His earlier encounter with Thane grew increasingly surreal as he replayed it in his head. Had he been so sleep-deprived that his mind conjured a new buddy to help him figure things out? Or was Thane, like Caleb, an angel sent from above to help him?

He wished he knew.

Turning his thoughts to more pressing matters, Bobby got off on the first exit after crossing into Hillsdale's town limits and turned left onto a busy thoroughfare called Grand Avenue before making turns onto progressively smaller streets where the homes and businesses grew progressively shabby.

The Pink Rooster came up so unexpectedly that Bobby almost passed it. He slammed on the brakes just in time and whipped the Nissan into the lot, choosing an empty spot by the door.

He studied the building before getting out. The Pink Rooster—not pink at all—was a one-story structure made of cinder blocks painted blue with lime green trim around the windows and door. Judging from the architecture, the building might have begun its career as an auto repair shop that was later remodeled to accommodate restaurant-style seating. He could even see where a bay door had been partly filled in with newer cinder blocks and fitted with a window.

Exactly what had drawn Mystery Woman to this place? It looked like the run-down sort of joint whose clientele might be comprised solely of "regulars."

Which might mean someone would remember the woman— again, assuming the receipts they'd found were hers.

He got out, took slow breaths to calm his nerves, and went to the door. In the split second before he pulled it open, something fluttered in his gut and the Spirit whispered, *Be vigilant.*

Praying he wouldn't be confronted by a seven-foot-tall thug who didn't like the looks of him, Bobby went inside.

Music that would have awakened a deaf man assaulted his ears as he shouldered his way into the establishment. Neon beer signs and hanging lamps with green shades lit the area. Just inside the door on the back of a booth was a movie-poster-sized painting of a pink cartoon rooster wearing sunglasses and taking a swig from a bottle of Blue Moon beer.

Bobby had only taken four steps into the room when blackness deeper than a starless night filled his mind. It was like his head was full of worms, millions and millions of them writhing over and under each other as they slowly ate away at everything pure and good.

Fear tightened his chest, and the sounds around him diminished until all he could hear was the beating of his own frantic heart.

It could mean only one thing: a demon had possessed someone. And that someone was somewhere in this room.

He gulped down fresh air and did his best to compose himself, though the black, wormlike aura did not abate. His hearing cleared, and he sent up a prayer of thanks.

Bobby felt about two feet tall as he approached the counter, where the bartender and a patron were watching a baseball game on a wall-mounted television while complaining about a player who had been traded to another team.

Neither of them was the source of the aura.

He breathed a small sigh of relief and said, "Excuse me."

The bartender, who had greasy black hair and about four days of stubble on his chin, drew his attention away from the television and smiled. Most of his teeth were yellow. The rest were missing. "What can I do for you today, son? Looking to celebrate your tenth birthday here?"

The man watching the game from his barstool let out a hearty laugh as he shoved a cheese-drenched pretzel into his mouth. "Vern, you're just getting old. Don't you know? This is what men look like these days."

Vern pretended to take offense. "If I'm old, you're a corpse. I'll bet you don't even last half a second anymore."

The man with the pretzels just snickered.

"Actually, I'm looking for someone," Bobby said as he placed the woman's picture on the counter while desperately trying to ignore the aura that continued to invade his thoughts. "I think she's been in here a few times and I wondered if you knew anything about her."

"Sounds like we've got a mystery on our hands." Vern swiped the picture off the counter with a flourish and fished a pair of reading glasses out of a pocket. "Now let me see here," he said as he put them on one-handed. "Do you know what day she was in?"

Bobby withdrew the receipts from his pocket and checked the dates. "Monday, Tuesday, and Wednesday."

"See, here's the problem. I'm not here any of those days. You want to know about her, ask my brother Chuck."

"Is Chuck here?"

"No."

Bobby refused to let disappointment take hold of him. "She could have been here other days, too. And I think she was with a blond guy."

"That narrows it down."

"Do you have any blond regulars?"

"It might be we do," Vern said. "And it might be we don't."

"Supposing you do," Bobby said. "Would one of them have a certain *thing* for women?"

"Son, you just described most of the folks who come in here. What specific thing are *you* talking about?"

Bobby took a deep breath. "He might be a predator. I think he might have befriended this woman here and then kidnapped her."

Vern shrugged. "It's not my problem if he did or didn't. I just work here."

"Do you know anyone named Phil Mason?"

"Sure don't."

Bobby believed him. "Thanks for your help," he said even though he hadn't really learned anything. "Do you have a bathroom?"

Vern pointed to a short hallway off to Bobby's right. "It's down that way. You can't miss it."

"Thanks." Bobby hurried into the hallway, which made a ninety-degree left turn about five feet in and led to five doors: two restrooms on the right and two doors marked "Employees Only" on the left. An exit sign hung over the door at the end. He didn't see any cameras.

Now that he was here, the aura dimmed.

It was possible, however remote, that Mystery Woman was being kept prisoner here.

Bobby made some quick calculations. Upon arriving he'd counted four other cars in the lot. Undoubtedly one belonged to Vern, one to the man sitting at the counter, and two to the other people he'd glimpsed sitting in booths. Unless one or more of them had carpooled with someone, there shouldn't have been anyone else in the building, so the actions he was about to take should go unnoticed.

Bobby opened the first door on the left and poked his head into a kitchen smelling strongly of grease. Stainless steel counters and appliances stared back at him, and a skinny guy in a flannel shirt stood at the grill flipping a solitary burger patty—someone had carpooled after all.

Strike one.

The second door on the left led into a dark storage room. He flicked on a light and saw shelves of cleaning supplies, boxes of napkins, unopened boxes of dishes, and dishcloths. A card table and metal folding chair sat against one wall. Above them hung a poster of a well-muscled nude woman riding a Harley.

Blushing like the ten-year-old that Vern had taken him to be, Bobby quietly switched off the light and backed out of the room.

He hurried into the men's room and did his business, then returned to the counter. "Do you have Sprite?" he asked.

"A teetotaler in a bar," said the man still nursing his pretzels. "Now I've seen everything."

When Bobby had his Sprite in hand and his own plate of pretzels and cheese dip a minute later (he was pleased to note that his drink was free of burnt matches), he gravitated toward one of the booths, where a man in his mid-twenties sat by himself with his head in his hands. The beer glass sitting in front of him had made a pool of condensation on the cardboard coaster, yet the man had only consumed half of it.

The black aura intensified as he drew closer to him, and though Bobby wanted to get out of there before he fainted or soiled himself from fright, a strange compulsion made him stay.

"Um, excuse me," he said to the man in a voice that shook too much. "Do you mind if I sit here?"

The man jerked his head up. He had a narrow face and pointed chin, hair so blond it looked white, and eyes a milky shade of blue. "What? No, I don't mind. I was just sitting here thinking."

Gingerly, Bobby slid into the opposite side of the booth. He would have to play this cool.

He held up Mystery Woman's picture. "Have you ever seen this woman before?"

Pale eyes moved back and forth as they scanned the image. "Yes."

"Here?"

"Where else?"

"Who's the man who was with her? You?"

A soft laugh. "No, but I watched them."

Bobby's heart beat faster. "What were they doing?"

"Drinking. Talking. Not much else to do here, is there?" A wicked glint shined in the man's eyes, but it vanished as soon as it had appeared.

"Can you tell me exactly what the guy looked like?"

"He smiled a lot. Average build. His shoulders slouched a bit. He comes here all the time but I don't know his name."

Before Bobby could formulate another question, his surroundings vanished and he was instantly transported to the hallway at his old high school, four years earlier.

He was inside a memory—one he had no desire to remember.

Greg Yates, a classmate he despised, had covered the combination lock on Bobby's locker with Vaseline not for the first time that week, and now Bobby was waiting for him with some tricks of his own in mind.

Greg appeared around the corner, swaggering like he owned the hallway. He'd popped the collar on his polo shirt. Bobby thought he looked like an idiot.

Bobby was taller than Greg, but since Greg participated in several school sports his bulk greatly exceeded Bobby's.

"Well if it isn't Knobby Bobby," Greg said, coming to a stop. "How's your day been, buddy?"

Without preamble, Bobby removed his hand from behind his back and smeared a thick glob of Vaseline right down Greg's face.

The vision ended, and Bobby was back in the booth sitting across from the blond man, who was staring at him with something like fear in his eyes.

*Get out of here*, a cruel voice hissed in Bobby's ear. *You're not good enough to do what you think you can.*

"Is there anything else you'd like to ask?" the possessed man asked, his tone oddly polite.

"Um, yeah." Bobby shivered. "How do you feel right now?" He threw a glance behind him and was pleased to see that both Vern and the pretzel eater had returned their attention to the baseball game and resumed their commentary on the players involved. The only other patron in the bar sat in a booth on the other side of the room flipping through a magazine.

With luck, the music blaring from the speakers in the ceiling would mask everything he planned on saying.

The blond man's attitude shifted faster than Bobby could count to zero. His lip curled, and his hands tightened into fists. "What does it matter?" he snarled. "I can do whatever I like and I don't have to explain myself to anyone."

Bobby considered leaving before he accidentally caused a scene but his rear had welded itself to the vinyl bench. "I—I know you've been going through some kind of trouble. I know some people who might be able to help you."

A spark of interest lit up the man's face. "What do you—"

The bar vanished again.

This time Bobby found himself standing at the edge of the fishing pond at Smithfield Park back in his Ohio hometown, minding his own business as he skipped rocks across the surface of the water to see how far they would go before sinking into the murk. The park was only a few blocks from his house, so he'd come here alone, as he often did.

He was twelve years old.

As he picked up another flat rock and positioned it in his hand so it would hit the water at just the right angle, footsteps came up behind him and stopped a few feet away.

He knew who it was without turning to look. "What do you want?" he asked as he gripped the rock tighter in his hand.

Eleven-year-old Rory Wells's voice consisted of a high-pitched whine that always made Bobby want to smash something, preferably Rory Wells. "I heard that you and Joel Fontenot are a couple of queers."

Bobby whirled around and glowered at the kid, who was four inches shorter than him and weighed about as much as a bag of potatoes. "Says who?"

"Says everyone. You two go *everywhere* together. I betcha want to get married someday and adopt a bunch of queer babies, too."

Joel's family had recently moved to the area from New Orleans. He and Bobby had discovered a mutual interest in music and scary stories, which Joel was happy to supply to him even though Bobby didn't believe a single one.

"It takes one to know one," Bobby said.

Rory crossed his arms. "What's that mean?"

"If you think Joel and I are queer, then you must be, too."

The kid's face became the color of a beet. "Am not!"

"Are you sure? Because you look like a little queer. You probably still wet the bed, too."

Rory's small hands tightened into fists. "If you keep up like that I'm going to go tell my—"

Bobby didn't let him finish. He lifted the rock and brought it down on Rory's head.

Rory crumpled to the ground wailing like a dying cat, but Bobby wasn't about to stop. He threw the rock aside, planted himself on Rory's chest, and pounded him in the face until his eye turned purple and began to swell.

Bobby gave a sudden halt, his heart racing so fast he felt dizzy. What had he just done?

Rory was sobbing, and Bobby got off of him. "If you tell *anyone* about this," Bobby said, hearing his voice tremble, "I'll kill you. You hear that? My dad's got a gun. Nothing's going to stop me from putting it against your stupid head and pulling the trigger."

In reality, he would never do such a thing—especially considering the fact that his father did not own a firearm of any kind. He just knew he'd be in some serious crap if anyone found out he'd nearly beaten Rory into a pulp.

Blood flowed from Rory's bottom lip as he nodded wordlessly. With a whimper, he got up and ran back in the direction of his house.

"—mean?" the blond man asked from the other side of the booth in The Pink Rooster.

Bobby returned to the present feeling ill at the memories the man's tormentor forced him to recall.

He had never told another person about that day at the park. Bobby had often wondered what lies Rory imparted to his parents in order to explain his injuries, but he would never find out. The following year a drunk driver slammed into Rory's side of the car when Mrs. Wells was taking him home from school. The driver got fourteen years in prison, Mrs. Wells got a coma, and Rory got a coffin and a nice headstone down in the graveyard at Holy Trinity Church.

Bobby stood, grabbing the wax paper that his pretzels nested in and twisting it into a parcel around them. "Never mind," he said. "I think I should go."

He rushed out of the bar without looking back.

Outside in his car, he leaned his head against the steering wheel. Tears ran down his cheeks, and every cell in his body burned with shame.

He'd often heard that the flapping of a butterfly's wings could alter the air just enough to start a hurricane on the other side of the world. Time and time again over the years he wondered what would have happened if he hadn't touched Rory, or if he'd simply stayed home from the park that day. If Rory hadn't been hurt, life might have gone on differently enough that he and his mother would have altogether avoided the accident that killed him.

Which was probably a crazy thing to think, but Bobby hadn't been able to help it.

It had taken Bobby ages to forget about Rory. In fact, he didn't think Rory had crossed his mind at all since Bobby left Eleanor, Ohio behind and shaken the dust from his feet.

Until now. The thing afflicting the man in the bar had read Bobby's mind like a book and held up a mirror to reflect the pages back at him.

"I'm not that person anymore," Bobby said aloud. Then, "Rory, I'm sorry. If you can hear me, I'm sorry."

Bobby fed himself a pretzel, started the car, and pulled out of the lot. He glanced in the mirror a few times to observe The Pink Rooster receding into the distance, wondering if he should have stayed with the possessed man and seen if there was anything he could do to help.

As he got back onto Interstate 5, he shivered. If just being near a demon could provoke such a reaction in him, what was going to happen the day he attempted to exorcise one?

He bumped up the radio to drown out his thoughts, but instead of getting lost in the melody blaring from the speakers, the faces of both Greg Yates and Rory Wells swam in the forefront of his mind as if demanding justice.

# 13

JACK DROVE through Hillsdale and then Autumn Ridge, trying to formulate a plan. Driving helped him think better than pacing back and forth across a room did. It let Jack see things he wouldn't otherwise: buildings, streets, parks, people. He would form connections and come up with new ideas, but so far determining how he would arrange for the capture of so many people in the next week was proving even harder than he'd expected.

Troy wanted him to get five.

Where in the world would he find them?

*And when did Troy become so demanding?*

One problem with communities like Hillsdale and Autumn Ridge was that neither was large enough for a man in his position to fully blend in with the crowd. Luckily for him, Jack had been born with an ordinary face and grew into a man with an ordinary build, and he wasn't into flashy attire, tattoos, or piercings that would proclaim who he was like a neon sign in a window. He guessed this was part of the reason he had yet to be apprehended for his part in

Randy Bellison's attempted murder: he was just too plain for people to remember him.

Yet arranging for five human beings to be abducted would draw attention to the most boring-looking man on the planet.

On the plus side, these towns weren't the type of place where law enforcement would expect such an illicit industry to take root. The longer their network stayed below the radar, the better.

When Jack had finally tracked down Graham, he'd been delighted to learn that the two of them had more in common than some measly strands of DNA and a penchant for the illegal. Graham had gained people's trust before murdering them, and Jack gained their trust before having one of his colleagues snatch them away. (On certain occasions Jack himself took care of said snatching. It all depended on the circumstances.)

But the central question remained: where would he find five easily-missed people during the next week? He would have to work quickly, but fast work tended to be sloppy. He couldn't afford to be caught.

*If only Trish were still here to help out.*

Trish Gunson, his late colleague, had been a reluctant recruit. She'd desperately needed the money and had resorted to finding vulnerable people at her college to send the traffickers' way.

Then she found out she had some lethal heart defect, and when Graham mentioned how much it would hurt Randy if a victim died during an exorcism, Jack happily donated Trish to his grandfather's cause. She'd always annoyed him, anyway, even though she did help get things done.

Jack had no desire to hang out at the college Trish attended. For one, he wasn't a student; and secondly, few people would be in class this time of year.

Back to square one.

He supposed he could drive into one of the seedier sections of town to see if any troubled girls—or boys—were looking for work. He might be able to get one or two that way.

But not five, and not so soon. Because someone in that seedy part of town would notice if five of their neighbors disappeared all at once, and if they were feeling extra ambitious, they might report it to the police.

As Jack turned down another street, he caught sight of colorful, fluttering banners announcing a summer festival that would take place in a couple of days. He tapped lightly on the brake and leaned over to peer out the passenger side window so he could see them better.

*10th ANNUAL AUTUMN RIDGE SUMMERPALOOZA!!!* one banner proclaimed in glaring red and orange letters. *RIDES! GAMES! FOOD! LIVE MUSIC! FUN FOR THE WHOLE FAMILY! FREE ADMISSION!*

Hmm.

Jack checked his mirrors and threw the car into reverse when he saw the coast was clear, then pulled into the park.

The parking lot was empty save for some overflowing recycling bins. The park occupied maybe twelve acres of land, half of which was wooded. A patchy field containing a baseball diamond sat between the woods and the parking lot. No rides or booths had been set up yet.

He placed his chin on his hand. He'd been to enough fairs and town festivals to know that the promise of free entertainment often brought the dregs of society crawling out of the woodwork like a bunch of hungry roaches. Could he really pull off what Troy wanted him to do at an event like this? There would probably be security on hand.

And lots and lots of eyewitnesses.

Jack got out of the car and slammed the door, hearing its lonely echo against the adjacent houses and trees. He inhaled deeply and closed his eyes.

A husky voice spoke inside his mind. *You're never going to be able to do what Troy wants. You know that, right?*

There was the truth, plain as day. Jack could see it now. Troy wanted him gone, and instead of saying it outright, he'd heaped this impossible task upon him that was guaranteed to fail. It took time to become acquainted with someone well enough to know whether or not he or she would be missed, and it took time to gain trust—

even Graham had known that when he found people on whom he would later conduct his twisted experiments.

Or maybe Troy really was offering Jack a promotion. It was too hard to read the man's mind.

Having nothing better to do, Jack walked toward the baseball diamond. Shiny bleachers sat beside it and Jack planted himself on the bottom row to brood.

He could always quit the business, go on the run from Troy, and find work elsewhere, but where would the fun in that be? Jack grew bored easily. He'd been that way for as long as he could remember. As a child his mother was often away at work, leaving Jack to fend for himself. Books, television, toys, and his sister had held little appeal for him, so he would hang out with the other children on their street. Jack had no emotional attachment to them. They'd simply been a means to an end.

One day when he was about ten, he and a younger neighbor boy named Tim had been walking down to a local ice cream shop when an unexpected voice in Jack's head plainly said, "Make him eat dirt."

An ordinary child would have been alarmed, but Jack welcomed the voice. He didn't know why it wanted Tim to do such a thing, but it suddenly seemed like the best idea in the world.

"Hey Tim," Jack said. "Have you ever eaten dirt?"

Tim halted on the sidewalk and turned. "Dirt?"

"You know, that brown stuff all over the ground."

Tim's cheeks had flushed. "Why would I do that?"

"The question is," Jack said, "why wouldn't you? It can't hurt you. All it is is dead plants and stuff." He grinned.

Tim looked uncertain. "It really can't hurt me?"

"Nope. And let me tell you a little secret." Jack leaned closer to Tim's ear and whispered, "We can't even grow up if we don't eat dirt. We'll just stay little kids forever and ever."

"Are you sure?" Now Tim's face had gone white, and the sight of it filled Jack with glee.

"I'm sure."

"Have you ever eaten dirt, Jack?"

"Lots of times. It's actually not that bad." Jack pointed at a bare patch of earth next to the sidewalk. "Go ahead. Try some."

"Okay." Tim bent over, picked up a small clod, and held it tentatively in his fingers. "What if there's bugs in it?"

"Who cares if there are? They add extra nutrition." Nutrition was something Jack's mother was always going on about, which probably meant it was supposed to be important.

Tim stared at the clod a moment longer, scrunched his eyes shut, and said, "Here goes!"

Jack watched in silent fascination as Tim popped the chunk of dirt into his mouth. His expression soured as he chewed, and Jack thought he'd throw up right there on the sidewalk. But then Tim shuddered and opened his mouth, revealing a brown tongue and bits of dirt stuck in his teeth. "That was nasty!"

Jack clapped him on the back. "The taste'll go away in a minute. Now let's get some ice cream!"

The feeling Jack had for the rest of that day was almost indescribable. He'd been able to convince someone to do something they never would have done otherwise. It was like he had a kind of power over Tim. For his entire short life, nothing had been under Jack's control—the shady men his mother brought home, the new apartments to which they moved, the new schools Jack was forced to attend, the constant rules imposed on him by his teachers. *Don't talk in class, Jack. Don't take Nicky's toys. Don't throw food at your classmates. Don't don't don't.*

Getting a taste of what it was like to take charge for once was a beautiful thing. And now that he'd tasted it, he wanted more.

After that he conducted similar experiments on other neighborhood children. He convinced a boy to run through the corner supermarket naked. He sweet-talked a girl into stealing a pack of cigarettes for him. He even got his own mother to buy him a brand-new video game system that he only played for a week before growing bored with it.

"Jack," she said one day while folding laundry, "you sure have a way with words."

Boy, did he.

In the present, Jack withdrew a quarter from his pocket and rolled it across his knuckles.

*Five. How in the blazes am I supposed to get five?*

---

I'M TRAPPED. *I'm for sale. I'm trapped. I'm for sale.*

Adrian's thoughts were stuck on repeat, and she felt as though she'd be sick.

At one point the brown-skinned woman returned with sandwiches and water for the three occupants of the windowless room, but Adrian couldn't eat. How could she in a place like this?

Marissa, the blonde, chided her in a low voice that wouldn't carry beyond the walls of the concrete room. "Starving yourself isn't going to help, you know."

Adrian hugged her arms against her chest and kept rocking back and forth on her cot. "I never should have left him. I should have just stayed home." Yuri had been right to advise her not to contact her children. If she'd stayed at his side like a good wife, she wouldn't be here.

She didn't even know where "here" was.

Neither did Marissa. She told Adrian she'd been there roughly three days, the Asian woman for two. When Marissa first awakened in the room, four teenage girls were there with her. None of them had spoken English. Illegal immigrants, Marissa guessed. They probably had either been restaurant workers or farmhands.

According to Marissa, two big men and a haughty-faced woman had come to the room and looked each of the women over. The woman had nodded and said, "I'll take these four."

The men had handcuffed the teenagers and led them sobbing from the room. Marissa never saw them again.

Adrian knew that the people who took the girls would be back. It was only a matter of time before they took her, too.

Adrian said, "Starving might be easier than whatever's outside that door."

Marissa shook her head. "It takes weeks of no food before you die. Besides, maybe it won't be that bad. Whatever they'll do to us, I mean."

Adrian gave her a doleful stare. "Honey, how old are you?"

"I'll be twenty-three next week. Some way to spend a birthday, huh?" Marissa shrugged. "The way I see it, the worst they could do is sell us to an illegal brothel. It might suck, but at least we won't be dead."

"You're a very naïve girl."

"Oh yeah?" Marissa stood up. "I'd rather have ten men a night than be murdered, and if they wanted *that*, we'd already be dead."

"They could be holding us for ransom. My husband—"

Marissa shook her head. "They'd be out of their minds to hold *me* for ransom. My parents don't have two cents to rub together. I haven't even talked to them in three years."

Adrian sighed. It was foolish to think someone in Oregon would have recognized her as Yuri's wife and abducted her in order to collect ransom money. Even if she hadn't run off, Yuri wouldn't have parted with his beloved wealth just to save her.

She felt a little wistful at that realization. Wealth was Yuri's one true love and had been all along. Adrian was simply a thing to be used for Yuri's convenience. Should she really have expected any different after what she'd done to her children?

Adrian picked up the sandwich and bit off a corner. It consisted of bologna and cheese so dry she could hardly swallow. "There has to be a way out of here."

"There is. Through that door. When they take you with them."

Awhile later—one hour, two hours, Adrian couldn't tell—the metal door swung open. Instead of the buyers Marissa described, a beady-eyed man and two with guns entered the cell.

Adrian averted her gaze and pretended to take great interest in the floor.

"This is all you've got?" the beady-eyed man asked.

*Please just leave*, Adrian prayed.

"Wait a few days, and we'll have more," one of the other men said.

"I don't have a few days." Beady Eyes let out a terse breath. "I was hoping for younger. A john blew my youngest one's head off last night and I don't like having empty rooms."

"Maybe you should start screening your clientele before letting them into your establishment. What you see is what you get."

Adrian found herself hoping against hope that the man would either leave empty handed or take the other women instead, which made her wonder if she was just as much of a monster as the people who had imprisoned them.

"Fine," the buyer said. "I'll take these two."

Adrian refused to look up as Marissa and the Asian woman were cuffed and led from the room.

Her stomach turned. *Please don't hurt them. Please, please don't hurt them.*

The heavy door swung shut and locked her in.

For the first time since she'd come here, she was alone.

She would not remain that way for long.

---

**BOBBY RAN** his hands over his face.

He had failed. Miserably. It had been a mistake to take Randy's place as the Servant, especially since Randy hadn't died after all. Randy could have found someone else to follow in his footsteps, preferably someone who didn't know the meaning of fear and had no past sins that could be thrown back in his face at inopportune moments.

At least the entity that called itself Thane didn't greet him upon his return home. He had enough to deal with without angels or hallucinations dropping in unannounced.

Bobby sank onto the squashed second-hand couch.

*Do you trust in me?*

A lump rose in Bobby's throat. He couldn't lie to the Spirit. "I want to."

*You have no reason to doubt.*

"I'm not good enough for this. You can't expect me to drive demons out of people when I've got this...this little punk inside me wanting to hurt people."

*You have been forgiven.*

Bobby blinked an embarrassing tear from his eye. "Okay. So what am I supposed to do?"

*Relax your mind.*

"Can you tell me who kidnapped that woman?"

*You know it in your heart. Relax your mind.*

Bobby understood now. Last week when he and Phil tried to figure out where Randy went to confront Graham, Phil helped Bobby move into an altered state of consciousness that helped Bobby determine where Randy could be found.

He supposed he could try a similar tactic now.

Bobby lay on his back across the cushions and took slow breaths. Blond guy. He needed to learn the identity of the blond guy.

He imagined he was walking along a sandy shoreline, and his consciousness wavered.

*Relax, Bobby. Relax.*

He put one foot in front of the other. Waves lapped against the sand to his left. The sun's blazing orb hung in the sky and seagulls circled and wheeled through the air around him.

At first Bobby could still feel the cushions pressing into him at the same time he was walking down the beach, but then the former sensation ceased.

The sound of soft footsteps accompanying his alerted him to the fact that he wasn't alone.

He jerked his head to the side, not quite surprised to see his father, the late Ken Roland, walking beside him. "You're back," Bobby blurted. "Just like when I did this before."

"But the question is," Ken said, "did I ever really leave?"

They continued walking.

"Dad?" Bobby asked after a time, casting his father a shy glance as his bare feet marked passage of their stroll through the sand. It felt like more than a decade had melted away and Bobby was a child again—albeit one whose mind was filled with very un-childlike thoughts. "Can I ask you something?"

Ken halted and planted his meaty hands on his hips. He looked just as he had in life. Thinning hair. A keg-like stomach that resulted from too many trays of late-night nachos. Eyes that twinkled even when he wasn't smiling. "Sure thing. What's on your mind?"

"Well, I was wondering." He broke off, not certain how to put it without the words coming across the wrong way. "I know I didn't hold up to your standards."

Ken's eyebrows rose in surprise. "What in the blue blazes are you talking about?"

Heat rose in Bobby's face. "I mean, you always went on and on about car stuff and working hard to be—what was it? A 'productive member of society,' and I ignored you just so I could do my own thing. I know you thought my music was a waste of time."

There. He said the words he'd wanted to say for years but couldn't.

Ken studied him. "Playing that guitar of yours made you happy though, didn't it? And that's what mattered to me more than anything."

Relief loosened some of the tightness in Bobby's chest. "You mean you're not mad at me?"

"Mad?" Ken laughed. "Course I'm not mad at you. Maybe I was worried about you becoming some sissy boy who couldn't do a thing for himself, but I was wrong about that, wasn't I?"

Bobby cast his gaze toward his feet. "I suppose so."

"You *suppose*. Bobby, what you did for those people is the best I ever could have asked of you." He was smiling now; his eyes twinkling more brightly than ever. "We're all proud of you. Not many could have done it."

"I was only doing what was right."

"Bobby, people are faced with choices every day of their lives. If you count the number of them who do the right thing instead of the things that are best for themselves, well, let's just say they won't be leading many polls."

Bobby remained silent, and they resumed their journey across the sand. The gentle waves lapping against the shore were almost hypnotic. "Have you always been watching me?" he asked after a length of time that could have been either a minute or a hundred years.

"Always."

"Charlotte and Jonas, too?"

"Of course."

"Can I ask you something else?"

"I'll bet I know what it is."

"Why is it that every time I try to meditate like this, I see you?"

A laugh. "Just because, son. Just because."

"And are you really here, or is this just a dream?"

"That's for you to decide. But does it matter?"

"I guess not." Bobby sidestepped a scuttling crab. There was something else he needed to know, but it had fled his mind.

"You need to love your mother," Ken said.

This was quite possibly the last thing he'd expected his father to say. "What?"

"I mean it. No matter what's happened, and no matter what *will* happen, you need to love her if it's the last thing you do."

"I don't understand."

"Yeah, you do."

The beach vanished, and Bobby was back in his living room.

In his mind he saw the face of Jack Willard, whose dishwater blond hair shined in the light spilling through the trees in the woods behind Graham Willard's house.

His mind scrambled to make sense of it.

Mystery Woman. Blond guy. Kidnapping.

He began to sweat. How could he have not realized that Jack Willard was the one who'd taken the woman? And if Jack could be callous enough to work with Graham, there was no telling what he might do to the poor woman who came to Oregon all the way from the Midwest for reasons Bobby had yet to learn.

# 14

BOBBY HAD never gone in to clean St. Paul's so early in the day. Voices interspersed with peals of laughter echoed down the hallways surrounding the inner sanctuary when he stepped into the entryway. A woman he didn't recognize was busy rearranging flyers on a bulletin board. Not wanting to waste any time by engaging in what would amount to meaningless small talk, Bobby hurried past her down the left-hand hallway to clock in and get started.

A voice startled him as he passed an open doorway. "Bobby Roland?"

He backtracked a step or two and ran a hand over his hair before entering the room.

A thin, middle-aged priest sat behind a desk on which sat a cup of pens and a tiny model sailboat. His hair appeared to have once been charcoal-black but was now mostly gray, and it was parted so neatly on one side that Bobby wondered if the guy used a ruler to make sure the line stayed straight when he combed it.

The priest regarded him with a mixture of friendliness and curiosity. "If you're Bobby," he said, "then please close the door and take a seat."

"What if I'm not?"

"Then I would have to ask why in the world you responded to Bobby's name."

Grinning, Bobby shut the door and sat in one of the chairs facing the desk. "So you're Father Preston."

A thin smile. "You're an astute one, aren't you?"

Bobby shifted to get more comfortable. Randy and Phil both liked the priest so he knew he'd be able to relax in his company. "Do you think I've been doing a good job cleaning the place so far?"

"I wouldn't say you're doing a bad job. You're here, right?" Father Preston folded his hands together on top of the desk. "I'm glad you came in early today. I've been eager to talk to you."

"You could have called me."

"I much prefer speaking with individuals face to face, especially when the topic turns to more sensitive matters." The priest cleared his throat. "Would you like some coffee? I just made some."

"Sure. Thanks." Bobby planned on staying up as late as possible tonight, so extra caffeine would be a blessing.

The priest rose and busied himself at a coffee maker sitting on a table by the window. "Creamer, sugar?"

"Just a little. Thanks."

Father Preston resumed his chair when he'd handed Bobby the cup. Wisps of steam rose from the surface of the brew and dissipated into the air like departing spirits. "I've heard some interesting things about you," he said, watching Bobby with the attentiveness of a scientist observing an experiment.

Bobby nodded, trying not to feel unnerved by the man's intense stare. Father Preston was just trying to get a sense of him. He needed to stay calm and not say anything stupid. "I hope they were good interesting things."

"Like leaving the church unattended to track down my assistant priest?" Father Preston laughed, but then his expression sobered. "I'm sorry about what Father Laubisch did to you. He's taken a leave of absence while he tries to sort out his priorities."

"I wouldn't say it was *me* he did anything to." Father Laubisch, a younger priest, had secretly been working with Graham Willard but sought to defy him by helping Lupe Sanchez. Bobby would never be able to trust him—not when Father Laubisch seemed to place his own wellbeing above everything else.

Father Preston folded his hands together again. "As they say, what's done is done." He sighed. "I understand you'll require the use of one of our meeting rooms sometime soon."

Bobby nodded and prayed that anxiety wouldn't creep back into his veins. "That's right." He sipped at his coffee, relishing the sensation of warmth traveling through him.

"You're frightened, aren't you?"

"I'm not supposed to be."

"But you are, and that's completely understandable."

"It feels wrong, though. Being afraid."

"I think," Father Preston said, "there's a difference between healthy fear and abject terror. Which one do you feel?"

Bobby thought about his encounter with the demoniac at The Pink Rooster. Instead of answering, he said, "Earlier today I ran into somebody who was, well, you know. Possessed."

Father Preston's eyebrows rose, and his face grew paler. "Where?"

"It was at a bar up in Hillsdale. And all the sudden I had these flashbacks about bad stuff I did to people a long time ago. I don't know how I could ever drive a demon out of anyone if I have those memories inside my head."

The priest fell into brooding silence. Then, "I suppose the real question is what do you fear more: the evil that lives inside this person you met, or the potential for evil that lives inside you?"

Bobby felt cold despite the Spirit's reassurances that everything would be fine. He took another sip of coffee. "I don't know."

---

**FATHER PRESTON** took a few minutes to show Bobby the empty room where he would eventually bring the possessed to be cleansed and then left Bobby alone so each could do their work without interruption.

Bobby fully intended to return to The Pink Rooster as soon as night fell so he could watch for Jack Willard. Unless the possessed man had lied to him, a man fitting Jack's description frequented the bar, and Bobby didn't see why Jack wouldn't do the same tonight.

Father Preston's words continued to haunt him as Bobby hauled a bag of garbage out to the dumpsters on the other side of the church building. What did Bobby really fear the most? Demons? Failure? His own inadequacies?

*Be strong*, the Spirit said.

But Bobby didn't feel strong. He felt like a child dressing in his father's clothes and pretending to be a man.

The row of three dumpsters butted up against a privacy fence so tall that the top of it lay three or four feet above his head. Bobby lifted the lid of the nearest dumpster and slung the bag into the growing mound of waste inside.

Raised voices on the other side of the fence made him freeze. A man and woman were arguing about something in Spanish. The woman spat out a word—*idiota*—that may or may not have meant what it sounded like.

Interesting.

He was about to search for a crack in the boards so he might spy on the pair and make sure one wasn't about to harm the other, but the ringing of his phone abruptly cut him off.

He yanked it from his pocket the same instant the voices fell silent.

It was Phil.

He jammed the phone to his ear. "Hey."

Phil's voice sounded choked. "Kimberly called me back with some news. Graham's awake."

At first Bobby wasn't sure how to respond to this proclamation, and he was vaguely aware of a door slamming somewhere beyond the fence. "Is that a good thing or a bad thing?"

"For him, it's a very bad thing. The aneurysm caused irreparable damage to his brain."

"And?"

"It completely paralyzed him."

Bobby leaned back against the dumpster, feeling dizzy. "He can't move anything?"

"Only his eyes. It's what they call 'locked-in syndrome.' That's when a patient has full charge of his or her mental faculties but can only communicate by blinking."

Bobby's mind conjured an image of the deranged old man lying in a bed while humming machinery kept him alive. "How much longer do they think he has?"

"Here's the thing. People can live for decades like that, and the state certainly isn't going to want to pay for Graham's long-term care. I don't even know if there's going to be a trial at this point. He might just end up being turned over to his family."

Bobby was silent for a moment. Despite the terrible things Graham had done, he couldn't help but feel some sympathy for him. "If you could heal him, would you?"

There was some hesitation in Phil's voice when he next spoke. "No."

"But you aren't sure?"

"Listen, Bobby. Graham deserves this. If I *was* able to heal him, I'd do it only to ask why he lied about killing so many people."

"He was probably going senile."

"I don't know about that."

An inexplicable wave of irritation rose up inside of Bobby. "Don't you know anything?"

Phil's tone became cold. "Excuse me?"

"You didn't know what to do when Trish died, you didn't know what to do when Randy went to confront Graham, and you didn't know what to do when Randy was in the hospital. Why can't you just accept that Graham was insane?"

"What's gotten into you?"

"Nothing." Bobby started walking back toward the church entrance, then stopped after traveling only half a dozen paces. "Why did you call me?"

"Why wouldn't I have called you? You're one of us now."

Bobby drew in a deep breath. "Sorry. I've had a bad day." Something in his gut made him turn back toward the fence. About four feet to the right of the end dumpster was a half-inch gap between the boards.

"Your day hadn't been going that badly when I saw you a while ago," Phil said as Bobby squatted down and held his eye to the gap, seeing a yard overgrown with weeds and foot-high grass. A nondescript white house and carport sat forty feet away from the fence. *No arguing people in sight.*

He straightened. "Well *maybe* I ran into a possessed guy and had crap I did to my classmates years ago blasted right back at me like a bad movie."

"You know it can't hurt you."

"It isn't me I'm worried about. I can't help anyone if I'm that screwed up inside."

"Haven't you asked for forgiveness?"

"Yeah, but—"

"Then you have nothing to worry about. You'll never be able to get over your fears unless you face them. If you choose to run away from the possessed instead of offering them help, then the world might as well be without a Servant for all the good you'll do."

Bobby's shoulders slumped. "I'm sorry."

"You don't need to apologize to *me*."

The sound of departing parishioners made Bobby turn back toward the church entrance. "I hate to cut this short," he said, "but I'm at the church right now and need to get back to work. I'll see you later?"

"I certainly hope so. And one last thing. The next time you run into an evil spirit, tell it that whatever it says or shows you can't hurt you. Do you understand?"

Bobby closed his eyes and nodded. "I think so."

# 15

"**THEY CAN'T** hurt me," Bobby said as he drove back to Hillsdale at ten o'clock that night. "They can't hurt me. They can't hurt me. They can't hurt me."

"That's the spirit," said Thane.

Bobby almost swerved off the road. "Dude," Bobby said as he straightened the wheel and threw a glance into his passenger seat, where the angel (*was* he an angel?) leaned back with his hands clasped behind his head. "Do you want me to be in an accident?"

"My apologies," Thane said. "Perhaps you would do well to be more alert."

"Perhaps *you* might consider not showing up while I'm barreling down the interstate at seventy miles an hour. Caleb wouldn't do that."

A shrug. "I'm sure he would if he had to."

"So you do know Caleb."

"I'm aware of his existence. From what I understand, he's been helping out the Servants much longer than I have."

Bobby's heart skipped a beat. "What do you mean?"

"Didn't anyone tell you? Caleb has been around for eons, showing up whenever the Servants have needed him. You shouldn't be so surprised."

Even as Thane said it, the idea began to make more sense. "Randy and Phil kept asking me a ton of questions about Caleb when I told them he'd disappeared." When Bobby's roommate vanished the week before, there hadn't even been indentations in the carpet where Caleb's furniture had been—a fact that had briefly made Bobby doubt his own sanity. "You think they knew who he was?"

"It's possible."

The excitement at this revelation dispelled the surprise of Thane's arrival. "And what about Graham? If Caleb helped out the Servants before, wouldn't Graham have recognized him when Caleb and I showed up to rent the bungalow?"

"Not if Graham never had a personal experience with him. And many people go by that name. He would have had no reason to assume the Caleb renting his house was the Caleb who aided his brethren in times of trouble."

"Do you think Caleb was protecting me from Graham?"

"His presence certainly didn't hurt you. After all, if you'd rented Graham's house by yourself, you would have been far more appealing as a victim."

Bobby shivered at the thought. "If you ever run into Caleb, tell him I said thanks."

Thane beamed. "Consider it done."

"So why are you here right now?"

"I was going to remind you that saving this woman might require you to do some things you're not comfortable with. You should do them anyway."

Alarm bells went off somewhere inside Bobby's head. "That doesn't sound like something Randy would have done."

"You're not Randy, and you're not Phil, either. You're Bobby Roland. You're your own man. Remember that."

Thane vanished. Bobby tried not to let it unnerve him.

*Don't do anything stupid,* the Spirit said.

"I'll do my best."

THE PINK Rooster's lot was so packed with cars and motor-cycles this time of night that Bobby had to park at an abandoned video rental next door.

He checked himself in the mirror on the back of the sun visor to make sure he still looked different enough from earlier in the day that he wouldn't be recognized at first glance. The bartender might have become suspicious if Bobby came back tonight, so he'd changed into one of his few pairs of black jeans and a plain black t-shirt and made a quick stop at Randy's house to borrow one of the decorative chains Randy used to adorn his pants.

Randy, not asking any of the questions that Bobby could prac-tically hear perched on the edge of his tongue, had also let Bobby take a chain necklace with a silver skull pendant and a pair of black clip-on stud earrings that Randy claimed to have worn as a teen-ager. Bobby then went into Randy's bathroom, wet his hair down, and mussed it up without combing it back out.

"You look like I did when I was about fourteen," Randy observed from his resting place on the couch.

"Gee, thanks."

Randy yawned and closed his eyes. "You're welcome. Just watch out, though, because I have an idea you're not dressing up just for kicks."

"Don't worry. I'm just going undercover."

"Make sure nobody kills you, okay?" Randy's tone held a hint of humor, but Bobby knew he was serious.

"I promise I'll come back in one piece. But don't tell Phil what I'm up to, because I have an idea he won't be as lenient as you."

Bobby got out of the car and crossed a grassy median between the two lots, feeling as conspicuous as if he had a spot-light shining upon him. He didn't want to look fourteen. He wanted to look tough.

"They can't hurt me," he muttered one last time before enter-ing the bar.

The establishment was dim this time of night. The music wasn't quite as loud as it had been that afternoon, but the babble of dozens of voices made up the difference.

Vern, the bartender, was too busy taking orders and filling glasses to look Bobby's way. Patrons young and old occupied stools at the counter. Each booth was crammed full, the tables in the center of the room were buried under card games, and a few leather-clad bikers slouched against the back wall draining glasses of beer. Many hard faces in the crowd made a nervous sweat form on Bobby's scalp.

Jack Willard and his aura did not figure among the throng.

Bobby would have to find a way to blend in while he waited for him to arrive. *If* he arrived.

He put his hands in his pockets and drifted over to a table where a foursome was engaged in a game of poker. Neither the players nor the few spectators crowded around the table paid him any notice.

Bobby pretended to take interest in watching the game. Every minute or so he risked a look at the front door, but none of the new arrivals was Jack.

He wanted to order something to drink since his mouth grew more parched by the minute, but Vern would see through his disguise at once. He couldn't even try to blend in better by ordering a beer since he wouldn't be twenty-one until November and he couldn't count on Vern to not ask for his ID.

A *thunk* and sudden yelling at one of the booths along the front wall startled Bobby out of his ruminations. A greasy-haired man stood up from the vinyl bench seat, his pants soaking wet from the glass of beer that one of his comrades had just knocked over. He came around to the opposite side of the booth, drew back a fist, and punched the other man in the jaw so hard that Bobby could hear the impact of flesh on flesh over the sound of the music and drunken conversations.

The man who'd spilled the beer blinked stupidly at his companion and staggered to his feet. "Whatcha do that for?"

The man with beer soaking the front of his pants like he'd waited too long for the bathroom replied by swinging his fist back again and striking the other man in the temple.

The other man swayed as if stunned and then crumpled to the floor.

Cheers went up all around. "Go Darren! You the man, Darren! That'll teach him!"

Darren shrugged and resumed his seat as if nothing had happened.

Bobby felt the urge to go help the man lying catatonic on the bar's hardwood floor, but to do so would draw unwanted attention to himself.

Could he really be that selfish?

No, he couldn't. He was going to help people now even if a premonition didn't tell him to.

He stepped away from the poker table and cleared his throat. "Isn't anyone going to help that guy?" he said to a curly-haired woman crossing the room holding a plate of chili cheese fries.

She had so much makeup caked on her face she resembled a clown. "What's it to you?" she sniffed. "Henry's always doing something to poor Darren. He's had it coming for weeks."

The woman may have been right, but that didn't ease Bobby's guilt at letting the man just lie there. Bobby gritted his teeth and hurried over to see what he could do to help before someone came along and trod across the man in drunken obliviousness.

Sometimes doing the right thing could really throw a wrench into one's plans.

Bobby kept an eye on the other patrons as he knelt beside Henry's still form. The curly-haired woman eyed Bobby with disgust as she set the plate down on a far table but other than that nobody gave him notice.

He turned his attention back to the victim.

Henry wore a torn denim jacket and had a scraggly beard full of crumbs. The places where Darren hit him were already bruising so much that if he had any dignity at all he'd go home and not leave the house for a week.

At least he was breathing.

Bobby grabbed his shoulder and shook it. "Hey. Wake up."

Henry let out a groan.

Darren, still sitting in the booth, cast his gaze down at Bobby and laughed. "Go ahead and wake him up. I'll just knock him out again."

"But he might be hurt," Bobby blurted. "He might have a concussion."

"So what if he's got a concussion? I'm gonna go get me another beer." Darren hefted himself off the vinyl seat and staggered off to the counter. The remaining occupants of the booth glanced Bobby's way for half a second before resuming their conversation.

Bobby silently cursed Mystery Woman for having come to this bar. If a man getting knocked unconscious didn't raise alarm among the customers, then it must have been far more common than Bobby would have liked.

Which made him wonder what other violent or illegal activities might be overlooked underneath The Pink Rooster's roof.

"Henry," Bobby said, giving the man's shoulder another shake. "You need to get up before someone steps on you."

Henry's eyes fluttered open. He brought a hand up and touched his temple, wincing. Then his eyes narrowed. "If you're the devil, I don't wanna be in hell no more."

"You're not in hell," Bobby said. "Just a bar."

Henry pulled himself into sitting position. "Man, Darren got me good this time. Last time he just gave me a shiner. You ever had one of those?"

"No, but a guy knocked me out last week, and that was close enough. Do you need help getting up?"

"I'll manage." Henry's eyes lit up, and he snickered. "You say someone knocked you out?"

Bobby absently rubbed his head in the spot where Jack had clobbered him. "Yeah. So I kind of feel for you."

Tears of mirth sprang into Henry's eyes. "He feels for me. Do you hear that? He *feels* for me!"

Bobby became aware of the fact that ten or more patrons now had their gazes fixed on him. His heart raced. He'd drawn entirely too much attention to himself. Now he wouldn't be able to linger around unnoticed while he waited for Jack to—

A blinding pain on the back of Bobby's head cut off all thought, and he hit the floor with all the finesse of a dropped sack of bricks.

The last thing he remembered before drifting away was a shadowy aura dancing in the back of his mind.

———————◆———————

BOBBY CAME to in a dark, unfamiliar place, feeling like someone had tried to brain him with a sledgehammer. He brought a hand to the back of his head, half expecting to feel gray matter leaking out through a fissure in his skull, but his hand came away dry.

*Please don't tell me I have another concussion. I can't afford to keep going to the hospital.*

He blinked to clear his vision, gradually becoming aware of the *crunch-crunch* of receding footsteps. Dark branches reached out to each other high over his head. The lights of unseen houses were visible as glowing specks in the distance, and a shadowy male figure meandered around silhouetted tree trunks as it moved toward the light.

Bobby counted off ten seconds before trying to stand. What had just happened? He'd been inside a bar, where a man lay unconscious on the floor...

It all came back in a rush. Bobby had tried to help the fallen man, and then someone had tried to kill him.

Okay, maybe they hadn't really tried. If someone wanted him dead, they would have shot him or stabbed him or kept pounding him on the head until his skull caved in.

A more likely scenario was that Darren had snuck up behind him to give him a little scare for trying to help Henry, and then he'd hauled Bobby outside and dumped him like a skinny bag of garbage. Darren was probably even the one he'd seen walking away through the trees—if that were so, then Bobby had only been out for a couple of minutes.

Any longer than that, and he would have had to call an ambulance.

*What a fine establishment Mystery Woman chose to visit.*

Earlier the Spirit warned Bobby not to do anything stupid. Going back inside the bar would be the epitome of such. There had been that shadowy aura at the last second, but Bobby suspected the blow to his head made him imagine it.

He would wait for Jack outside.

Bobby turned in a wobbly circle to try to pinpoint the location of the bar. A mercury vapor lamp outside a building a short distance away illuminated painted blue cinder blocks.

Bobby brushed off his shirt and pants and set off toward it like a moth drawn to a bug zapper.

He walked in a weaving line back to the video rental lot and clambered into his Nissan, then monitored the bar's front door for well over half an hour. It felt like his skull had sprouted a lump the size of a golf ball. He'd be sleeping with an icepack tonight if he ever made it to bed.

Bobby checked the time. Eleven o'clock. Where could Jack be? Would he even show up?

He leaned his head back into the headrest to get more comfortable while he waited and immediately regretted doing so when a spike of pain hammered into his scalp. Blinking away tears, he looked over at The Pink Rooster's door just in time to see a blond man swagger out into the night.

*Jack Willard.*

He blinked. The aura *had* been Jack's. But where had he been hiding?

He watched as Jack got into a car. Its engine turned over and headlights winked on. Heart thumping, Bobby stuck the key in the ignition and eased out of the parking space.

Jack's car made a left onto the street, and when it passed the video rental, Bobby pulled out behind him.

"Please don't let me lose him," Bobby whispered. He gripped the wheel so hard his hands hurt. With luck, Jack would lead him to Mystery Woman within the hour.

How Bobby would free her was another issue entirely.

# 16

BOBBY DEVELOPED a violent case of the shakes as Jack led him north for five blocks and east for five more. If Jack had so gleefully aided his grandfather in his mission to torment and kill Randy, what in the world might he to do Bobby? If Jack caught him trying to free his prisoner, Bobby might find himself at heaven's door trying to explain to God that he'd truly had the best of intentions and hadn't meant for the world to fall into further ruin since he'd croaked before finding a replacement.

Jack finally turned into an apartment complex aptly-named Shady Grove for the thick stands of trees surrounding it. Red-lettered signs posted on the fence standing between the parking lot and road announced that there should be No Trespassing and No Soliciting.

Bobby drove in anyway.

He chose a spot far from the lit, open stairwell in the nearest building. Jack parked closer to the light, got out of his car, and sauntered up the stairs.

Bobby almost called the police then. Jack had been at large for a week, and here he was, walking around right out in the open where anyone with eyes could see him. Did he have no fear that someone might recognize him from the mug shot they kept showing on the news?

Bobby pulled out his phone, entered the first three digits of the local sheriff dispatch, and hesitated. He couldn't call the police unless he knew precisely where Jack was staying.

Bobby fumbled with his seatbelt and dashed across the lot before he lost sight of Mystery Woman's abductor, his stomach queasy from the pain in his head. He took the stairs two at a time and got off on the second floor, where Jack paused outside a door on the right hand side at the end of a long hallway.

A key appeared in Jack's hand, and he let himself inside.

"God, help me," Bobby whispered.

He felt a slight boost of encouragement. He crept down the hall, stopped outside Jack's unit, and pressed his ear to the door.

His heart gave a flutter of surprise when a woman's voice issued from within, and he strained to hear better. "—to hear about your grandpa. I know he means a lot to you."

Footsteps crossed the floor inside the apartment. "I'm not sure what he means to me."

"What do you mean?"

"Forget about it. Where are my cigarettes?"

"I thought you took them with you."

"Why would I do that? The government won't even let a guy smoke in a *bar*, and Vern and Chuck have been brainwashed into enforcing it." Something slammed—maybe a cabinet.

More footsteps. "So about your call to me earlier. What's the scoop with Troy?"

"The *scoop* is that Troy wants me to bring in five by next Saturday or I'm gone."

"Is he high, or something?"

"He says if I succeed, I get a promotion. For the love of *God*, I need a cigarette."

"Chill out, Jack. I can run down to the corner and pick up a pack for you."

"Get me some Bud, too. A whole case of it."

"Weren't you just down at the Rooster?" A long silence. "Okay, I'll get beer, too."

Bobby nearly wet himself when he realized the woman in the apartment would be coming through the door any second.

There was no place to hide in the hallway. Without thinking, he raced on light feet to the closer set of stairs and up to the third floor.

He paused at the top and listened. The sounds of a door opening and closing and the jingling of keys carried up to him, and footsteps receded toward the other end of the building.

Bobby waited another minute before moving. Certain the woman had reached the parking lot after that length of time, he slid a hand into the pocket of his jeans and closed his fingers around its contents.

"Dad," he whispered, "please pray for me."

He crept back to the second floor and stopped outside Jack's door, which had been painted a glossy white and bore gold numerals indicating that this was unit 212.

Logic told him he should call the police now, but the woman who'd gone on a beer run might have been involved with the kidnapping, too. If she returned and saw police cruisers outside, she might run for it.

Seconds ticked by as Bobby stood indecisively in front of 212. He glanced to his left and right. No visible cameras monitored the floor.

Sweat broke out all across his body. He raised his left hand and knocked on the door, hoping he hadn't just made the worst mistake of his life.

Footsteps approached the door. Bobby's attention was drawn to the peephole just below the numbers. Though he couldn't see it, he knew Jack's eye was peering out at him.

When the door swung open, Bobby whipped his right hand out of his pocket and flicked the blade out of the pocketknife, a motion he'd practiced a few times at home before coming to the bar.

Jack stood in the doorway with his arms hanging loosely at his sides. His blondish hair shined in the reflection of the hallway lights, and his blue eyes bore a dangerous glimmer.

The shadowy aura—not nearly as intense as that of the demoniac at the bar—filled Bobby's mind.

Jack's gaze traveled to Bobby's knife. "What are you going to do, poke me to death?"

This wasn't quite the reaction Bobby expected. "Where is she?" he asked, taking half a step closer to Jack.

"I'm afraid you'll have to be a little more specific. You look a little crazed right now, so I don't think you're thinking clearly. Nice earrings, by the way."

"You put the picture and notes on my door. You must have been stalking me to figure out where I live now."

"Maybe I did. Maybe I didn't. Maybe I wanted to see how badly your feathers could be ruffled. It's funny what a few pieces of paper can do to someone, isn't it?"

"Cut the crap. You wanted me to track that woman down, and now I'm here. Is she locked up in there?" Bobby craned his neck to see around Jack and caught a glimpse of a couch and coffee table on which sat a scattered newspaper, a pair of scissors, and a bottle of Elmer's glue.

Jack might have shut the woman away inside a bedroom.

Jack's eyes flashed. "Do you really think I'd tie someone up in an *apartment*?"

"You could have bound and gagged her so she wouldn't make any noise."

"Nice theory, but you're still wrong."

"I've got my phone with me. I can call the cops right now."

"But if you do that, you won't get to ask me all the questions buzzing around in that little head of yours. How does it feel, by the way? A blow like that had to hurt."

Bobby's stomach squirmed. "You did that?"

"No, but I admit it was rather entertaining seeing that buffoon knock you senseless the second I walked in the door." Jack smiled. "Let's make a deal."

*Don't do anything stupid.*

"What kind of deal?" Bobby tensed his muscles in anticipation.

"I'll tell you everything I know."

Bobby sensed a trap coming. "What's the catch?"

"You forget you ever saw me. You don't call the cops, we go on with our lives, easy peasy."

Bobby tightened his grip on the knife. "How will you know if I've called the cops?"

"Presumably if they show up at my door. But that's not the issue. I'll only tell you what you want to hear if you promise in front of my face you won't tell anyone where you've found me— cops included."

"I can break a promise."

"Can you? I know about your kind. *Grandpa* told me all sorts of things about the people he used to hang out with. He said the Servants can't commit evil deeds in order to save anyone—and I know you're the Servant now because I heard what Bellison said to you in the barn. Now what's it going to be? Do we talk or do you let the cops take me away to a place where you'll never learn what you want to know?"

Bobby hoped he wouldn't regret his next decision. "Let's talk." Then, though it pained him to say it, he added, "And I won't tell anyone where you are."

Jack looked like he'd just won the Mega Millions jackpot. "Excellent. But I'm not going to flap my gums out here. Let's go to your car."

Bobby heard a tremor in his voice when he spoke. "You'll kill me out there."

"I solemnly swear I won't, though I do find it tempting. It's your fault I can't go back to my own apartment and your fault I'm wanted by the law."

*Yeah right, it's my fault.* If Jack hadn't broken any laws in the first place, the cops would have no interest in him, but of course Jack wouldn't see it that way.

Straightening his shoulders, Bobby gave Jack what he hoped was a stern glare. "Turn out your pockets."

Jack shrugged and did as Bobby requested. Both pockets were empty.

"Now turn around."

"Are you going to stab me in the back with that thing you call a knife?"

"I want to make sure you don't have anything in your back pockets."

Jack rolled his eyes, held up his hands, and turned to face the interior of the apartment. "See? Nothing."

Jack's back pockets lay too flat to have contained anything, so Bobby said, "Fine. We'll go to my car. But if you try to hurt me, I *will* call the cops."

"That's fine with me. Where did you park?"

Bobby pointed at the far set of stairs. "That way. But you're going to walk in front of me."

To Bobby's delight, they passed no one on their way out to the car—at this hour, many of the apartment's residents would either be in bed or enjoying a night out on the town.

When they reached the Nissan, Bobby gestured at the front passenger door. "You get in first."

Shrugging, Jack obeyed without hesitation.

Bobby smelled a rat. People like Jack weren't this cooperative unless they had some kind of ulterior motive in mind.

*Do not let his words get to you.*

Dreading what might come next, Bobby got behind the wheel, shut the door, and switched on the dome light.

The first ten seconds were filled with silence. Bobby wondered if this was what it felt like to be locked in a cage with a tiger. He had to remind himself that Jack was nothing more than a man—one not much older than himself.

Jack was casually examining his fingernails. "That was you in the parking lot at the Sanchez woman's place last week, wasn't it?"

He nodded. Bobby had driven Randy there to be with Lupe after her emotional breakdown and waited in the car for over an hour until he realized someone occupied the vehicle next to him.

"It's interesting how one of my grandfather's tenants ended up joining the very people he despised."

"You're stalling."

"Why, yes—yes I am."

Jack's glib manner dialed Bobby's anger up a notch. "Why did you kidnap a woman I don't even know and stick her picture on my door?"

Jack cocked his head to the side and studied Bobby with those unnerving blue eyes. The shadows that filled Bobby's mind swirled and intensified as if their conversation was stirring up the evil being that influenced Jack's thoughts and actions. "I didn't kidnap her," he said.

"I don't believe you."

"You can disbelieve me all you want. And before you ask, I don't know where she is, either."

Bobby tried not to let despair take hold of him. If Jack was indeed providing him with honest answers, then he'd reached a dead end. "You were still a part of it, though."

"Of course. Otherwise we wouldn't be having this little chat."

"So what's your part in all this? You find women and have somebody else kidnap them for you?"

Jack focused his attention on the windshield, onto which a single green maple leaf had fallen and stuck. "Remember what your God will do to you if you break your promise to me."

Bobby gulped. "Who are you, really?"

"That's the million-dollar question, isn't it? Who am I? Seems to be the topic of many an existential crisis. I'm a number of things. A human being. A free thinker. What answer would you like?"

"That wasn't a trick question."

"Of course, of course. You want to know what I *do*, not who I am. People always want to know what you do. It's one of the first things people ask when they meet you. *What do you do, Jack?* Even Grandpa wanted to know, but I didn't tell him because I didn't trust him to keep his mouth shut. But you'll keep *your* mouth shut because you're afraid of failing your Maker."

It was all Bobby could do not to hold his pocketknife against Jack's throat and demand that he get on with it.

Thane's words echoed through his mind in that moment. *I was going to remind you that saving this woman might require you to do some things you're not comfortable with. You should do them anyway.*

*God help me,* Bobby thought as he pointed the knife at his passenger. "Look. If you don't hurry up and tell me what I want to know, I'll slash your stupid throat and dump you in the woods."

Jack's nostrils flared. "If you think you've got the guts for it, go ahead and kill me. I'll be able to tell you all kinds of things when I'm a corpse."

Bobby lowered the knife. "Then get on with it."

"Fine. I met the woman. Sweet-talked her a bit like I do with all of them. This one said she'd been in the area for a week or so and was looking for some work. So I told her I knew some people in need of help over on Oakland Avenue but they wouldn't be home until after midnight, but unfortunately her car broke down so she had to walk there all the way from the McDonald's on Ridge Avenue. I guess she was waiting out on the sidewalk in front of their house when someone came along and nabbed her."

"Let me guess," Bobby said, his voice shaking. "There weren't any people she was supposed to meet about a job on my street."

"That's what it looks like."

"Why did you do it?"

"A man has to make a living somehow. And what's one of the biggest commodities out there? Women."

Bobby swayed in his seat. "What are you talking about?"

Jack wore an expression of triumph. "Don't you know? Normal men have needs. I help them obtain the objects they desire in order to meet those needs."

"Women, you mean."

"Mostly. We deal in young men, too, but not as many."

"Women aren't objects."

"Aren't they? Some of them are so vapid it's almost as if God gave them no brains."

It almost took more willpower than Bobby was able to muster not to swing back a fist and knock the smile off of Jack's face. "So you...you *trick* women into thinking someone is going to help them find work, and then someone else nabs them. Then what?"

"Then buyers show up where they're being held and purchase the ones they think will benefit them the most. I take a cut of the sale."

"And you're just admitting all of this to me like it's nothing?" A high-pitched whine rang in Bobby's ears. He'd heard of such things, of course, but never had it occurred to him that something so vile could be happening right where he lived.

"It's making you angry, yes? It's so easy to press your buttons. I can tell you anything I want because you already promised you wouldn't report me."

Bobby gnashed his teeth together. Jack was right, and Bobby hated it. "So why did you make that woman go to my street? Why did you put her picture on my door?"

"Are you really so dense that you haven't figured it out yet?"

"You're just getting back at me for calling the cops on you and Graham. What's her name, Jack?"

"You should know it."

Bobby brandished the knife at him. "I said, what's her name?"

"Why don't you know what it is?"

"Because I've never seen that woman before in my life."

Jack laughed. "And that's where you're wrong. The two of you used to be rather close."

"You're lying."

"See, you think that because of who I am, I'm incapable of telling you the truth."

"You've got me mixed up with someone else. I don't know her."

Jack gave him that Cheshire Cat grin. "Really. What if I told you her name is *Adrian*?"

Bobby's heart was beating so hard he thought he might faint. "Adrian who?"

"Adrian Pollard. She told me when we met at the bar."

Puzzle pieces clicked into place in Bobby's mind, forming a picture he had no desire to see. His voice sounded far away when he next spoke. "Pollard. Like, that's her maiden name?"

"I would assume so. She certainly didn't call herself Adrian Roland, but that's because she never married your father. Right?"

The whine in his head grew increasingly louder. Bobby pointed at the door. "Get out of my car."

Jack didn't budge. "Poor old Adrian came all this way to see her precious baby boy—the one she abandoned oh so many years ago. Imagine my surprise when she told me her baby's name." He laughed. "I hope she's having a good time wherever she is. I wonder how many men she'll have before one of them does things a little too rough and kills her."

"I said get out!" Bobby lunged toward Jack and held the tip of the knife a millimeter from his throat.

Jack held up his hands. "No need to get so upset. You asked for the truth and I gave it to you just like you wanted."

Bobby wished that Jack was lying but knew he could only have known Adrian's name and what she did to Bobby's family if he'd actually spoken to her. "Get out now."

A flash of headlights lit up the interior of the car. Jack's eyes flicked toward the parking lot entrance. "Oh, look. My friend is back. It was lovely talking to you, Bobby. We'll have to do this again sometime." He opened the passenger door and, without further ado, vanished into the night.

Bobby sat there for a long time without moving. *How could you do this to me?* he thought as shameful tears spilled from his eyes. *I've never done anything to deserve this.*

The Spirit didn't respond.

# 17

DISCONNECTED MEMORIES swirled through Adrian's head. Driving down the interstate, passing the Welcome to Oregon sign, stopping for gas and picking up Mountain Dew and beef jerky to snack on for the rest of the trip, stretching her legs at a rest area, taking some travel brochures advertising parks and attractions in the area, checking her wallet to see how much money she had left, realizing she would need to find employment before she ran out of funds...

And then a blond, blue-eyed man young enough to be her son who'd seemed so interested in her story. Adrian reached out her hand to him like one drowning in a lake. *Please help me. Something's gone wrong. Please help. They've got me.*

Adrian was startled awake by the sound of the metal door swinging open. She blinked to adjust to the light given off by the bare bulbs hanging from the ceiling and watched in wordless horror as the cell's newest occupant arrived in the arms of one of the men she'd seen before.

*Mother of God, have mercy on us all.*

Another man helped lay the girl's still form on the cot previously occupied by the Asian woman who had departed for horrors unknown. The Hispanic woman followed them with folded arms and observed the scene wearing a smirk, throwing a sneer at Adrian when the men had their backs turned as if to say, *Don't like it? Try doing something about it.*

How any woman could sit idly by while others were locked up and then sold like cattle was beyond Adrian's comprehension. This woman's eyes were cold, like a pair of lifeless brown marbles. Did she have no pity?

*She's just like you,* a voice whispered. *You care more about yourself than anyone else.*

But Adrian would never kidnap anyone or lock them away.

*But if you knew a woman had been kidnapped, would you ever try to help her?*

Adrian wasn't sure she wanted to answer that, so she looked to the girl on the cot the moment the threesome departed.

The girl had dark hair tied into a wild bunch of braids fastened with pink ties, coffee-colored skin, and looked no older than nine—the age when little girls were supposed to live in blissful worlds of tea parties and dress-up. Adrian's chest tightened. This child would likely never know such innocence again. What kind of person would snatch one so young and then sell her so men with too much money to spend could...could...

Adrian scrunched her eyes shut. The fact that girls this young ended up here meant that demand existed for them. Forget why a woman would work here. What *man*—who might be a father himself and read his kids stories and tossed baseballs to them—would choose to destroy a child's purity? Could someone truly be that selfish?

*Look at yourself, Adrian.*

She bit her lip in anger. Abandoning her children had destroyed no one's purity. Their self-esteems, yes; and maybe even their faith in the goodness of humanity, but Adrian's actions had never caused anyone direct harm.

She sat up on her cot and continued to stare at the girl. She wore a bright pink shirt that had a stain from a spilled drink, purple pants, and yellow sneakers that stood out like a pair of rubber-soled highlighters. Her chest rose and fell with shallow breaths, and her eyes rolled around behind closed lids as she dreamed of terrors that Adrian hoped she would forget upon waking.

Any person who tried to hurt this child for his or her own pleasure was selfish beyond any kind of reason.

And Adrian had been selfish for leaving her children behind with their fathers; to be left wondering why their mother had not loved them enough to stay.

"I won't be like those men," she said in a low voice as blood simmered in her veins.

She stood. Looked at the girl, then to the door she couldn't open.

"Honey," she said, though since asleep the girl couldn't hear her, "I'm going to get you out of this place. I'll get you out if it's the last thing I do."

---

**MORNING LIGHT** roused Bobby from slumber, but he refused to climb out of bed, in part because of the headache raging behind his eyes.

He rolled over and jammed a pillow over his head. Why did he have to wake up so early? Heck, why had he awakened at all? A lot of good a new day would do him, considering what he'd learned last night.

*Don't just lie there,* the Spirit chided. *Get up.*

"No. I'm kind of mad at you right now."

Though Adrian's kidnapping had not been the fault of God. It had all been Jack's doing.

He knew full well why Jack had gone into detail about what he did to Adrian specifically and women in general. He'd wanted Bobby to know what horrors his birth mother would be suffering that very moment. Jack was right: he did know how to push Bobby's buttons, and there wasn't a thing Bobby could do about it.

Bobby had the sudden mental image of holding a gun to Jack's temple and pulling the trigger, and he relaxed.

The sound of an approaching engine outside grew too close before falling silent. *Please be at the neighbor's house.* The thought of having to talk to anyone right now made him cringe.

Light footsteps moved up the driveway and onto the porch, and though he expected it, he made an involuntary flinch when a knock sounded on the front door.

"Go away," he muttered. "I'm not home."

The knock came again. "Open up, Roland. I know you're in there."

Groaning, Bobby swung his skinny legs over the side of the bed and got to his feet, lightly tapping the back of his head with one hand. The knot he'd received at The Pink Rooster had shrunk overnight but the pain was still sharp and raw.

He wobbled a little as he crossed the tiny front room and undid the chain and deadbolt before swinging the door open. Carly awaited him, her auburn hair tied back and gleaming in the sunlight.

"You look terrible," Carly said, thoroughly assessing him in about two seconds.

Bobby dragged a hand over the stubble on his chin. "You don't look too great, yourself." Carly's face was pale, and she had uncharacteristic bags under her eyes.

At least she wasn't crying.

She smirked and shoved past him into the house. "You're not supposed to say that kind of thing to a lady, you know. You're supposed to lie and tell me I look beautiful."

Bobby's head throbbed even harder as he closed the door. "But when I do that, you tell me I'm full of crap."

"At least you're learning what to expect from me. We have to be on the same page now that we're working together."

Bobby went to the freezer and got out a fresh icepack. He wrapped it in a dishtowel and pressed it to the lump beneath his hair. "Dang, my head hurts."

"What happened? Take a nasty spill?"

"Not exactly." He recounted what happened in The Pink Rooster, and by the time he finished, Carly held a hand over her mouth in shock.

"That's awful!" she said. "You should have reported the creep before he hurt someone else!"

"I was a little too busy to call the cops." Bobby moved over to the coffee maker and dumped in a scoop of grounds without checking to see if the filter basket was in place. Thousands of tiny brown granules scattered across the countertop and onto the floor.

He was grateful that Carly didn't make fun of him. "Here. You sit down and I'll take care of it. You're lucky you have a lump. Phil told me it's bad if a hit like that doesn't swell because it means it's swelling inside your brain instead and can potentially kill you."

"That's nice. And thanks." Bobby lowered himself into one of the chairs and closed his eyes as the chill from the icepack moved through the towel and into the lump. "Why are you here?"

Carly bustled around behind him as she cleaned up the spilled coffee grounds. "Because we're still looking for Mystery Woman, right? I figured I could help you brainstorm some more ideas."

Bobby's stomach gave a turn. "I think I'm done looking for Mystery Woman," he said, opening his eyes and staring at the crumpled image of Adrian Pollard he'd thrown onto the table upon returning home last night.

"What? Why?"

"Because if she really is locked up by some creep somewhere, she deserves it." Even as he said the words, he felt ill. *Does anyone deserve that?*

Carly fell silent. Shock appeared on her face for the second time in as many minutes. "How could you say that?"

"I found out that Jack Willard's the one who had her kidnapped, and he told me who she is, only I swore I wouldn't tell anyone where I found him so I can't even call the cops on him."

Carly pulled out the other chair and sat down across from him, giving him a stare so sharp that Bobby felt it cutting him open. "Well? Who is she?"

"You wouldn't know her."

"Obviously." She raised an eyebrow. "What's her name?"

"Adrian Pollard." The name came out of his mouth sounding flat, and he gave a start when he realized he'd never uttered her full name aloud to anyone in his life.

"That's pretty. Now why do you think Adrian deserves to be locked up? To be honest, I really don't think that's something you should be thinking right now. Certain entities might end up using it against you."

Bobby tightened his free hand into a fist. "I can't help how I feel. If you knew anything about her, you'd want her to be locked up, too." He stood up abruptly and went back to the coffee maker, which Carly had yet to set. He whisked the filter basket out of the dish strainer, shoved it into the top of the coffee maker, and dumped in a fresh batch of grounds.

"You know," Carly said as Bobby poured half a pot of water into the machine, "it's okay to talk to me."

"I am talking to you."

"You know what I mean."

The brew trickled into the pot. Bobby watched it rise past the first two lines on the side of the carafe. Carly didn't need to know about all the emotional baggage he'd long ago shut away in a closet somewhere in the back of his mind—a closet he'd not opened since he left Ohio two years before.

And while he'd never thought about it, maybe Adrian was part of the reason he'd left Ohio in the first place. Putting so many miles between him and the ghost of what might have been had been his way of erasing the pain he hadn't acknowledged in years.

And now Adrian was here. In Oregon. To find him. Her son.

*Charlotte told her where I am*, he thought as a new lump rose in his throat.

"Bobby?"

He turned. Carly's expression had softened, and for some reason her demeanor made hot tears spring into his eyes. "What?"

"Who's Adrian?"

There was no point in keeping it a secret. "She's my mother."

At first Carly gave him a quizzical look, but then she clapped a hand to her forehead. "Oh my gosh. I didn't realize you were adopted."

Bobby gave a hollow laugh. "Oh, I'm not adopted. She ran off when I was a few days old and we never saw her again. My dad had to hire a nanny to take care of me while he worked, and he ended up marrying her a few years later."

"Bobby, I'm sorry. I didn't know."

"It's not something I wear like a badge."

"But you're from Ohio. How did she end up out here?"

"I'm assuming she drove."

Carly's mouth formed a thin line. "So Graham's grandson is the one who kidnapped her? It's too bad you promised you wouldn't call the cops."

Bobby didn't feel like going into all the details he'd learned from Jack last night. "He arranged for her to be kidnapped and sold to a brothel after they ran into each other and she told him who she was. He says he doesn't have a clue where she is."

"Do you believe him?"

He thought about the things Jack had said about what he did for a living. Someone who sold women into what amounted to modern-day slavery might not want to know everything about the network they were a part of so if one of them was arrested, they wouldn't be able to confess everything and bring the whole ring down.

"Yeah," he said. "I do." When the coffee maker beeped, he grabbed two mugs off the tree on the counter and filled them both to the top.

"What are you going to do about it?"

"Nothing, I guess." Inwardly, he cringed. Sure, he could do nothing, but his conscience would never let it go.

"You know that's not right. If she came out here, that means she wants to see you. Maybe she's trying to put things right."

Bobby accidentally sloshed coffee out of both mugs when he plopped them onto the card table. "What's the point after all this time?" He drew in a deep breath. "Do you have any idea what it's like growing up knowing your mother was a deadbeat? Charlotte was always nice to me and treated me like her own kid, but for my entire life I always felt like the odd man out. Her family never accepted me. They knew Adrian before she ran off because she grew up on the same street where Charlotte's parents lived, and it's like they thought I had some kind of disease since she's the one who gave birth to me. Just imagine going to her parents' house every Christmas Day. Your brother gets about seven hundred gifts from them because he's their real grandkid, and you're lucky if you come away with a wrinkly ten-dollar bill stuffed inside a card. Charlotte used to go off on them about that but they didn't care."

Carly's face grew even whiter. "I'm sorry."

Bobby wasn't finished. The closet he'd kept locked for so long had broken open and couldn't shut because of the tidal wave of garbage washing out of it. "In school kids knew I didn't live with my real mother and they'd keep asking and asking what had happened to her, and I finally just said she died a long time ago so I didn't remember anything about her. She might as well have been dead, and sometimes I hoped she really was. Is that bad?"

"It's bad if you feel that way now, but you were just a kid."

"I can't help how I feel."

She was silent for several long moments. "Can you?"

"Put yourself in my shoes and see how *you* feel."

Carly opened her mouth as if to say something else but then closed it. Her brow scrunched, and she nodded a few times to herself.

"What?" Bobby asked.

"You promise you won't go off on me?"

Bobby braced himself for a lecture. "I'll do my best."

"Good. Now I'm going to ask you to listen without interrupting or blowing another fuse. Bobby, everyone gets hurt at some point. I've been hurt. You've been hurt. Randy's been hurt. Phil's been hurt. Even Lupe and Allison and my parents have been hurt. Now tell me what you've seen in each of them. What are they all like?"

"Phil worries too much."

"Uh-huh."

"And Randy's a lot mellower than Phil, but I think he worries a lot, too."

"He also finds humor in things more than Phil does. It's a good coping mechanism. Randy has every right to hate the world, but instead he does his best to have a positive outlook."

Bobby took a sip of coffee and winced when he discovered it was still too hot. "What's your point?"

"I want you to think about what you're going to do with your pain. Are you going to let it fester inside you like some kind of cancer, or are you going to use it to improve yourself and grow?"

"I don't know."

At once Bobby remembered part of the exchange he'd had with his father in his vision the day before.

*You need to love your mother.*

*What?*

*I mean it. No matter what's happened, and no matter what will happen, you need to love her if it's the last thing you do.*

Now Bobby understood.

He put his head into his shaking hands and stared into his coffee cup. "God help me," he said. "I don't know what I'm going to do."

# 18

CARLY'S PHONE rang in her purse, dispelling the heavy silence that lay upon the room. She withdrew it and accepted the call, her face brightening. "Hey, Mom! Uh-huh. That's great!" She moved the phone away from her mouth, eyes sparkling, and Bobby had the sense that some great weight had just been lifted from her chest. "Bobby, my parents are just a few hours away from here. They'll be home by lunchtime."

"Cool." Bobby sipped on his coffee some more, not particularly caring about the Jovingos' return to Autumn Ridge. In fact, the only thing he found himself caring about at the moment was trying to find a way to get Carly to leave him alone so he could properly sulk in silence.

Carly redirected her attention to the conversation with her mother. "I'm at Bobby's right now, but I can hurry home and throw some stuff in the crockpot so you don't have to fix anything tonight. Is that okay? Great! Love you, Mom. Bye."

Bobby breathed a sigh of relief as Carly ended the call. "Did she say where they went?"

"No, but I'm guessing I'll find out once they get back. Knowing Dad, he probably picked another random town to go preaching in. I wonder if he got two black eyes this time instead of just one."

Bobby's stomach turned at the thought of someone slugging Frankie Jovingo in the face. "Someone gave him a black eye?"

"It doesn't happen too often. Most people who hear him at least listen patiently, even if they don't agree with anything he says."

"But still."

Carly drained her cup of coffee and set it in the sink before shouldering her purse. "It doesn't bother him. He knows he's doing God's work, and it makes him happy. It's just fun to tease him about it. The next time you see him, mention the word 'Portland' and see what happens."

"Portland. Got it."

Bobby followed her to the door. "Remember what I said, Bobby," she said when she put her hand on the knob.

"About what?"

"What will you do with your pain?"

*I want to put a fist through a wall*, he thought, but he said, "I'll figure it out later."

She smiled. "That's a start."

Bobby waited until her car departed from the driveway before storming back into the kitchen. "Is this all some kind of joke?" he said to the ceiling. "Because I don't think it's very funny." And to think he'd devoted most of the previous day to tracking down "Mystery Woman" when he could have been doing something important like...

Like what?

Like going to the gym and lifting weights like Phil wanted him to start doing. He had to be physically fit in order to be the Servant since driving out demons amounted to something like a small battle.

Or he could have tried to jog around the block a few times. Or he could have gone someplace like Walmart or McDonald's or Autumn Ridge Safari Adventure Golf in search of another demoniac to freak him out so he could run home crying like a kid again.

Had Randy and the others gone through anything like this when they first became Servants?

He wasn't sure he wanted to ask.

Even though he didn't want to, he picked up Adrian's picture. Now that he thought about it, he did look a bit like her. Since his father had been overweight for as long as Bobby could remember, he'd often wondered why he always stayed so skinny regardless of whatever he shoveled into his mouth, and here was the answer.

Charlotte was about the same size as the woman in the picture but well-muscled because she worked out pretty much from the instant she got home from the daycare where she worked until she went to bed.

She began her vigorous exercise regimen shortly after Ken's death. It was interesting how the passing of a loved one could so alter one's own existence. Charlotte became more conscious of her health, and Bobby became afflicted with premonitions of tragedy that haunted him day and night.

He gritted his teeth. *Charlotte.* Adrian must have slunk back to Eleanor, Ohio for God knew what reason and talked to Charlotte, who had then directed her to Oregon.

Bobby retrieved his phone and dialed Charlotte's number.

His fifteen-year-old brother Jonas answered. "Hey."

"Hey," he said. It always startled Bobby to hear his brother's voice on the phone. Jonas had only been thirteen when Bobby left home. His voice had deepened since then, and it was almost like the young man on the phone was a stranger now. "Is Charlotte there?"

"She's out weeding the garden. How's Oregon?"

Bobby didn't know how to respond. Just how *was* Oregon? "It's interesting," he said, and that was true enough.

"Before you moved out there, I didn't know anyone even lived in Oregon. I mean, what do you *do* out there? Are there any girls?"

"Some."

"I have a girlfriend now. Remember Candy Wallace? We've been dating two weeks."

If Bobby remembered correctly, Candy was some little pigtailed girl in Jonas's class, but he supposed she wouldn't be so little anymore. "It isn't a date if neither of you are old enough to drive."

"Ha, ha, ha, I'm laughing so hard. I bet you still haven't worked up the guts to ask a chick out."

"Can you please put Charlotte on?"

Jonas sounded triumphant when he next spoke. "I knew it!"

In the background Bobby heard a door open and close. "Jonas," he said, "I would really love to speak to your mother right now."

"Hey, take it easy. You know I'm just messing around. Here she is."

Muffled sounds indicated that the phone was being passed from one hand into another. Then, "Bobby?"

A lump rose in Bobby's throat at the sound of his stepmother's voice. "Hey, Charlotte."

Charlotte's voice was full of relief. "Bobby, I'm so glad you called. We've all missed you so much."

"Sorry."

"Don't say that! You're a grown man who wants to find his own way in the world, and nobody should stop you from doing that." Bobby heard her hesitate for a moment. "But I would like it if you called more often. I want to know what my boy's been up to."

"He's been up to his neck in deep crap," he blurted.

Charlotte's tone changed in an instant. "Why? What's happened?"

"Nothing," he said too fast. "I mean, something has." He swallowed and counted off a few beats. "Charlotte, did you tell someone where I am?"

A long silence. Then, "I take it you talked to her?"

"No."

More silence. "I don't understand."

"She's in trouble," Bobby said. "Bad trouble."

"That's terrible!"

"I want to know what you said to her."

It sounded like Charlotte let out a long breath through pursed lips. "She showed up here out of the blue two, maybe three weeks ago."

"What was she driving?"

"This little teal thing. Might have been a Ford Escort. It looked like if you poked it too hard it would fall apart. I was out front watering the flowers when it pulled in, and she just sat there behind the wheel for a minute not doing anything, so I came around to her window to see what was going on. I asked if I could help her, and she asked me if Ken still lived here. I just about broke down then. She must have known what happened without me saying because she broke down, too." Charlotte sniffled. "I told her I was sorry and asked if she was an old friend of Ken's, and she said no, they were together for a couple years about twenty years ago, and that's when I realized who she was. I hadn't seen her in so long I didn't even recognize her."

Bobby's hands were shaking. "You grew up on the same street as her, right?"

"Right, but we didn't know each other well. She was a few years behind me in school. We went into the house and I poured her some tea and we sat and talked for hours. First we mostly talked about your father, but then we started talking about you. She was... upset when I told her you'd moved away."

"She didn't seem too upset about leaving me and Dad."

"People change, Bobby. She was a mess. She cried so long, I don't know how she didn't run out of tears. She kept going on about how stupid she'd been and how she wished she could put everything right."

So Adrian thought she was stupid for running away? She must have developed a little self-awareness in the past twenty years. "It's too late to put everything right," he said.

"Bobby, you have every right in the world to be angry at that woman, but don't be too hard on her. You probably don't want to hear this, but look at the good things that came out of what she did. I met your father. We fell in love. We had Jonas." Charlotte's voice became choked. "I loved your father more deeply than I've ever loved another human being. I thought about killing myself after he died. I'd shut myself in the bathroom, thinking how easy it would be to end it all so I could see Ken again, and then I heard you talking to Jonas out in the hallway and I knew I could never be so selfish as to end my own life even though it hurt so bad to keep on living. You boys needed me. And I needed you."

Bobby blotted his damp eyes on the back of his hand. "What does this have to do with Adrian?"

"She screwed up, Bobby. Screwed up big-time. But God likes to take all the broken pieces that other people leave behind and put them back together in a new way."

Bobby had the idea that Carly would form a fast bond with Charlotte if they ever met. "Why did she come back?"

"She said she had some kind of rude awakening and that she wanted to see each of her other childr—"

Charlotte broke off awkwardly, and a cold chill filled Bobby's veins as he pieced together what she'd been about to say. "Children?"

Silence stretched for a brief eternity before Charlotte said, "I'm sorry, Bobby. You have three siblings you've never met. Adrian said she wanted to find each of you and tell you she was sorry. You were the last one she had to meet. She said she isn't asking for forgiveness."

"Then what in the world does she want?"

"I'm afraid she'll have to tell you, herself. I really do hope she's okay."

"Yeah," Bobby found himself saying, though the words tasted bitter on his tongue. "Me too."

<hr/>

**BOBBY GOT** off the phone and started pacing. Charlotte's words had stirred up a sea of emotions that no amount of sulking was going to settle.

So Adrian felt bad about leaving Ken and Bobby behind? Good. She deserved to feel that way.

Unless her sorrow and regret were just an act. Maybe Adrian was broke and wanted some money. Would she really trek all the way across North America to find him just to beg for some cash?

Probably not. But Bobby didn't know her, so he couldn't know what crazy thoughts went through her head.

"What am I going to do?"

The Spirit surprised him by saying, *Go outside. Now.*

Gritting his teeth, he walked barefoot onto the porch, which felt warm beneath his feet in the growing heat of the late July morning.

"Okay," he said. "Now what?"

Most of the houses on the opposite side of the street had two floors. One of the neighbors over there had a ladder propped against the front of his house and was busy blasting a second-floor window with a hose he'd carried up with him. The only other person in sight was a woman with a ratty ponytail squatting in the flowerbed of the next house yanking out weeds and tossing them into the grass behind her.

Was one of them in some kind of danger? He didn't feel any of the urgency he associated with a premonition.

The sound of an approaching vehicle made Bobby turn his head as a white work van emblazoned with the logo of the Trautmann Electric Company turned onto his street.

His heart gave a flutter as the van slowed and pulled into the driveway of the house where the woman was weeding the flowerbed. She stood up, brushed off her hands, and went to the van's window.

Bobby caught snatches of conversation between gusts of wind: "...fixture's gone bad...Pete says he wants...check wiring in the basement..."

The driver, a thirtyish man in a white shirt and jeans, got out and opened the doors in the back of the van, withdrawing some kind of work kit. He and the woman disappeared into the house.

Bobby's mind buzzed. Someone driving that same type of van had kidnapped Adrian and taken her away to places unknown. Randy said that Bill Trautmann, the company owner, had been friends with Graham. Could Bill, like Graham, have a penchant for hurting others? Perhaps they were partners in crime, and if Bill had been introduced to Jack, then they might have formed a fast friendship as well.

Thing was, Bobby couldn't imagine why anyone would be so stupid as to use their own company van to conduct a kidnapping.

Bobby followed the sidewalk and stopped three houses down from his, eyeing the company phone number stenciled on the side of the van and committing it to memory.

Then he walked home, put on some fresh clothes, and picked up the phone.

# 19

THE TRAUTMANN Electric Company sat on Autumn Ridge's southern edge on a quiet street lined with trees so old their stumps could have been used as dinner tables. On the phone, Bill Trautmann explained that he and his wife lived behind the company headquarters and to come right on in if Bobby wanted to chat.

Bobby passed a parking lot filled with more work vans as well as a squat, brown building with a sign jutting from the grass proclaiming "Trautmann Electric Company. Always Reliable. Always On Time." The driveway Bill indicated on the phone appeared on the right just past the office, and Bobby turned.

The side of the blacktopped lane not facing the office was lined with tall evergreens that had dumped needles all over the pavement. An old-fashioned two-story house with indigo siding and cream-colored trim appeared on the right behind the office. Bobby pulled up beside a silver Lexus that had a vanity plate reading "FISHMAN" and got out.

He eyed the house with trepidation. Bill sounded friendly enough over the phone, but Graham had been friendly to him, too.

White wicker furniture with indigo cushions matching the siding sat on the wide porch. Pink flowers of a variety Bobby didn't recognize waved their heads at him from a ceramic pot perched on the porch railing. Not exactly the kind of place he'd expected an electrician to call home.

For some reason, the tidy appearance of the dwelling put him even more on edge. Bobby strode up to the door anyway and pushed the doorbell. *He's going to have a demon,* he thought. *He's going to have a demon, and he'll kill me.*

The door swung open. A trim black man with patches of gray hair around his ears stood in the opening.

"Bill?" Bobby ventured.

"That's me!" the man said, holding out a hand, which Bobby shook. Bill was in his early seventies and wore an orange Izod polo tucked neatly into his slacks.

He didn't have an aura.

But apparently neither had Graham.

"I'm sorry if it seems like I'm intruding," Bobby said. "I just didn't know who else to talk to."

"Oh, don't you go apologizing to me. Your reason for coming is perfectly understandable. Now come on in."

*Is it understandable?* Bobby wondered as Bill led him through an entryway into a spacious study that looked out onto a flower garden in full bloom. When Bobby had called the electric company, the woman who'd answered patched him through to Bill, and Bobby had to come up with a decent reason for calling. At Bobby's first mention of Graham, Bill had invited him right on over.

"Nice place you've got," Bobby said when Bill seated himself behind a giant polished desk and Bobby sat in a chair facing him.

Bill beamed at him. "What you see here is the result of decades of hard work. When I was a boy in Tennessee all I ever heard was how a black man could never amount to anything, and it made me so mad I vowed to make something decent of myself if it was the last thing I did. I moved here, learned the electrician's trade, saved every dime I could, and eventually started this company." He laughed. "Regina and I were so poor those first few years we were in business, we had to sell our furniture to pay the bills and ate off the ironing board instead; and now I have forty employees and a fleet of twelve vans, and life's never been better. But I'm sure you didn't come here to listen to an old man tell you his life story."

Bobby tried to figure out how he could steer the conversation to the missing work van without being too obvious about it but decided he would just go with the flow. "I don't mind. It's cool that your business got so big."

"It's all about how you treat other people. All my men and women know they have to be polite with our clients and do the best job possible. I get one complaint about an employee, they get a warning; two and they're fired. I have a very low tolerance for poor conduct."

*But do you have a low tolerance for abduction, too?* "No offense, but I think I might be afraid to work for you."

Bill threw his head back and let out a hearty laugh. "I've only had to can two people in the last ten years, and I can't say I enjoyed it either time. But if you want your company to keep a decent reputation, you have to cut off any part that deviates from it."

Bobby found himself nodding. "So I was wondering about Graham."

Some of the cheer evaporated from Bill's expression. "Right. I'm sorry you ended up as one of his tenants. If I'd known where he was..." He stared past Bobby's shoulder, and a shadow crossed over his face. "If someone had told me what he'd end up becoming, I'd have said they were crazy. Graham was one of my best buddies for years."

It was interesting hearing about Graham from someone who hadn't previously been a Servant. "How did you meet him?"

Bill took a moment to clear his throat. "We had booths next to each other in the commercial building at the county fair about thirty-five, forty years ago. He was promoting his drug store and I was promoting my company, and we got to talking about how we both got started, and first thing you know we were going out for drinks every so often and then our wives met each other and would go out shopping, and then we'd invite each other over for parties and things, and the rest is history."

"He seemed like a nice guy to me. You know, when he was my landlord."

"He was nice, on the outside at least. When I heard he'd shot that boy he took in like a grandson, I was sure it had been a mistake. You might say I was in denial. But then I thought, what did I really know about Graham, after all? I don't know what sort of things were festering deep inside that head of his." Bill's mouth formed an unhappy line. "For all I know, each and every one of us has a little crazy inside. It's just a matter of making sure nobody lets it out."

Bobby thought about what Phil learned from Graham's notebook. "Apparently the crazy didn't start until about six years ago."

Bill's eyebrows rose. "Six years, huh?"

"Did something happen to him six years ago aside from Randy moving into his house?"

Bill shifted his weight and set his chin on his hand. "Let me think." His forehead creased. "That would have been 2009. Hmm."

When Bill lapsed into silence, Bobby pondered what he'd learned so far. It seemed unlikely that Bill had been the one to pluck Adrian off the side of the street. But who, then? Who had taken the van and spirited Adrian away?

Bill snapped his fingers. "Nate," he said.

Bobby whipped his head back to face the man. "What?"

"That's the year Graham met somebody named Nate. He wouldn't stop talking about him, like Nate was the best thing to ever come into his life. We used to tease him and ask if Nate was his new boyfriend."

Bobby had no idea where this conversation would lead. "So, who *was* Nate?"

"Somebody Graham befriended. He had one of those funny Armenian last names, but I can't remember what it was. Bag something. Bagdalasian? No, but it was something like that. I never met the guy. Graham was so fixated on him that it kind of felt like I did know him, which is strange because I don't know what Nate looks like or even how old he is. Does that make sense?"

"No."

"What I mean is he kept talking about things Nate said to him. Like, 'Nate told me the funniest joke the other day' and 'You know what Nate said about the President?' Things like that."

"So what did Nate say?"

"I don't remember. I guess I didn't care enough to remember since Nate was nothing to me. Graham stopped mentioning him after a few months. We'd ask what Nate was up to and Graham would just shrug."

"Didn't you think that was strange?"

"Of course I did! But life went on and I didn't think much of it."

Bobby wondered if Nate was Graham's first victim. He shivered.

"Do you believe in demons?" Bill asked.

Goosebumps rose on Bobby's arms. "Why do you ask?"

Bill sighed. "It's just something I wonder now and again. I know that God Almighty put us on this earth and that forces are out there trying to screw everything up, which brings me back to Graham. Yes, it's possible he went crazy from a tumor or dementia or something. But sometimes when I lie awake at night I can't help but wonder if his murder attempt on that boy was caused by something else."

"Graham wasn't possessed," Bobby said. "I'm pretty sure of that."

Bill raised an eyebrow. "Are you, now?"

The faces of Trish, the woman who'd died in Randy's basement last week; and the nameless demoniac at The Pink Rooster flitted through Bobby's mind. "Let's just say I've run into some people who are, well, you know."

A look of understanding dawned on Bill's face. "Ah. You're one of them."

Bobby's pulse quickened. "One of who?"

"Let's just say I know a thing or two about Graham's old crowd. Not much, mind you, because what I learned was by mistake and it wasn't my place to pry any deeper into it than I had to." He gave Bobby a piercing stare. "You best be careful. If you are one of them, you know what's out there."

# 20

CARLY LET herself into the house feeling like the biggest hypocrite who'd ever walked the earth. "What are you going to do with your pain, Bobby?" she asked when she set her purse down on the kitchen table. "Heck, Carly, what are you going to do with yours?"

She tugged the crockpot out of a bottom cabinet and plopped it on the marble countertop between the sink and stove. She just needed to let it *go*. Cassandra, the woman who'd so drastically altered her family's life, couldn't hurt her anymore. What she'd done was long ago, in the past. The past was not now. Now was today, and today her parents were coming home from another Frankie Jovingo Mission Trip, and she was going to get dinner ready for them even though it wasn't even noon yet.

Carly swung the freezer door open to rummage for vegetables to toss into the pot. Corn, peas, carrots, beans. She found a package of frozen steak chunks and decided it would be good to add that, too.

She tore the packages open and dumped the contents into the pot. She could understand why Bobby was so upset to learn that

Mystery Woman was his own mother, but if he was going to be a good Servant, he would have to let it go.

It wouldn't be easy for him. But the important things in life never were.

"Face it," a voice said behind her. "You want Cassandra dead."

Carly's body went rigid and her chest tightened like a giant had just enclosed her in its fist. Someone had broken into the house while she visited Bobby, and now he was in her kitchen standing right behind her.

She forced herself to face the intruder, hoping against hope he didn't have a weapon.

Her heart skipped a beat when she laid eyes on the male figure standing in front of the fridge. He had auburn hair like hers. Plain clothing. A winning smile.

It was the same man who'd appeared at the top of the privacy fence and then behind the bench the day before. Carly was certain he hadn't been in the kitchen when she first walked in.

"Who *are* you?" she croaked.

He went on as if he hadn't heard her. "Cassandra ruined you. Don't you remember what it was like? You and Jackie, as happy as could be. The birthday girls. You both were at an age when you thought you'd live forever."

Carly's pulse pounded in her ears. This man couldn't be real, yet here he was, standing before her as clearly as the rest of her surroundings.

"And then Cassandra came along. She wanted to kill her husband but dear, sweet Jackie got in the way of things. I suppose every war has collateral damage."

Tears filled Carly's eyes as his words conjured forth memories of that terrible day. The excitement. The laughter. Moments before it all ended.

"How do you really feel about Cassandra?" the man asked.

It was madness, hearing these words from a stranger's mouth.

"Who are you?" she repeated, wishing he would make some reply instead of going on about Jackie and Cassandra.

The man tilted his head to the side. "Cassandra is free now. Doesn't it make you angry knowing she's alive while your sister rots in the ground feeding the worms, forever a child, while you've grown into a woman?"

Carly's legs went weak beneath her. She reached for a red plastic ladle sitting in the dish strainer and brandished it in front of her, knowing she looked about as dangerous as a kitten. "Get out of here."

"It won't be that hard to find Cassandra, you know. Autumn Ridge isn't that big of a city. You could track her down, wait until nightfall, slowly creep up to her door with a gun in hand, and pay her back in kind for what she did. And it'll feel so *good*."

Her purse sat on the table between her and the man. She considered lunging for it and digging out her phone, but the man might try to attack her before she was able to dial 911.

The image of Carly standing above Cassandra's bleeding corpse filled her mind with such abruptness that she let out a startled "Oh!"

Cassandra lay sprawled on her back in a doorway, her spill of dark hair doing little to mask the new hole in the center of her forehead. *You want this, Carly. Oh, yes, you do.*

Carly blinked. She still stood in the kitchen between the sink and the table, only now the auburn-haired intruder had come around to her side and towered over her, his triumphant grin so wide she could see almost all of his gleaming white teeth. "If you kill her, you'll be ridding the earth of a monster. What's going to stop her from killing another child? You, Carly. Only you."

Carly swung the ladle at his head. It passed through him as if he were made of air.

He winked.

Something snapped inside her. She swung again and again, and each time the ladle made no impact because nothing was there but the image of an auburn-haired man who was either a figment of Carly's frazzled mind or a ghost.

The man darted past her, and by the time she turned, he was gone.

Then something fell over up in her bedroom on the second floor.

Carly ran, taking the stairs two at a time. She braked in her bedroom doorway, feeling the color bleed out of her face.

The framed photograph of her and Jackie on their tenth birthday that had sat on her dresser for years now lay in the middle of the floor, the glass cracked in a jagged line right down the middle, separating her from Jackie: a foreshadowing of the more permanent separation they would undergo three years later.

Well, it wasn't exactly permanent. Carly would die someday too, either today or sixty years from now, and then she and Jackie would be together once again.

Then Jackie's favorite stuffed bear, a red furry thing she'd named Valentino, flew off a shelf and landed next to the broken frame, a seam down its back unraveling and spewing stuffing all over the carpet and braided rug.

At the same instant the crucifix hanging over the bedroom window jumped from its nail and went smashing into the dresser mirror, shattering it into hundreds of glimmering shards, the weight of the ladle changed in Carly's hand. She found herself holding a Taurus Model 605 snubnosed revolver—the same one her father kept locked in the gun cabinet in his study.

*This can't be happening. I don't even know the combination to get into the cabinet.*

Her hand slowly brought the nose of the revolver to her right temple.

*It's you or Cassandra. Cassandra or you.*

Something warm rolled down Carly's cheek as Cassandra's dead face swam in her mind's eye.

———◆———

IN THE morning Jack headed westward into the mountains to the place where Troy—thanks to Vincent—had opened his newest enterprise. Jack didn't officially work there, but he'd visited enough times that everyone there knew him.

Troy called it the Domus. Latin for "house," it was technically a country club with highly select membership. Membership was granted by invitation only, and Troy had one of his most trusted employees (unfortunately not Jack) carefully screen each new member before granting them entry.

The Domus sat at the end of a two-mile-long gravel lane accessible only by a winding logging road that saw little traffic. Hidden among thousands of square acres of evergreen forest, the nearest human dwellings were easily five miles away. The building that became the Domus had been a spiritual retreat back in the seventies, long before the owners went bankrupt and foreclosed on the property. Troy had snatched it up when he got into the logging business, knowing that the building could someday be of use to him.

It had needed some obvious upgrades, and he'd completely remodeled some of the floors to better suit his needs. Jack suspected that some of the workers Troy hired had probably never been seen again once reconstruction was complete.

At least that's what he'd have done if he were Troy. It paid to cover one's tracks.

Jack's car jolted as he turned into the lane, which was blocked by a plain white gate but no "No Trespassing" sign, as the latter often tempted people to do just the opposite. He put the car in park, climbed out, and walked up to a log post jutting from the ground beside the lane.

He pushed a brown button embedded near the top and eyed the tiny black pinprick where a camera had been hidden in the post.

A voice squawked out of an unseen speaker. "Password?"

Jack rolled his eyes. "Inkblot." The password changed on a weekly basis. Farley, the man in charge of Domus security, said he chose the passwords by using a random word generator online.

Jack personally found the whole idea of passwords absurd.

Farley coughed a few times through the speaker. Then, "Name and purpose."

"Jack Willard, and I work for Troy, which you very well know. It's not like I haven't been here several dozen times before."

"Hey, man, I'm just following orders."

The white gate swung open, and Jack got back in the car.

It was a long, bumpy ride back to the Domus. The lane finally opened out into a wide gravel lot that fronted the great log structure. The Domus boasted two upper floors, a basement, and a sub-basement and could accommodate up to fifty guests at a time.

An in-ground swimming pool and tennis court were visible off to the left of the building. A middle-aged woman in a black swimsuit and giant sunglasses lounged in one of the chairs beside the pool while paging through a novel. Jack knew her as Carol, but it wasn't necessarily her true name. Many members signed up under aliases. Only Troy and the employee who screened them knew their true identities.

Jack strode up to the massive wooden doors. Cool air washed over him as he entered the tile-floored lobby where the ceiling extended up to the second floor.

Giselle, the young receptionist, stood up behind the counter. Today she wore a skin-tight black top, a faux-pearl necklace, and blood red lipstick that stood out sharply against her pale skin and curly platinum blonde hair. "Jack!" she exclaimed with a blush. "We weren't expecting you today."

"I'm just full of surprises, aren't I?"

Giselle let out a giggle as he approached the counter. Jack knew she'd had a crush on him from the moment she'd started working there. "So what can I do for you today? Looking for a little voyeurism or something dirtier?"

"I wanted to know if Vincent was busy right now. I'd like to talk to him."

Giselle's expression soured. "Good. Maybe you can talk some sense into him. I assume you heard what he did?"

"Troy said he wants to take a vacation."

"Then you haven't heard the latest. Vincent got out last night."

Jack's stomach flipped. "What?"

"He disappeared after the evening show, and his chip must be malfunctioning because they couldn't track him. Farley and the others combed the woods, and at eleven o'clock they found Vincent blundering his way back to the building. Apparently he got scared and came back."

*Interesting.* "Where is he now?"

"As far as I know, he's waiting for the morning show to let out." Her lip curled. "I hope you convince him not to do anything rash again. If he escapes, I'm out of a job."

*Unless Orin and Theo find another like him.* "I'll see what I can do."

Jack strode toward the western corridor and descended the first flight of stairs he came to. As he traversed the carpeted lower hallway, he could hear the faint sound of excited voices coming from the room that was his destination.

He pushed open the door and slipped into the darkened theater-style room. Ten or so men and women occupied the descending tiers of seats. Jack recognized the Staffords, a gray-haired couple in their sixties who traveled the country in their free time; a brunette twentysomething named Ella who claimed to be working on a psychology degree; and a thirty-year-old maintenance man in overalls named Louis. The others were strangers to Jack, though one man appeared to be dressed like a banker and another woman wore a summer dress and too many bracelets.

All stared enraptured at the spectacle unfolding behind the six-inch-thick layer of Plexiglas positioned in the place of a movie screen.

Jack took a seat in the back row to watch.

Behind the Plexiglas lay a small room that was empty save for two individuals: a muscular man and a boy of perhaps ten. Blood flowed from the boy's nose and over his lips and one of his eyes had swelled shut, but the man continued to pound him relentlessly in the face. The boy's eyes were dead, and he took the beating without so much as lifting a hand to stop it.

One final swing and the boy crumpled to the floor.

There came a smattering of applause as curtains drew themselves shut over the Plexiglas. The exhilarated audience stood up, commenting to each other about the highlights of the display before filing out of the room.

Jack's gaze lingered on the curtains. He'd never been able to understand the voyeurs even though he'd sat here among their number time after time. They wouldn't dare lay a hand on a child themselves, yet they had no problem watching someone else beat one into unconsciousness. Jack attributed it to cowardice.

The voyeurs would probably deny it.

Jack followed them out and went to the next door down the hallway, where he punched in a code on a keypad. The door beeped and unlocked, and Jack let himself in.

Two assistants were laying the unconscious boy out on a table while Vincent—dressed in a plain white t-shirt and black skinny jeans—stood nearby, wringing his slender hands together. The eyeliner he'd put on that morning had run. Looked like sissy boy had been crying. Again.

The man who had knocked the boy out would have been taken to a different room so he could shower and put on clean clothes.

"All right," Larry, one of the assistants, said. "He's all yours." Heavy bags hung under Larry's eyes. Jack suspected he was one of the employees who'd stayed up late looking for Vincent.

Larry and the other assistant, Joe, stepped back while Vincent came up to the table and placed a hand over the boy's black eye. When he removed it, the swelling and discoloration had vanished, and the trickle of blood coming from the boy's nose drew to a stop. "It's finished," he whispered before shrinking back against the wall.

Larry proceeded to wipe the blood off the boy's face. His eyes fluttered open, and Larry spoke to him in soothing tones: "It's okay, buddy. You're all back to normal so you can be ready for tomorrow's show."

The boy made no response.

Jack cleared his throat. "Vincent?"

Vincent jerked his head toward Jack, and his face paled. "Oh. I didn't see you come in. What are you doing here?"

Jack noted that Larry and Joe made a point of not acknowledging Jack's presence. "I wanted to talk to you," Jack said, ignoring them in turn. "You do have time for that, right? Or are you going to spend the next few hours sobbing like a baby?"

Vincent glared at him. Then his expression softened. "If you want to talk, let's go outside."

"So you have a better chance of running away? That bimbo at the front desk told me what you did."

"Jack, you don't understand."

"Then enlighten me."

———◆———

MINUTES LATER, Jack found himself sitting next to Vincent out by the swimming pool, Carol having gone inside. "So you wanted to run away," Jack said.

Vincent put his head in his hands. "You don't know what it's like not being allowed to leave because *you* can go anywhere you want. It's eating me up. I—I don't think I'll survive much longer if I stay."

"Yet you came back."

Vincent grimaced. "They made me do it. I can't resist them."

"Few could."

"They whisper things to me. Awful things. And—" Despondency wrote itself across Vincent's face, then he suddenly seemed calmer. "What is it you wanted to talk about?"

Jack took a moment to collect his thoughts. Upon waking that morning, he'd known he needed to come out here and do something but wasn't sure what it was. At first he'd thought he wanted to clear up his foul mood from last night when the Roland dweeb showed up at the apartment and pulled a knife on him, but once he'd reached the outskirts of town he realized his trip to the Domus was meant to be something more.

"What would you do," Jack asked, "if a little punk came to your house and threatened to stab you if you didn't do what he wanted?"

"Troy would destroy him."

"I'm asking *you*."

Vincent's expression deepened into a frown, and a new glint shined in his eyes. "We would destroy him, too. You shouldn't have let him go. You could have ended him once and for all."

It unnerved Jack only a little hearing another entity's words coming out of Vincent's mouth. He knew that one of them was often with him, as well. It even gave Jack encouragement from time to time. In fact, it was just that encouragement that made him decide to track his grandfather down using the information provided by Kerry, a hacker employed by Troy. Kerry had wormed his way into records showing an illegal change of identity for Graham, who had taken on the name of David Upton; the real David Upton having died in a car accident in Florida at the age of five.

Jack knew that one or more of the others had also helped him evade the police last week when they showed up to arrest him and Graham. Always coming in handy, they were.

Jack cleared his throat. "It would have been too risky to kill him there. We would have been seen, and it'll be a cold day in hell before they lock me up again." He paused. "I've been thinking about something Troy said. He wants to give me a promotion but I can only do it if I pull off the impossible."

"Then you should think outside the box."

"I've been trying."

"Destroy him."

"What?"

"Destroy him." Vincent's body gave a massive lurch as if he'd been shoved from behind, and he blinked wide, wondering eyes as if awakening from a dream. "Sorry, Jack. I must have dozed off for a minute. What is it you wanted to talk about?"

---

BOBBY REGRETFULLY left Bill Trautmann's home without having broached the subject of the missing van—changing topics from Graham's insanity to vehicular theft would have been so jarring that Bill's suspicions would have been roused.

Instead, when he pulled out of Bill's driveway, he made an abrupt turn into the electric company's lot and parked between two of the vans.

Not sure what he would find, he killed the engine and got out.

Four spaces down from his, a mechanic had the hood of another van popped up and was rummaging around in its engine.

Bobby took a deep breath and casually walked around the side. "Hey."

The mechanic gave a start and studied Bobby with coal-black eyes. In one hand he held a slender wire that was wet on one end, and in the other was a paper towel. He wore a white t-shirt with the Trautmann Electric Company name and motto printed over the left breast, and beneath that was embroidered the name "Angel."

"What do you want?" Angel asked in a Mexican accent much thicker than that of Lupe Sanchez.

Bobby couldn't take his eyes off the guy's name.

"It's pronounced *AHN-hel*," the man said, reading Bobby's mind. "I said, what do you want?"

"Have you worked here long?" Bobby asked, saying the first thing that came to mind.

Angel's eyes narrowed. "Four years. Why?"

"I just wondered what kind of boss Mr. Trautmann is. I've heard he has a low tolerance for poor conduct."

The man gave a nod. "Ah. *Sí*. You are looking for a job, no? Bill, he is a nice man, but tough." Angel gestured at the van before him. "Like this van disappears yesterday and turns up in its spot a while ago. Bill says, 'Angel, go make sure it's safe to drive.' Like someone stole it just to mess it up a bit. So I check steering, brake fluid, now oil...what?"

Bobby's heart stuttered. "You said *this* is the van that was stolen?"

"*Sí*, and now it is back. Someone must have had a change of heart. If only more bad men were like this one, the world would be great place, no?" He grinned.

"What makes you think a man took it?"

Angel shrugged and wiped a bead of sweat off his forehead with the back of the hand clutching the paper towel. "It is a man sort of thing to do."

Bobby took a few steps backward and squinted in through the passenger window. Clean gray seats. Shining steering wheel and dashboard. No trash or dirt on the floor. "Did you clean it out before checking the oil and stuff?" he asked.

"No."

"Do you care if I have a look in the back for a minute?"

Angel's amiability was replaced with his previous suspicion. "What is this about?"

"I'm nosy."

Angel's mouth tightened, and he glanced over his shoulder in the direction of Bill Trautmann's house, which was mostly obscured by a thick stand of fir trees lining the lot. "Maybe I am nosy, too. Tell me what you really want, and *then* you can look inside."

Like Bobby was going to tell Angel that the woman who'd birthed him had very likely been held in the back of this van for an undetermined length of time. "I just thought there might be some clues back there about who might have swiped it. You know, so you can tell the police."

Angel seemed to think this over for a moment or two before saying, "Very well. Take a look. But you will not find anything."

"Thanks."

Bobby slid the passenger side back door open and climbed in. Goosebumps rose on his arms and the back of his neck when Angel's words replayed themselves in his mind. All he could see through the windshield was the van's open hood and brief glimpses of Angel moving around on the other side of it.

Could Angel have been the one to take the van? As a company employee he would have had a key, so Bobby couldn't dismiss the possibility. But would he really be that obvious if he were the kidnapper?

The inside of the van smelled like Windex. The gray carpet on the floor appeared to have been vacuumed. A toolkit and some coils of wiring sat neatly on one side of the empty space.

He had the idea that even if the police came along checking for stray hairs and fingerprints, they wouldn't find much of anything. Adrian Pollard's abductor had known what he was doing.

But who was her abductor?

It startled him when he realized he'd become fully immersed in his search for her once again. *She's nothing to me,* he thought. *Just someone who needs a bit of saving.* When he did find her, they would simply acknowledge each other's existence before peacefully parting ways. Bobby certainly didn't want to start a mother-son relationship with her. Her other children wouldn't have done that. They would have been hurt, too.

The idea that he had siblings he'd never met made him feel strange, as if he'd just learned that the earth actually had four moons or that there was a secret continent in the middle of the Pacific Ocean that nobody ever talked about. He wondered how old his siblings were, where they lived, and if they were anything like him.

*No.* He couldn't let himself think about that. He would have to crush those questions before they seeded themselves in his brain and began to grow. To learn the answers, he would have to sit down and have a long chat with Adrian, which was out of the question.

Bobby backed out of the van and slid the door shut. "Nothing," he said. "I guess Bill will never get to find out what kind of creep stole his van."

Angel stood beside him with his arms folded across his chest, his face warped into a scowl. "Get out of here before I decide to tell my boss you're just here to snoop around."

Bobby caught a glimmer of something in the man's eyes, and he thought, *Aha!* "Are you talking about Bill or somebody else?" He continued before Angel could answer. "I see how it is. You know somebody who needed a van since using their own might have been incriminating, and you lent this one to him to use instead. They probably even paid you for it. Right?"

Angel opened his mouth to voice what probably would have been some kind of objection, but the ringing of Bobby's phone cut him off.

He wanted to ignore it, but his gut told him he needed to take the call. "Excuse me," he said, and stepped over to his Nissan.

Frowning, Bobby held the phone to his ear. "What's up?"

"I need you to come over here," Carly said in such a flat tone that Bobby almost didn't recognize her voice. "Now."

Alarm bells went off in Bobby's head. "Did something happen?"

"Just come over here. Please."

"I've never been to your house. I don't know where it is."

"We live at 900 Waterstone Drive off of Skyline Avenue. Do you know where that is?"

"I think so." Bobby swallowed and glanced back in Angel's direction. The man was rummaging around under the hood once more. "Do you need anything?"

"Just you. I mean; to talk to." She paused. "God help me, I sound like an idiot. Just get over here soon, okay? I'll talk about it then."

The line went dead.

Coils of dread snared him. Just what in the world was going on?

———◆———

WHEN THE little girl who'd joined Adrian first awakened, her gaze darted wildly around the concrete room before coming to rest on Adrian's face.

The haunted look in the child's eyes tore Adrian's heart in two.

Adrian had probably looked the same when she first came to in this place, only unlike this child, she had a far better idea of what would happen to the both of them if she didn't come up with a plan of action, and soon.

She crossed the small room and sat on the edge of the cot next to the girl and tried to smile at her just to provide her with a shred of hope, but for some reason she couldn't work the muscles in her face to change her expression.

"Honey," she said, "everything is going to be okay."

Fat tears welled up in the child's brown eyes. "I want my mom."

"And we'll get your mom, honey. But first we have to find a way out of here."

Adrian knew that the odds of completing a successful escape without any weapons other than her own two hands were next to nothing, though the child didn't need to know that. Telling her that she wouldn't be freed from this prison until someone came along to do unspeakable things to her would have been a cruelty, which Adrian dared not inflict upon one so young.

So Adrian did the only thing she could in the meantime: she talked.

"Honey, what's your name?" Adrian asked.

"M-Monique."

According to Monique, she was eight years old, not nine, and she lived with her mother and little brother in a place called Eugene. Monique's father had "up and left" one day to go live with "some blonde tramp," and Adrian almost laughed hearing such adult words come out of the child's mouth but quickly swallowed it back.

"Do you know how you got here?" Adrian asked.

Monique started to shake her head but turned it into a nod, the plastic balls on her hair ties bobbing up and down. "It was Wanda."

"Wanda?"

"She's a real nice lady. My mom always says not to talk to strangers but Wanda wasn't like them."

"She wasn't like who?"

"Other people. Other people look at you funny like you smell or something and just keep on walking. But Wanda was nice and talked to me. She gave me a doll one day and my mom got mad and asked where I got it, but Wanda told me not to tell anyone, so I told my mom I just found it somewhere."

Adrian could see it clearly in her mind. Monique's mother must have had to work a lot to support two young children on her own, leaving Monique and probably her brother to roam unattended. This Wanda must have been one of the vultures who helped stock this underground prison. She would have seen Monique out somewhere, decided she was easy pickings, and pretended to befriend her so it would be easier to kidnap her.

"What else did Wanda do?" Adrian asked, afraid that her voice would break if she tried to speak any louder.

Monique drew her knees to her chest and gazed at the dirty cot. "She took me to get ice cream. We even saw a princess movie, and all the ladies wore these pretty crowns and dresses." A look of dreamy contentment passed over the child's face, as if the thought of being a real life princess was the most wonderful thing in the world.

*It's not all it's cracked up to be*, Adrian thought. She had practically lived like royalty in the years she'd been with Yuri—she'd had all the clothes, jewelry, and alcohol she'd ever wanted—and all it gave her in turn was a mountain of regret.

It all seemed so juvenile now. It was as if Adrian had been a child her entire life and was just now coming to understand what it meant to be an adult.

She first laid eyes on Yuri when he and his colleagues came to a benefit dinner at the golf course clubhouse where she worked. Adrian's job that evening had been to work behind the bar counter filling glasses of wine.

When Yuri came back through the line for his fifth glass, she realized he wasn't just doing it for the alcohol. He wanted to see *her*. It was just like with Ken and all the others all those years ago. A man had seen her, and he liked what he saw.

"You are so beautiful," he said, a slur in his speech from the four glasses he'd already consumed. "What's your name?"

At first she'd blinked stupidly at him like he'd just said something in a foreign language. Well, he did have some kind of accent. Something European, maybe. His hair was so pale it was almost white, though he wasn't at all old; and he wore a crisp, clean suit with a shiny blue tie.

"I'm Adrian," she said as a blush warmed her cheeks. "Is there anything else I can get you, sir?"

One of the men she'd seen sharing Yuri's table stood behind him in line, laughing. "You watch out for this old dog," he said. "He barks up a lot of trees."

Yuri ended up staying late after the benefit was over and walked Adrian to her car. He told her he'd grown up in Kiev in the Ukraine and was now the chief executive officer of a financial consulting firm based here in southern Michigan. He slipped her a business card and told her that if she was ever lonely, to just give him a call.

Then he'd slipped away into the night like a shadow fading into darkness, and Adrian felt giddy inside to know that someone with such standing in their city would take an interest in her.

She'd called him the very next morning, and they were married three months later.

"Adrian?"

The sound of Monique's voice snapped her back to attention. "What is it, honey?"

"You look sad."

"Well, maybe I am sad." She shivered, wishing her mind would stay in the present since finding a way out was far more important than lamenting about her years with Yuri. "How do you know Wanda is the one who brought you here?"

Monique's bottom lip trembled. "She said we were going to the zoo. I've never been there before. But we kept on driving and driving, and then I said I was thirsty so she gave me a drink, and then my head got all funny and then I was here."

A new wave of anger flared up inside of Adrian as she pictured the scene. She looked to the metal door. It could only be opened from the outside since there was no knob in here, but what if there was a way to get the bolt to disengage by sliding something into the paper-thin gap between the door and its frame?

Monique followed her line of sight. "How will we get out?"

"I'm not sure."

"Do you think someone will come save us?"

*No*, Adrian thought, but she said, "Maybe."

# 21

BOBBY PULLED up in front of the Jovingos' two-story house, parking beside Carly's Aveo and wondering what in the world could have happened since she left him less than an hour ago.

Was this how life would be now that he was the Servant? One crisis after another after another without end?

His heart banged against his ribs as he hurried up the flower-lined walk onto the porch.

He rapped on the door and waited.

And waited.

"Carly?" he asked in a loud voice, hoping she'd hear him through the walls. "Open up."

No response came, and the storm cloud of dread hanging over him darkened. He felt a stirring within him. *Just go in.*

He sucked in a breath that didn't sufficiently fill his lungs. *Here we go.*

The house exuded an eerie stillness when he stepped over the threshold and closed the door behind him. Directly before him lay a kitchen with a table in the center of the open space, on which sat

Carly's purse, a napkin holder, and a candle in a jar. A crockpot had been set out on the counter, and empty packages of frozen vegetables sat beside it.

Bobby treaded lightly as he moved into the kitchen. He almost expected to find Carly passed out on the floor (or worse), but his fear proved to be unfounded since Carly wasn't there.

His mind jumped backward into last week when he, Randy, and Phil had arrived at Lupe's apartment to protect her when they'd learned that Graham was on the loose. Randy had unlocked the apartment and they'd all gone inside to find it vacant, though Lupe's purse had been left behind on her coffee table.

Could Carly, like Lupe, have been abducted? Bobby wouldn't put it past Jack to do something else to get even with him, but if Carly had been forcibly removed from her home, how in the world had she been able to call him from there?

A faint sniffling from up above met his ears, flooding him with both fear and relief. He returned to the entryway, eyed a carpeted flight of stairs, and ascended them to an upper hallway running perpendicular to the stairs.

He hung a right and halted in the open doorway of a bedroom, his pulse breaking into full gallop once more.

Carly sat cross-legged on a braided rug in the center of the room, rocking back and forth with her eyes scrunched closed. The landline phone she'd used to call him sat in its cradle beside her on the floor.

Not having the faintest idea of what to say or do, Bobby flipped on the light. "Are you okay?"

She shook her head. "What do you see?" she asked, keeping her eyes firmly closed.

"Is this a trick question?"

"I'm not laughing, Bobby. Go on. Tell me what you see in here."

"I see you sitting on the floor."

A grim smirk tugged at her mouth. "At least I know I'm still here, then. What else?"

Bobby made a quick appraisal of the room. Neatly-made bed with a cerulean bedspread and fuzzy, sky-blue pillows. A dresser. A desk and chair. Photos and knickknacks and stuffed animals. "I see a bedroom?"

Carly's eyes opened. They were more bloodshot than Bobby had ever seen them. "Bobby, I have to step down as counselor."

This was just about the last thing he expected to come out of her mouth. "What? Why? I thought you liked doing that."

"Why?" She gave a hollow laugh. "Because I'm losing my mind. Heck, I even thought I was holding a gun, but I guess I wasn't or you'd have mentioned it."

For the first time Bobby noticed the red plastic ladle lying across her lap. "I don't get it," he said, the sight of the utensil deepening his unease.

"It's not that hard to understand. I can't counsel anyone if there's something wrong with me."

"Okay." Bobby swallowed. "What's wrong with you?"

"Are you blind?"

Despite his concern, irritation rose within him. "Look. You call me upset, I come here and see you sitting like this, and you expect me to figure out what's the matter without you telling me? I'm not a psychic."

At first he thought she'd go off on him like she had on the day they'd met, but instead she said, "I need help. For three years I've helped people work through their problems, and I can't even work through my own."

"Why do you think you're losing your mind?"

She mustered a few ounces of resolve. "A man was in the kitchen."

"I didn't see anyone."

"He isn't here now."

"Where did he go?"

"Heck if I know." She shivered.

Bobby licked dry lips. "He...he didn't try to hurt you, did he?"

"Not physically."

Bobby couldn't see how a prowler would make Carly question her sanity. "Do you know who he was?"

"No, but yesterday I saw him peeking over the privacy fence when I was eating lunch outside, and when I went to tell him off for spying, he disappeared. When I went to go back to the bench, he was behind it like he dematerialized and reappeared yards away in just a few seconds."

"And then he reappeared today in the kitchen?"

"Right. And he said awful things to me. Things he had no way of knowing." She drew in a deep breath, and Bobby had the sense that a number of unspoken thoughts rested on the tip of her tongue but she was too afraid to say them.

While he waited for Carly to work up the courage to share the rest of her ordeal, Bobby's attention drifted over to her dresser, on which sat a framed photograph of a much-younger Carly and another girl he didn't know. The other girl had a stockier build and darker hair than Carly, though he could tell they were related. The girls sat side by side behind a cake that had orange icing and a bunch of lit candles stabbed into the top.

A new chill snaked its way into Bobby's veins.

Carly followed his line of sight. "Her name was Jackie," she said, her voice thick with tears.

Carly hadn't mentioned a Jackie before. "She's your sister?"

She nodded. "You didn't think I was an only child, did you?"

"It sort of crossed my mind. Um, what happened to her?"

A shudder passed through her body, and in his mind Bobby saw himself sitting down and putting his arm around her to give her a boost of strength, but instead he just stood immobile like some dummy in a shop window. "It was the day after our thirteenth birth-day," she said.

"You were twins?"

"Fraternal twins. She was bigger-boned than me, like our dad, and I got the petite genes from Mom. People always thought she was the older sister." She closed her eyes and took slow breaths. "Jackie was always the mild one. She wasn't nearly as hotheaded, as, well, you know. She loved to help people."

"So do you."

"Not then, I didn't. Back then I was way more concerned with other things. Looking pretty. Fitting in. Your typical adolescent woes." Carly glanced down at the ladle in her lap and gave a start as if she'd only just noticed it was there. Face flushing, she set it aside on the rug. "The day after our birthday, we went to the Family Fun Zone. It's closed now—I think they turned it into a hardware store—but it's where you could play arcade games and skee ball and things and win tickets you could trade in for crappy prizes. We went every year and thought it was the best thing in the world." She paused, her face lined with pain. "There was this woman who'd just lost custody of her kids because she was mentally unstable. Her ex-husband took them to the Family Fun Zone the same day we were there. Cassandra—their mother—showed up to kill her ex-husband, but Jackie saw what was about to happen and jumped in front of the guy a split second before Cassandra pulled the trigger."

"You can't be serious."

"I am."

"What kid just jumps in front of a gun?" Bobby would have scampered if he'd been in Jackie's place. He'd *still* scamper, to be honest.

"Here's something you have to understand," Carly said. "Dad raised us to be fearless. Even when we were little he'd pound it into our heads that we couldn't be afraid of everything like Mom is. He'd read us stories about martyrs and praise their bravery in the face of death. Well, I guess Jackie was braver than I am. You don't see me taking bullets for people."

Her words left a hollow feeling in Bobby's gut, and he felt the weight of her grief pressing down on him. He wanted to say something—he *needed* to say something—but what in the world could he possibly say that would make her feel better, especially when it seemed to him that Frankie had tried to brainwash his own kids?

Nothing. That's what. So he kept his lips sealed and waited for her to go on.

"Cassandra was just let out of prison," she continued. "I saw her in the store the other day and she smiled at me. She must be one of those people who remembers faces."

"Why'd they let her out?"

"Good behavior, I guess. It's not like she meant to kill Jackie, but she never showed an ounce of remorse for what she did."

"I think I kind of understand why you were upset the other night."

Her lips formed a faint smile. "The thing is, I thought I was over all of this. But now this man I saw...it's like I've flipped my lid. Him going on about how I really want to kill Cassandra to get back at her for killing Jackie. But there's no man in here. It was all in my head."

The image of Thane sitting in Bobby's kitchen flashed through his mind. "Wait a minute. What did he look like?"

Carly's eyes narrowed. "Why?"

"Did he have sort of reddish-brown hair?"

"Yeah, and he smiled too much." She looked up in alarm. "Where have *you* seen him?"

"In my house and car."

"What the heck? Did you tell anyone about this?"

Bobby's face flushed. "Just you. I thought he was an angel."

"What in the world would make you think *that*?"

"Because he was trying to help me." *Wasn't he?*

"Bobby, this is bad. You should have known that's not what he is."

"Well, what is he, then? A ghost?"

"A ghost. Very funny."

It hit Bobby like a kick in the stomach. "You're saying Thane is a demon?"

"Oh, so he has a name? Nice."

Her snide tone struck a nerve. "He didn't try to hurt me, okay? For all I know, he's an angel and whatever you saw in here was a demon who looked just like him. I mean, don't demons try to sow confusion? Your dad said something like that in our meeting the other day."

Carly nodded. "And confusion sows discord."

"Sorry."

"It's not your fault. You didn't summon the thing here."

Something about this situation still didn't sit right with Bobby. "There wasn't an aura," he said. "Shadowy *or* black."

"So? You'd only see that in someone who's possessed."

"Are you sure? Because I'd think that if a demon appeared like a human, I'd at least pick up some kind of signal telling me what it really is."

"A demon is the only thing it could be."

"Or we could both be having hallucinations."

"Yes, and pigs now have wings and can fly. Is the Spirit saying anything to you about this?"

Bobby paused and listened. *Any advice?*

In response, the image of Randy sitting at the desk in the church office flitted into his mind.

It wasn't the answer he was looking for, but it would have to do. "We need to talk to Randy."

"Now?"

Bobby nodded. Randy had been the Servant for six years. Surely that was enough time for him to have seen and heard just about everything, so he would know what to do.

# 22

LUPE SANCHEZ bustled around the kitchen while Randy sat in an armchair beside the window gazing out into the side yard, which was in dire need of mowing since he didn't yet own a lawnmower.

He would get one eventually. All things in their time.

Lupe poked her head into the living room. "You need me to get you anything?" Her long, black hair was swept back into a ponytail, and her brown eyes were bright, but Randy could still see the sorrow that lay behind them like a shadow. He knew that the guilt over her betrayal of him was eating her alive.

It was yet another obstacle they would work through together.

"A good, stiff drink sounds great about now," he said.

"Like you need that with your painkillers. I'll get you water instead."

Lupe disappeared into the kitchen again, and he heard her filling a glass at the tap. She brought it out, set it on the small table beside him, and gave him a peck on the forehead. "Everything will be okay, you know."

Randy knew she was right, though news of Graham's condition had jarred him more than he thought it would, considering the terrible things Graham had done to him.

Yet Graham had taken him in all those years ago. Randy's teenage years had been filled with more pain and emptiness than most people would ever know. His classmates would talk about things they'd done with their parents and siblings, trips taken and parties celebrated, and Randy would swallow back his pain like a bitter medicine and think about whatever family he'd been stuck with that month, hoping against hope that one would love him enough to adopt him.

But they didn't.

He'd aged out of the system at eighteen—April Fool's Day, 2007—and felt like a boat that had lost its anchor. Now he had no hope of finding a family because he was a grown man. Who in their right mind would adopt an adult?

He brought this up with an elderly coworker at the sporting goods store he'd worked at for two years, and she suggested that he join a church to see if he liked it.

"Because even if they aren't of your blood," she'd said, "sometimes new friends can become so close they feel like family."

So for months Randy shopped around for a church he liked, trying out a nondenominational church a few times that was so huge he felt like a grain of sand on a beach. After that he tried a Baptist church and a Methodist church and finally settled on St. Paul's since it was smaller than the rest and he didn't feel overlooked amid the throng, and he was very glad he did.

He'd met Graham and Frankie at a church picnic that took place in a park across town. Later they introduced him to Phil, Roger, and Frank the First.

Phil took a peculiar interest in Randy and kept grilling him about his newfound faith.

Little had Randy known Phil's reason behind it all.

In the present, Lupe said, "What are you thinking?"

"Who said I was thinking?"

She smirked. "You're always thinking."

*Isn't that the truth?* "I feel awful about Graham."

Lupe's expression darkened. "Don't think about that man. It's over. We never have to worry about him again."

Randy looked out at the sunshine so she wouldn't see the tears in his eyes. In those final moments in the barn when Graham was about to kill him, Randy had seen something black and fluttering in the pupils of Graham's eyes. Perhaps Randy had imagined it, but he didn't think so.

"You're thinking about him again," Lupe scolded. She put her hands on either side of his head and swiveled his face around so their noses were barely an inch apart. Tears glistened on her eyelashes.

She planted her lips fully on his, and the tension left his muscles. Lupe let out a soft moan that set Randy's nerves aflame.

Randy pulled his mouth away from hers to draw a decent breath. "You're making it kind of difficult for me here."

A wicked gleam shined in Lupe's eyes. "Five years, Randy. For five years I've waited for you to find a replacement so we can get married."

"This hasn't been easy for me, either."

Lupe stepped back and crossed her arms, letting out a frustrated sigh. "I know. It's just..."

The sound of an approaching vehicle crunching in the gravel outside made Lupe turn.

"Who is it?" he asked.

Lupe squinted out the window. "It looks like Bobby." Her eyes widened. "And Carly's with him."

Two car doors slammed, and Lupe pulled open the door to admit a pale-faced Carly, who was then followed by Bobby, whose wide blue eyes met Randy's the instant he stepped over the threshold.

Great.

"Carly!" Lupe exclaimed as she threw her arms around her younger friend. "What happened to you?"

Bobby broke away from them and moved toward Randy. "We kind of have a problem," he said in a low voice.

Randy brought his hands up and kneaded his eyelids. Might as well get this over with. "Okay, folks. Spill it."

Carly stepped away from Lupe. "Bobby, you're the one who saw it first. You tell him."

Bobby cleared his throat and shuffled his feet. "Can a demon manifest itself as a human?"

The room became so quiet that Randy could hear his own heartbeat, its tempo ever increasing. "Yes."

"You've seen one?"

"Before we go any further into this, may I ask what this is all about?"

"We saw something." Bobby and Carly exchanged quick glances. "Independently of each other. And we wondered if that's what it could have been."

It seemed Bobby was being intentionally vague. "Listen," Randy said. "If you want me to give you any kind of advice, you're going to have to be completely clear with me. No beating around the bush, no dodging questions. Okay?"

Bobby sighed. "Please don't be mad at me."

Bobby went on to tell the tale of a man who had appeared in his house and later, his car; and Carly talked about how she saw what seemed to be the same man at her house and hallucinated that her bedroom was being trashed. When Carly finished, Bobby said, "So what was it? An angel, a ghost, or a demon?"

Randy leaned his head back and closed his eyes, wishing he could still hear the voice of the Spirit as loudly as he could before. "You said there wasn't an aura."

"I didn't see one. It's not like Carly could, anyway."

"Let me think here." Randy opened his eyes and stared at the ceiling. What were they missing? In a human being, a gray, shadowy aura indicated that the individual lived in collusion with an evil spirit or spirits, and a black, writhing aura showed that the person was possessed and in need of cleansing.

When Randy had been in training under Phil, he'd asked why the auras he picked up inside his head weren't the other way around. "Wouldn't the darker aura tell me who's evil?"

"No," Phil replied in his usual stern tone. "The darker the aura, the greater the individual needs your help."

If Randy guessed right, the presence of an actual demon minus a human host would cause Bobby to sense a shadow in his mind. Unless...

"Do you think the guy I talked to could have been an angel?" Bobby asked.

"Not if he tormented Carly."

"But what if it was two different people who just happened to look alike?" Bobby shivered. "I mean, a demon might have known how an angel appeared to me and appeared to Carly the same way so I'd doubt the advice he gave me."

"Which was what? To save your mother in any way possible?"

Bobby winced, and Randy couldn't blame him. Bobby had been forced to provide some backstory when talking about the entity that called itself Thane, so now Randy knew about Bobby's abandonment as an infant. "Do you think it's possible?" Bobby asked, ignoring his question.

"Of course it's possible. Just about everything is." Randy frowned. "This is a trying time in your life, and I apologize for that because it's partly my fault. I didn't give you much of a choice back in the barn. I knew you weren't ready for something like this, but I didn't know what else to do."

Instead of objecting, Bobby just nodded.

"But," Randy continued, "we can't undo what's already been done. The powers of darkness will be trying to get at you in any way they can."

"Really? I never would have guessed. So...how do I deal with this?"

"If either of you run into this Thane character again, I want you to do a little test in order to determine what he is."

Bobby blanched. "Test?"

"Don't worry, it's not the bar exam." Randy reached backward into his memory to draw forth what he'd learned from his predecessors long ago when he was as green as Bobby was now. "If Thane really is a demon, he'll find certain things repulsive. Crucifixes.

Bibles. Basically any reminder that he's one of the fallen. You can even say a prayer to see what happens. If he's an angel, he'll probably want to pray with you."

"And if he isn't?"

"Then he might become violent. You'll need to invoke the power of the Spirit in order to drive him away. Carly, you can do this too."

Carly bit her lip and nodded. She said, "In the name of the Father, and Jesus Christ his son, and the Holy Spirit, depart from this place and torment God's people no more."

"Looks like your dad got a head start on me."

Her cheeks flushed pink. "When I became part of the fold, he warned me I might be in for a bit of trouble for helping you." She swallowed. "I guess I was pretty lucky until now."

Boy, was she. As far as he knew, Carly had never previously been tormented with disembodied noises, apparitions, or objects thrown by invisible beings as others of their circle had in the past.

He'd always tried not to envy her for that.

Randy returned his attention to Bobby, who'd taken great interest in the floor. "Hey there, Roberto. Do you understand what I'm asking you to do?"

Bobby bowed his head. A serious look entered his eyes. Randy smiled. The kid was finally learning.

# 23

PHIL MASON jerked awake early that morning from a dream that rendered him incapable of returning to sleep.

Based on what he could remember, the dream had begun in a normal enough manner. He'd been sitting outside on a wide lawn lush with real grass—not the mishmash of weeds that occupied his yard in the real world. A pond sat a short distance away at the bottom of a hill, and beside it grew a stand of weeping willows whose branches swayed back and forth in a breeze he couldn't feel.

A distant voice called to him from the woods on the other side of the pond. "Phil!"

Unnerved, Phil cupped a hand around his ear to hear better.

The voice came again. "Come on, Phil! I want to talk to you."

Phil took one step in the direction of the tree line and halted. "Then come out where I can see you."

"Nope. You're coming to me, buddy. If you can't do that, we don't get to chat."

Well, if that's how things were going to be...

Phil straightened his shoulders and set off around the curve of the pond, and soon he was in the woods, the trunks and limbs of the trees pressing close on either side of him.

"I'm here now," he said. "What is it you'd like to talk about?"

"You'll have to come in a little farther."

Sensing that he was stepping into a trap, Phil proceeded at a slow pace, keeping his eyes wide for signs of trouble.

"A little to the left, Phil." Then, "Now veer a bit to the right. Uh-huh. You're almost there."

Phil found himself in a place utterly devoid of light. He held his hand in front of his face and wriggled his fingers, seeing nothing other than the black void that now engulfed him.

His heart began to race and sweat trickled down his forehead and back.

"Open your eyes, Phil."

"They are open."

"No, they're not. If they were, you'd be able to see."

Phil tried blinking, yet he could still see nothing. Then he could hear something breathing behind him. "What's the matter, buddy? Afraid of the dark? Nothing here is going to hurt you. All you've got to do is open your eyes, and all the lights will come on."

But try as he might, he couldn't figure out a way to see.

"Here. Maybe I can help."

Something seized his arm then, and Phil was so startled that he flailed out of its grip and fled. His feet raced over uneven ground, and he was grateful he didn't careen into any trees in the darkness.

Feet crunched on the forest floor behind him, and he had the sense that his pursuer was gaining ground. No. He couldn't let that happen. He had to get out of this dark place before—

A hand closed around Phil's wrist again and whipped him around, and a sudden light blossomed so bright that at first Phil couldn't make out who had grabbed hold of him.

"Don't you see?" said the voice. "It's me."

Phil blinked some more, and the figure of a man came into view. He had sandy hair mussed up by wind, freckled cheeks, wore cutoff blue jeans, and had a bullet hole in his bare chest right over top his heart.

It was Martin Hampstead, Phil's predecessor who had been murdered in 2002 while helping a single mother in need.

"Martin," he choked, hardly able to draw his gaze away from the wound that had ended the young man's life—Martin had been taken from the world at twenty-seven. "What is it I need to see?"

"I need you to see me." Martin beamed. "I'm okay, Phil. I think you'd forgotten that. So get rid of the long face."

Tears rolled down Phil's cheeks. Memories of their friendship rushed back to him: talking about girls they liked, discussing which local craft brew was superior to the others, wondering how God would help them use their gifts, and a dozen more. "I lost my ability."

"That's not such a big deal, is it? Look at you. You have a family now. Think of them, not what you've lost."

"But why did I lose it? I can't figure out what I've done wrong."

Martin's boyish face grew solemn. "If you think that our Father would punish you like that, then you've lost all understanding of how things are."

"Do you know why I lost it?"

"Of course. Someone needs to come home, and it isn't you."

"Then who is it?"

"You'll see."

That's when Phil awoke in the early morning darkness, soaked in sweat. "Martin," he whispered as his friend's face vanished into the smoke of dissipated dreams. "Come back."

Allison stirred beside him and pushed her hair out of her face. "What is it?"

"Nothing," Phil said, staring up at the ceiling. "Just a dream."

———————◆———————

UNLIKE MOST Phil had, this dream didn't fade into obscurity once he rose for the day. He showered, shaved, and dressed, then helped his daughter with her letters as they sat at the breakfast table while Allison prepared sausage and biscuits for them, but all the while Martin's face hung heavy in his mind like a storm cloud.

"Daddy?" Ashley piped up once the breakfast dishes had been cleared away. "Why are you sad?"

Phil forced a smile as he regarded his daughter, whose hair was tied into blonde pigtails. Her blue eyes were wide and bright with curiosity. "What makes you say that?"

Ashley tilted her head to the side and studied him. "You just are."

Sometimes Phil found his daughter far too perceptive for a five-year-old. "Daddy's just missing an old friend right now," he said, and decided to leave it at that.

Allison turned away from the sink with a plate and dishcloth in her hands, raising her eyebrows in a silent question.

"Do you mean Randy?" Ashley asked. "Because he'll get better soon. I know it."

"No, I don't mean Randy." Phil sighed. "This was a different friend. One who went away a long time ago, way before you were even born."

"Did he die?"

Phil's throat constricted. "Yes."

"What happened to him?"

"Ashley," Allison said in a tone of warning. "Don't you think you should get back to your schoolwork?"

Technically it wasn't "schoolwork" since it was July and Ashley hadn't yet started kindergarten, but the child was adamant that that's what it was. "No," Phil said, "it's okay." He cleared his throat. "Martin—my friend—was helping someone, and a very bad man didn't like it so he hurt him."

He could actually see the sorrow well up in his daughter's eyes. "Why would somebody do that?"

"That's just how some people are."

Ashley frowned, and her forehead creased. "Well, I won't ever be that way."

"That's a very good thing to hear."

"I'll be nice to people even if they're mean to me. That's what Father Preston said to do."

"You're right. And do you know who else said it?"

Ashley's mouth widened into a grin that was missing two of its teeth. "Jesus did."

"That's right." Phil leaned back in his chair and sighed, thinking back to his dream. He knew it had been symbolic—he doubted that Martin would return from paradise with a bullet in his chest just to haunt Phil's dreams—yet what did it mean? God wanted Phil to open his eyes and see something, but it seemed Ashley had outpaced him by far in the perception department.

Before Phil could say more, Ashley grabbed up her lined pad of paper and resumed copying the alphabet, her focus intense.

*Father, help me,* Phil prayed. What was it he needed to do?

---

AROUND LUNCHTIME, the slamming of car doors startled Phil from his continued reverie about the dream. He switched off the television, which he hadn't even really been watching, and went to the door.

"Frankie," he breathed when he saw who had pulled into the driveway. "Thank the Lord."

He pulled the door open to admit the former Servant and his taciturn wife, but then he noticed that an unfamiliar pickup truck with Idaho plates had parked beside it. A dog stuck its head out the passenger window and started barking at the same time a pudgy, washed-out man with straw-like hair unfolded himself from the vehicle.

Frankie was doing the same, but Janet remained inside their car, looking anxious.

Nothing new about that.

Phil strode outside and halted beside Frankie, who towered over him. "What's going on?" he asked, not wanting to mention that he'd been worried almost to the point of illness about the man's absence. "Where have you been?"

"Idaho," Frankie said, as if that explained everything. His black hair riffled in the wind, and his cheeks were rosy with excitement. "I hate to barge in like this, but could we tie Kevin's dog out in the back so Janet feels safe to get out of the car?"

*Yeah, right, you hate it.* Frankie never felt bad about any of his actions. "Kevin who?" he asked, glancing over at the man who'd gotten out of the truck and remained lurking by its door, wearing an expression of utmost uncertainty.

The man took one step forward. "I'm Kevin Lyle," he said in a thin voice. "You must be Phil."

It took several moments for the name to register in Phil's mind. "Wait a minute. You're Frankie's successor?"

Kevin bobbed his head in a nod. "And God knows what I'm doing here now. I must be crazy. Yeah, that's it. Crazy. So, is it okay if I tie Chet out back?"

"Sure," Phil said as he narrowed his eyes at Frankie. "Go right ahead."

Once a stake had been driven into the ground in the backyard and Chet, the dog, had been affixed to it with a long chain and provided with a bowl of water, the unlikely group gathered in Phil's living room.

"All right," Phil said as he stood at the front of the room with his hands on his hips. Everyone else had taken seats in various armchairs and the sofa. "Would anyone care to enlighten me about what's going on?"

Frankie cleared his throat and rose. "We're in need of a healer."

Phil gave an inward wince. "Why?"

"I didn't think you would've needed to ask me that."

"Spare me the insults, Frankie, and I'll rephrase. What makes you think we need a healer now?"

"It's simple: an angel visited me and said we would need one."

Phil could already feel a headache coming on, which wasn't uncommon whenever Frankie was around. "You're sure?"

"I would never lie to you, or to anyone else." Frankie's face became grim. "Something will be going down soon, but I don't know when. I just knew I had to find Kevin and bring him back here before it's too late."

"You're serious about this."

Frankie bowed his head. "So if you could, would you please summon our new Servant? I feel it's time to have another long chat with him." He paused. "And call Randy and Roger, too. Might as well get everyone involved."

"What about your grandfather?"

Frankie hesitated. Then, withdrawing his car keys from his pocket, he said, "I'll go get him myself. Come on, Janet. Let's go."

# 24

BOBBY AND Carly had still been hanging out at Randy's house when he got a call from Phil instructing him and Randy to come over as soon as they could.

Holding his phone to his ear, Bobby said, "Don't you think he should stay here?"

Phil sounded unfathomably tired. "I'm afraid that's not an option. Frankie's adamant that everyone be here, and it's just not worth arguing with him. Trust me on that."

Randy, still sitting in the chair by the window, looked exhausted. The simple acts of sitting up and talking for the couple of hours Bobby and Carly were there had evidently worn away what little energy he possessed. "What is it now?" Randy asked.

"Phil says Frankie wants everyone to meet up at Phil's house. Even you."

"Is Frankie aware that I have about seven hundred stitches in my chest?"

Bobby knew the number was an exaggeration, but he repeated Randy's words to Phil anyway.

He could hear Phil let out a sigh. "Tell Randy that if he comes, he won't regret it."

---

PHIL'S DRIVEWAY was so packed when Bobby arrived with a heavily-sedated Randy that he had to parallel-park along the edge of the road with the two right-side tires in the grass. Carly and Lupe stayed behind at Randy's.

"Maybe I should have waited until after I got here to take more pills," Randy said with his eyes closed. "I don't know if I can get up."

"Do you want me to help you walk?"

Randy's Adam's apple bobbed up and down, and his bloodshot eyes fluttered open. "Just give me a minute. I'll manage somehow or another."

Bobby hopped out and came around the side of the car, opening the door for Randy while the man fumbled clumsily at his seatbelt. Once freed from the restraint, Randy grabbed onto the doorframe, started to his feet, and sank back to the edge of the seat, shaking his head. "Sorry. This is more moving than I've done in a while."

"Here." Face flushing, Bobby held out his hand for Randy to take. "You've only got about thirty more feet to go."

"Thanks for the reminder." Randy latched a callused hand around Bobby's thin one, took a deep breath that made his face go white, and staggered to his feet, swaying a bit once he was out of the vehicle. "God forgive me for saying this, but if Frankie just wanted me to be here so he could say hi, I'll kill him."

It was slow going from the car up to the one-story brick house because Randy had to keep stopping and leaning against whichever vehicle was closest to him so he wouldn't keel over. Just as Bobby opened his mouth to suggest that Randy wait there while he went inside to get some help, Phil appeared on the porch and rushed out to meet them.

"Sorry." Phil came around to Randy's other side. "I didn't see you pull up."

Randy gave a silent nod and put his arms around Phil's and Bobby's shoulders as they completed their journey to the door, which flew open the moment they made it to the porch.

"Randy!" Frankie Jovingo strode out to meet them. "My apologies. I didn't realize your condition was still so poor."

Randy gave him a withering smile, but Bobby sensed amusement hiding behind it. "It's good to see you, too, Frankie. Now can you help me inside?"

Bobby stepped aside and allowed Carly's father to lead Randy into the house. A wave of dislike washed through him at the sight of Frankie, who resembled a human Easter Island head with hair. Didn't he care that Randy had been shot and cut open and was currently doped up on pills?

He followed them inside. Allison Mason waved at Bobby from in the kitchen, and he sheepishly waved back.

"Bobby!" a voice called from the back of the living room. "I see you haven't run off yet."

Eyeing heavyset Roger Stilgoe playing a game of solitaire with shriveled Frank the First, who had recently reached his one hundred and first birthday, Bobby squeezed past Randy and the others and went to join them.

Roger had salt-and-pepper hair that was thinning on top and was dressed in a Hawaiian shirt and tan Bermuda shorts in sharp contrast to the formal office attire he had worn to the meeting during which Bobby had met him.

No one could ever claim the former Servants weren't a motley group. Randy, for instance, was wearing another black t-shirt covered in skulls.

"No," Bobby said to Roger. "Not yet."

"That's good to hear. So how are you?"

"I'm good." He threw a glance over his shoulder at Randy, who was lowering himself onto the couch with the aid of Frankie and Phil. "But Randy isn't."

Roger's eyes sparkled with mischief. "He will be soon enough. Just you watch."

Not having the faintest idea of what Roger meant, Bobby noticed a pale man in blue overalls for the first time. He was seated in the chair beside the couch where Randy planted himself, wringing his hands together and wearing an expression of such torment that Bobby would have thought he was possessed.

Frankie moved to the front of the room and cleared his throat. "Thank you all for coming today. I know this was short notice—"

"You can say that again!" Frank the First barked, looking away from his card game. "I swear I don't know what the world's coming to when your own grandson drags you out of your apartment kicking and screaming to go to a *meeting*." He winked.

"Don't worry," Frankie said, wearing a smirk. "I'm sure we'll make this worth your while. But now that we're all here, it's high time we make some formal introductions."

Bobby saw Allison take little Ashley's hand and lead her down the hallway at the other end of the house before disappearing through a doorway and closing it behind them.

"Anyway," Frankie continued, scanning the room's remaining occupants. "For years our circle wasn't complete because one of our members felt it necessary to leave the state, but now he's back. Bobby and Randy, meet Kevin Lyle, my successor."

The pale man lifted his gaze and nodded at Bobby, then at Randy. "Hello."

Bobby nodded in return, noting that nobody had ever mentioned Kevin when discussing former Servants.

Frankie went on. "I knew we would need Kevin soon because of the ability he's been blessed with. You can imagine my delight when I learned it hasn't diminished."

Randy's tired eyes lit up as he turned his gaze to Kevin. "Wait a minute. You're a healer, aren't you?"

Kevin gave a slight nod. "Frankie made me prove it still works."

Randy looked back to Frankie. "Good grief, what did you do? Cut your hand off and have him stick it back on for you?"

Frankie folded his arms. "You mock me."

"No offense, but it's not that hard to do." Randy refocused his attention on Kevin. "So if you can, will you?"

Kevin hesitated but then nodded. "Give me your hand."

Bobby watched in fascination as Randy reached out his left hand. Kevin closed the fingers of his right around it and closed his eyes. Moments later, Randy's skin took on its original tan color and the lines vanished from his face.

Randy lifted up his skull-patterned shirt and goggled at his torso, which was now free from injury but still contained dozens of stitches marking where the deep cuts had been. His voice sounded choked when he next spoke. "Thank you."

"Not a problem," Kevin said, bringing his gaze down to the carpet.

"Wait a minute," Bobby said, the knot on the back of his head throbbing as if to remind him of its presence. "Can you heal me, too? I mean, I kind of bumped my head yesterday, and it really hurts, so..."

Kevin looked up at him with watery eyes and nodded. "Come here, then."

Bobby felt all eyes on him as he crossed the room and stopped in front of the man. He reached out his hand as Randy had done, and when Kevin took it the low throb on Bobby's scalp ceased. He didn't need to touch his head to know the lump was gone. "Thanks," he said, backing away.

Phil, who had taken a seat next to Randy on the couch, removed his black-framed glasses and rubbed his eyes in a gesture of utmost weariness.

Frankie scanned the room, his expression stern. "May we proceed?"

All heads swiveled to face Bobby, who swallowed. It felt odd that these people were looking up to him. "So what's going on?" he asked.

"What's going on," Frankie said, "is that an angel visited me and said we would need Kevin to be with us again."

"Was his name Thane?" Bobby blurted, and as soon as the words came out of his mouth Randy gave his head a sharp shake.

Frankie's eyebrows rose. "Why do you ask?"

Heeding Randy's unspoken warning, Bobby said, "No reason."

Not appearing convinced, Frankie went on. "Now Bobby, I have to ask you this, and I need you to be honest. Are you planning on doing anything rash?"

"What do you mean?"

"It seems to me that the only reason we would need Kevin's ability so urgently is if you're in mortal danger."

Randy spoke up before Bobby could reply. "Are you sure? I was in mortal danger for months."

"This isn't about you, Randy." Frankie waved a hand at him in dismissal. "Well?"

Bobby's pulse quickened as he raced through everything that had been on his mind in recent days. "I don't think I'm planning anything rash." Was he?

Frankie gave him a grim smile. "Based on what I've heard from some of the individuals in this room, rashness comes as easily to you as breathing comes to other people. That isn't always a bad thing."

"So what am I supposed to do? Coat myself in bubble wrap and not leave the house?"

"I want you to be careful and use your head. It would be most unfortunate if harm were to befall you so soon as the Servant."

"I'm not a babysitter," said a sharp voice.

Kevin was sitting up straighter in his chair.

"What was that?" Frankie asked coolly.

Kevin's gaze darted back and forth among the room's occupants. "You just want me to be here to make sure this boy stays out of trouble. I don't want to be any part of that."

Frankie opened his mouth but then closed it as he looked toward the hallway where Allison and Ashley had gone. "Let's go to the back," he said, moving toward the kitchen. "I don't think our voices will carry as much from there."

Shrugging, Bobby got in line behind Randy as the group filed through the kitchen into a solarium sitting at the back of the house. The many-windowed room was filled with white wicker furniture covered in blue cushions, and five of the men took seats in them. Bobby remained standing and watched as Frankie quietly closed the door.

"What exactly is going on here?" Bobby asked.

Frankie let out a sigh and planted his large hands on his hips. "It pains me to say this, but in the faith department, several members of this group are severely lacking."

Guilt wormed its way into Bobby's conscience. "I'm sorry."

"I wasn't talking about you, but if that's the way you feel, then I advise you to listen as well." Frankie eyed each man in turn but only addressed two of them. "Phil, what is it you're so worried about? You used to believe that no harm would come to you even if you should die, and now you carry that gun around like it's your only friend. And Kevin: why the long face? God's Spirit once filled your veins, yet you still doubt that he has plans for you."

The air was heavy with the silence of unspoken thoughts. Roger exchanged a glance with Frank the First, who shrugged and kept his focus on his grandson.

Frankie went on. "Randy, even you doubted when you boarded up your windows and pretended no one was home. You feared that God wouldn't protect you from Graham, yet he did, even when Graham tried to kill you."

Randy bowed his head. "I know."

Frankie held his palms up, and Bobby was startled to see tears shining in his eyes. "This flesh is fleeting. Your *pain* is fleeting. It will be gone in the blink of an eye." He drew in a breath. "Think of the glory of what will come. To be united with our Maker once and for all. To see Martin again. And Gary. And Jackie, and all the others. So tell me," he said in a softer tone. "Why is your faith so weak when you know very well that God will save you no matter what happens?"

As Frankie's words lodged themselves in Bobby's mind and took root, he thought he understood why the man came across as someone to be disliked: in contrast to Bobby's constant anxiety, Frankie literally feared nothing, not even the pain of death—a trait Carly claimed he'd passed down to his late daughter.

Perhaps part of Bobby, who feared many things, envied Frankie for that.

Bobby tried to swallow back a lump of emotion that had formed in his throat, but it stuck there, rendering him speechless.

"Let's all sit in a circle," Frankie said as he moved to the side of the room and plucked a jar candle and lighter off of a shelf. "Bobby, you may sit by me."

As if the men had done this before, they each picked up whatever chair they sat in and dragged them all into the middle of the room, forming a lopsided circle. Frankie lit the candle and set it in the middle of the ring, then gestured for everyone to sit back down.

Bobby lowered himself into the chair to Frankie's right, feeling a nervous excitement build inside him even though he had no inkling of what was about to happen. Phil took a seat on Bobby's other side and grabbed Bobby's hand. Before Bobby could ask what he was doing, Frankie said, "No. Let Kevin sit there."

Shrugging, Phil got up and switched places with Kevin. The older man settled into the cushion, hesitated, and took Bobby's hand.

Frankie did the same on Bobby's left, and likewise so did everyone else.

A giggle welled up in Bobby's chest as he observed the six other men shamelessly holding each other's hands like a group of kids around a campfire, but he quickly stifled it.

Frankie bowed his head. "Father, your Son endured the pain of the cross so that we, your children, might find everlasting life with you in a place free of pain, free of torment, free of sorrow, and full of peace. Let these men, your Servants, remember your love and protection. Grant them healing from their pain." He gave Bobby's hand a hard squeeze. "Bobby? Would you care to lead us?"

Bobby was so surprised he almost jerked his hand out of Frankie's grip. "Lead us in what?"

"Listen to the Spirit. You'll know."

"Okay." Bobby stared at the flickering flame dancing in the jar on the floor. It reminded him of how he would sometimes light a candle and meditate when things got rough in his life.

Then unexpected words formed on the tip of his tongue, and he said, "I'm sorry for doubting my place here. I know I was chosen for a reason, even if I don't understand it." Tears welled in his eyes. "I trust you'll show me the way even when the way is dark." He thought he might say more, but decided that those words had been enough.

Phil was the next to speak. "I'm sorry for missing Martin so much." His voice became strained. "He was my best friend. And when I thought you'd take Randy away, too, I...I'm sorry. Never let me forget that what's here now isn't permanent and never will be."

Then Randy: "I knew I'd be okay in the end, but I feared you wouldn't protect me from pain. Well, you didn't, and I'm still here, right?" He gave a sheepish smile. "But thank you for sending Kevin along to help. I appreciate it."

A palpable sense of peace rose from Phil and Randy, and Bobby found himself smiling. He understood now. Their doubts and fears festered within them when left unspoken, and now that they'd admitted their shortcomings, they no longer hid their shame.

Bobby expected Kevin to speak up next, but the man kept his jaw clamped shut, and his breathing quickened as if he were starting to hyperventilate.

"It's okay," Bobby whispered to him. "Say whatever you need to. I don't think anyone here is going to judge."

Kevin stood up so abruptly that the wicker chair scooted backward several inches. His wide eyes darted around the room. "No," he said. "No, no, no." Then he eyed a door leading out of the solarium into the backyard and fled through it, slamming it shut behind him.

Bobby and the others sat there in stunned silence as they watched Kevin sink onto a stone patio bench and place his head in his hands. "This might be a dumb question," Bobby said, "but what's the matter with him?"

A look of sorrow passed over Frankie's face. "You're the Servant now. Why don't you go find out?"

# 25

KEVIN HAD his elbows propped on his knees and was staring glumly at a chained brown and white spotted mutt happily chewing on a Nylabone.

"Hey," Bobby said. "Are you all right?"

Kevin didn't lift his gaze. "You're nuts. You know that, right?"

Even though it made him uncomfortable, Bobby took a seat on the unoccupied end of the bench. "Isn't everyone?"

"Heh. Maybe you're right." Kevin straightened. "If you're smart, you'll scram before things get worse. Just find a replacement and get out of here."

Bobby offered him a wide-eyed stare. "Worse?"

"You'll know soon enough if you don't already. I used to be something like you. Young. Stubborn. Thought I could change the world if I tried hard enough." Kevin pressed the palms of his hands against his eyes and shook his head. "I was just a young chump."

Bobby couldn't believe what he was hearing. "Randy and Phil and I aren't chumps. And Frankie..."

"Called me a coward before I left."

Frankie sure wasn't one to mince words. "Are you a coward?"

Kevin's demeanor changed in an instant. "He never went through what I did. None of them did. They think Kevin Lyle is just some big pansy who didn't have enough faith in God to do what he was supposed to, but it isn't like that at all. They don't know what happened. I couldn't bring myself to tell them."

Bobby feared asking but knew that he had to in order to get to the root of Kevin's distress. "Well, what happened?"

"That can of worms doesn't need opened again. I put a lid on it ages ago."

"Maybe if you open it, the stuff inside won't bother you anymore." Lord, now he was sounding like Carly. "You know what I'm saying?"

"Does spilling your guts make *you* feel better?"

Bobby sent up a silent prayer that Carly would never catch wind of what he was about to say. "Maybe. Sometimes."

"Why should I tell you, anyway? It's not like we know each other."

Bobby thought of Joanna, the woman he'd met last week at the safe house who'd basically told him her life story despite the fact they'd just met. "I think maybe it's easier to talk if people don't know you because strangers aren't going to judge you as much as your friends."

"Oh, geez." Kevin gave his head another shake. "Do you really want to know?"

"Only if that's what you want. And it's not like I'm going to tell anyone if you do."

Kevin lapsed into silence. The solarium's occupants craned their necks to watch his and Kevin's exchange.

Bobby wondered how well they could hear their conversation through the glass.

"I never told anyone," Kevin said finally. "I mean *anyone*. I guess maybe because it hurt too much. Maybe not talking about it is just one way of coping. You know?"

It didn't sound like Kevin had been doing much coping at all, but Bobby nodded. "Sure."

"I was doing some work up in Seattle one summer. I'd just cleansed a guy. I found him in Seattle and we'd come back to Oregon so I could take care of him, and when he was better I went back to Seattle with him so I could find someone else who needed me. Let's just say I was feeling pretty good about myself since he was so much happier now that *they* weren't tormenting him anymore. I really felt that God had called me all the way up there for a reason." Pain was evident on Kevin's tired face. "Only now I look back and wonder if the voice I heard inside of me belonged to the devil instead."

Bobby's mind tried to conjure a scenario that might cause someone this much grief. His experiences of witnessing his father's death and finding his neighbor's bullet-riddled corpse had stabbed him in the heart, but he hadn't been so traumatized that he'd moved to another state and stopped talking to everyone he knew.

Well, actually, he had. He'd left his hometown behind as soon as he was financially able, and he hadn't lingered in New York after his neighbor had been shot.

Were he and Kevin really that much alike?

"So what happened in Seattle?" Bobby asked, not wanting to answer his unspoken question.

Kevin's eyes were bloodshot. "I—I was walking down the street, maybe five or so in the afternoon. All the sudden I heard this ruckus in an alleyway I'd just passed so I stepped back a bit to see what was going on and saw a couple dogs getting into some trash that fell out of some knocked-over cans. I walked back there to scare them off because I didn't want them to make a huge mess for someone to clean up later, and when they'd scampered I stood the cans back up and was about to start shoving all the garbage back into them when I saw..." Tears sprang into Kevin's eyes, and he shook his head again and again as if to dislodge his memories from the forefront of his mind. "Oh, sweet Jesus. I wish I'd never gone back there. I should have kept on walking."

"What did you see?"

Kevin's Adam's apple moved up and down, and his eyes took on an expression that gave him the appearance of one who had long ago lost his way. "A hand."

Bobby wasn't sure he'd heard him right. "A hand?"

"Yeah. A human one, about the size of my pinky nail. It was lying on the ground beside a torn trash bag."

Bobby felt an icy chill as he tried to process this information. "You mean like a baby hand?"

"Smaller than that. My dad was an OB-GYN so he had all kinds of baby models and stuff lying around the house when I was a kid. The best I can guess, the hand was from a second-trimester fetus."

"I'm sorry," Bobby said somewhat lamely. Kevin's words had conjured a crystal-clear image of the scene in his mind, and he forced himself to focus on the man beside him rather than become weighed down by the scene of Kevin's pain.

"That wasn't all, though. I sort of lost it a bit; started looking around for the rest of, you know, the body. So I moved the bag aside and found, well, more parts, and I got this crazy idea that I could use my ability to put them all together again so the baby might have another chance. I—I *touched* it, and prayed, only of course I can't raise anyone from the dead, and I was crying so hard, and then I realized there were too many parts there for just one baby, so I went nuts and opened the bag the rest of the way, and..." Kevin's shoulders shook. "I ran around to the front of the building to see what in the world kind of place would have *that* in their trash, and then it hit me. I was so. Flipping. *Naïve*. I—I ran back to the motel where I was staying and scrubbed my hands until they bled." Kevin blinked as if only just remembering that he was sitting on a bench in Autumn Ridge, Oregon and not crouching down beside a garbage can in Seattle, Washington. "Why do you do it?"

"Why do I do what?"

"Help people. You do do that, right?"

The picture of Adrian Pollard walking out of the shower house flitted through his mind. "I help them because I care about them," he said, feeling a shred of guilt at how angry he'd been when Jack told him who Mystery Woman was. Bobby cleared his throat. "When I was a kid I wanted to be a superhero. I was going to grow up and become Rescue Man."

Kevin allowed himself a soft chuckle. "Rescue Man, huh?"

Heat washed over Bobby's face. "I know it sounds dumb. But I guess it's all because if I was in trouble, I'd want someone to care about me."

"How old are you, Bobby?"

He didn't see how his age pertained to the conversation, but he said, "Twenty. I'll be twenty-one in November."

"Good Lord, you could be my kid." Kevin's gaze drifted back over to the dog, who had paused in the gnawing of the Nylabone to stare at Kevin with his ears perked up. "So I hear you have the gift of Prophecy."

"That's what they tell me." Bobby felt a stirring inside, and he knew he had to steer the focus of the conversation back to Kevin. "I'm sorry about what happened to you. But you can heal people. I don't think God wants you to hide from the world when there's so many more out there you might be able to help."

"But it's so much easier not to care. To not have to worry about who might not make it no matter how hard you try to save them." Kevin paused to run a finger across the skin below his eye. "I wanted to get help, but I couldn't just waltz into a shrink's office and tell him why I was falling to pieces. He would've pried into too many things and I would have ended up telling him about who I am. What I do. And then he'd think I was some sort of nutcase and have me locked away."

"I'm really the first person you've told about all this?"

A nod. "I found a replacement, passed the mantle on to him, and left. I've been in Idaho ever since. I do farm work for a guy I know out there. It's peaceful."

"So Frankie called you a coward because you didn't want to be the Servant anymore?"

"I kept having flashbacks. I could be doing the dishes and *bam*, I'd be back in that alley. Whenever I'd try to cleanse a victim, the demons would throw the images of it all right back into my face. And then the dreams..." Kevin shuddered. "I couldn't handle it any-more, which probably seems crazy considering some of the things I'd dealt with before that. It's like...it's like I let my guard down in that alley, and the demons found an opportunity to creep into my heart. I knew I had to get out for the sake of the possessed. I was afraid I'd accidentally hurt one of them. So yeah, call me a coward, because I guess deep down that's what I really am."

It sounded to Bobby like Kevin was suffering from some sort of post-traumatic stress. It was no wonder he'd been so agitated while he was sitting with everyone else inside the house. Being in the presence of his old comrades would have brought back too many memories of his time as one of them.

Carly's words from earlier in the day returned to him. *What will you do with your pain?*

He understood then. If he didn't let go of the hurt that Adrian inflicted upon him by leaving him in the care of a single father, it would poison him. Maybe he'd end up being a wreck like Kevin.

Bobby swallowed. *Please help Kevin get over his pain.* "I don't think you're as cowardly as you think you are," he said.

"Why's that?"

"You came back here even though you didn't want to, right?"

Kevin stuck out his bottom lip. "I did, didn't I?"

"It seems like a step in the right direction."

"I hope so."

Bobby stood. "I'm going back inside. You're welcome to come with me."

"Nah, I think I'll stay out here awhile longer. I need the fresh air."

Bobby turned to go in and screeched to a halt five feet from the glass door.

Thane stood behind it, looking out at him.

Smiling.

# 26

FEAR ROOTED Bobby's feet to the ground. "Uh, Kevin?"

"What?"

"Do you see anything odd behind the door?"

"No. What's the matter?"

"I'm not sure." The devilish grin that spread across Thane's face dispelled any thought that Bobby beheld a benevolent being. But was it the same being that had visited Bobby's house? Again, the idea that there were two Thanes crossed his mind. It was crazy to think that a demon might masquerade as an angel just to confuse him, but Bobby had witnessed enough crazy things in the past week to know it wasn't outside the realm of possibilities.

He closed his eyes to see if he could pick up even a whisper of an aura and came up with nothing.

"Bobby?" Kevin said, his voice full of concern. "Are you okay?"

Inside the solarium, the former Servants were deep in discussion once more. Nobody seemed aware of the auburn-haired man standing feet away from them.

"Come in," Thane mouthed.

Bobby shivered. "Yeah," he said to Kevin. "I'm fine."

His pulse pounded in his ears as he freed himself from the grip of paralysis and opened the door. Thane glided off to one side, giving Bobby room to pass. "You know," Thane said once Bobby was inside, "you won't get very far as the Servant if you fear every single thing you don't understand."

Bobby pretended he didn't hear and directed his attention to Frank the First. "And I said, Frankie, what in the world do you think you're doing? And he said..." Frank broke off when he made note of Bobby's gaze, and his wrinkled forehead creased even further. "What's the matter? You act like you've never seen a hundred-and-one-year-old man before."

Bobby cleared his throat. "There's a man standing behind me."

As one, the other four men stared at him.

Frankie, who didn't look pleased to have been the subject of whatever story his grandfather had been telling, gave him an unimpressed stare.

Randy's eyes grew round. "Does this have to do with something we were talking about earlier?"

Bobby nodded. Sweat beaded on his scalp. From his current position, he couldn't see Thane. The guy could be doing anything behind him. Like getting ready to stab him with a knife no one else could see, either. To Frankie, he said, "I sort of have this problem. I keep seeing this guy, but I don't know if I can trust him or not."

"What Bobby's saying," Randy said, "is that he doesn't know if this person is an angel or a demon."

The color drained out of Frankie's face. So something *did* scare him. "Show me exactly where he is," Frankie said, rising from the wicker chair.

Bobby went to point and let out a mild curse when he beheld the empty space Thane had occupied moments before. "He's gone."

"Allison," Phil breathed as fear flooded his face. He rushed across the room to the door leading into the kitchen and disappeared through it.

"Call Thane back here," Frankie said.

"Are you crazy? If he's a demon—"

"Then you've been granted authority over him. Listen to the Spirit. You'll know what to say."

"Oh, crap."

"Just do it. Please."

Bobby's teeth chattered. This was insanity.

"Do you think any of us found this easy in the beginning?" Roger said, still seated in one of the chairs. The armpits of his Hawaiian shirt were soaked. "If we could do it, so can you."

"But I'm not—"

"Ready?" Roger gave a soft chuckle. "You'll never be ready if you don't dive in."

Bobby realized there was no way out of this. If he didn't just suck it up and order Thane to show himself, Frankie would accuse him of being a coward just like Kevin.

He took a deep breath. "Thane?" he said, trying to ignore the sudden churning in his gut. "In the name of God, I command you to show yourself to us."

Nothing.

Phil slipped back into the room and remained standing near the door. Randy folded his hands together and bowed his head. The two Frank Jovingos and Roger did the same.

Okay. Time to try again. "Evil spirit!" Bobby said in a louder voice as a blush warmed his cheeks. "In the name of God, I command you to manifest yourself to us."

"You really think you know everything, don't you?"

Thane materialized half a dozen feet away from him, and if Bobby was to judge from everyone's reactions, this time Bobby wasn't the only one to see him. "What is it that I think I know?" Bobby asked, hating the tremor in his voice.

Thane held up a finger. "First of all, you think I'm a demon."

"There's nothing else you could be."

"Bobby," Frankie said, moving to Bobby's side and placing a hand on his shoulder. "You can't let him talk to you like this. You have to remain in control."

"That's cute," Thane said. "Really cute. What is there to control? You see me because I want you to, not because some higher power forced me to."

This time when Frankie spoke to Bobby, he bent down and whispered so softly into Bobby's ear that he almost didn't hear him. "You have to banish him back to the pit. And you have to believe that you can do it through the power of God and no power of your own."

Bobby nodded, keeping his gaze fixed on the entity standing before him. *Okay*, he thought. *You've got to help me do this. You've got to send him away and not let him bother anyone again.*

He said, "Thane: In the name of the Father, and of Jesus Christ his son, and of the Holy Spirit that fills me, depart from this place and torment us no more."

Thane let out a soft snicker. "When will anyone believe me when I say I'm not a demon? You're such a stubborn bunch, but I guess I can't do a thing about that."

Bobby tried not to let the demon's words get to him. Thane was just trying to distract him and sow doubt in his mind.

He repeated his last admonition: "In the name of the Father, and of Jesus Christ his son, and of the Holy Spirit, depart from this place and torment us no more."

Thane's features twisted into a scowl. "Fine. You don't want me here? I'll leave. But before I go, I should mention that Jack Willard has something nasty up his sleeve. And Bobby? I can't believe you still haven't figured out where your mother is. You must not be as smart as I thought."

He blinked out of existence with the swiftness of someone switching off a light.

"What in the world is this all about?" Phil said, coming up to Bobby's other side. "*I* never had anything like this happen."

"I would be surprised if anyone here has," Randy said, looking perturbed. "But each of us is affected differently. When I was the Servant mostly all they did was throw things at the windows because they knew it would drive me up a wall. They obviously know that won't work with Bobby because when they tried it at his house, it just sent him back to me, so they upgraded to apparitions. It's that simple."

Bobby didn't think it sounded simple at all. "So the rock thing only happened to you and me?"

Randy bowed his head. "We're all different, so it's only fair that different things will drive us over the edge."

They were all silent while Bobby's mind returned to the previous week, when he had been hounded by what he thought were poltergeists. He would take apparitions like Thane over invisible rock-throwers any day because at least then his adversary had a face.

"Do you think he's right about Jack?" Bobby asked.

"Look," Frankie said. "Whatever this thing is, it's evil. It's going to do everything within its power to make sure you fail as the Servant. And what was that bit about your mother?"

Like Bobby was going to talk about the whole Adrian ordeal with him. "Nothing."

"If it was indeed nothing, he wouldn't have brought it up."

"Okay, it was nothing important." Bobby paused, thinking about how Jack had seemed entirely unruffled by Bobby's arrival at the apartment last night. Could Jack really be planning some way to cause him harm?

Randy was rubbing his chest. "I don't know. I'm concerned about what he said about Jack. That guy is bad news."

"For all we know," Frankie said, "he's in Long Beach right now sipping margaritas. Forget about him and let's move on."

"Actually," Bobby said, the weight of guilt pressing down on him, "he's in Hillsdale."

"How could you possibly know that?"

Bobby swallowed a knot of fear. They were going to be upset about what he did, but there was no changing what had happened. "I sort of found where he was hanging out and followed him home. But then he made me promise not to tell anyone where he's been staying."

"Hold it," Phil said. "You mean to say you found where the man who shot Randy in the leg lives and didn't do anything about it?"

"Yeah."

"Why didn't you call the police?"

"Like I said, he made me promise. I needed information and the only way he was going to give it to me was if I said I wouldn't tell anyone where he is. I didn't know what else to do."

Phil looked like he was about to cry. "This is like last week all over again." He looked to Frankie. "Randy promised Graham he wouldn't tell us where he was going to confront him, and as a result he almost got himself killed."

"The key word being 'almost.'" Randy gave Bobby a pitying smile. "It stinks, doesn't it? Wanting to tell so badly but refusing to compromise your principles."

"Yeah. I guess it does."

Frankie cleared his throat. "You're forgetting something."

Randy turned his attention to him. "Yes, dear Frankie? And what might that be?"

"If Jack is coming, Bobby will know. Unless I've been misinformed about what his ability entails."

Randy shook his head. "You haven't been misinformed. I've seen firsthand what he can do."

A nervous tremor shook Bobby's hands so he jammed them into his pockets. "Yeah," he said. "If Jack's going to hurt one of us, I'll know." *I think.*

The only problem was that his premonitions didn't occur at a uniform length of time preceding whatever tragedy he was supposed to prevent. Sometimes he knew something bad would happen hours in advance. And sometimes, like with Randy in the church parking lot, he had only seconds to figure out what to do.

It really depended on how much work he had to do to save the person involved.

So for all he knew, Jack could be coming down the street that very moment.

"I have a question," Bobby said as a new idea took shape in his mind.

Frankie's dark eyebrows rose. "What's that?"

"If you knew that someone was going to hurt someone else, is it okay to hurt them first before they can actually do it? You know, to stop them?"

"Just what is it you have in mind?"

"Nothing. Just a hypothetical idea I had." He envisioned himself returning to Jack's apartment with a baseball bat and slugging him in the head so he wouldn't be able to harm a woman or child again, but Jack would just wake up and hunt down more women anyway.

"Is it okay if I talk to Randy and Phil alone for a few minutes?" Bobby said, looking from Roger to the two Frank Jovingos.

"Surely we can hear whatever you have to say," Frankie said with a scowl.

"It's something personal."

Frankie seemed to weigh this before nodding. "Very well. But this meeting is not adjourned." One by one, he, his grandfather, and Roger filed out of the room. Outside, Kevin was still gazing at what had to be his dog with the despondency of a lost soul, completely oblivious to what was going on in the solarium.

"Okay," Randy said when the others were gone. "Spill the beans."

Bobby looked to Phil. "Jack found my biological mother and had somebody kidnap her."

The room filled with silence for several beats. Phil frowned. "You're talking about the woman in the picture left on your door?"

"Yeah. It turns out Jack left it there to taunt me. He has to have been spying on me all week to know I'd moved."

"Why didn't you recognize your own mother?"

Now wasn't the time to explain every single detail about his past, so Bobby just said, "It's a long story. But Jack said he targets people and arranges for them to be kidnapped and sold into...into slavery. He said he doesn't have any idea where Adrian—my mother—is, because he's not the person who takes the women to wherever it is they're taken."

Phil uttered a soft curse and closed his eyes. "And you promised this monster you wouldn't tell anyone where he is."

Desperation made Bobby's heart race. "I didn't know what else to do!"

"There has to be a way you can let someone know without breaking your promise."

"It was an apartment in Hillsdale. That's all I'm saying."

Phil opened his eyes and gave Bobby a piercing stare. "You knew that Randy and Lupe were at different houses."

"What?"

"Last week. You meditated on where Randy and Lupe were. Why haven't you done the same with your mother if you'd like to find her so badly?"

Bobby clapped a hand to his forehead. "Because I'm an idiot."

Randy and Phil exchanged glances. "Do you want to try to meditate right now?" Randy asked. "Because if that's how you ended up saving me, I say go for it."

"I guess I can give it a try." Bobby shivered. Would it work a second time?

"Here," Phil said. "Lie down on the couch."

The solarium jutted out from the rest of the house, and at the end farthest out into the yard a faded couch sat parallel with the windows. Bobby crossed the room, sank onto a squashy cushion, and eased himself onto his back.

He tried to slow his breathing. *Relax. Just relax. You've done this before. You can do it again.*

"Do you need us to help you?" Phil asked.

"Not yet. I'm going to try this on my own."

The sunlight coming through the windows made colors dance behind his closed eyelids. He willed his limbs to go limp.

*Please help me find her,* he prayed. *She might have been stupid, and maybe she still is, but she doesn't deserve to be locked away and treated like a piece of meat.*

Because even though Adrian had abandoned him, she must have felt some shred of love for him since she'd allowed him to be born.

Lying in that position made him realize how exhausted he felt. Last night's conk on the head had not made for restful slumber, and now he could feel himself drifting away on a river of fatigue.

*I can do this.*

218 | J.S. BAILEY

In his mind, he saw himself pulling into the parking lot of the apartment complex where Jack lived.

In the distance, he heard a door open and close. "What's going on in here?"

"Shh. Bobby's trying to go into deep meditation."

He did his best to ignore Phil's and Kevin's voices so they wouldn't distract him. Now he was at St. Paul's hauling a giant bag of garbage out to the bins along the tall, wooden fence, and then came arguing voices in another language.

Voices. Arguing. Fence. Behind the church.

*A woman standing along the curb in the dark, snatched away by someone in a work van.*

The man named Angel tinkering around under the hood.

*The voices. The fence.*

Bobby's body gave an involuntary lurch, and he snapped back into the present. Kevin stood beside Randy and Phil wearing an expression of utmost fascination.

"Any luck?" Randy asked.

Phil snorted. "Yes. Because luck is what we should place our faith in." But the look in his eyes was hopeful.

"I'm not sure." Bobby reviewed what he'd seen. "I kept seeing the fence along the back edge of St. Paul's property."

"Do you think she's in one of the houses on the other side?"

"I don't know. I'd like to find out."

Phil glanced toward the door that led to the kitchen. "How soon do you want to leave?"

"Now would be nice."

"Frankie isn't likely to want you to go just yet."

"I don't care what Frankie wants."

Phil smirked. "I don't, either."

"In any case, I'm not letting you go alone," Randy said to Bobby. "I can have your back as long as we make a quick stop at my house so I can pick something up."

"Would this something be kind of sharp?"

"You know me too well."

Phil looked torn. "I'd go with you, but I don't want to leave Allison and Ashley here alone with that Thane creature on the loose." He bit his lip. "You should probably go out the back so Frankie won't try to stop you. And Bobby, whatever you do, make sure you don't hurt yourself."

# 27

ADRIAN WENT over every inch of the concrete room in search of a thin object that could be slid into the crack between the door and its frame and came up with nothing. Whoever owned this place wasn't stupid. They would have thought of everything ahead of time and made sure that escape was more difficult than interstellar travel.

Monique watched her with wide eyes the whole time she conducted her search, and when at last Adrian returned to her cot and sank hopelessly onto the thin cushion serving as a mattress, Monique said, "If someone comes, you can hit them on the head."

"With what, honey? My hands?"

Monique scanned the room with her dark brown eyes. "You can throw a cot at them, and then we can run away."

If only things could be that simple! To make the child think she hadn't yet lost hope (which she was perilously close to doing), Adrian stood and lifted one side of the cot. Its frame must have been made of aluminum because it wasn't quite as heavy as she'd expected. Maybe she could find a way to take the cot apart and use a piece of the frame like a club.

Just as she was thinking this, the door's lock disengaged with a loud click and it swung open, admitting the woman who always brought food. This time she held a paper plate in each hand, both of them bearing a sad-looking peanut butter and jelly sandwich and a few slices of apple that were already turning brown from exposure to the air.

Adrian was too hungry to complain.

This time the woman stayed while they consumed their meals and then took the empty plates before moving over to the closed door.

A mad compulsion came over Adrian as she watched the woman's casual manner. Before she could convince herself to do otherwise, she charged at the woman, who was several inches shorter but probably thirty or forty pounds heavier than her.

The woman dropped the paper plates in surprise as Adrian hooked a skinny arm around her neck and looped the other across the woman's midsection to try to pin her arms into place. The woman struggled, and Adrian tightened her grip, but then the woman slammed her head backward into Adrian's face, sending a spike of pain through her nose. Blinking tears out of her eyes and trying her best not to let go, she said, "I want you to let us out. I have a lot of money. I'll pay you whatever you want if you let us free. I won't even tell anyone who you are or where this place is." These were all lies, of course, especially considering that Yuri had most likely found a way to prevent her from accessing their accounts now that she'd left him.

The woman let out a snicker. So she understood English after all. "You don't know how tempting it is to let you go," she said in a heavy accent. "You are a waste of space and resources. Our customers want the young, supple ones. If I'd known ahead of time how old you are, I would have put my foot down." Her body shook with laughter. "We could always kill you, maybe feed you piece by piece to the next ones who show up here. At least then you'd be useful."

This wasn't going well at all. Adrian willed every ounce of strength into her right arm to restrict the woman's airflow, and just as she was thinking that she might be able to crush her throat and use the cell phone to call the police, the woman managed to worm her way out of Adrian's grip and slapped Adrian so hard across the face that another wave of tears sprang into her eyes.

Her captor slid the phone out of her pocket and made to dial it but Adrian jumped forward and knocked it out of her hand. It skidded across the floor, Adrian dove for it with the intensity of a bird of prey closing in on a rodent, closed her fingers around it, and punched in 911.

Pain exploded across her head before she could send the call through, and her vision wavered. Somewhere close by a child was crying, and the lights grew dim, and my, how her head hurt! And then...

———◆———

ADRIAN AWOKE flat on her back, feeling sick to her stomach. Ropes bound her to the cot so tightly that she couldn't even sit up. *My God I can't throw up I'll DROWN if I do I can't I can't—*

Monique sat on the cot across from her, her expression blank. Two new men had entered the room with the evil woman at their side.

One of the men—a guy with frizzy red hair and too many freckles on his face—pointed at the child. "This one," he said, as if he were observing a household product sitting on a grocery store shelf.

Adrian strained against the rope and felt it chafe against the bare skin on her arms. This wasn't supposed to happen. She was going to save Monique, not watch her get dragged away to a living hell. "Stop it!" she screamed. "Don't hurt her! Take me, instead!"

The red-haired man laughed. "Looks like you've got a feisty one here, Rayna. I know some people who might like that."

Adrian's queasy stomach turned a somersault.

"You be quiet!" Rayna, her captor, snapped at the man. "Hurry up and finish your business. There's someone I need to go talk to."

Adrian watched helplessly as the other man seized Monique, forced her onto her stomach, and bound her small hands behind her back. Her eyes burned with tears. If only there was something she could say to the men that would give them an instant change of heart—a magic spell of sorts!

"What if she was your daughter?" she croaked. Monique wasn't even putting up a struggle, and Adrian prayed that she would block this out of her memory so that if she survived, this horror wouldn't haunt her for the rest of her life.

Eyes blazing, Rayna strode over to the cot, swung her foot back, and kicked Adrian so hard in the side she swore she heard a rib crack. Red-hot pain seared through her and she tried not to be sick. "Monique," she said. "I'm sorry. I'm so, so sorry."

———◆———

LUPE'S WHITE Prius still occupied Randy's driveway when Bobby pulled up in front of the ramshackle garage and killed the engine.

"I was kind of hoping Lupe and Carly would have decided to take an impromptu trip to Miami or someplace like that," Randy said as he unbuckled his seatbelt.

"Because it's about as far away from Jack and Thane as you can get without leaving the country?"

"Exactly."

Bobby followed Randy to the door, his nerves tingling with excitement. "Do you think it was dumb to promise Jack I wouldn't let anyone know where he's been staying?"

Randy pulled the door open, lifting his eyebrows. "You're asking *me* that?"

"Point taken."

Carly and Lupe were conversing in low voices at the kitchen table when they stepped inside. Lupe eyed them and rose. "Hang on, I'd better go help—" She froze, blinking in disbelief. "Randy? You're—"

"All better," Randy said as he led the way into the kitchen. "It turns out an old Servant is in town and still in the business of working miracles." He grinned.

Lupe yanked his shirt up so she could see where Graham had cut him. She clapped a hand over her mouth. "There aren't even scars! Let me find some scissors so I can get all those ugly stitches out of you."

Randy held up a hand. "That can wait. Bobby and I have some urgent work to get done in town. Now if you'll excuse me, I need to go get something out of my room." He disappeared into the back hallway and Bobby heard him ascend the creaking stairs.

Carly, who had been gaping at Randy the whole time like he'd just been raised from the dead, cleared her throat. "What kind of urgent work?"

At first Bobby hesitated, not wanting to go into another long explanation, but instead he said, "I think Adrian is being kept in one of the houses behind St. Paul's."

Her eyes grew round. "And you're going to get her out? Isn't that dangerous?"

He swallowed. "Of course it's dangerous. But how else am I going to save her?"

She gave him an appraising look. "Bobby, I mean absolutely no offense when I say this, but you're not exactly tough. There's going to be people guarding her. They could kill you if you try to get past them."

"I thought you were on my side here!"

A pink tinge filled her cheeks. "I am on your side. I just think you should let professionals handle this."

"I have to know if she's really there before I give any kind of 'professionals' a call."

Randy entered the kitchen with his hands hidden behind his back. "Who's calling professionals?"

"Bobby is when he finds out if his mother is at this place or not." Carly put her hands on her hips and arched an eyebrow at Bobby.

"Remember that the Titanic was built by professionals. Bobby, pick a hand."

"What?"

"Left or right."

"Um, left?"

"Good call." Randy brought his hands forward. He held a leather-sheathed knife in each one.

Bobby gulped. Even though he'd known that's what Randy had come here to pick up, he said, "Stabbing someone seems kind of up-close and personal." *Like that mattered when you went to visit Jack.*

"You don't say." Randy handed him one, and Bobby slid it out of its sheath. Six inches of glimmering metal. A razor-sharp edge.

With luck, Bobby wouldn't have to use it.

He put it back into the sheath and stuffed it in his pocket. "I wish we could do this at night instead. I don't want someone to catch us spying on the place."

"I can act as lookout," Carly said.

"But you had that bad scare this morning," Bobby said. "You should stay here where it's safe."

He could practically feel her glare burning a hole in him. "I said I'm stepping down as counselor while I work things out. I didn't say I couldn't help out in other ways in the meantime."

Lupe's face paled. "If Carly's going, then I am, too."

Randy looked stricken. "Bobby, this is your call."

"Might I remind you," Carly said, "that Lupe and I aren't damsels in distress? I counsel people who had *demons* feeding on their souls. I think I can handle sitting in a car and calling to let you know if some thug is sneaking up behind you with a tire iron."

"And I survived being imprisoned by Graham," Lupe added, though a shadow passed over her face when she said it.

"But that's different," Bobby said.

Now both of them were glaring at him.

"Fine," he said, sensing defeat. "You can both act as lookout. Maybe nothing will even happen." *And maybe it will.*

THE FOUR of them squeezed into Bobby's Nissan—the men in the front and the women in the back. Bobby took some reassurance from the fact that he had yet to experience a premonition, though one could hit at any moment.

"The question is," Carly said once they were on the road headed back to Autumn Ridge, "how are we going to communicate with each other while you two are scoping this place out?"

"You said you could call us," Bobby said.

"That might not be a good idea, though. People might hear you talking."

"How about text messages?" Bobby tightened his grip on the steering wheel. His heart pounded harder and he forced himself to take slow breaths before his vision went gray with dizziness.

"But those don't always go through right away," Lupe said from her place behind Randy.

"We'll set our phones to vibrate and use them like walkie-talkies, but only if we have to," Randy said. "That should be easy enough."

"That still doesn't solve the problem of being overheard," Bobby said.

"Then we'll talk quietly."

During a brief spell of silence, yet another Trautmann van passed them in the northbound lane heading out of Autumn Ridge.

"Not to change the subject," Bobby said, thinking of his meeting with Bill Trautmann, "but did Graham ever mention a friend named Nate?"

"Nate?" Surprise colored Randy's voice. "Not that I remember."

"Graham sometimes talked about a Nate when he forced me to chat with him," Lupe said. "He met Nate at Arbor Villa Nursing Home. He had a strange last name. Bagdasarian, I think."

They stopped at the first light on that side of Autumn Ridge, and Bobby took the opportunity to crane his neck around to look at her. "Was he a resident or an employee?"

Her forehead creased. "I don't think he said. All I remember is him talking about things Nate said to him. Like..." She paused. "That's strange."

"Let me guess," Bobby said as he recalled Bill's words from earlier in the day. "You can't remember."

"No." She then murmured something in Spanish, to which Randy replied in the same fashion.

"*Yo no hablo español,*" Carly muttered as the light changed to green and Bobby turned onto another street. He made a mental note to ask Lupe more about Graham's friend once their business in town was finished.

They completed their journey in silence. Bobby pulled into the parking lot at St. Paul's, figuring that this would be a safe starting point. "Great," he said. "We're not alone."

"I hate to break it to you," Randy said while Bobby drove past a dozen parked cars toward the lot on the other side of the building, "but this is a church. People do church things here."

Bobby parked beside the row of dumpsters and looked back at the church. Two women stood conversing at the front entrance while another woman and her small son wearing a Cub Scout uniform squeezed past them from within the building.

"They might not notice us," Randy said.

Bobby thought the women would have to have a severe vision impairment not to observe what he planned on doing. "Okay," he said, facing the three other occupants of the car. "I think the house might be on the other side of this fence here. What I need is for Randy to stand on one of these dumpsters and wave over the top of the fence so I can tell where he is when I drive over to the next street."

Carly shook her head. "All we need is a big dog and a hippie van and we've got ourselves one bad episode of Scooby-Doo."

Randy sighed. "I hate to say this then, but let's split up, gang." He opened the car door and climbed out, giving them a grim salute.

As Bobby dipped his head in reply, he had the sense that something more than the mantle had just been passed to him. As if Randy had officially acknowledged that he was no longer in charge, but merely a supporting player.

*It's all on me now.* Bobby set his jaw. *So I'd better do this right.*

He backed the car up and drove back out to the road.

Bobby wasn't wholly familiar with this end of town since he'd only been employed by the church for a week, but he knew he'd have to find a cross street as soon as possible and turn down it to find the street on which Adrian's prison lay.

Assuming he was right about where she was.

He turned left onto the first street past St. Paul's. The nearly identical houses were sandwiched together so closely that if one caught fire the whole block would go up in flames. Would traffickers work in such a populated area?

He swung another left and slowed to a crawl, keeping his gaze fixed on the left-hand side of the street to try to spot Randy.

The homes on this street sat farther apart than on the previous one, but an unforeseen problem soon presented itself.

"Who lets their hedges get so tall?" Carly asked as Bobby parallel-parked along the opposite curb so he could plan his next move.

"People who want to hide something." He stared out at the row of houses, many of which were mostly obscured by twelve-foot hedges growing across the fronts of their lawns.

"How are we going to see where Randy is?"

"Easy. I'm going to climb on top of the car and hope I can see over all that crap."

"*That's* not going to look suspicious."

Bobby didn't have the energy to work up a retort. He checked the street for oncoming traffic, climbed out onto the pavement, and prayed that his legs would stop shaking.

*If only this could have been at night instead.* Not all of the houses were hidden behind hedges. Any number of people could be watching him from gaps in the curtains.

Any number of them could be connected to the trafficking ring with which Jack Willard worked.

Setting aside his fear for Adrian's sake, Bobby scrambled up onto the hood of his Nissan.

Dread began to build inside of him: the start of a premonition.

Randy's face flashed through his mind.

He took a deep breath and crawled onto the car's roof, hoping he wouldn't slip off. He got his feet under him and wobbled a bit as he slowly stood. Heart pounding, he scanned the properties on the other side of the street.

Disappointment smothered his hopes.

He still couldn't see over the hedges.

His sense of urgency increasing, he slid out his phone and dialed Randy's number.

Randy picked up before the phone had the chance to ring in Bobby's ear. "Where are you?"

Bobby's heart thudded. "I'm standing on the roof of my car. There's a bunch of hedges blocking the view, so I can't see you. I—I think you might be in danger. Be careful, okay?"

"Great." Randy's voice sounded flat.

"There's a few houses it could be. All I can see is their roofs, and they all have the same gray shingles." The residences hidden behind the hedges had paved driveways also lined with hedges, and it looked like the driveways curved around behind the houses so that nobody on the street would be able to see anyone getting out of their cars.

Very fishy.

He relayed this information to Randy, who said, "Ah, the benefits of tract housing. Do you want me to jump the fence and walk out to the end of the driveway? It'll be a bit of a drop, but I'll manage."

Terror slammed into Bobby's gut so hard he almost toppled off the roof and onto the ground. "No, don't! If you do that, something bad is going to—"

Randy's voice was firm. "Short of renting a helicopter and flying over the place to scope it out, this is the only way for you to be absolutely sure you've got the right house."

"But if you do that, you'll—"

"Die?" He gave a soft laugh. "Then come save me."

A click told Bobby that Randy had ended the call.

Crap.

There was no time to explain to Carly and Lupe what was going on. The adrenaline surging through Bobby's veins made him feel like he could run a marathon, which was strange considering that Bobby rarely ran at all.

He leapt down from the roof and raced to the opposite side-walk. "Don't let anything bad happen to him," he prayed.

Bobby chose a driveway at random and raced down it, feeling like he'd entered a short maze. The hedge-lined driveway made a sharp left, and he ground to a halt when he heard the vicious barking of dogs close by.

A startled cry behind him sent chills down his spine. He was at the wrong house!

He dashed back to the cracked sidewalk running past the prop-erties and raced down the next driveway, which appeared virtually identical to the first.

As he rounded the corner, the breath left his lungs. Randy had his back pressed against the fence, which he had evidently jumped with greater ease than Bobby had expected, and four growling retriever-sized mutts wearing red collars prevented him from going anywhere.

Randy had pulled out his knife.

Like that was going to help him.

"Just go," Randy said, and at first Bobby thought he was talk-ing to the dogs. "You know this is the place. I'll keep these guys distracted while you call the cops."

Another surge of fear told Bobby that Randy wouldn't see the light of another day if Bobby chose that course of action. One of the dogs took a step closer to Randy, its growl deepening in its throat. All four looked ready to spring at a moment's notice.

"You don't trust the cops," he said.

Randy threw him a pleading look. "In this situation, you don't have any other choice but to call them."

Bobby gritted his teeth. This should not be a zero-sum game. He did not need to choose between saving his mother and saving his friend.

He was Bobby Roland, God's chosen Servant. He would find a way to do both.

The Spirit gave him a surge of courage, and Bobby withdrew the borrowed knife from his pocket.

He really wished he didn't have to do this.

Randy had already caught on. "Bobby, don't. I don't want you to turn into dog food."

"I don't want you to turn into dog food, either." He took four steps closer to the dogs and halted when two of them broke away from the others and faced him. Sweat trickled down his scalp. All those sharp teeth...

"Better me than you. I'm not the Servant anymore. I can die in peace."

*More like dying in pieces.*

Bobby's two new canine friends growled at him, and he almost lost his nerve. What was one knife going to do against two attack dogs?

A warm sensation filled him then, and he knew it was the Spirit giving him the signal to go.

"Sorry," he whispered as he lunged at the dog on the left, blade extended.

Bobby had never enjoyed killing things. Even as a child Jonas had made fun of him when he found himself too squeamish to even smash a house centipede that raced around their living room one night like a thirty-legged escapee from hell.

His squeamishness hadn't stopped him from beating the stuffing out of Rory Wells all those years ago, though. And it hadn't stopped him from snatching up the fireplace poker and racing around the yard at his old rental bungalow in search of phantom prowlers.

Drawing on that ruthlessness, he tried to stab at the canine's throat, but he wasn't fast enough. The dog clamped its jaw onto his hand and shook it with a violence Bobby hadn't expected. White-hot pain spiked through him with such intensity that his vision went black.

When it cleared he realized a thin scream was escaping his throat. The dog still hadn't let go, and its companion had latched onto Bobby's leg so tightly that he couldn't even begin to work his way out of its grip.

Something wet ran down his face.

Tears.

"Help!" he cried when he realized he wasn't going to get out of this on his own. Over by the fence he caught a glimpse of the other two dogs attacking Randy, who wouldn't be able to help him now, either.

Now Bobby was on the ground, blood oozing out of his hand and leg, but the dogs still wouldn't let go. They had probably been trained to fight until their victim was dead.

If only Phil was here with his gun. Bang-bang, and their problem would be over.

Something in Bobby's brain began to shut down from shock. So this was how his short life ended: in someone's backyard behind St. Paul's Church, barely a week after he'd taken on the mantle of Servitude so he could help free the possessed.

*Don't worry,* the Spirit whispered. *It isn't over yet.*

# 28

CARLY WATCHED with wide eyes as Bobby leapt down from the roof of the car and dashed across the street like a madman. He disappeared down one driveway, came back seconds later, and vanished down the next without returning.

Minutes ticked by.

Long, nerve-racking minutes.

Somewhere close, dogs were barking. The sound of it turned Carly's stomach.

"I don't like this," Lupe said, her face pale.

"Me neither."

"I can't stand not knowing what's going on." Lupe's eyes glistened. "I'm going to call Randy." She pulled out her phone and tapped in the numbers, then held it to her ear and waited.

After several seconds she let out a curse in Spanish.

This wasn't good at all. "I'll try Bobby," Carly said, but he didn't answer, either.

Lupe bit her lip. "We need to call the police."

"What are we going to say to them? That Bobby was trespassing on someone's property and never came back?"

"We could report a...how do you say? Disturbance."

"But then they'd ask for details, and we don't have any of those."

"Those dogs were barking. That is a detail."

Lupe was right, and it bothered Carly. What if there were attack dogs somewhere behind the house? They could have been penned in by an invisible fence.

"Fine," Carly said. "I'll make it anonymous." She did a quick search on her phone for the local dispatch and dialed that number instead of 911, then tried to compose herself while she waited for someone to pick up.

A woman's voice came on the line. "Cascade County Sheriff's Dispatch."

"Um, yeah. I'm calling to report a disturbance on, um..." She held the phone away from her ear. "What street is this?"

"Locust," Lupe said without hesitation.

"Locust Street in Autumn Ridge," Carly said to the dispatcher. "At..." She squinted at the fortress of hedges across from her. "Well, I don't know the house number because there isn't a mailbox and there's all these hedges out front, but it's the third house with hedges on the left."

"Ma'am, what type of disturbance was there?"

"Tell them we heard screaming," Lupe whispered. "Like someone was being attacked."

Carly cringed. Her parents would kill her if they ever caught wind of the fact that she'd fibbed to the police. "Well, there was all this barking, and I think maybe someone was screaming back there, too, like dogs were attacking them."

"Ma'am, could you please give me your name and number? We'll need to—"

Carly ended the call before the woman could proceed. "I'm getting in the front," she said.

Lupe nodded, and they each climbed out of the back of the Nissan. Carly sat in the driver's seat and Lupe took the seat beside her.

Carly was thankful that Bobby had left his key in the ignition. "You think they went in together," she said.

"There's no other reason Randy wouldn't have answered. He would have climbed over the fence if he heard that Bobby was..." Lupe scrunched her eyes shut and shook her head.

"They'll be okay," Carly said, though a hollow feeling inside of her told her she was lying to Lupe and to herself.

Ten more minutes passed. Carly tried calling Bobby three additional times, with no success.

Lupe leaned her head back, closed her eyes, and was praying softly in Spanish.

Just as Carly was thinking that at least the Thane-creature hadn't yet shown up to complicate things further, an Autumn Ridge police cruiser turned onto Locust Street and slowed to a crawl.

"Lupe, look."

Lupe shifted and leaned to see out the driver side window. "I hope they don't try to talk to us."

As far as Carly could see, the individual driving the cruiser wasn't even glancing their way. The cruiser paused in front of the place where Bobby disappeared; then swung into the driveway and around the corner of hedges so they could no longer see it.

"Why didn't he park out front?" Lupe asked.

"Probably so he has easier access to his car if something goes wrong." Carly gave an inward cringe. "I hope he doesn't run into any attack dogs."

She shifted positions and kept her gaze trained on the driveway entrance. She itched so badly to go back there and learn what, if anything, was happening. If only those blasted hedges weren't in the way!

Ten more minutes came and went with cold indifference. Lupe let out a little gasp. "He's coming back!"

Sure enough, the police cruiser emerged from the sort-of hedge maze and departed the driveway at a leisurely speed.

No backup had been called. No ambulance. Not even a fire truck, which always seemed to show up at emergency scenes whether one was needed or not.

If Bobby and Randy weren't injured, why weren't they picking up the phone?

"That's it," Carly said. "I'm walking back there to see what's going on."

Lupe gaped at her. "Do you want to be eaten by a dog?"

"For all we know, the dogs were somewhere else and it only sounded like they were back there."

Lupe's eyes lit up. "And maybe Randy and Bobby went into someone else's yard." Her face fell again. "And got attacked by dogs there."

"There's only one way to find out. Let's go."

"Wait." Lupe popped open the glove box and rummaged around in Bobby's insurance papers and roadmaps.

"What are you doing?"

"Looking to see if he has a gun."

"If he did, he would have taken it with him."

Lupe slapped the glove box closed. "I'm an idiot."

"If you're an idiot, I'm a moron. Come on." Completely weaponless, Carly stepped out onto the street, her mind firmly set on the task before her.

"What if something comes after us?" Lupe asked as they crossed over to the opposite sidewalk. She had taken a flashlight from Bobby's car and gripped it like a club.

"We run like heck back to the car." *And then we pray that Bobby and Randy show up all in one piece.*

Carly estimated the paved driveway to be about forty yards long before it turned sharply to the left. The thought that she was making a huge mistake intensified with each footfall, but she refused to turn back until she'd learned something or was chased away.

Lupe had straightened her shoulders and held her head up high. Carly noticed she was making a point to stay as close to her side as possible.

They both stopped by unspoken agreement a few feet before the driveway turned. Fear lined Lupe's face. "It is now or never," she said.

Carly nodded, and before she took the step that could very well be one of the dumbest things she'd ever done, her mind conjured an image of her and Lupe rounding the corner only to see the lifeless bodies of Bobby and Randy lying spread-eagled on the ground.

Which was stupid, because if that had been the case the cop who'd shown up would have called in reinforcements.

She took a deep breath and stepped forward.

The paved driveway ended at a leaning carport stationed behind the shabby two-story house. White aluminum siding was stained with spots of gray, and a tired wind chime hanging by the back door made sad clinking sounds in the light breeze.

A kennel sat at one end of the yard, which was speckled with days' worth of dog doo, but there were no dogs in sight.

There weren't any people, either.

The next thing Carly noted was that the walls of hedges completely blocked this yard off from the neighbors on either side. The privacy fence that divided this property from the back parking lot at St. Paul's lined the rear of the yard.

Lupe stepped toward a picnic table sitting in the grass, which hadn't been mowed in weeks.

She halted and gasped. "*Sangre.*"

"What?"

"Blood. In the grass."

Fear seized Carly's heart as she rushed to Lupe's side. She crouched down and swallowed back bile. Sure enough, something dark and sticky glistened on the uncut blades of grass.

Lupe folded her arms across her chest and glared at the blood as if it had caused her some sort of grievance. "That stupid cop didn't even look at this. He must have stayed in his car the whole time he was back here."

"Maybe he's afraid of dogs," Carly said, only half-jokingly. Her own mother had severe panic attacks if she even came into contact with a breed as innocuous as a basset hound.

"Hmm." Lupe put a hand on her chin, forehead creased. "We don't know that it's human blood. Maybe we should..." She broke off the same instant a muffled sound issued from a shed sitting beside the carport. "What was that?"

Carly was already creeping through the high grass over to the shed door. It appeared latched but not locked. She held an ear against it and listened.

Something inside let out a plaintive whimper that sent goosebumps cascading over her arms. "Something's alive in there." *Like an injured Bobby.*

"Are you sure?"

Carly nodded. "Step back. I'm going to open the door."

Lupe moved back several paces. Carly saw her grip tighten on the flashlight.

Carly tensed her muscles, preparing to run at a moment's notice in case whatever lurked in the shed wasn't human. *Okay,* she told herself. *Go.*

She slid the metal latch away from the loop and swung the door open.

Four dogs with coats of varying colors bounded straight out at her, and she instinctively brought her arms over her face to protect herself. *Please don't hurt me please don't hurt me oh please...*

All four ran past her toward the driveway and started pacing back and forth at what had to be the edge of the invisible fence.

Carly lowered her arms. *What the heck?*

Two of the dogs had minor lacerations as if someone had tried to fight them off with a knife. Yet if these dogs had truly tried to attack Bobby and Randy, why weren't they attacking Carly and Lupe? Had they only been trained to attack men?

And how had they gotten in the shed?

That question could wait.

Carly pushed the shed door closed and wiped away the sweat running down her forehead. "I have another idea," she said, unable to remove her gaze from the pacing dogs. One had laid down on the edge of the driveway with its ears perked up. All seemed oblivious to her and Lupe.

"What is that?" Lupe asked.

"I'm going to see if anyone's home."

Lupe whirled around and gaped as if Carly had just suggested they both go dancing naked in the street. "Why?"

"Why not? Bobby and Randy have to be somewhere close. They could have gone in the house."

Lupe's face took on a sickly hue. "I'm going to wait out here."

"Holler if you need me." Trying to stifle the jitters, Carly strode to the back door and knocked. When nobody came to answer it, she turned the knob and pulled it open.

Uncertainty prodded at her. If this house was a waystation where human traffickers imprisoned women, shouldn't there have been better security?

Unless Bobby had been wrong about where his mother was being kept.

Or maybe the dogs had been the extent of the house's security system.

Carly said a quick prayer and stepped over the threshold into a dim room that smelled of stale cigarette smoke. Her hand found a light switch and flicked it on.

A dingy couch looked as though someone had spilled drinks on it repeatedly and never bothered to clean it up, an ashtray sitting on the dusty coffee table overflowed with cigarette butts, and dozens of empty Mountain Dew bottles lay heaped beside the couch.

All the comforts of home.

"Bobby?" she whispered. "Randy? Is anyone here?" She scanned the carpet for signs of blood, and even though it was so dirty she couldn't determine the original color, it didn't look like anything red and wet had dripped on it in recent minutes.

She proceeded to the next room through an open archway and passed a dining room table and chairs. Next she entered the kitchen and learned that whoever stayed here wasn't fond of doing the dishes or taking out the garbage, either, as waste overflowed from a can in the corner. Fat flies buzzed around a bag of apples on the counter. One tried landing on her arm.

"Is anybody home?" Wrinkling her nose, Carly moved on from the kitchen and found flights of stairs going down and up.

She chose up and arrived at a landing off of which lay a single bedroom and a bathroom. No sooner had she done so when a scratching-fluttering-flapping sound issued from somewhere above the ceiling. *Oh, yuck. Something's alive up in the attic.*

Ignoring the sound, Carly stuck her head through the bedroom doorway. "Hello?"

No reply. She stepped further into the room and switched on the light.

A four-poster bed had been neatly made and covered in hot pink blankets and pillows. To the left sat a dresser, and on top of it sat a white jewel box and a sort of metal tree on which hung a bunch of necklaces.

Could Bobby's mother have been staying in this room? Perhaps the woman's kidnapping had all been a ruse to kidnap Bobby, which seemed farfetched but not impossible. Adrian may very well have traveled all the way across the country to see Bobby, stayed at the campground, and met up with Jack Willard at that nasty bar in Hillsdale for the sole purpose of finding someone to help orchestrate Bobby's capture.

Heck, Adrian and Jack might even be *friends.*

Her lip curling at the thought of anyone befriending the man who'd helped hurt Randy, Carly yanked the top dresser drawer open only to see a collection of Victoria's Secret's finest. After making a vow to scrub her hands when she got the chance, she moved the lingerie aside and found an expired driver's license that had been issued to Rayna Vasquez Robles in the Mexican state of Sonora.

Rayna had dark hair, a deep brown complexion, and a conceited smile—or maybe Carly was just seeing things based on her own assumptions.

"Don't you know what these people do here?"

Carly froze at the sound of Thane's voice. He was here. Right behind her. Trying to make her doubt her sanity once more.

She wasn't going to fall for it.

She dropped the license and slid the drawer closed before opening the next one. If she continued to ignore Thane, maybe he would go away.

"Come on," Thane said. "I know you can hear me. You want to know what these people do here. I know you do."

Carly steadied her shaking hands as she went through more of Rayna's things. She didn't need a demon to tell her what all went on within the walls of this hovel. She could use her own wits and figure it out herself.

The next drawer contained an amethyst geode that sparkled from purple facets. Next to it sat a small soapstone box, and shoved in the back of the drawer was a framed photograph of Rayna and four other Hispanic women sitting at a table in a restaurant.

"Nothing to see here, is there?" Thane went on. "That's because they hide it well. They'll tell you one thing when the truth is something else, but I suppose that's the way of humanity. We all wear a mask, though some wear it better than others. Graham wore a mask. Jack still wears it. And you do, too, even though you won't admit it."

Carly took a deep breath, straightened her shoulders, and turned. Thane, dressed all in white this time, was sitting at the end of the four-poster bed with his legs dangling over the side. His weight made no impression in the bedspread.

She walked out the door without even giving him a nod of acknowledgment.

Her next stop was the basement. She swallowed a knot of fear. As she descended the stairs and took the next flight down to the basement, she realized that deep down she'd known she wouldn't find Bobby or Randy here at all.

Carly clapped a hand over her mouth as the basement steps terminated at a gray cement floor. A dark-haired woman who could only be Rayna Vasquez Robles lay crumpled just feet away, a pool of dark red congealing beneath her.

The smell of blood made Carly gag. How long had the woman been lying here? Was she alive when Carly called the police or had someone dropped by earlier in the day to end her life?

"Help..."

Carly's heart fluttered at the sound of the heavily accented voice. She approached the woman on light feet and crouched down beside her.

Rayna's eyes were open in a hollow stare, but something in them sparked to life when Carly entered her field of vision.

"What happened here?" Carly asked. "Where are Bobby and Randy?" *And Adrian?*

Confusion entered Rayna's eyes. "Compromised."

"What?"

"This...location." Rayna winced, and sudden anger filled her eyes. "It must be you. The reason I have to die."

"Did you trap women here?"

"It is...none of your business." Her eyes closed. She said something in Spanish before becoming still.

Carly felt a pang of sorrow despite Rayna's apparent association with the network of traffickers.

Thane appeared on the staircase. "You still don't know everything. Pity that."

If only there was a way to shut him up!

Continuing to pretend Thane didn't exist, Carly moved past the dead woman down a bare hallway. A thick metal door sat ajar on the left. Carly peered inside and saw a collection of dirty cots and a bucket that might have doubled as a toilet. One of the cots was overturned as if some struggle had occurred there, and a coil of rope lay beside it like a dead snake.

She went back into the hallway. Further down on the right was another door, this one closed.

She gulped and stepped forward.

Behind her, Thane snickered.

Her mind filled with the image of her holding a gun and standing over Rayna's lifeless body. *You killed her, Carly! It's your fault she's dead!*

She gritted her teeth. *No it's not.*

The image dissolved, and she was back in the basement hallway. Thane was just trying to screw around in her head again. He couldn't hurt her unless she let him, and she wasn't about to give in now that she knew Thane was just a demon who had chosen to manifest as a man.

"I'm not a demon!" Thane called. "I'm your worst nightmare."

"I doubt it," Carly muttered as she opened the door.

And she was right. Thane was just an unpleasant dream. The real nightmare lay in the room before her.

# 29

BOBBY WAS sitting in the living room recliner in the rental bungalow owned by Graham Willard, alias Dave Upton. His presence there gave him a jolt. Everything was just as it had been during the year he'd lived in the small but comfortable house. Boxy television set in the corner. Coffee table. Quantum mechanics textbook sitting on the end table. Squashed secondhand couch, on which sat Caleb Young, his geeky roommate who had vanished in an air of mystery the week before and never returned.

Caleb's eyes were large behind the lenses of his thick glasses; his face as emotionless as always. "It's about time," he said as he drilled Bobby with a stare.

Bobby sat up straighter. The chair felt solid beneath him. "Is this a dream? I don't live here anymore."

Caleb shrugged. "Dream or not, you're here."

"Okay," Bobby said. "And what about you? You're not even human. I figured that much out on my own."

Caleb didn't answer. He leaned forward and steepled his fingers together. "You've found yourself in a bit of trouble."

Bobby tried to think back to what had been happening just before he showed up here but drew a blank. "Oh yeah?"

"I want to remind you that you must do your best to preserve your own life, even at the expense of those you may care about. You are the Servant. *You must not die.*"

This didn't sound good at all. "So you're saying it's better if Randy or Phil or whoever's around me dies?"

Caleb tilted his head to one side. "Dying isn't going to hurt them. All of your kind must die eventually."

Bobby crossed his arms. "I don't want anyone to die."

"I don't want anyone to die, either, but if it comes down to it, better them than you."

"That sounds so harsh."

"But it's the truth." Caleb cleared his throat. "I advised another Servant not to go out one day. He ignored me and soon found a knife in his heart, which I understand is not the most pleasant feeling one might experience."

Bobby gulped. *Hans Mueller.*

Caleb continued. "More recently, I advised a Servant who had a morbid fear of flying insects to stay home. He'd left the windows down in his car and didn't know that bees had been attracted to a can of Pepsi he'd left in the cup holder. He left anyway and crashed into a utility pole when they flew out of the can." He allowed a grim smile. "Luckily that Servant had already found a replacement before he died."

Bobby found himself nodding. It was strange hearing Caleb go on like this when in the year he'd known him, Caleb hadn't been the chatty type. "So basically your job is to protect the Servants."

"Yes, but only if they listen."

"How many Servants have there been?"

"Many more than you could ever keep track of."

"And what about Thane?" Bobby asked. "Is he like you, or something else?"

A shadow darkened Caleb's face. "Thane has let his own arrogance get to his head. The only thing you can do for him is pray."

"That doesn't tell me what he is."

Caleb seemed to ponder something. Then, "You're about to wake up. Be vigilant and don't be afraid." This time he really did smile. "I know you can do it."

The next thing Bobby knew, he was lying on his back on something soft in a place devoid of light.

Someone close by let out a moan. "Argh. I think someone tried to brain me."

Bobby sat up. "Randy?"

"That's me. You okay?"

"I think so. What about you?"

"I feel like I have a hangover." Randy paused. "Someone's lying next to me. I can hear them breathing."

"Who is it?"

"If I had night vision goggles, I might be able to tell you. Wait a minute." Randy's voice faltered. "Those dogs. I thought we were goners."

The memory of sharp teeth tearing into Bobby's flesh made him wince. He rubbed the back of the hand that had taken the brunt of the first dog's fury and found the skin perfectly smooth. "Kevin must have healed us."

"Kevin wasn't with us. Remember?"

"Maybe he followed us at a distance to keep an eye on me."

"Our dear Mr. Lyle seemed a little too distraught to think of something like that. Even if he did follow us and got to us in time, it doesn't explain how he was able to get past the dogs, and it doesn't explain where we are."

"Maybe Kevin's the person lying next to you."

"Dear God, I hope so."

The pitch-darkness was starting to give Bobby the creeps. Either they had been out for so long that night had fallen, or they were somewhere underground. "I'm going to find a light."

Bobby swung his legs to the left. He found the edge of the mattress on which he sat and gingerly tapped the floor with his feet. It felt like tile.

He got to his feet and held his arms out in front of him. *Show me the way to go.*

Bobby took baby steps across the room and managed to stub his toe on something that made him gnash his teeth together. Where in the world were his shoes?

Ten steps after he got up from the bed, his hands made contact with a wall. He patted around for a switch and found one.

The light was so bright in contrast to the blackness that at first Bobby couldn't see a thing.

Behind him Randy said, "Oh!"

Bobby blinked. They were in what appeared to be a large, windowless storage room with white walls. An assortment of junk including broken lamps, stained pillowcases, and a dismantled table was jammed without regard to order on some nearby shelves.

Bobby had lain on a dirty twin-sized mattress, while Randy and their unknown companion shared a king-sized one. Were they in a hotel?

Randy was eyeing the unconscious form beside him. Whoever it was had curled up into a ball. Bobby saw a spill of long, dark hair, and his stomach flipped.

As though they had taken on minds of their own, his legs carried him across the room and stopped beside the mattress. His eyes glued themselves to the woman's face. Her chest rose and fell with quick exhalations, and her eyes fluttered frantically behind closed lids.

"Is it her?" Randy asked.

Bobby nodded. Here lay the woman who had captivated his father all those years ago. The woman who had been the light of Ken Roland's life until she had a kid and realized parenting would just be too much trouble.

Anger welled up inside of him and manifested itself as tears.

Randy nudged Adrian in the side. "Hey. Wake up."

Bobby wanted to tell him to stop. If Adrian awoke, he would have to talk to her. But what else had he expected? He had wanted to rescue her from the house behind St. Paul's where dogs had nearly killed him. Did he really think he would have been able to get her out without engaging in any kind of conversation?

Adrian stirred and let out a string of garbled words.

Then her eyes fluttered open and stared directly at him. Astonishment lit up her face. "Bobby?"

Bobby's ears rang. "How did you know that's what they call me?" he asked, which seemed a lousy greeting but was a lot nicer than most of the things he could have said.

An echo of Carly's voice flitted through his head once more. *What will you do with your pain?*

And then his father's advice from the vision: *Love your mother.*

Adrian sat up. Her blouse was stained and wrinkled. She'd probably been wearing it for days. "Charlotte told me. She showed me a lot of pictures of you over the years, too. We had a very long talk." An expression Bobby hadn't expected shined in her eyes: remorse. Her blue-eyed stare penetrated his. "I'm sorry."

While Bobby tried to come up with something to say that wouldn't make him sound like an idiot, Randy got up and tried the door. It didn't open. "Of course," Randy muttered.

Bobby took a deep breath. "Do you have any idea where we are?" he asked Adrian.

"I wish I did. The last thing I remember is a cop coming in and clubbing me on the head. I was surprised because Rayna said they didn't want me. They thought I was too old."

"The traffickers, you mean?"

She nodded. "She said their clients prefer the young, supple ones." Her face paled. "Monique! Oh, God. They took Monique."

Monique, whoever she was, must have been imprisoned with her.

Randy strode over to a dinged-up dresser and started yanking open drawers.

"What are you doing?" Bobby asked, shaken.

"Seeing if anyone was thoughtful enough to leave a sledgehammer in here so we can break down the door."

Adrian let out a choked sob. "That poor little girl. For them to do that to her..." She marched over to the door, giving the knob a violent yank. She continued to tug and tug even though she would have needed to be a bodybuilder to tear the door out of its frame with her bare hands.

Bobby gaped at her, and even Randy paused in his search of the dresser to stare at the woman's antics. The sound of the door jiggling probably carried throughout the entire dwelling. Whoever was in charge here might drop in to see them at any moment.

Strangely, he felt none of the urgency he associated with an oncoming premonition. It was possible that some kind soul had rescued them from the dogs and taken them here to recuperate.

Yet why was the door locked?

*And why are our wounds healed like they were never there?*

Adrian ceased trying to bring the door down and backed up several steps. "Someone's coming."

A hush fell over them all, and sure enough, the approach of light footsteps issued from beyond the door.

At once a black, writhing aura filled Bobby's mind like a pulsating ocean of death. He braced himself against attack, willing his painful memories to be kept at bay.

It seemed an eternity before the lock disengaged and the door swung inward.

A gaunt, dark-haired man in his late twenties stood in the doorway. He had large dark circles under his eyes, which were ringed in eyeliner. "Welcome," he said in a soft tone as he stepped inside and closed the door behind him. "How are you feeling?"

Bobby knew that this man was a victim, unlike Jack, whose aura didn't have a tenth the intensity of this one. "Who are you, and why are we here?"

"My name is Vincent," he said, wearing a vague smile as if he knew the punchline of some joke Bobby wasn't aware of.

*Keep asking him questions*, the Spirit urged.

Bobby licked dry lips. *Might as well.* "What do you do here?"

Vincent's smile broadened, and in some corner of Bobby's mind he could hear the man's tormentor snickering. "I'm a healer. I healed you."

A cold voice cut into Bobby's thoughts. *Stop prying, little rat. He's ours.*

Bobby said, "All right. What exactly did you heal?"

250 | J.S. BAILEY

"Your wounds, of course. One of you had a broken nose, some bruised ribs, and a concussion, and some animal had attacked two of you and you'd both lost a lot of blood. I couldn't let you die." His dark eyes sparkled. "That would have been terrible."

"What's the point of keeping us alive?"

Vincent gave a soft laugh. "We don't deal in death here. Not usually, anyway."

Bobby's skin crawled. "Usually?"

"Accidents happen, of course, but that could be said about anything." Vincent winced. "I keep praying for one to happen to me."

*Interesting.*

Randy folded his arms and glared at the man. Since he was no longer the Servant, he wouldn't know Vincent was possessed—if he did, Bobby suspected he'd regard Vincent with greater sympathy. "What exactly is this place?"

Vincent's face became radiant, and the black aura intensified in Bobby's head. "We call it the Domus. It's where the dreams and desires of many come true."

Bobby tried not to smirk. Vincent's words held the false tone of one repeating lines from a script.

It would be nice to know who'd written it.

"Where..." Randy's voice faltered.

"What is it?" Bobby asked him, keeping half his attention on Vincent in case he made any sudden moves to harm them.

Randy shook his head. "Nothing." But the look in his eyes told Bobby otherwise.

"I have been told," Vincent said, "to take you to a nicer room now that you're awake. Some of our staff prepared it just for you."

That didn't sound reassuring at all. "Is it going to be a storage room, too?"

"Oh, nothing like that." Vincent gave a soft laugh. "I just know you're going to love it."

# 30

CARLY WOBBLED, and her vision went gray.

"Isn't she pretty?" Thane asked.

Carly saw no need to reply.

The much-cleaner room held similarities to the living room upstairs. A television hung on the wall. A loveseat sat before a coffee table on which lay a collection of syringes. There was even a pinball machine and a Space Invaders arcade at one end of the room.

The room itself wouldn't have given Carly much pause, even with the syringes lying on the table.

The upside-down crucifix hanging on the wall did. About five feet long, it showed off the remains of either a child or a very short adult—Carly wasn't sure which because the individual mounted on it had no head.

The person had been hanging there for a long time. The skin looked brittle as though mummified, and the pink shirt and denim skirt were threadbare and full of holes.

*Please just be a very convincing dummy.*

"She's real, all right," Thane said as he stood beside her and crossed his arms.

Carly swallowed, unable to pull her gaze from the corpse. She yearned to run from this place and never return again, but her feet remained planted to the floor.

*I must be fearless.*

"Her name is Layla," Thane said. "She's been up there twenty, twenty-five years."

*I must not be afraid.*

Carly faced him, more angry than saddened by Thane's offhand manner. "Okay. So you want me to talk to you. Are you going to just be a jerk and ignore everything I say, or are we actually going to have a conversation?" She was treading dangerous territory by communicating with this monster, but he knew more than she did so she might as well get as much information out of him as possible.

"You're more interesting when you have an attitude." Thane gazed lovingly at the corpse on the wall. "Layla was one of the trafficker's children. Some of them became quite intoxicated one night and thought it would be funny to, well, you know." He gestured to where Layla's head should have been. "People get the most peculiar ideas in their heads, and speaking of those, the individuals responsible for this burned her as an offering to whatever deity they were worshipping at the time. This was after years of sexual abuse. Even the child's own mother couldn't get enough of her. You might say Layla's death was a blessing."

*I must be fearless.* "How do you know all of this?" Carly's voice quaked.

"Because I know everything. Just like I know that deep down you've never gotten over your sister's death. Don't you know? Jackie's in a better place. You should be happy for her. Now Cassandra, on the other hand..."

"Carly?" Lupe's voice, high-pitched with fear, carried down the stairwell. "Is everything all right?"

"Don't come down here!" Carly darted back into the hallway, thoroughly shaken by Thane's words. Lupe didn't need to see the late Rayna Vasquez Robles lying on the floor, and she certainly didn't need to pay Layla a visit, either.

"Why?" It sounded like Lupe was in the kitchen. "Did you find anyone?"

Carly skirted Rayna's body and climbed the stairs. "Not exactly. We have to get out of here." She reached the top of the stairs, welcoming the sunlight coming through the windows.

Wide-eyed, Lupe stood by the counter, still holding the flashlight in a death grip. Her face fell. "No sign of them?"

"No, but I can tell someone was held down there against their will. I found a room full of cots." *And a dead little girl named Layla who'd be older than both of us if someone had let her live.*

Lupe was silent for several beats. "We need to tell Phil."

Carly nodded. "And Dad. Oh, geez. He's going to have a conniption when he finds out we lost them."

---

FRANKIE INHALED deeply, doing his best to maintain some semblance of inner peace.

He'd been angered when he learned that Phil encouraged Bobby and Randy to skip out on the rest of the meeting, but then he realized that if God had called Bobby to perform a certain task as the Servant, it wasn't Frankie's place to stop him.

Roger had then driven Frank the First home so Frankie could stay behind and have a long talk with Phil about his faith problem. Kevin returned to the bench outside and stared dolefully at the ground. Frankie was starting to wish he'd left him back in Idaho, but he knew that Bobby needed Kevin too badly for him to have done that.

And then Carly and Lupe showed up claiming that Bobby and Randy had vanished into thin air.

The four of them—he and Phil, Carly and Lupe—stood facing each other in Phil's living room. "How foolish could you be," Frankie said, "to have let them out of your sight?"

Carly's eyes were red from crying. "We tried to act as lookout. We didn't know they'd disappear."

254 | J.S. BAILEY

Frankie's voice shook. "Carly Jovingo, you are twenty-one years old. Did you really think *you* would be able to handle something like this?"

She sniffled. "You don't have any problem with me counseling people at the safe house."

"Teaching people to pray is not the same as going after a group of human traffickers. I thought you were old enough to know the difference."

"That's right, Dad. Keep insulting me for making a mistake. Nobody can be as perfect as you, right?"

Frankie stiffened at his daughter's defiance. Where had that come from?

Lupe's eyes blazed. "Arguing like a group of...of *schoolchildren* is not going to bring either of them back! Phil, tell him we were right in doing what we did."

Phil had removed his glasses and was rubbing his eyes with the weariness of a chronic insomniac. "I can't make that call until I see the outcome of this." He turned his attention to Frankie. "Are you up to investigating this house to see if they're trapped inside?"

"Don't go in there!" Carly shrieked before covering her face with her hands. "I—I looked around. Nobody's there."

Frankie could hear what she'd omitted as loudly as if she'd shouted it. "But something else is."

She nodded.

"Would you mind sharing it with us?"

"Yes, I mind," she said. "We need to focus on finding Bobby and Randy. And please don't ever ask me about what I saw again."

———————◆———————

WHILE FRANKIE continued his attempts to pry information out of his daughter, Phil slipped down the hallway and closed himself in his bedroom so he could clear his head. He could hear the murmurings of Allison and their daughter through the walls, and knowing they were safe from harm at the moment brought him a small measure of comfort.

"Father," he whispered, "let me have the faith that Randy and Bobby will both be unharmed." *And Martin, if you could put an extra word in with the Big Guy, that would be great, too.*

Then he slid out his phone and dialed Randy's number.

No answer.

He dialed Bobby's and got the same result.

Staring blankly at the muted sunlight spilling through sheer drapes, he tried to come up with a plan. He'd never been the planning type. Randy was always the more likely one to brainstorm new ideas, and Bobby seemed even better at that task than Randy.

Hopefully that meant Bobby would think a way out of whatever situation he and Randy had gotten themselves into. And since Kevin had healed Randy, maybe Randy would be strong enough to incapacitate their foe and free himself and Bobby from wherever they'd been imprisoned. Because they had to be imprisoned somewhere. Where else could they be?

But Carly and Lupe had found blood on the ground. Wherever the two younger men were, at least one of them was hurt.

Even though he knew it was pointless, Phil dialed Randy's number a second time.

Still, nothing.

Phil returned to the living room, feeling defeated. During his few minutes of absence, his three bickering guests had taken seats and had been joined by Kevin.

"Welcome back," Frankie said to Phil as he sat next to Lupe on the couch. His face was grim, and Lupe kept biting her lip. "We've had a new development since you went back there."

"I hope that 'new' in this instance means 'good.'"

Frankie frowned. "Carly, tell him what you told us."

Carly lifted her gaze to Phil's and cleared her throat. "When I was checking out that house behind St. Paul's, Thane came back. I tried to ignore him but I finally got fed up and got a conversation going with him. He told me about some bad things that happened there." Pain flashed through her eyes. "He says he knew about it because he knows everything."

"Because he's an evil spirit," Phil said, not sure where she was going with this.

Carly's forehead creased. "I thought he was, but now I'm not so sure. It was something he said." Her face strained with the effort to remember whatever the monster had said to her. "One room in the house looked sort of normal inside, and I was thinking that it didn't look like a horrible person would live there, and then he said, 'They'll tell you one thing when the truth is something else, but I suppose that's the way of humanity. We all wear a mask, though some wear it better than others.'" She paused and looked at Phil, then at her father. "If he was a demon, he would have said *you* all wear a mask. But he didn't. He said *we*. I—I think Thane is a human."

Phil opened his mouth to object but then closed it. Carly's theory was nonsense, of course. An evil spirit like Thane would have said that just to confuse her.

Frankie was thinking along the same lines. He said, "Explain to me, then, how this *human* can appear and disappear at will and read your thoughts like they're written in a book."

"It's a gift," someone said softly.

They all looked at Kevin, whose eyes held a gleam of revelation.

"A gift," Frankie repeated, his tone oozing disbelief.

"Frankie, hear me out." Kevin lifted his head higher. "Some of us can see the future, or at least get the gist of it. Some of us heal. Some of us understand languages we were never taught. Well, what if there are evil gifts given to people who serve, well, the other side? Kind of like anti-Servants."

It felt as though someone replaced all of Phil's blood with ice water. He thought Frankie would say something snide but saw that the man's face had gone white.

"This is not good," Lupe said.

# 31

**DESTROY HIM.** *Destroy him. Destroy him.*

Vincent's words to Jack at the Domus had taken root in his mind, sending their tendrils deep inside of him.

He couldn't believe he'd never thought of it before. The very thought excited him almost as much as seeking out new victims did. It wouldn't be that hard to do, and in the meantime he could even tie up a loose end that had been bugging him.

"Jack? What are you doing?"

Jack set his comb down after slicking his hair back and examined his reflection in the mirror over the dresser in the bedroom where he'd been staying all week. Wanda Livingston, a fellow employee of Troy Hunkler and the apartment's sole legal tenant, stood a few feet behind him, her black eyebrows raised in a question.

"I just got a call from Troy." He flashed a grin at her. "He told me to come see him as soon as I could."

In reality, he and Troy had not spoken. Jack had, in fact, made some calls of his own in order to make certain arrangements, and much to his surprise things were working out in his favor far more than he'd expected them to.

His unseen comrades must have been working hard to help him.

Wanda tossed her curly hair over her shoulder and smirked. "Maybe someone exceeded their quota so you won't have to bring in five this week."

"I doubt that. You can come with me to see him if you want. It's up to you."

She weighed this for a few seconds. "Fine. But afterward I'm going to dinner. There's this Thai place on Hillsdale Boulevard I've been wanting to try out."

Jack stiffened. Sometimes Wanda could be almost as much of an airhead as Trish Gunson had been. "If I go anywhere," he said, "it'll be to The Pink Rooster. At least there I won't run the risk of having a cop spot me." The Hillsdale Police Department knew better than to show up at Vern and Chuck's place. If a cop stepped through their doors, he was bound to have an unfortunate accident.

Wanda folded her arms. "I didn't say you were invited."

"I thought you were fonder of me than that."

She let out a hollow laugh. "Me, fond of you? You're not that special. I only let you stay here as a favor to Troy."

*Is that so?* Jack straightened the collar of his sky blue polo shirt and winked at his reflection. "We'd better hurry. I don't want to keep him waiting."

Wanda shouldered her purse and led the way out of the apartment. As Jack closed the door, he wondered if he'd ever see it again.

If all went according to plan, he'd have a much nicer place to spend his days from here on out.

He slid out his phone and dialed a number. "Angel," he whispered as they descended the stairs to the parking lot. "Are you busy?"

A radio blaring music in the background fell silent. "No, *señor*. Listen, some skinny kid came by earlier and started asking too many things about the other night. This whole thing, I knew it was a bad idea."

"When you say 'skinny kid'..."

"He had dark hair. Maybe a little younger than you? He was very nosy; it made me nervous."

Sounded like Bobby Roland had been doing his homework. "Forget about him," Jack said. "We won't have to worry about that 'kid' anymore after today." Jack's invisible helpers had seen to that.

He opened the passenger door of Wanda's car and climbed inside. Still speaking to Angel, he said, "Tell your boss you need off early and that you need to take a van because your car won't start, so you should probably fiddle around under the hood and break something in case he checks. If you come up with a decent enough excuse for leaving, he might feel sorry for you and let you go."

"You need a ride, *señor*?"

"Meet us at the park and ride as soon as you can. We'll be waiting."

He ended the call, knowing that Angel would do exactly as Jack requested. If he didn't, Jack would report him to the police for at least one of the crimes Jack knew he'd committed, and then *adios, amigo*.

"Why are we ditching the car?" Wanda pouted, her eyes full of suspicion.

"We're not ditching it. I just feel better having Angel behind the wheel than either of us."

"Fair enough." Wanda let out a sigh. "I hope this meeting with Troy doesn't take too long. I'm starving."

"Me too," Jack said, though not for food.

⸻◆⸻

ADRIAN FOLLOWED Bobby, his friend, and the other man out into a black- and gray-carpeted corridor that she suspected was underground like her previous prison. It made her think of a hotel, though it wasn't nearly as lavish as ones she'd visited with Yuri. The air held a funny odor, like a mixture of perfume and disinfectant.

Charlotte had shown her many pictures of Bobby but it was another thing entirely seeing him in person. She could see traces of her father in Bobby's face—maybe if Rob Pollard hadn't died so long ago, his presence in her life would have encouraged her to stay with Ken and raise Bobby like a responsible woman would have done.

*Now you're just making excuses. The only person whose fault this is is you.*

Bobby lagged behind the others and fell in step beside her. She'd expected him to look older than he did. Right now he just looked like a scared kid desperately trying to keep it all together. "Why did you leave us?" he asked in a low voice.

Adrian forced herself to hold her tears in check. "Because I was too selfish to look beyond myself and care for another person."

He nodded in agreement, and it sent a knife through her heart. "Charlotte told me you did this to other people, too."

*Dear God, don't let him hate me.* "We shouldn't talk about this here. Not with anyone else listening."

They descended a flight of stairs into what must have been a sub-basement and found themselves in a grim corridor decorated with more garishly patterned black and gray carpet, smoky gray wallpaper, and pewter wall sconces flickering with cold light. At first she thought they held candles, but closer inspection revealed small, battery-powered tea lights.

How much lower would they go before their strange guide brought them to their destination? Then another, crazier thought came to her: What if she'd died and this was her own version of hell?

Bobby's jaw tightened. "We might not get another chance to talk. I mean, I haven't had a premonition yet, but—" He broke off, his face flushing.

"What do you mean, premonition?"

"It's nothing." He winced. "Sorry."

Perhaps the stress of their situation was taking its toll on him. It was certainly taking its toll on her.

Their guide brought them to a halt outside a carved mahogany door engraved with the number seven. Pewter sconces were mounted on each side at shoulder height, flickering away like the rest she'd seen. Adrian could imagine them continuing to fill this gray hallway with light for all of eternity, indifferent to the passage of time, until no one was left alive to observe them.

"We're about to enter one of the special guest suites," Vincent said in a soft tone. "It's stocked with food and drink and all the comforts of home."

"What's the point of taking us here?" Bobby's stocky friend asked, his muscular arms folded across his chest.

"I'm just following orders. If you need anything, feel free to ring the bell. You'll find it just inside the door." He opened the door to the suite, which was blacker than pitch inside until Vincent threw a switch and illuminated a lushly furnished room that was more reminiscent of the hotels she'd seen. Unlike the grays and blacks Adrian had expected, burgundy and gold comprised most of the colors therein.

"Are you going to lock us inside like you did in the other room?" Bobby asked, gaping at the small crystal chandelier hanging over the sitting area.

A suspicious glimmer entered the man's eyes. Without a reply, Vincent glided back into the corridor like a shadow and closed the door.

Bobby's friend let out a sigh through pursed lips. He held a hand out for Adrian to shake. "I might as well introduce myself, seeing as we're all stuck here together. I'm Randy Bellison. Bobby and I met last week when he came in for an interview at the church where I worked."

Adrian raised her eyebrows and glanced from Randy to Bobby, who'd finally torn his gaze from the elegant light fixture. "You've only known each other a week?"

"A lot's happened since then. I'm sure Bobby could tell you a little bit about it if he wants to."

But Bobby must not have been interested in talking, because instead of replying he went to the door and pulled it open. "It *isn't* locked," he said as a furrow formed in his brow. Then he straightened. "He's trying to lead us into a trap. Or maybe he wants us to think it's a trap so we stay here, where the real trap is." Bobby peered up at the golden ceiling. "You think they've got cameras watching us?"

"Oh, I hope not." Adrian wringed her hands together. Upon waking she'd been relieved to find she was no longer in the cement room with the cots and reeking pail, but that relief had fled the instant she realized she was still trapped. A prison was still a prison, even if it resembled a room in the Hilton. "I just don't understand why that cop would have knocked me out and brought me here. You two were trying to get me out?"

Bobby nodded. "I got a, uh, tip that you were in a house behind the church. I tried to sneak in, but the dogs...never mind."

It pained her to know he was keeping things from her, but she knew she deserved it. "Bobby, we need to be open with each other."

The color rose in his face. "Why? Because you happened to give birth to me, or because we're stuck in this place together and have no idea where we are?"

"She's right, you know," Randy said, giving the room a visual sweep. "Adrian, Bobby and I were attacked by dogs in the yard behind the house where you were kept. *Viciously* attacked, I might add. And when we woke up here, there wasn't a scratch on either of us even though we'd practically been mauled."

"That man said he's a healer," Adrian said, uncertain. "How long can we have been here for him to have completely healed us?"

Randy's face darkened. "That's what I'd like to find out. But anyway, the cop who hurt you must have dragged us along to punish us for trespassing."

Adrian took in the plush burgundy sofas and armchairs and eyed the kitchenette off to the right. An unopened bottle of wine and a corkscrew sat on the marble countertop next to a trio of upside-down wine glasses. "Some punishment." Her curiosity getting the better of her, she went to the stainless-steel refrigerator and found a meat and cheese tray stashed on one of the shelves inside.

If she knew with absolute certainty that the food didn't contain drugs or poison, she would have dug right in. It had to be dinnertime by now—her hunger pangs confirmed that fact.

She returned her attention to the wine bottle. She hadn't heard of the brand, but the year on the front said 1998.

Seventeen-year-old wine wasn't likely to come cheap.

"What kind is it?" Randy asked.

Adrian read the label. "Pinot Noir." Then, darkly, she said, "Do you want me to pour you a glass? They left one for each of us."

Instead of replying, Randy's mouth twisted into a frown. "Is there anything else on the label in a foreign language?"

She rotated the bottle and scanned the back label. "The whole thing looks French. Why?"

"Hand it to me."

Adrian relinquished the bottle to Randy, whose eyes took on a haunted look as he scanned the label. "I can't read it."

"So what?" Bobby ran a hand over his short, dark hair and then froze. "Wait. You understand languages. That's your gift."

Randy nodded as he set the bottle down. He opened his mouth, closed it, opened it again, appeared to strain for a moment, and then went over to the nearest sofa and put his head into his hands.

Bobby's voice took on an agitated tone. "What's the matter? Can't you do it anymore?"

"No."

"What would make your ability go away like that? You were just speaking Spanish in the car!"

"I don't know." Randy sat up straighter, his face white. "Have you had a single premonition since we woke up in this place?"

"No, but that might just mean we aren't in any danger. Except the Vincent guy kind of has some invisible company."

"Wanted or unwanted?"

"Definitely unwanted. I—I wish I could help him."

Adrian felt as though she'd dropped into the middle of a conversation between two madmen. She was about to ask what in the world they were going on about when a soft sound issued from the hallway leading to other rooms in the suite.

Bobby's eyes grew round. "Did you hear that?"

"Shh." Randy rose from the couch and let his hands hang at his sides.

The suite became so quiet that Adrian could hear her pulse pounding away a frantic beat in her eardrums. Somewhere else in the hotel (*was* this a hotel?) a man was laughing, a distant object fell over with a thump, high-heeled footsteps echoed on a far-off floor, and from the back of the suite a young, female voice said, "Are you coming or not?"

A chill washed over her. The three of them goggled at each other before returning their attention to the hallway. Several more mahogany doors led off of it but the lighting was too dim back there for her to see into them.

Bobby nodded in response to something she hadn't heard and said, "I'll go back and see who's there." He picked up the wine bottle by its neck and held it like a club.

Smart kid.

———————◆———————

**BOBBY'S LEGS** turned to rubber as he stepped into the dimly lit hallway, expecting bullets to tear out of the darkness. This could be the trap he'd imagined: because if something about this place had put a damper on his and Randy's God-given abilities, he had no way of knowing what lay in wait for him until he laid his own eyes upon it.

He tightened his grip on the wine bottle.

The hallway terminated at a door that had been left half an inch ajar. Faint light spilled around the edges and he caught a whiff of some scent he couldn't place.

The Spirit said, *Open the door. She will not hurt you.*

He did as he was told, and the breath fled his lungs.

The room behind the door was furnished with a queen-sized bed and a nightstand on which glowed a peach-colored jar candle that sent shadows dancing across the tile floor. The deep blue bedclothes had been folded aside as if the room's occupant had been about to retire for the night, but instead she sat at the foot of it eyeing Bobby with interest.

All intelligent speech left him so he just said, "Hi."

The girl could have been no older than ten. She wore a green plaid skirt, a white polo, had her hair done in pigtails, and wasn't in the least bit possessed, which was just about the only positive thing Bobby could have said about the situation that lay starkly before him.

"Hi," she said. "Are you ready to begin?"

Bobby dumbly patted the wall for a switch, but when the light came on overhead it didn't dispel any of the gloom that had settled upon his heart. The royal blue wallpaper didn't help, either. "Begin?" he squeaked.

She shrugged her small shoulders. "If you're not ready, take your time. I'll be waiting."

Bobby looked helplessly back at Randy standing in the doorway. Adrian stood behind him, looking anxious.

"Keep talking to her," Randy whispered.

Even though Bobby had always felt he had the conversational skills of a socially-awkward amoeba, he said, "What's your name?"

"Lily. Would you like to start?"

Bobby's initial revulsion was instantly replaced by anger at whoever had put this girl here. "I'm not here to 'start' anything."

"You're not?"

"I'm stuck here just like you. I mean, I'd never set foot inside a brothel. At least not to do *that*. I—I have too much respect for people." He was practically blubbering now, and while at one time this would have embarrassed him, he found he no longer cared. Hot tears filled his eyes as he thought of the things this child must have been through. "I guess nobody has any respect for you."

All at once he saw himself as he'd once been: a frustrated eighteen-year-old who had left home in search of something better. He'd thought he was looking for a place where his music career could get off the ground, but in reality he must have been searching for something more.

That "more" sat at the foot of the bed in the form of a girl named Lily.

*This is my purpose.*

In spite of the heavy atmosphere, Bobby felt light inside. *My purpose.*

"This isn't a brothel," Lily said, breaking his train of thought.

"Then what is it?"

"Troy calls it the Domus. It's where people's dreams come true."

*Not that again.* "So what's your job here?"

Lily blinked. "Why don't you know? Isn't that why you're here?"

"I think somebody wanted to surprise me and my friends by putting us here. We don't know anything." Bobby set the bottle on the tile floor beside him and crossed his arms. Why would a bedroom have a tile floor, anyway? It made him think of a hospital.

"You don't know," Lily said, staring down at her bare feet. Bobby could practically see the gears turning behind her eyes as she tried to comprehend that simple fact.

*I could use a little help here.*

It came to him then. "Lily?" he said. "I want you to tell me what happened the last time someone came in here to—to visit you. What did that person do to you?"

She frowned. "The last time?"

"If you can remember."

She appeared to strain as she called the memory forth. Maybe whoever was in charge here (Troy?) kept her doped up so she'd be more docile, and the drugs compromised her memory as a result.

Which might not necessarily be a bad thing.

She licked her lips. "The last time, a man cut my throat."

"What?" Bobby said even though he'd heard quite clearly. Her throat showed no sign of recent injury.

"He did," she insisted. "And it hurt so bad, but not for long because Vincent watches and comes to save me."

Bobby swiveled his head toward the ceiling. In one corner a black speck indicated where a tiny camera had been installed.

Lily continued. "Some beat me up until I can't move. Some do gross things and try to choke me. One time a man choked me so hard I couldn't breathe at all and Vincent came in really angry and made him leave. When Vincent made me better he said that man would never be allowed to visit again."

Adrian let out a sob and shouldered her way past Randy into the room. "Oh, honey, how long have you been here like this? We've got to get you out!"

Puzzlement entered Lily's eyes. "Vincent's my friend. He takes care of me and the others."

"How many others?" When Lily didn't respond, Adrian grabbed her by the shoulders. "How many?"

Randy gently pulled Adrian away from the child and knelt down at the foot of the bed. "There are other kids here like you," he said. "Yes?"

A nod.

"Can you tell me their names?"

Another nod. "Ashlynn, Priscilla, Kay, Joan—Joan is older like Vincent—Martha, Ellie, Syd..." She rattled off another dozen or so names, several of them male. "And there was a Millicent, too, but she went away and never came back."

*Probably because some creep killed her,* Bobby thought savagely. He was beginning to understand the purpose of this "Domus." Children were kidnapped and brought here. Then people would come and let out their frustrations by torturing the kids in whatever way pleased them the most. Once they were finished, Vincent would come and put them right again so the kids would be healthy enough for the next customer.

He turned to the microscopic camera. "Is this what you wanted us to see?"

A laugh crackled through a hidden speaker. "How do you like this place, anyway? I'll bet you never knew something like this existed right under everyone's noses."

Bobby would have known that voice anywhere: Jack Willard. "You lied to me," he said, clenching his hands so tightly his nails dug into his palms. "You said you didn't know where Adrian was."

"You trust people too much. I've known where she was the whole time."

"Where are we now?"

"I could tell you, but would it be the truth or a lie?"

"Bobby," Randy whispered, "don't engage him. Last week in the barn..." He closed his eyes and took slow, deep breaths. "He'll just twist your emotions into a knot and laugh while you squirm."

"I didn't know you could be so poetic," Jack sneered.

Randy kept his eyes closed and made no reply.

Something clicked inside Bobby's head. "You sent Thane after us."

Jack paused. "What?"

"You know, that smiling demon who showed up in my kitchen acting like my best friend before terrorizing someone I know. I mean, you live in the company of a demon. You must have sent it after us."

For the next fifteen seconds the speaker issued only silence. Then, "I don't have a clue what you're talking about."

"Don't you know that a demon is with you all the time? I can see its aura. It's like a gray shadow."

"Bobby, don't," Randy said as Adrian's blue eyes grew round with disbelief.

"I know no one named Thane," Jack said, his voice dangerously low. "Perhaps your demon is a freelancer."

Bobby's mind whirled. Here he thought he'd finally figured out where Thane came from, and now he was back to square one.

Jack's voice jarred him back to the present. "You might consider cracking open the wine. My boss wants to see you."

# 32

PHIL OFTEN carried a zippered tote bag with him containing various medical supplies including a first-aid kit, a thermometer, a stethoscope, several over-the-counter medications, finger and arm splints, and a surgical needle and thread in case he ever needed to stitch anyone up on short notice.

If only the bag's contents had the ability to mend their current situation. It was Phil's fault that Bobby and Randy had vanished. He was the one who'd encouraged them to leave.

Allison and little Ashley emerged from the hallway, the former halting at the sight of everyone's grim expressions. "What's happened?"

"We don't know where Randy and Bobby are," Phil said, praying that his overly astute daughter wouldn't become upset. She didn't know Bobby well yet, but whenever Randy came to visit he would read her stories or tell her lame jokes that always made her giggle.

Allison lowered her voice. "Is there anything I can do?"

"I wish there was."

Allison opened her mouth and hesitated. "I was going to take Ashley to the library before it closes, but I can stay here if you need me to."

"We're going to get the Boxcar Children!" Ashley piped up. "Mommy says they're kids like me who solve mysteries."

Phil forced a smile. "Go ahead and do that." He lifted his gaze to Allison. "If anything else happens, I'll call you."

Allison gave him a tight squeeze. "Be careful." Then, in a lower voice, she said, "I'm sure they'll turn up. They can't have gone far."

When she and Ashley left, Phil, Frankie, Kevin, and the girls went into the solarium and closed the door. Phil clasped his shaking hands together in front of him. "We need to summon Thane." As terrible as it sounded, it was the only course of action he could think of.

Frankie whirled to face him, just as Phil knew he would. "Might I ask why?"

"Carly says he knows everything, or at least he thinks he does. If that's true, he can tell us where Bobby and Randy are."

"Even if Thane is human, he's still evil. We can't rely on someone like him to tell us the truth."

Phil gave a curt nod. "Very well. We'll just leave Bobby and Randy alone and see if they come back uninjured."

"But he's the Servant!" Kevin said in a high-pitched voice. "It's our duty to keep him safe!"

Frankie scowled. "You're telling me this?"

"Dad, we don't have any other choice." Carly maintained a defiant pose, and Lupe nodded in agreement.

"I say we put it to a vote," Lupe said. "All in favor of calling Thane, raise your hand."

Everyone but Frankie lifted a hand into the air. "It looks like that settles it," Phil said, secretly pleased that Frankie hadn't gotten his way.

Splotches of pink formed on Frankie's cheeks. "It settles nothing! Carly, you and Lupe have never been Servants and never will be Servants. Your opinion doesn't matter."

"Even if that is the case," Lupe said coolly, "you are still out-numbered two to one."

Frankie looked from Phil to Kevin and frowned. "I won't have any part of this. If you're going to summon a monster, I won't be held responsible."

With that, he turned on his heel and stomped out of the solarium. The front door slammed seconds later.

Phil rubbed his eyelids.

"Are we ready, then?" Kevin asked, looking terrified once more.

"We're as ready as we'll ever be." Phil cleared his throat. *God, don't let this be a mistake.* "Thane? If you can hear us, show yourself."

Nothing.

"Why are you ignoring us if you wanted us to see you before?" Carly asked.

"Maybe he's busy," Lupe whispered.

Part of Phil hoped that Thane would stay away. They really had no business getting involved with someone like him. But what else were they supposed to do?

To his surprise, Kevin spoke next. "Who are you, Thane? And why were you here before?"

"You don't want me to be here," hissed a voice. "You only want to know what I know."

Thane was sitting in one of the wicker chairs with one leg crossed casually over top the other. Phil swallowed and conjured forth every ounce of courage he could muster. "We have some questions for you."

"So I've heard." Thane's dark eyes narrowed. "Why should I tell you anything? It's not my concern if your men die. The world would be much better off without them, especially the scrawny one."

"Where did you come from?" Kevin asked.

"Don't you know about the birds and the bees? No, you don't. You've never had a woman in your life because in reality you're a *queer*. You looked at all those men when you were a boy and wanted them oh so much, but then you found *Jesus* and vowed to never have sex with anyone because that would only lead to sin." Thane winked.

*He's redirecting the focus away from himself,* Phil realized. Thane wanted to make Kevin forget the question he'd just asked.

Kevin's breathing quickened. "Stop. Just stop. You know I haven't done anything."

"Oh, but you wanted to. You must be crushed with loneliness, wanting someone to love but knowing you shouldn't."

Somehow a look of determination appeared on Kevin's face. "If you want to pick on me, why don't you come do it face to face? I know you're not really here. That means you're too afraid to show up and speak to us in person."

Thane's expression soured. Kevin must have struck a nerve.

"So what are you?" Carly asked, her arms folded tightly across her chest. "A ghost?"

Thane shot her a filthy look. "I might as well be."

"What is your name?" Lupe asked. "Your full one, that is."

"Like I'm going to tell you, *whore.*"

It seemed Lupe wasn't going to fall for the distraction. "So Thane isn't your name?"

Thane rose and stood directly in front of her. "You know what I can't stand?" he asked. "People who can't mind their own business."

Lupe looked as though she'd been struck. She blinked wide eyes at the apparition. "No," she whispered.

Phil sensed that something was horribly wrong. "Lupe? What is it?"

Thane vanished. Phil made an instinctive turn, half expecting to see Thane rematerialized behind him, but they appeared to be alone.

He turned back to Lupe. "What's going on?"

She straightened her spine, looking resolute. "I'm not sure. But we need to go. Now."

---

BOBBY DIDN'T know what to expect when Jack fell silent. Was Vincent going to come back and escort them to wherever Jack and his boss were waiting, or would they come to them?

The Spirit told him nothing other than to be vigilant.

That, he could do.

"Don't drink the wine," Randy said as he cast a glance to Lily. "You'll want full control over your senses."

Bobby nodded. He wasn't about to eat or drink anything that he found in this place, anyway.

"We should go up front and wait," Bobby said, tension squeezing his chest.

They filed out of the room, Randy holding the wine bottle and Adrian leading Lily by the hand. Bobby found the gesture jarring. He hadn't thought it possible for Adrian to care for a child, especially a stranger.

Just as Bobby was about to plant his rear on one of the chairs in the living area, Adrian beckoned to him. Gritting his teeth, he went to her side just as she let go of Lily's hand.

"What?" His voice came out terse, and it made him feel ashamed. Acting like a moody toddler wouldn't improve their situation.

Adrian's blue eyes glistened with tears. "I know you don't want to, but I'd like to talk to you alone."

He glanced toward the entrance to the suite. "But—"

"We can talk in the back."

"It's okay," Randy said. For a fleeting second Bobby saw wistfulness in his expression. "I'll keep an eye on Lily. And on the door."

Bobby sighed—there was no getting out of this. "Okay," he said. "Let's go."

They returned to the bedroom where they'd found Lily and closed the door, then faced each other. Adrian dabbed a hand at her eye and cleared her throat. "I'm not asking for your forgiveness."

"Okay."

"There's no excusing what I did."

He wondered where she was going with this. "I know."

"I—I just wanted to see you. And apologize."

Bobby had no fitting response to that, so he said, "Where have you been all these years?"

Her expression tightened. "For a long time, I've been in Ann Arbor. After I left Eleanor I bounced from town to town for a while." She closed her eyes and let out a long breath. "Your siblings...they didn't receive me as well as you have."

He felt a twinge of pain at the mention of her other children. *What's done is done. Just let it go.*

Color rose in her cheeks as she continued. "Peter looks a lot like you, only his eyes are brown. His last name is Imbus. He wouldn't talk to me." She shivered. "Then in Michigan there's Kylee Turkelson and Jenna Lyman."

Bobby's heart ached. "How old are they?"

"Peter's eighteen, Kylee's sixteen, and Jenna's fourteen. None of them knew that the rest of you existed." Adrian leaned back into the wall and ran her hands over her face. "I married a man in Ann Arbor but we didn't have any children. He was very much against me coming to see all of you, so I left him in the middle of the night and set out on my own. I was afraid he might try to come after me, but he seems to have been the least of my worries. Do you think we'll get out of here alive?"

"I don't know," Bobby said with all honesty, remembering Caleb's warning to preserve his own life over everyone else's.

Adrian put a hand on her chin. "We could try to overtake whoever shows up. Your friend looks like he has some muscle."

Bobby pasted on a grim smirk. "We've got the wine bottle. Randy can crack someone over the head with it." Only after he'd spoken did he remember the camera and speaker in the ceiling. He silently cursed himself. No doubt someone was listening in to their plans and would come in with guns blazing.

He gestured for her to follow him out of the room. "Let's go into the bathroom," he whispered.

Adrian nodded.

Once inside the bathroom, Bobby checked the ceiling and saw no visible cameras, which didn't necessarily mean anything. "Okay," he said. "We'll each need to find something to use as a weapon. Randy can take the wine bottle, you can use that candle back in the bedroom, and I can use..." His gaze traveled to the ceramic soap dispenser perched at the back of the marble vanity.

Bobby picked it up and tested its weight in his hands. Could he throw it in such a way to knock someone out with it?

Adrian disappeared through the doorway and returned with the newly-snuffed jar candle, which was now unfurling wisps of smoke. "I hope this works."

*Me too.*

Bobby led the way back to the living room and recounted his plan to Randy, who nodded. "Lily," Randy said, "I need you to shut yourself in the bathroom right now. We don't want you to get hurt."

Lily appeared entirely unfazed by Randy's warning. "If I do, Vincent will save me."

"But Vincent isn't here right now. So will you please go back to the bathroom and close the door?"

Lily shrugged and headed down the suite's hallway. The bathroom door clicked shut.

"All right," Bobby said to his two companions. "I'll listen at the door. If I hear someone coming, Randy should be ready with the bottle raised and Adrian and I will move into the kitchen with the other stuff ready to throw at them. Sound good to you?"

"Not really," Randy said, "but right now I think it's the best we can do."

They moved into position. Adrian held the jar candle from her place in the kitchen and kept blowing on it to harden the wax, Randy picked up the wine bottle and held it like a cudgel beside the door, and Bobby pressed his ear up against it to listen for the approach of feet.

*Please help us,* he prayed. *Don't let anyone hurt us.*

A minute or two crept by. Bobby's pulse continued to quicken, and he prayed he wouldn't pass out.

From somewhere beyond the door, another door opened and closed, followed by the sound of many footfalls.

"They're coming," he whispered and dashed into the kitchenette beside Adrian.

An eternity passed before the knob turned and both a gray and a black aura reappeared with the same intensities as before.

Bobby tightened his grip on the soap dispenser, hoping his aim would be true.

The door swung open. Randy lunged forward and brought the bottle crashing down onto the head of the first person who entered. A slender figure crumpled to the floor like a dropped marionette.

It was Vincent.

Bobby had hoped it would be Jack.

Randy repositioned his hands on the neck of the unbroken bottle as voices moved toward the door.

A familiar dishwater blond head came through the opening. In unison, Bobby and Adrian launched their makeshift projectiles at Jack the moment he stepped over Vincent. The candle bounced off of Jack's shoulder, and Bobby's soap dispenser whizzed over Jack's head and hit Randy in the chest before cracking in half on the floor and oozing a puddle of orange soap onto the carpet.

Jack laughed. "See, Troy? We didn't have anything to worry about. They're harmless as flies."

A straw-haired man in a blazer stepped in behind him, and bringing up the rear was a seven-foot tall chunk of human muscle carrying a gun. The former scowled. "Harmless? Look what they did to Vincent."

Jack squatted down beside the healer and held his hand to Vincent's neck. "He's got a pulse. No worries."

"No worries? We need him awake for tonight's show."

Something about the word "show" made the hairs on Bobby's arms stand on end.

"About the show," Jack said. "I thought we could spice things up a bit and use these instead." He gestured toward Bobby and the others. Adrian threw him a look of alarm.

"Show?" she squeaked. "What kind of show?"

The man called Troy shook his head. "You've overstepped, Jack. They aren't the right type. I can't believe you even had them brought here."

"Then give them each their own room." Jack smiled.

Bobby's thoughts went to Lily sitting on the end of the bed in the tile-floored room, as calm as a lamb, waiting patiently for someone to cause her unspeakable harm.

"What exactly do you do here?" Bobby asked, his voice coming out in a growl.

"I have an idea," Jack said. "Why don't we show them the interview video?"

"How about not? This is wasting my time. There's a meeting in Corvallis I have to get to by nine." Troy pulled up his sleeve to check a watch.

Jack shrugged, pulled out a gun, and shot Troy point-blank in the head before the man could put up any kind of resistance. He crumpled to the floor beside Vincent, blood trickling from his temple.

Adrian let out a shriek, Randy blanched and flinched away, and Bobby stared dumbly at the dead man as ringing sounded in his ears.

The giant with the gun let out a grunt. "I wish someone had done that months ago. Twerp's been demanding way too much of us lately."

Jack held onto his own weapon, and at first Bobby feared he would shoot them next. Instead, he holstered it. "It's time things changed around here," he said, looking at each of them in turn. "If the three of you want to see tomorrow, you'll follow me out of here and let Farley bring up the rear. If you try anything, you'll end up like Troy."

Bobby remained rooted to the floor. "Where are we going?"

"To my new office. You should have stayed away, *Bobby*. If you'd left me alone, I might have done the same with you." Jack stepped out into the hallway. "Now come on."

Bobby's skin crawled at the implication of Jack's words. Thane had wanted Bobby to go after Jack. And because he'd listened to Thane, this had happened. Had Thane known this was where Bobby would end up?

They turned down another gray corridor lined with sconces and doors that probably led to more suites. Jack halted outside an unmarked door and keyed a code into a pad mounted out front.

Bobby wanted to ask what would happen to them now but knew it would be better to keep his mouth shut.

Inside the room was an ordinary desk and sitting area with a flat-screen television mounted on one wall. "I like Troy's offsite office better," Jack said as he sauntered to a shelf full of DVDs, "but this one will have to work for now. Lucky for you he kept copies of his videos here to pass the time." He pulled out one DVD, examined its label, and nodded.

"Why not just kill us?" Randy asked. "You didn't have any objection to that last week."

Jack moved toward a DVD player stacked on top of an old VCR on a low table beneath the television. "It's what Graham paid me to do. Now Graham's a vegetable, and I can do whatever I want."

"Which is what, exactly?"

Jack put the disc into the player. "You'll see."

# 33

LUPE GOT behind the wheel of Bobby's Nissan, and Carly clambered into the passenger seat while Phil and Kevin piled into the back. "Where are we going?" Carly asked as Lupe whipped the car backward out of Phil's driveway.

Lupe threw the car into forward gear and pushed the gas pedal to the floor. The fire of determination burned in her eyes. "A place Graham told me about."

"Can you please slow down?" Kevin wailed. "You're going to get us killed!"

Lupe eased off the gas a bit but maintained a steely grip on the steering wheel.

"It won't help things if we get pulled over," Phil commented from behind Carly as Lupe ran a stop sign. Carly could hear the fear in his voice, immensely grateful that her father wasn't there to chastise him.

"We won't get pulled over," Lupe said in a dark tone.

And she was right. Ten minutes later, they arrived in the parking lot at Arbor Villa Nursing Home. Without providing an explanation, Lupe strode to the front door with purpose in her step.

Carly turned to an equally-clueless Phil and shrugged.

Lupe was already talking to a woman sitting behind a reception desk when they came through the entrance into a lobby with butter-yellow walls and a tile floor that made Carly's shoes squeak. "Yes, he's here," the receptionist said to Lupe. "Are you a relative?"

*A relative?*

Just what was going on?

"No, but a—how do you say?—mutual friend is sick and we thought he would want to know. Can we see him?"

"Wait one moment, please." The woman disappeared through a doorway on the other side of the desk.

"So what's the big secret?" Carly asked, staring after her.

Lupe shook her head, her expression tight. "I don't want to say until I know for certain."

Just then the woman reappeared wearing a smile. "He says to come on back. He's in room 39. Do you need someone to show you the way?"

"No thank you."

Again, Lupe set off ahead of them. Dread gnawed at Carly's insides. Something terrible was going to happen. She just knew it.

Carly eyed the numbers above the doors on the right-hand side of the hallway. Twenty-one, twenty-three, twenty-five. Some of the doors they passed sat several inches ajar, and Carly caught glimpses of frail, stooped figures huddled beneath blankets in beds. A few of the nursing home residents had visitors, but the rest Carly saw were alone. Maybe those people's families weren't home from work yet. Or maybe they didn't have families at all and they were living out the remainder of their lives without loved ones to care for them.

As they passed room 35, Carly's surroundings vanished in a swirl of color and she found herself in a bustling place crowded with people and happy voices.

It took several moments for her to get her bearings. She was standing in front of a prize case containing stuffed animals, novelty basketballs, colorful change purses, and more.

"Dang it, I *still* don't have enough tickets to get anything good!" a familiar voice said beside her. "Come on, let's go play the UFO game."

Carly blinked. Standing at her side was her sister Jackie, who had a huge wad of pink tickets bunched up in her hand. "You go play the UFO game," Carly said. "I want to go try something else."

Carly's pulse raced with the realization that she was two Carly Jovingos at the same time: a twenty-one-year-old trapped inside a thirteen-year-old's body.

Together she and Jackie turned to go back to the gaming area. Several yards away a man and his young children stood in front of an arcade with flashing lights.

"Daddy, show me how to play!" a little girl in pigtails said, standing on her tiptoes to better see the arcade screen. A boy who must have been her younger brother stood beside her wearing a Spiderman shirt and yellow Crocs.

Their father appeared distracted as he dug around in the pockets of his cargo pants. "Hang on a minute, baby. Daddy needs to see how many tokens he has left."

"Aw, they're so cute," Jackie commented, then halted. "Hold on a sec. I want to ask Mom something."

*No. No. Don't do it.*

But there was no stopping it, because this was the past and the past could not be changed.

Jackie let out a funny little noise. Confused, the thirteen-year-old Carly made an about-face to see what the matter was, and her blood ran cold.

A thirtyish woman with dark hair was standing with a gun pointed at the man accompanying the children at the arcade, blind to everything else but them.

"Oh, no," Jackie whispered as a glint of determination shined in her eyes, so much like their father's. Then, at the same moment the gun fired, Jackie leapt in front of the woman and collapsed to the floor with the wad of tickets still clutched in her twitching hand.

The memory ended, and Carly was back in the hallway at the nursing home. Beside her, Kevin was sobbing, Lupe was trembling like she'd just faced down a monster, and Phil's face had gone deathly white.

They were still outside of room 35.

"What happened?" Carly whispered.

Phil cleared his throat, making a visible effort to regain his composure. "Something just made me relive the day Martin died."

Lupe's jaw quivered. "I betrayed Randy again."

"I saw the alley," Kevin said somewhat enigmatically, though Carly knew that whatever he saw had hurt him, too.

Lupe shook her head as if to clear it and glanced back up at the numbers over the doors. Room 39 was two doors down, and it sat open about an inch, seeming to beckon them. Together, they continued to the door and pushed it open.

*I must have no fear.*

Carly's first impression was one of comfort. Faint strains of classical music issued from an iPod dock sitting on a table beside an empty bed. The walls were painted lilac, and here and there copies of famous pieces of art hung on them, including Van Gogh's Starry Night.

The wide window at the end of the room opposite the door offered a view of a lush courtyard. A fortyish, auburn-haired man in an electric wheelchair sat in front of it facing away from them. "Come in and close the door," he said, his tone soft.

Phil hesitated, but he clicked the door into place anyway.

Then, ever so slowly, the wheelchair turned to face them.

The man's limbs appeared frail and immobile, his head leaned back at an odd angle, and Carly saw that he wore some kind of black earpiece like a Bluetooth.

It was Thane.

His eyes shot daggers at them.

Carly saw that his tongue was pierced when he next spoke. "You'll regret coming here."

"I don't understand," Phil said to Lupe, looking shaken. "How did you know where to find him?"

Lupe cleared her throat. "Graham told me he used to visit this nursing home to keep the residents company. He said he made a new friend here named Nate Bagdasarian. He told me Nate couldn't stand people who can't mind their own business."

Hadn't Bobby asked about a Nate while they drove to the house where he and Randy subsequently disappeared? "That's funny," Carly said, having trouble reconciling the man in the wheelchair with the Thane who'd been haunting her in recent days. "He can't stay out of ours."

Lupe continued, speaking to Thane this time. "Your full name is Nathaniel, isn't it? Nate and Thane are your nicknames."

Thane's lip curled. "I can paralyze you the same as I did to him."

Alarm bells went off in Carly's head. At one point Phil had mentioned that Graham had been so damaged by his aneurysm that he couldn't even speak. "We need to get out of here," she said, wanting to put as much ground between her and Thane as possible.

A spark of amusement lit up Thane's face. "I can hurt you from anywhere. It's part of my gift."

"And what exactly do you call this 'gift' of yours?" Phil asked, reaching for his gun.

A non-paralyzed version of Thane appeared two yards in front of the one in the wheelchair. "We call it the gift of Thought."

Kevin swayed where he stood. "I was right. God help us, I was right."

Phil pointed the gun at the real Thane's head. "Tell us where Randy and Bobby have gone."

Thane's apparition gave a little sniff. The actual Thane's eyes were scrunched shut in concentration. "Why should I do that?"

"Because if you don't, I'll kill you."

"And risk going to prison for murder? You'll probably get the chair for that, murdering a poor, innocent cripple who can't even lift a finger to defend himself."

Phil seemed to weigh this. Then he lowered the gun and put it back in the holster he hid under his shirt.

"That's better," the apparition said with a smile before vanishing.

The real Thane opened his eyes. "So there you have it. I can make you see whatever I want."

Even though every cell in her body urged her to make a beeline back out to the car, Carly boldly stepped forward. "Why do you do this to people? You have this ability. Why not use it to help people?"

"Because that's not what it's for." A glimmer of malice shined in Thane's eyes. "You want to know where your friends are? Have the fat one heal me, and I'll tell you."

Kevin blanched. "Me? No. I won't do that. Not for someone like you."

"I didn't think you would," Thane said. "What a pity. That's fine, though, because my father made me a promise. I'll walk again when my work here is done."

At the same moment Carly said, "Your father?" Phil said, "What work?"

Thane just laughed. "I didn't realize you'd be so eager to learn from me. Very well. Sit down, and I'll tell you a little story."

---

FARLEY—THE GUARD with the gun—ordered Bobby, Randy, and Adrian to take seats in front of the television. Then he moved to the door, blocking their only means of escape.

"Troy made everyone watch a video like this when screening them for membership in this little club," Jack explained as the DVD began to play. "It was to gauge their reactions and make sure they weren't undercover. If they were, they would have been killed."

Bobby's palms grew sweaty.

*Be strong,* the Spirit urged.

A bird's eye view of a bedroom like the one in which they'd found Lily appeared on the screen. A young girl—not Lily—sat on the edge of the bed, and a middle-aged woman came into view holding a knife. The woman swung the knife back and plunged it into the girl's arm, pinning it to the bed.

Bobby scrunched his eyes shut and received a prompt slap on the back of the head. "None of that," Jack said. "You're going to watch this."

Figuring it was best to obey since doing so might preserve his life, Bobby forced his eyes open and watched the woman tugging the knife out of the girl's arm. The girl shuddered as blood pooled on the bedclothes, but she put up little resistance.

The woman proceeded to stab the girl again, and again after that. Adrian retched, and Randy's face deepened to a shade of crimson.

Then, abruptly, the video clip ended.

"What are you trying to prove to us?" Bobby managed to say. The image of the suffering child was going to be forever branded in his mind like a burning scar.

"I'm not *proving* anything. I'm explaining what we do." Jack folded his hands together in front of him. "Carol, who you just saw in the video, always struggled to contain her violent tendencies. When my dear late boss founded this club, he offered Carol a way to release that energy. Nobody even has to die."

"Because Vincent heals them," Bobby said.

"Obviously. You might say this club provides a valuable service. It keeps the violent contained since they can let it all out here without repercussions."

Randy had murder in his eyes. "Has violent crime gone down since this *club* opened its doors?"

"I'm afraid I don't know, nor do I care. But I wasn't finished. Some members are simply voyeurs. That's what the shows are for. They sit in a theater and watch other members vent their energy onto our subjects."

"Who Vincent then heals," Randy said.

Bobby could no longer contain his growing anger. "This is torture you're talking about! Don't you even think about what those kids go through?" The girl in the suite acted like part of her was missing. Like she was an empty shell of a person without a life and without hope.

Jack shrugged. "Why should I care?"

Bobby wanted to hurt him. To throw something heavy at him, to put his hands around his neck and squeeze the life out of him.

To shut him in a room like Lily and have a creep come and put an end to him so he could never hurt another soul.

"So what happens now?" Bobby asked, struggling to maintain his composure. Since Jack had admitted what went on here, they would never be allowed to leave.

Jack paced casually back and forth as he spoke. "Troy and I didn't always see eye to eye. Not everyone here is satisfied with the services offered because they just aren't quite what some of the clients want." He turned to the guard. "Farley? Take them to one of the confinement rooms. I have some things to work on."

The giant guard gave a curt nod and stepped toward Bobby, who flew out of the chair before the guy could get hold of him.

As if he'd been planning it the whole time, Randy jumped up, grabbed his chair, and swung it hard at Farley, who let out a surprised "Oof!" when the chair slammed into him. Farley staggered to the side and pointed his gun at Randy, his finger moving toward the trigger.

"Don't kill them, you idiot!" Jack screeched as he reached for his own gun. "Our clients can pay us ten grand to do it themselves!"

Not trusting Farley to obey Jack's command, Bobby dropped to his stomach and crawled around to the other side of the desk, praying that he would find a phone, and fast.

In the front part of the room, Adrian was grunting and huffing as she joined the fray. Another gun fired, nearly making Bobby empty his bladder. Chips of plaster and dust drifted down from the ceiling, and Bobby sneezed.

Crouching behind the desk, Bobby yanked open drawers. Papers, binders, lewd magazines, handcuffs, a packet of Q-tips. *Nothing useful here.* He forced back the panic that threatened to overtake him, and as he did, a sense of peace trickled into its place like a soothing balm.

*Thanks*, he thought, feeling strangely detached from the fight occurring only yards away.

All at once he knew he had to reach his arm up above the top of the desk.

Without the slightest bit of worry, he blindly patted around on the smooth surface and felt a box.

He pulled it down and set it in his lap.

It was an old King Edward cigar box. Bobby lifted the lid and blinked.

Nestled inside were his and Randy's phones as well as the two knives they'd brought with them to the house behind St. Paul's, all of which must have been confiscated when he and Randy arrived.

Bobby dialed 911 on both cell phones and set them on the floor in the space beneath the desk. Hopefully the cops would be able to trace the origins of the calls, because Bobby didn't have the faintest idea where the Domus was.

Still maintaining his newfound inner peace, Bobby took a knife in each hand and stood up to assess the situation.

Randy had a struggling Jack in a headlock, and Farley had shoved Adrian up against a wall, his hands squeezing her neck.

Her hands had a death grip on the man's wrists as she tried to force him off of her.

She might as well have been fighting off a mountain.

Bobby's vision narrowed to a point. Feeling no fear, he passed Randy and Jack, snuck up behind Farley, and plunged both knives into his back, pulling them out again just as quickly.

The man let go of Adrian with an animal yell and flailed around as blood splattered on the floor.

Adrian rubbed at her neck, which showed signs of bruising.

Bobby ducked a blow from Farley and dashed to one side. He'd thought that stabbing Farley might put him out of action, but it only made him madder. Farley's eyes blazed, and he lunged at Bobby again with his hands out to choke him, too.

Just as Farley was onto him, Bobby eyed the man's abandoned gun lying on the floor—it seemed to have been left there just for him.

His stomach squirmed. He didn't have a problem with hurting someone, but killing them?

*No.*

Unfortunately, he could see no alternative. Farley was a big guy, and even though he was dripping blood everywhere, he might still have the strength to kill Bobby.

Caleb had warned Bobby to preserve his life at any cost.

Had Caleb known things would come to this?

Eyes stinging, Bobby ducked away from the massive guard, snatched the gun off the floor, and turned it on him.

He pulled the trigger the second Farley's hand touched his throat. Farley jerked backward, then sat down hard on the floor as blood oozed from the front of his muscle shirt.

Something began ringing far away inside Bobby's head. This was a terrible mistake. He shouldn't have done that. He could have just darted past the man and run out into the hallway to get away from him. Nobody should have had to die.

Bobby hunched over and threw up, but it had been so long since he'd eaten that the only thing that came out was acid.

Randy was still struggling with Jack, whose livid eyes bulged out of his head. "A little help here?"

Bobby felt cold inside. "I'm not going to shoot him, too."

"Why not?"

"I—I can't." Bobby was shaking so badly he almost couldn't get the words out.

"Then don't, but for the love of God, do *something*."

Jack managed to spit out a swear word that only made him appear juvenile.

"Wait a minute," Bobby said, remembering the handcuffs he'd seen in the desk. He retrieved them, and together he and Randy shoved Jack onto his stomach and wrenched his arms behind him. Bobby forced the cuffs onto Jack's wrists and clicked them into place.

Randy sat on his back, looking as satisfied as a cat who'd finally caught his prey.

"You realize," Jack said, his voice muffled, "that Farley and I aren't the only people who worked for Troy? As soon as you open that door you'll have to face the others."

"I'm not too concerned about them right now." Bobby thought of the phones still hidden under the desk. His gaze traveled to Adrian, who had backed into a corner and held her head in her hands. His chest lightened a little. He may not have felt any love for his mother—how could he, when he didn't even know her?—but he was glad to see that for the moment, she was okay.

She lifted her head, wearing a faint smile. "Thank you."

"Don't thank me yet." Bobby tried not to look at the body of the man he'd just killed. If he'd had any innocence left within him, it was surely gone now.

A languid whisper filled his head. *You asked for this,* Servant. *We wanted you to leave and never come back.*

On the floor, Jack snickered, and the shadowy aura in Bobby's mind fluttered as if laughing with him.

"It was *you*," Adrian said, looking at Jack. "I remember now. Someone must have drugged me and made me forget."

"What is it you remember?" Randy asked, still sitting on Jack's back with no apparent desire to stand up.

"That man." She pointed. "He said he was going to find me a job since the money I brought with me was running out."

"I hate to break it to you," Randy said, "but he lies."

Bobby decided to search the room for his shoes (if his phone had been in here, surely they'd be here, too) and came across a black wardrobe-sized cabinet behind the desk. He opened the doors and felt himself deflate.

The wardrobe contained five shelves. Each was heaped high with personal items—everything from plastic jewelry and brightly-colored hair accessories to wristwatches and shoes, most of which were quite small.

Bobby grabbed his gym shoes and Randy's Doc Martens off the top of the stack, then saw a pair of women's Nikes sitting with them and took them, too. "Here," he said. "I found our stuff."

As everyone put on their respective pairs of shoes, Jack let out a little sigh that made Bobby want to kick him in the head.

Ignoring him, Bobby went to the other side of the desk and retrieved the cell phones, then pocketed them. "Okay," he said as he returned to the front and plucked the bloody knives off the floor. "We should head out."

"If I stand up," Randy said, "this little punk is going to get up and try to stop us."

Bobby let out a huff of frustration. "Fine. Club him in the head with the gun."

"Gladly," Randy said, cutting off Jack's immediate objection. Bobby handed Randy the gun, and he smashed the butt of it into Jack's temple. Jack's body went slack.

A cruel little voice inside Bobby's mind hoped Jack was dead. Better Randy to kill him than Bobby, who couldn't stomach two kills in one lifetime, much less two in one day.

Randy stood and eyed the motionless form on the floor. "You have to wonder what made him this way."

"Who cares?" Bobby moved toward the door. "Let's get out of here."

Before heading out, Randy passed the gun to Adrian and took a knife for himself.

Bobby grabbed hold of the knob and pulled the door open as his heart tried to beat a hole through his chest. *Please warn me if someone's coming.*

He stepped out into the vacant hallway and was greeted by a writhing black aura that flooded his mind.

The face of Rory Wells started to appear in his thoughts, but with Bobby's sheer willpower he forced it away.

At the distant bend of the hallway, a rather dazed Vincent staggered around the corner holding his hand to his head. He caught sight of them and froze.

*Help him,* the Spirit said.

*Help him how?* Bobby thought wildly. He wasn't ready to drive out the demon that afflicted the healer. He was ready to find a way out of this awful place and book it back to Autumn Ridge. *Or are we in Autumn Ridge?*

Adrian lifted the gun and pointed it toward Vincent.

"No," Bobby said. "He's a victim, too. Just like the kids." Someone—the late Troy, perhaps—had found Vincent and took the opportunity to use his ability to start this abhorrent enterprise.

Maybe Vincent's gift resulted from his possession. If Vincent was freed from demon kind's grip on his soul, he might lose the ability to heal wounds.

Bobby set off toward Vincent at a fast clip. "Hey!" he said. "Vincent?"

Vincent halted and blinked; his eyes appearing out of focus. He probably had a concussion after his altercation with the wine bottle. "Yes?"

"I want you to help us, but first I want to help you."

A look of suspicion entered Vincent's eyes. "What is it you need?"

"First let's go back to Lily's room. Okay?"

Vincent nodded, then grimaced.

They followed him back to the suite.

The body of the man named Troy still lay on the floor in the suite's living area. Bobby skirted the still form without looking at it. *No wonder Vincent acted like he didn't want to come back here.*

Vincent led Bobby and Randy into a small study close to the back of the suite. Adrian left them to sit with Lily.

"Why do they have these suites?" Randy asked.

Vincent's eyes darted back and forth between them. "Some guests stay long term and conduct their business from here when they're not...you know."

"How much do they pay to be here?"

"I don't know. Troy doesn't—didn't—tell me that kind of thing. I'm sure it's a lot. Not that I ever see any of the money."

Bobby wanted to hurry, but at the moment his priority was to learn more about Vincent's past. "How did you end up here in the first place?"

"I—I worked with a man in Salem. He had a shop. People came to him for readings and advice. If they were sick or hurt, I'd heal them. Troy must have heard about me from someone I healed. Offered me a huge salary if I'd come with him. It's been years now, though. I haven't left this place since then. I couldn't even tell you how long it's been because I lost track of the time."

"You don't want to be here, then," Bobby said.

"I hate it here! I—" Vincent shuddered, and his voice was harder when he next spoke. "This is where he's meant to be. He has no other life but this."

Bobby knew that what was speaking now wasn't Vincent at all. "He used to have another life, though. He needs to have it back."

Randy closed his eyes and silently moved his lips in prayer.

A black tendril entered Bobby's thoughts. *You're not going to save him or any of the others. They're going to stay here and rot for all of eternity, forever and ever and ev—*

"No!" Bobby shouted, fighting off the negative thoughts. Remembering what the former Servants had coached him to say, he said, "In the name of the Father, and of the Son, and of the Holy Spirit, identify yourself."

Technically the first step was to get the entity to reveal its presence, but this one had done that on its own.

Vincent made no response. His eyes took on a faraway look as he gazed at a painting of fruit hanging on the study wall.

"Do it again," Randy whispered.

"Spirit!" Bobby shouted, feeling somewhat silly even though nothing about this situation should have been considered such. "In the n-name of the Father, and of the S-son, and of the Holy Spirit, I c-command you to state your name."

Vincent sat down in a chair and gave a nervous twitch. Then his face broke into a smile. "What's the matter with everyone?" he said with genuine surprise. "You act like there's something wrong with me."

Bobby's first instinct was to reply, but the advice of Roger Stilgoe, who had helped coach him in what to say in this very situation, flitted through his mind. *They will do everything in their power to distract you from your task,* Roger had said in between sips of coffee as the group sat out in Phil Mason's solarium the previous Sunday. *Sometimes they try to engage in meaningless banter. Don't give them the pleasure of responding. As the Servant, you'll*

*need to focus intensely on what you're doing. And it's never wrong to
ask the Spirit for help.*

Bobby could certainly use some of that help now. *Tell me
what to say.*

The unnerving smile pasted on Vincent's face warped into
something far more malicious. "I'm fine," he said before Bobby could
continue. "So can we leave now? I need to go see if Lily's okay."

"You will not distract me," Bobby said in a low voice as energy
grew within him. "In the name of the Holy Spirit who gives me
strength, I command you to state your name."

All at once a memory so old he'd forgotten it existed entered
his thoughts. He had been a boy of three playing in the sand pit
behind his house with one of the neighbor boys while Charlotte and
the other boy's mother sat in the shade at the picnic table. Bobby
could remember how the sand felt in his hands as he scooped fist-
fuls of it into a yellow pail. Life had been simple then. He knew
no struggles. He knew no grief. He had no conscious inkling that a
woman who'd carried him for nine months ran away.

With a pang of sorrow, Bobby realized that that boy and his
simple world of sand castles were gone forever.

Tears dampened his cheeks. "You will identify yourself to me,"
he said, fighting against the darkness in his mind. "In the name of
God, state your name."

Vincent's jaw clenched, and his eyes rolled back into his head.
"We are Sarcio."

Relief at this apparent success made Bobby want to let out
a cry of victory, but it would take days to completely drive out a
demon so he couldn't count this as a success just yet.

Bobby nodded. "Sarcio—in the name of God the Father, let
Vincent speak."

Tremors racked Vincent's body. "No, no, no, no, no—"

"Vincent?" Bobby said, ignoring the plaintive note in the
man's voice. "Can you hear me?"

A slight nod. Vincent brought his hands to his face. "Get them
out of me!"

"I will. I promise." And he meant it.

"They're trying to hurt me."

Bobby hoped this was only a psychological hurt and not a physical one. "Start praying for them to leave you alone," he said. "Because right now we need you to help us get out of this place."

"What's in it for me?"

"If you get us out, I'll make sure nobody uses you for their own gain ever again."

Vincent gazed longingly toward the door but seemed to weigh Bobby's words. "I tried to get out but they wouldn't let me leave the property. They want me to be trapped here forever."

"Nobody's going to be trapped here anymore. You just have to trust us and help us find a way out."

"Bobby really can help you," Randy said, his prayers evidently concluded for the time being. "So what's it going to be?"

Vincent bit his lip. "I can get you out. But it's going to be hard."

# 34

FRANKIE DID his best not to explode when he returned home. They were fools, the whole lot of them. To summon an evil entity for help? How could Bobby ever become a successful Servant if those on whom he relied went to such measures to save him?

*Father, keep your child Bobby safe from harm. Randy, too.* Though it wouldn't be as big a tragedy if Randy died saving Bobby. Sad, yes, because Frankie had grown fond of the most recent Servant, but Randy's death would no longer be a disaster.

Frankie still couldn't understand where Kevin came into play. The angel Caleb wanted Kevin with them instead of in Idaho. Could it be that Randy had needed Kevin to heal him so Randy would be there to give his life for Bobby? Or was Frankie's vision of Caleb nothing more than an ultra-realistic dream?

Frankie went into his and Janet's bedroom and found her sitting on the edge of the bed in tears.

What was going on? Had someone called her to say that Bobby and Randy were gone?

"What is it?" he asked, sitting down beside her.

"Oh, I'm just being silly," she said with a sniffle. "Don't mind me."

"Janet, tell me."

Janet cleared her throat. "I was thinking about how nice it would have been to have Kevin around the day that Jackie...you know."

Frankie nodded. His throat tightened. "I know."

"But he'd have had to *be* there when it happened. Because Phil could have done it, too." She shook her head. "See? I told you I was being silly. I need to just stop thinking and get on with things."

That was the kind of advice Frankie himself would have given, but Janet's words had taken root inside his head. (He didn't want to think about the fact that his own parenting methods had influenced Jackie's decision to take a bullet for a stranger.) If Kevin or Phil had been there to heal Jackie as the life faded from her body, everything would be different today. Carly might not have wanted to help the Servants. She might have gone to college in another state and never learned the Servants existed.

When Frankie left the bedroom, he went to his private study where he often meditated upon returning home from the financial planning firm where he worked, and shut himself inside. He stared at the two dozen Bibles placed on the shelves with care and then at the family photo taken when the girls were nine.

What kind of father was he to have left Carly when she was about to summon Thane? Had his own stubbornness left his only living daughter vulnerable and in harm's way?

Was his judgment finally slipping away from him?

Frankie made an abrupt turn and strode out of the study. He would go back to Phil's house and stop whatever was happening there, even if he was met with staunch objection from everyone else. He could not let his daughter be harmed.

———◆———

**FRANKIE RAPPED** on Phil's door for a full minute before deciding nobody was there, even though Phil's car and van occupied the driveway. Where could everyone have gone? Were they all out back and couldn't hear him knocking?

As he went around to the back of the house to peer in the solarium windows, his cell phone rang.

He answered it so quickly he almost dropped it. "Hello?"

"Dad?" Carly said in a whisper. "Can you hear me?"

Relief almost brought tears to his eyes. "Where are you?"

"I'm in the ladies' room at Arbor Villa Nursing Home. Dad, Thane is a man, and he lives here at the nursing home. Lupe connected the dots. Phil and Kevin are here with us."

Frankie blinked. Carly might as well have been speaking Japanese for all the sense her words made to him. "I don't understand."

"Thane told us he was paralyzed in a car accident twenty years ago, which is why he lives here. He says he has something called the gift of Thought. He can read people's minds and make them think they see him when he isn't really there."

A chill crept into Frankie's heart. "What else?"

"He says he won't tell us where Bobby and Randy are unless Kevin heals him. We thought you might have some advice."

For once Frankie was at a loss for words. If what Carly said was true, they were facing a human adversary far more powerful than any that the living Servants had ever encountered. "Do you know if he has any weaknesses?"

"The fact that he's paralyzed from the neck down might be considered something like that. He said he's the one who caused Graham's aneurysm. He could kill any of us at any time if he wants to."

"Why is he doing this?"

"He said he read Graham's mind when he first came to the nursing home to keep the residents company. That's how he learned about the Servants. Thane said that his 'father' will let him walk again if he destroys the Servants."

Frankie started to tremble. "If he could cause Graham to have an aneurysm, why didn't he just kill Randy the same way?" *Caleb*, he thought then. The angel Caleb, or one of his kin, must have been with Randy to protect him.

A long silence. "I don't know, Dad. But I don't know what to do. Thane could even be listening to us right now."

"And we still don't know where our Servant has gone."

"Right."

Frankie's mind raced to come up with a solution. Bobby and Randy had vanished from a house behind St. Paul's Church when Carly and Lupe sat across the street watching. They'd called the cops when they heard vicious barking, but the officer who came to the scene left without calling in any backup.

The truth came to him then. "That officer who showed up," Frankie said. "He came to that house, found Bobby and Randy, and must have put them in the back of his cruiser to take them away."

"But he was the only one in it," Carly said.

"They could have been on the floor behind the seats."

"They wouldn't just let some dirty cop tie them up. They would have been two against one."

"You heard dogs barking and found blood in the grass. They attacked our men, Carly. Bobby and Randy wouldn't have been able to put up much resistance if they were injured." Frankie's heart sank. Such a cop would not have taken Frankie's young successors to a hospital.

"You think they're dead," Carly said in a flat voice.

"Not necessarily." *Father, don't let it be so.*

"What are we going to do?"

"First you're going to get out of that nursing home."

"But Thane said he can hurt us from any—"

"I don't care what he said. Come home as soon as you can. Bring the rest of them with you."

---

"THERE'S A stairwell that the cleaning staff uses," Vincent explained as they left the study, the entity that tormented him temporarily kept at bay. "We might be able to get to the ground floor that way without anyone seeing us."

"Are there security cameras anywhere other than in the suites?" Bobby asked.

"I'm not sure. It's not my job to know that kind of thing."

"Okay. Once we get out of the stairwell, what will we see?"

"A long hallway. We can either take it to the reception area up front or out the back."

"And what will we find if we go either way?"

Vincent's sweaty forehead creased. "Giselle is in the front behind the reception counter. We might see some guests coming and going. Out back is a patio area. Deliveries come in that way."

Bobby was about to say that leaving through the rear of the building was a no-brainer, but Randy spoke first. "The man Jack shot—he was in charge here?"

Vincent nodded. "His name is Troy Hunkler. Was."

"Did he report to anyone?"

"No. The Domus was all his idea." He shook his head. "I'm glad he's dead."

"Is there anyone else in a higher-up position?"

"Farley is head of security."

"Farley's dead now, too," Bobby said, his stomach squirming. Once again the thought that he'd made a terrible error in killing the man flitted through his mind.

*Quit that,* he told himself. *You know he would have killed you if you hadn't stopped him.*

Another nagging voice jumped in to drown out the other: *You can't know that. You could have clubbed him in the head like Randy did with Jack.*

Hope flickered through Vincent's eyes at Bobby's announcement. "And Jack?"

"He's alive but unconscious," Randy said. "Who else do we have to worry about?"

"Assorted staff, but not many. A couple of the higher-ups went out of town and haven't come back yet. And then there's the guests."

"I'm going out the front," Randy said.

Bobby goggled at him. "Seriously?"

"Seriously. I have a plan. But first I have to get that nasty gun back from your mother."

RANDY HATED guns.

Back in the olden days he didn't have much of an opinion of them one way or the other, but getting shot tended to change one's perspective.

He tried not to recoil as he pointed the gun at Vincent's head. The possessed healer had allowed them to tie his hands together behind his back using strips they tore off the sheet in the suite's bedroom. Then Randy discovered how to remove the bullets from the weapon so he wouldn't accidentally kill the young man who so desperately needed Bobby's help.

"Turn left," Vincent whispered as they walked down the long, gray corridor.

Randy did, and they came to a metal door with a push bar.

"This is it."

Randy turned back toward Bobby and Adrian, the latter of whom wore a pasty-white look of fear. Bobby, however, seemed to have mustered some determination. He gripped a knife so tightly that the knuckles on his bony hand were turning white like his mother's face. "You ready?" Randy asked.

Bobby started to shake his head but then nodded. "Yeah. Let's go."

<hr>

CARLY SLIPPED back into Thane's room.

"Why the pierced tongue?" Phil was asking as she closed the door behind her.

"It's an experimental device that acts like a joystick," Thane said. "It helps me move my chair, among other things. I used to have to blow into a straw to get around, but when I heard about this technology, I volunteered myself to be part of the study to test it.

"I have no sensation below my neck," Thane went on, eyes blazing. "I can't even cough or sweat. Do you know how humiliating it is to live like this? I'm like an infant. My own family sent me to live here so they couldn't be bothered by my disability. I was their star child, and when I couldn't be that person anymore, they doted on my siblings instead."

"I'm sorry to hear that," Carly said as she came up beside Phil, who had his arms crossed. "Doesn't anyone ever visit you?"

"Graham did. He was such a kind old man." Thane smiled.

Carly's mind raced. Her father wanted them all to leave right now, but she couldn't keep thinking about that because Thane would see into her thoughts and know they were going to come up with a way to stop him.

Her stomach let out a whine. *I want to leave because I'm hungry,* she thought. *I'm so, so hungry and I have to leave now so I can get something to eat.*

Hopefully her thoughts of hunger would drown out all others. "Phil?" she said quietly. "I'm hungry."

Phil tilted his head her way. His face was ashen. "Do you want to leave?"

She nodded. "There's nothing else we can do. Our work here is done."

Lupe whipped her head around and gaped at her. "Have you lost your *mind*? He hasn't told us where Randy and Bobby have gone!"

"And he's not going to," Carly said. "So let's just go."

"I've been waiting for someone to say that since we got here," Kevin said, looking relieved.

They made to leave when Thane said, "They're not going to survive, you know. Their bones will rot in the middle of nowhere until kingdom come."

"Whose kingdom, Thane?" Phil said in a cold voice. "God's, or yours?"

Thane just scowled at them.

Phil slammed the door without looking back.

"Let's go over to my place," Carly said as they walked back to Bobby's car, trying to focus on food and only food. "We can eat supper there."

"How can you think of food at a time like this?" Lupe asked, sending her a bewildered look.

"Because I'm hungry and need to go clear my head."

"I think I know why she's thinking of food," Kevin said with a frown.

"Me too," said Phil.

———◆———

FRANKIE'S CHEST flooded with relief when a silver Nissan pulled into his driveway and spilled out its passengers. Carly took the lead and held the front door open while the others filed into the Jovingos' house.

"I've called Roger and my grandfather," Frankie explained to them once all were gathered in the front room. "They're not coming, but said they would be praying for Bobby and Randy." *And all of us, too.*

Janet stood in the archway to the kitchen with her arms folded tightly across her chest. "What are we going to do about this man?"

Nobody said a word. Carly and Lupe exchanged glances, then shrugged; Phil scratched at his temple; and Kevin stared hard at the floor.

The lack of a response seemed to deepen Janet's desperation. "We have to do something!" she said, giving Frankie a pleading look. "How do we know he isn't listening in right now?"

"We don't," Phil said.

Kevin lifted his head. "I have an idea."

"Yes?" Frankie said, praying that the healer would at least have something useful to say.

Kevin's Adam's apple bobbed up and down. "Let's kill him."

Frankie thought this would be met with immediate objection from all present in the room but to his surprise, nobody batted an eye. "Explain," he said.

"His sole purpose is to destroy us. I think I know why he didn't just kill Randy by fiddling around inside his brain. He wants to poison us from the inside out and ruin everything we've worked for. Phil told me Graham thought he killed more people than he really did. Thane must have done that so you'd all think Graham's heart had been in the wrong place the entire time. Then you'd start doubting each other, wondering if one of you was going to turn back on the things you'd believed in."

"But Graham really did start killing people," Phil said. "Do you think Thane forced him to do it?"

Kevin gave his head a slow shake. "I don't think so. The Graham I remember was kind. Helpful. Inquisitive. Thane must have seen Graham's weaknesses and used them against him. Graham's gift was Ministry, right? He wanted to help people. So due to Thane's influence, Graham decided to find sick people and end their suffering, not realizing that he was actually murdering them."

Phil's eyebrows knit together. "I suppose that makes sense in part. But Graham tortured Randy in that barn last week. Carved a bloody cross into his chest. You're saying Thane made Graham do those things?"

"Not necessarily. Thane must have pointed Graham in a certain direction and gave him a big push to keep him going that way. And the question is, how do we know that Thane hasn't done the same to us?"

Phil gave a wan smile. "Kevin, I wish you hadn't gone away all those years ago. We could have used a thinker like you."

Spots of scarlet formed on Kevin's cheeks. "Thanks."

Frankie cleared his throat. "You mentioned killing Thane."

"Right!" Kevin snapped back to attention. "I don't see any other way to deal with him. He isn't going to leave us alone now that we know about him."

Frankie pondered this. It was a sin to murder others. Would ending Thane's life be considered murder, or would it be considered self-defense since the man's death would protect the Servants from harm?

He didn't like the conclusion this line of thinking presented to him. "We cannot kill him," Frankie said, "unless we know specifically that he is going to kill someone else."

The room erupted with arguing voices.

"—but Randy—"

"How can you even—"

"There isn't any other way to stop him!"

Frankie held up a hand. "We are not a group of vigilantes. Killing Thane would make us no different than him."

"This stinks," Carly mused.

Lupe let out a strangled sniffle and pressed the palms of her hands into her eyes, shaking her head as if to dispel thoughts too terrible to utter. "What are we going to do?"

"Absolutely nothing," said a new voice that filled Frankie with dread. Thane's apparition, dressed in black slacks and a black button-down shirt with sleeves rolled up to the elbows, leaned calmly against the wall next to the fireplace. "It's been cute listening to you plot my demise."

Frankie drilled him with a stare. "What do you want?"

Thane's lips twisted into a wry smile. "I just thought I'd let you know that your *Servant* and his buddy are trapped in a lodge up in the mountains west of town. It's a place where little girls and boys are tortured for fun, which makes me wonder what they'll do to your men. If they ever get out of there—which I doubt—you probably won't even recognize them."

Before anyone could reply, Thane vanished.

# 35

RANDY AND Vincent emerged from the stairwell first. "You'll want to turn left again," Vincent said softly. "The hallway ends in the reception area."

Randy nodded to Bobby and Adrian and set off toward the front of the building, Bobby heading off in the opposite direction.

This had better work.

The hallway carpet—a swirling pattern of brown and forest green, unlike the gray and black of the floors below—muffled the sound of their footsteps. They passed a series of numbered doors that probably led to more suites. Daylight from up ahead spilled down the hallway toward them, providing Randy with a sense of hope. *Move toward the light, Randy. Just keep moving toward the light.*

Right before the hallway opened out into the reception area, one of the suite doors swung open and a gray-haired man in swim trunks and a t-shirt stepped into Randy's path. At first he gave Randy a blank stare but then his eyes widened. Without thinking, Randy swung the gun away from Vincent's head and pointed it at the other man. "Don't you even think about raising an alarm," Randy said in a cold voice.

The man slowly put his hands up, and a wry grin tugged at the corner of his mouth. "Is this a new act they didn't tell me about?"

Of course. If this was a place where people were injured for sport, the sight of someone with a gun wasn't going to raise many eyebrows.

Maybe getting out of here would be easier than Vincent claimed. Odd that the man didn't act concerned about Vincent, though. Perhaps Vincent stayed mostly behind the scenes so the guests wouldn't recognize him.

Randy lowered the gun and grinned. "I'm Randy. Adrian and I are new here, and this guy is showing us around. Isn't that right?"

"Uh-huh," Adrian squeaked from behind him as Vincent gave a wordless nod. With luck, the man wouldn't notice Vincent's bound wrists.

The man's grin broadened and he stuck out a hand. "Nice to meet you, Randy. I'm Tom. What's your deal?"

Randy tried to keep his composure. Tom wanted to know what sort of things Randy did to the victims trapped within the walls of this anti-sanctuary.

Jack's gloating face flitted through his mind. "I like to beat them until they're unconscious," he said.

Tom gave a nod of understanding. "You're one of the tamer ones, then." He glanced furtively up and down the hallway before lowering his voice. "There's one fella here who likes to drink their blood. He's almost bled a few of them dry. Kinda creepy if you ask me, but who am I to judge?" He laughed. "I'm off to the pool. See you around, I suppose."

"See you around."

When Tom passed them by, the three of them let out a collective sigh of relief.

"Nice guy, huh?" Randy whispered to his companions before continuing down the hallway. He prayed they'd run into no further delays. It was best they keep moving.

**FEAR KEPT** creeping back into Bobby's heart after he split off from the others according to plan, and he knew it was from the entities that dwelled within the healer and those who influenced Jack. They smothered his courage like a wet blanket over a fire.

It would take a lot more than simple fear to make him give up, though. The only thing that could stop him now was death.

As he darted down the corridor, he kept repeating one thought: *Please keep me calm. Please keep me calm.*

He froze in his tracks when he heard a man talking to Randy further down the corridor and held his breath to hear better, but the bend in the hallway as well as the hum of the air conditioning system made it hard to make out the words.

At least Bobby wasn't in a position where he could be seen.

The Spirit prodded at his thoughts. *Keep moving.*

He kept an eye out for the set of doors Vincent had described to him, then smiled when he saw the wooden double doors off to his right. Vincent said they led straight out the back of the building and that Bobby would have to take cover in the woods as quickly as possible before he was seen by any guests who might be lounging outside in the late afternoon sunshine.

He doubted he looked tough enough to pass for a member of their crowd. Not that he wanted to.

After checking behind him to make sure nobody was coming around the corner, Bobby shoved open the doors and stepped into a small vestibule where a set of metal doors with windows provided entry into the outside world. He pressed his face against the glass to get an eye for his surroundings. Part of a tennis court was visible way off to the left. Directly in front of him was a stone patio with a built-in wooden pavilion giving shelter to a table large enough to seat twelve or more guests.

It didn't seat anyone at the moment.

"Okay," he whispered. "Let's go."

The metal doors squeaked when he shoved through them. For several seconds he stood motionless on the patio, trying to get a sense of where exactly he was. Birds chirped in the evergreens surrounding the property but no man-made noises like traffic or low-flying aircraft met his ears.

Just where in the world was he?

Voices off to the left nearly made his heart go into orbit. Without thinking, Bobby dashed off the patio into the trees and took refuge behind the largest trunk he could find. Then he peered back the way he'd come to see what was going on.

A man and woman came from the direction of the tennis courts at the same moment a gray-haired man in swim trunks emerged from the building. A grayish aura poured off of the woman but not the men.

"—tonight's show—"

"Oh, I completely understand."

Their voices cut off when they entered through the doors Bobby had just exited. The man in trunks paid no attention to them and rounded the corner of the building, disappearing from view.

Bobby's timing couldn't have been better.

He studied the sky for a sense of direction. The sun hung low at one end of the sky, so if that was west, it must have been about five or six o'clock. But was it the same day he and Randy had gone to search for Adrian in the house behind St. Paul's, or had a much longer span of time passed?

The answer to that could wait.

Narrowing his gaze, he assessed the best route out of here. Vincent said the lane leading off the property was "long," but the healer didn't know how far it extended since he wasn't permitted to leave and hadn't seen it for himself. Bobby's plan was to stay far enough inside the trees while following the path of the gravel lane so that nobody driving on it would immediately catch sight of him.

Keeping beneath the trees, Bobby passed around the side of the Domus, which looked like a giant lodge made of cut logs. Someone flying over the Domus in a plane would probably assume it was some kind of mountain resort.

A hundred steps further and the front parking lot came into full view. A Trautmann Electric Company van sat in a spot near the door.

*Leave*, the Spirit urged.

But the sight of the van sparked something in his mind. If a key had been left inside, he might be able to drive it out of here with Randy, Adrian, and Vincent.

*Leave!*

"In a minute," Bobby whispered as he strode boldly toward the van. Maybe if he didn't act so furtive, nobody would suspect him of doing something wrong.

Bobby put a hand on the driver side door handle and pulled it open.

Angel, the Trautmann employee he had so recently interrogated, was slumped to the side behind the wheel.

Dead.

And he wasn't alone. An equally lifeless woman with curly black hair sat in the passenger seat. Both she and Angel appeared to have been shot execution-style in the temple.

He thought of Jack shooting the man in the suite. Looked like Graham's beloved grandson was trying to clean things up as he took over.

Recoiling from the scene, Bobby made to dash back to the trees when a window in the front of the Domus exploded into a thousand glimmering shards.

*Leave, leave, leave!*

*Okay, okay. I'm out of here.*

Gunfire had erupted inside the building. Bobby hunched over and scuttled back under the cover of the evergreens, then took up a post to see what would happen.

A woman inside was screaming, men were shouting, things were breaking, and Bobby was trembling so badly he thought he would break, too. He couldn't just let Randy and the others stay there to be killed. It was against everything he'd ever stood for.

*You need to let them go. Get out while you still have a chance.*

"But they'll die."

Caleb's words of warning returned to him then. Caleb said that he must preserve his own life.

*You have to think of the bigger picture.*

Images of a world at war filled his mind. If Bobby died saving his friends, the world would be without a Servant, causing another disruption like the one that happened more than a century ago.

*You need to leave NOW.*

Even though he didn't want to, Bobby tore his gaze away from the great log structure and stumbled off through the woods in search of civilization.

———————◆———————

**IT FELT** like he'd been walking for hours, though he knew a much shorter length of time had passed. Every so often Bobby mustered up his reserves of strength and jogged for a few hundred feet before his strength ebbed. His body wanted to pass out every time he exerted himself and he had to force himself to keep going even when his vision threatened to go gray.

He understood more than ever why Phil wanted him to get into shape. If he made it out of the woods here—literally—he would start up a regular exercise regimen. He would have to start out small, of course, and slowly work up his stamina.

Too many people's lives would depend on Bobby's strength.

At last, when long fingers of shadow stretched across the forest floor, the sound of an engine carried through the trees. He jerked his head up and caught a glimpse of movement traveling from right to left up ahead.

*A car!*

He broke into a run.

Sixty seconds later, the trees ended at the edge of a curving road and continued on the other side, where the ground stretched upward into a low mountain.

Twelve or so yards to his right, the gravel lane leading back to the Domus was blocked off by a nondescript white gate.

He returned his attention to the road. Right led uphill, and left led downward. The road made a gentle curve to the right half a mile downhill.

No vehicles were coming from either direction; the car he'd glimpsed a minute before now long gone.

*I can't give up hope.*

He would have to sit and wait for someone to pass by—hopefully someone completely unassociated with the Domus.

So he stood there. Waiting.

And waiting.

After ten or so minutes, it occurred to him that if the police were going to follow up with the 911 calls he had placed, they would have been here already. But he'd walked parallel to the lane as he made toward the road. No emergency vehicles had entered the premises.

That meant no emergency vehicles were coming.

And with all that gunfire...

Tears filled his eyes. Randy had removed the bullets from the gun he was going to point at Vincent so he wouldn't accidentally kill him. If someone had started firing at him, he had no way to defend himself.

*God, help them.*

Though at this point it was likely they were beyond any kind of physical help.

He pulled out his phone anyway and made to dial 911 again but discovered that the phone had no reception.

Maybe there hadn't been any to begin with and the calls hadn't even made it through.

He pocketed the phone.

Off in the distance, the whine of an engine approaching from the right echoed off the mountainside and through the trees.

Bobby waved his arms like a madman.

A red pickup truck roared around the bend and was gone before Bobby's brain could properly register the fact that the driver gave no indication of having seen him.

The silence of nature settled around him once more, but only briefly. Another distant whine carried through the trees from the same direction. Knowing the action he was about to take would seem drastic, Bobby stepped out onto the pavement and waved his arms again.

A logging truck heaped high with felled tree trunks barreled around the curve toward him. "Help!" he shouted, stepping off the pavement. "Please help me!"

Brakes squealed and the truck slowed, coming to a stop on the gravel shoulder a quarter of a mile downhill. A pair of hazard lights blinked on.

Bobby checked for oncoming traffic and jogged toward the truck, praying with every cell of his being that the driver wasn't one of *them*.

The driver sported a short Mohawk and wore a muscle shirt that revealed sleeve tattoos on his arms. He rolled the window down and peered at Bobby in trepidation. "You all right, man?"

"No," Bobby panted, rubbing a stitch in his side. "That lane back there—there's people trapped. Prisoners. I just got out."

The driver's eyes grew round. "You're serious?"

"Yeah, and my phone won't work. Is there a way you can radio in to someone to get help?"

The driver blinked. "I don't have a radio like that in here. Get inside and let's talk before someone comes along and creams you."

Bobby obeyed, climbing into the cab's passenger seat. A plastic bobblehead skull sat on the dash.

"My name's Dusty," the driver said.

"And I'm Bobby. Do you think you can remember where that lane is?"

"Sure, man. I pass it every day. We've been working about ten miles back. I was taking this load to the mill and was about to call it a day when you showed up."

"Where's the nearest town? I need to call the cops."

Dusty's brow scrunched. "There's a little place at the bottom of the mountain called Peabody. There's a gas station that might let you use their phone."

"How much farther?"

"Maybe fifteen minutes?"

"Take me there. Please."

"No problem, man." Dusty let off the brake and pulled back onto the road, throwing a worried look into the left mirror. "There's really people trapped back there?"

"Unfortunately. That's why we've got to hurry."

# 36

ADRIAN'S HEART occupied her throat when she, Randy, and Vincent arrived in the high-ceilinged reception area that looked, for all intents and purposes, like the lobby of any ordinary hotel. A skinny blonde twenty-something sat behind the counter chewing gum and reading a romance novel when their presence caught her attention.

At first the girl gave them a blank stare, but then horror filled her eyes as she slowly laid the book down. "What are you *doing*?"

Bobby's dark-haired friend jammed the barrel of the gun into Vincent's temple. Adrian tightened her grip on the knife Randy lent her, hoping she wouldn't have to use it.

"You're going to let us out of here," Randy said, ignoring the girl's question. "If you don't, I'll blow a hole in this loser's head."

Vincent winced. The blonde, who must have been the Giselle whom Vincent referred to in recent minutes, looked uncertain. "What's he to me?" she asked innocently, already recovered from her initial shock.

"He's the reason you're employed, right?"

Giselle gave a little sniff. She leaned over and pushed an intercom button with a delicate white finger. "Farley? Jack? Get up here now!"

Adrian edged her way closer to the set of front doors, hoping to make a sudden run for it.

Giselle bent below the top of the counter, and when she straightened, what looked like a machine gun had appeared in her hands.

Pure instinct dropped Adrian to the floor. The windows in the front of the building blew out in a spray of glass as the weapon chattered away, leaving Adrian momentarily deaf. Her limbs felt frozen like she'd seen snake-haired Medusa and turned to stone.

Then all went silent. The sound of her ragged breaths was as loud as a gale-force wind in her ears.

Behind the counter, Giselle was swearing at her weapon, which must have run out of ammunition.

Running footsteps came down both hallways leading to the reception area. *We're dead*, Adrian thought, and scrunched her eyes shut.

A sudden commotion of voices made her jump.

"What's going *on* out here?" A man, elderly by the sound of it.

"*God*, Giselle, why'd you blow out the windows?" This, from a woman.

Giselle panted her reply. "Intruders were trying to run off with Vincent! Look on the floor. I think I hit one of 'em."

Adrian's heart skipped a beat as footsteps approached where she lay. Bobby's friend couldn't be dead. They were going to get out of this place together and run for help.

Her mind raced. If Randy really was dead beside her, there was no use in sticking around. She would have to get out on her own, call for help, and send the cavalry back here to rescue the children—because she couldn't make the assumption that Bobby would escape unscathed.

She cracked open one eyelid. Three feet away from her, Randy trembled as blood seeped down his left arm. Vincent's glassy eyes stared up at the ceiling. His left arm had shoved up against Randy's right one when they fell, and as Adrian watched, the flow of blood from Randy's other arm ceased and a bullet popped out of the wound and rolled to a stop on the floor.

So Vincent had the magical ability to heal others, but not himself.

A woman in a black one-piece bathing suit came up to Adrian's side. She looked like Carol, the woman from the video they'd all been forced to watch down in the office. "You missed this one," she said, wearing a smirk.

Adrian launched herself to her feet, drew back a bony fist, and planted it squarely in the woman's astonished face before she could put up a hand to block the attack. Carol staggered backward as blood flowed from her nose.

Adrian hadn't felt so satisfied in ages. She bent down, snatched up the knife she'd dropped, and poised herself to spring.

Carol just laughed as she wiped away the blood with the back of one hand. The three other people who had entered the room at the sound of gunfire stood off to the side looking amused. And why wouldn't they? This sort thrived on violence as if it were food.

Giselle remained behind the counter with her arms folded tightly across her chest. Her face was troubled. Poor dear was probably worried about why poor, dead Farley wasn't showing up to take care of those who had survived.

Suddenly Adrian no longer felt afraid. Carol wasn't holding a weapon—neither were the other new arrivals.

"If you don't let me out of here," she breathed, "I'll slit your throat."

Carol smirked again. The sight of more blood running from her nose turned Adrian's stomach. "You think you have it in you?"

*I do now.* Adrian lunged at her with the blade pointing outward.

"Stop!" a voice said from behind her.

She halted and gave her head a slight turn.

Randy was standing up, his face white. The skin where a bullet had so recently penetrated his arm looked smooth and new. "Vincent's dead," he said. "You do know who that is, right?"

Two of the new arrivals, Carol included, nodded while the others simply looked puzzled.

"And do you know *why* he's dead?"

Silence.

He pointed a shaking finger at Giselle. "Because this woman thought she could save him by shooting at us. She's clearly never used a weapon like that in her life. By trying to save him, she murdered him." Randy paused. "Your Domus no longer has a healer. I'm afraid you're out of business."

One of the guests fidgeted and glanced down at her feet.

Randy continued. "You're all going to end up behind bars now that word's getting out about what went on here."

The Domus guests swiveled their heads toward Giselle, who took an involuntary step in reverse. She clasped her hands together in a pleading gesture. "It—it was an accident," she said lamely. "Farley told me to use the gun in case of emergency." Her face twisted into an unexpected grin. "But some of them are out looking for someone else like Vincent. Where there's one, there's another, as they say. So we won't be 'out of business' for long."

"Are you sure?" Randy said, eyebrows raised.

"Why wouldn't I be?"

"Because you don't know what happened downstairs."

Carol snickered as she wiped more blood off her face. "Giselle, he's just stalling. Ignore him."

But it seemed Giselle was going to ignore her, instead. "Enlighten me," she said to Randy.

Randy put a finger on his chin and pretended to think. "I don't know, maybe I shouldn't. You probably wouldn't believe me if I did."

"Just what did you do?"

"It was Jack, not us. He killed Troy. I think he wants to take this place over for himself."

A flush of excitement warmed Giselle's pale cheeks. "Jack killed Troy?"

"Did you want him to?" Adrian saw Randy's confidence waver for a moment.

Giselle didn't answer. "Farley is going to be thrilled!"

"About Farley," Randy said, a note of genuine sorrow entering his voice. "We had to kill him."

Adrian was grateful he didn't mention anything about Bobby. As far as she knew, three of the Domus people who knew about Bobby were dead and the fourth was trussed up in the basement office, hopefully still out cold.

The guests glared at Randy. Uncertainty had filled Giselle's eyes once more. Her finger hovered near the intercom button but she must have realized there wasn't anyone else for her to contact because she drew it back. "Is Jack...?" she said, leaving the sentence unfinished.

"I don't know," Randy said. "He took an awfully hard hit on the head. For all I know, the blow killed him."

"Where is he?" Giselle screeched, her eyes shooting daggers at Randy.

"Troy's office. We—"

Giselle darted out from behind the counter and ran wailing down the hallway in a pair of black stilettos. "Oh, please no, not Jack..."

Randy cleared his throat. "Adrian?"

"Yes?"

"I need you to help me."

The guests who'd arrived to observe the commotion hadn't moved a muscle in the past sixty seconds. One of them, a man in his seventies wearing a crisp black suit, had coal-black eyes that bored into Adrian as if he were entertaining sick fantasies of which she was the subject.

The guests claiming no knowledge of Vincent looked afraid.

"What do you need me to do?" Adrian asked in a low voice.

"Go behind the counter and tell me what you see."

Keeping an eye on the others in case one made a move to stop her, Adrian hurried past Vincent's lifeless form and passed through an opening between the counter and the wall. Half a dozen drawers had been built into the counter. Adrian yanked them open one by one and recited the contents to Randy as she rummaged through them. "Binders, a stapler, some kind of log book, something that looks like pepper spray—"

"Give it to me and drop to the floor. And the knife, too."

Adrian fumbled with the small black device and passed it over the top of the counter into Randy's hand along with the knife.

Two of the guests had already started running toward the shattered windows.

Randy ran after them with the pepper spray in hand. Adrian wouldn't have to duck for cover after all.

Adrian stared at the two who remained—Carol and the old man. "Are you just going to stand there, or are you going to run like cowards, too?"

Enraged, the old man lunged at her over the top of the counter. Adrian picked up a metal waste can and in one fluid movement brought it down on his head. Tissues and empty Sun Chips bags scattered across the countertop and floor.

The man swore at her and backed off, but now Carol was coming at her, fists curled.

Adrian prayed that the commotion wouldn't draw the attention of anyone else who might be on the premises.

The can crashed down onto Carol's head with a glorious clang. The old man was sitting on the floor a few feet away rocking back and forth gripping his bleeding forehead, the skin of which appeared to have split open upon impact.

Righteous rage seemed to have turned Adrian into Super Woman. "This is for Monique!" she screamed, bashing Carol again and again until she staggered away in a daze. These people were pathetic. They could torture children for fun but couldn't even put up a decent fight to defend themselves.

Her eyes stung. Outside the broken windows, Randy blasted the other women with the pepper spray and dashed out of sight, and the wind wafted some of it into the building. From Adrian's vantage point she could see that the women had their hands clapped over their eyes as they staggered blindly out of sight.

Now if only there was a way to tie them all up before they recovered.

Trying to keep at least part of her attention on the injured guests, Adrian began another frantic search behind the counter but found nothing that could be used as bindings. "Randy?" she coughed. "Can you hear me?"

No reply came. Maybe Randy had run for the road in order to flag down a passing vehicle.

Carol moaned from where she sat hunched over on the floor. "Oh, my *head*..."

Adrian wanted to kick her. Again the thought that Adrian was really no worse than these people flitted through her head but she quickly batted it away. No, she wasn't like these people. Something important set her apart from them: regret.

Her chest lightened. *I regret what I did to my children. That makes me the better person.*

Adrian strode around to the front of the counter gripping the knife and came to stand between Carol and the old man. "If either of you try to get up, I'll kill you," she said, unsure if she was bluffing or telling the truth. Then, "Randy?"

The sound of rapidly approaching footsteps made Adrian's heart skip a beat. To her relief, Randy clambered through a now-empty window frame with a tangle of what looked like shredded netting piled in his arms.

"Tom and one of the women got away," he explained, panting, as he dumped the netting on the floor. "I tied the other one to one of the chairs by the swimming pool." He refocused his attention on Carol. "It's best if you give me your full cooperation while I tie you up. I don't want to have to hurt you."

Carol glowered at him.

"Adrian, give me a hand here and make sure she doesn't try anything."

Adrian held the woman's arms in place while Randy tied the strips of cut netting around her wrists. Randy clapped her on the shoulder when he finished. "That wasn't so bad now, was it?"

"Go to hell."

Randy's face grew solemn as he regarded her. "I've already been there." Randy proceeded to tie the old man who, due to his injury, was far less coherent.

He stood up and brushed his hands together when he was finished. "We're lucky they have tennis courts out there. I cut up the nets." Randy's gaze traveled to Vincent's motionless form, and his hazel eyes filled with tears. "I wish we could have saved him."

Adrian's throat felt too choked with emotion for her to speak so she just nodded. The young man did not look peaceful in death, but frightened as if he saw something unbearable the split second before he passed.

Adrian shivered. "We should go look for the children."

"Good idea."

# 37

AS THEY backtracked along the hallway that he, Adrian, and Vincent had so recently passed through, Randy prayed that Jack would remain unconscious and that Giselle wouldn't return with another weapon to use on them. Randy counted himself lucky that his physical contact with the dying Vincent had healed the new bullet wound in his arm, but now that the healer was dead, Randy would have to be extra vigilant.

Or was he lucky that Vincent had healed him? Ever since awakening in the storage room down below, he'd felt drained. When Kevin healed him in Phil's living room, it was as if an infusion of energy had entered his veins. If Vincent's gift had been demonic, the possibility existed that something had been removed from him instead.

Holding Lupe's face in his mind, Randy tried to conjure a thought in Spanish and ran into a brick wall. He tried French, Thai, Afrikaans, Farsi, Italian, Galician, Mirandese, German, Walloon, Korean, and a dozen more both common and obscure.

Nothing. The sea of languages he could summon without conscious thought had run dry.

Not that only knowing English would bring him harm, but Bobby had been healed by Vincent, too. If Bobby's gift of Prophecy had been obliterated by Vincent's gift, was there a way for him to get it back?

They stopped at the first guest room door. Randy banged on it with a fist. "Anybody in there?"

No reply.

He tried the knob and the door swung open. Apparently those in charge of the Domus had seen no reason for the guest rooms to be locked as they were in ordinary hotels. The room that lay beyond wasn't nearly as lavish as the suite in the basement: a four-poster bed, dresser, and small bathroom were all it offered for guests who might stay here. This type of room was for the "voyeurs," then—the ones who came only to watch the children suffer.

They went to the next room and the next, finding luggage in the one where Tom had emerged, but no children.

All rooms on the first floor—even a kitchen and communal dining area that had to have seated at least fifty people—revealed the same.

They ascended the stairs to the second floor. Randy swept his gaze across a large rec room stocked with pool tables, ping-pong tables, one blackjack table, a dartboard, and a television. Sprawled on the floor between the pool tables was a middle-aged man dead from a bullet wound to the head. Feet away a woman curled into fetal position lay in a pool of congealing blood. The smell of it made Randy ill.

A janitor's cart and vacuum sat near the bodies. The vacuum was still plugged in.

"Do you think Jack did this?" Adrian whispered, looking from the dead woman to the dead man.

"I don't know. He may have wanted to clean up a bit before killing his boss."

"Why did he leave some of the others alive, then?"

"I don't know. Listen." Randy placed his hands on the slender woman's shoulders, hoping she would remain calm enough to keep her head. "I had the misfortune of running into Jack last week. There isn't time to explain all of it right now, but he loves to be in control. The fact that he's wiped out his boss and some of the other employees doesn't surprise me. Control is his weakness."

"He tried to control me," Adrian said, eyes downcast. "And I was too foolish to realize it. He acted like he cared about me. I should have known it was too good to be true." She sniffled. "I wanted to make a good impression on Bobby, and Jack—he called himself John—said he could help me do that."

"He did it to get back at Bobby for something that happened last week. You must have told him Bobby's name."

Adrian blanched. "That's why I was kidnapped?"

"Yes." Adrian opened her mouth to object, but Randy held up a finger. "But because of that, we found out about this place. So don't beat yourself up over it. Okay?"

"Okay." She smiled, but hesitantly.

They returned to the stairwell and commenced their descent to the ground floor. Randy found himself wishing he had Bobby's ability because he had no way of knowing how many Domus employees Jack had spared. One could be creeping up the stairwell toward them that very minute, quiet as a cat.

Randy sent up a prayer of thanks that Lupe didn't know what kind of situation he'd gotten himself into. She would be worrying herself to the point of illness right now (especially since the chaos of last week was still a fresh wound in their minds), but at least she could always entertain the possibility that Randy was safe wherever he was and that the reason she couldn't reach him was because his phone was dead.

"They're all in the basement, aren't they?" Adrian asked as they passed the set of doors leading to the first floor and continued downward past them.

"Looks like it."

"You don't think Jack...?" Adrian left the question unfinished.

Randy cleared his throat. "Lily was alive, right? So I don't see why the others won't be, too."

---

BOBBY THOUGHT Dusty was taking the curves too fast in the logging truck, but his nerves were wound too tightly for him to object. Ten hair-raising minutes later—not the fifteen that Dusty had estimated—the road leveled out and the trees gave way to small patches of farmland. A faded green sign on the side of the road read "Peabody," the town of which consisted of about four houses and the aforementioned gas station that sat off to the left.

"This is it." Dusty pulled onto the opposite shoulder of the road. "Truck's too big to fit in their lot. I'll wait here if you need me to."

"Thanks." Bobby scrambled out of the cab and crossed the road. A lone car sat at the pumps while an attendant filled the tank.

When he burst through the station's glass doors, Bobby eyed a wall-mounted phone behind the counter. He yanked it out of the cradle and dialed 911, certain he'd just broken the record for emergency calls made by a single person in one month.

An operator squawked the customary greeting in his ear. "This is 911. What is your emergency?"

---

THEY WERE in the basement.

Again.

Adrian could hear faint male voices coming from behind a mahogany door as soon as they exited the stairwell into the top-most level of the basement.

Gripping the knife with one hand, Randy held a finger to his lips.

He pushed open the door.

Two men Adrian hadn't seen before—one with a ponytail and the other bald—stood just inside, apparently deep in discussion. Each wore a gray t-shirt and nondescript gray slacks. Their expressions morphed into ones of astonishment when they laid eyes on

Adrian and Randy, but what was more astonishing was the number of children, teenagers, and twenty-somethings gathered in the large room behind them. Rows of cots lined the walls, all covered in identical gray pillows and blankets.

Several of the children—and even some of the ones well into their twenties—were sucking their thumbs as if they had the mental capacity of infants. The sight of them made Adrian want to cry, but she held back so she wouldn't show weakness to the men who stood between her and the children.

"Put your hands up," Randy ordered the men, stepping forward with his knife pointed outward.

Ponytail Man let out a high-pitched laugh that betrayed his nervousness at their unexpected arrival. "I thought people were only supposed to say that if they had a gun."

Randy's voice took on a dark tone that sent goosebumps racing down Adrian's arms. "Knives don't run out of ammo."

Bald Man snorted. "Get back to your suite, buddy. Guests aren't allowed in here."

Adrian and Randy exchanged glances. "We don't have a suite," she said. "At least not by choice."

Ponytail Man gave her a suspicious look.

"We were kidnapped," Adrian explained. She tensed her muscles, ready to spring the moment the men made a move toward her, but both remained still.

Ponytail Man's bald counterpart stared at them long and hard. Then he glanced back at the children. "So let me get this straight," he said, lowering his voice. "You were brought here against your will, and instead of doing the smart thing and finding a way out, you came in *here*?"

"We're not the only prisoners in this building," Randy said, "and I intend to free the rest of them. Troy and Farley are dead, by the way, so if you're hoping for backup, you're not going to get any."

Instead of the anger that Adrian expected, the bald man looked hopeful. "Joe, go get Lily out of her suite," he said to his comrade.

Joe's eyes grew round. "Are you crazy? How do we know this isn't some trap Troy put these people up to?"

"I really don't think—"

"I won't do it! Not until I have proof they're dead."

"If you go get Lily," Randy said, "you'll see part of the proof with your own eyes."

"I wish I could believe you." Joe ran his trembling hands over his face. "Of all the times I thought I might be able to outsmart them and get away from here just to remain stuck in the end..."

The bald man cleared his throat. "Troy wouldn't hire guests to test us. Now are you going to get Lily or will I have to go do it myself?"

Joe hung his head. "Fine. I'll get her. But if I find out it's all a lie, I'll...I'll...oh, God help me." He hurried past Adrian and Randy and disappeared into the hallway. Randy, eyes narrowed, made no move to stop him.

"How do we know he isn't going to come back with a gun?" Adrian asked him. "He obviously doesn't trust us."

"Because we aren't allowed to have them," the bald man said.

Some of the younger children had taken notice of Adrian and crept up to her with the timidity of deer. The older ones remained in the back, sitting on cots or on the floor, waiting to be taken to a suite while wearing expressions as blank as unpainted pieces of canvas.

Lily, though naïve, did not appear to be as damaged as some of these other children.

Perhaps she hadn't been here as long.

Adrian returned her attention to the bald man. "So you're going to help us get out?"

He locked his brown-eyed gaze onto hers. "Yes."

———◆———

JACK CAME to feeling nauseated. His face pressed into carpet, and he could see nothing but shadows and a horizontal yellow line where light peeked out from under a closed door.

Where in the world was he? Certainly not at home, since he couldn't hear Chloe arguing with their mother like she did on a constant basis. So if he wasn't at home, then...

He blinked, groaned, and rolled onto his side. It felt like his wrists were fastened together with handcuffs.

Handcuffs...

*You're in Troy Hunkler's Domus office*, something whispered to him. *And now that you've killed him, it's your office.*

His office. That was right. It was coming back now in bits and pieces. He'd had it with Troy. He'd had it with a lot of people. Killing Angel and Wanda out in the van had made him nervous but had ultimately satisfied him. Wanda had acted excited when he told her about the Domus on the drive over but he couldn't let her live knowing about it because she might blab it to someone else. And Angel was expendable.

All of them were expendable.

Except for Vincent, unless Orin and Theo found someone else like him soon.

Upon arriving, Jack had gone around to the back of the lodge, entered through the rear to avoid immediate detection, and went to the top floor to search for more expendables. He'd blown away two members of the cleaning-slash-kitchen staff and relished the sensation of control that ending their lives had given him. It was more powerful by far than the feeling he'd had when he made the neighbor boy eat dirt all those years ago. It was even more powerful than when he'd taunted that holy man Bellison in the barn.

It was as if he'd become invincible.

After killing the cleaning staff, Jack stopped in the reception area to flirt with Giselle and then met up with Farley in the guard's basement office, where dozens of screens monitored suites and Domus property. He'd told Farley what he did upstairs and recounted the rest of his plan to him. Farley had then summoned Troy, who had stopped by the Domus on one of his periodic checks to see if things were running smoothly, and then, with Vincent, they all went down to meet the Roland dweeb and his ilk.

Jack had almost been ecstatic when he shot Troy. This was the ultimate control he'd desired deep down where he hadn't even known it. Hunkler Enterprises would become Willard Enterprises, and Jack would never have to listen to anyone again. Instead, they would listen to him. Could life be more perfect?

Jack wasn't feeling so ecstatic now, though. Bobby, Randy, and the dark-haired bimbo he'd had kidnapped off the sidewalk would run into trouble trying to get out of the building, but who was going to come looking for *him*? Why hadn't he thought about that before? Had he been too blinded by his recent accomplishments to even consider the fact that too many employees might not be left alive to come free him?

His fears proved unfounded when the office door swung open and flooded the room with light, revealing Farley's cooling corpse lying feet away from him.

"Jack!" squealed Giselle. "Are you okay?" The overhead light came on, causing Jack to squint. "Oh my God, *Farley...*"

"Do I look okay?" he spat. "Go open the top left drawer of the desk. The handcuff key should be in there."

She hurried around to open the desk. Jack blinked again. Randy had clobbered him so hard he was surprised his skull wasn't fractured. If Jack found the punk, he would put an end to him once and for all. No more taunting. No more gloating. Just one swift gunshot to the temple and that would be it.

"I found it!" Warm hands touched his wrists, and the cuffs popped open. "I can't believe they did this to you. How's your head?"

Jack didn't answer. Very carefully, he pulled himself to his feet and tried not to feel disoriented. "Did they get out?"

"You mean the shaggy-haired guy and the woman?"

Interesting how she made no mention of Bobby. Maybe the little pipsqueak freaked out after shooting Farley and hid in some cranny because he was too chicken to encounter any more of Troy's employees. "That would be some of them."

"I don't know if they got out or not!" Tears glistened in Giselle's blonde eyelashes. "Jack, I did a terrible thing. I accidentally killed Vincent."

At first Jack just stared at her. Vincent. Killed. Accidentally. "Would you mind telling me," he said, "how you can *accidentally* kill someone so important to your employment status?" He'd actually planned on keeping Giselle alive since she knew so much about each client and his or her needs. Yet she had done this stupid thing. This *moronic* thing that effectively brought an end to half of Jack's plans. Because how likely was it for another healer like Vincent to be found?

Giselle made an unsuccessful attempt at blinking away her tears. "The guy held a gun to Vincent's head. He said he was going to kill Vincent so I picked up the gun I keep under the counter and started shooting. I—I didn't know it would jerk so much in my hands."

Jack's face heated up as anger continued to rise within him. The odds of Theo and Orin finding a replacement for Vincent in a timely fashion were next to nothing, and Jack wasn't about to be in charge of a Domus that had no healer since not every client was going to choose murder as a pastime. What was he going to do, keep a steady stream of kidnapped brats coming in and bury them each in a mass grave whenever a client was done with one?

He stepped closer to Giselle and put his hands on her shoulders in a gesture of mock tenderness. "You've been a very bad girl."

She nodded but didn't speak.

"I don't have any use for bad girls."

Her head jerked up in alarm, but it was too late for her. Jack gripped her neck in both hands and squeezed tight, his fingers digging into her soft flesh so hard his joints hurt. She kicked and struggled against him for only a minute or two before her body went slack and he released her.

She crumpled to the floor in a lifeless heap. Jack swayed as a spike of pain arced through his head where Randy had hit him.

Jack set his sights on the door and staggered toward it. *Randy,* he thought as he arrived in the hallway, *I'm going to kill you. And I'm going to love every minute of it.*

---

JOE AND Bald Man, who introduced himself as Larry once a white-faced Joe came back with Lily, explained that they'd been duped into working at the Domus and weren't allowed to leave.

Larry had been a delivery driver and shuttled food and other supplies to the Domus for Troy. At the time he'd thought the Domus was just "a private club for rich snots."

"Just shows what I knew," Larry said, his tone oozing bitterness.

Joe, on the other hand, was an electrician Troy had called in when some wiring in the building needed updated. Both he and Larry had been roped into caring for the children who were brought here.

"Why didn't you try to get out?" Adrian asked, hardly believing that two grown men would choose to stay in a place like this.

Joe's face turned even whiter. "Troy had us microchipped like a couple of dogs. Anywhere we go, he knows. And there was a third guy who left against Troy's orders. Farley caught him, and Troy made us all watch while Farley..."

"We don't need to talk about that now," Larry said, cutting him off. "You two are absolutely sure Troy and Farley are dead?"

"Troy is, at least," Joe said, casting a wary glance in the direction of the door. "I had to step around him to get into the suite."

"And Farley?"

"He was shot in Troy's office," Adrian said. "I'd swear it before a judge."

"Lady, I sure hope you're right." Larry cleared his throat and turned to the children. "Hey. Listen up, all of you."

Every prisoner turned his or her head to face the man. It was eerie seeing them act as one, as if they only had one mind between them.

The fact that the men in charge of the children were actually going to work with her and Randy seemed too good to be true. Part of Adrian wondered if it was some kind of trap they were traipsing into like a couple of blind fools.

Larry continued. "We're all going to take a trip outside, okay? Now we need you all to be very quiet so we can leave without anyone hearing us..."

Joe nervously sidled up beside Adrian and Randy and dropped his voice while Larry went on. "I'm glad the creeps are dead."

"That seems to be a common sentiment," Randy mused.

"We're stuck with these kids pretty much twenty-four seven. Some of the things I've seen...it gives me nightmares."

"I hear you," Adrian said. She looked back to the thirty-odd children, who were obediently arranging themselves into two single-file lines.

"Do you have weapons?" Randy asked Joe.

He shook his head. "I wish. Like I said, we're basically just babysitters. Who'd have thought a guy like me would end up watching kids all day?" His hollow laugh conveyed no humor.

"No offense," Randy said, "but it seems strange that Troy would have hired men for this line of work."

A shrug. "Whenever a new kid gets sent here, they tend to fight back before what's done to them breaks them down. Troy thought we'd be tough enough to handle them. But some days I wonder..."

Randy frowned and scanned the room's many occupants. "Not to change the subject, but if everyone's accounted for, we'd better get going. Joe, I'll take the lead with you, and Adrian and Larry can bring up the rear. Got it?"

A wide-eyed girl a few years younger than Lily cast her gaze up at Larry, whose bald head now glistened with sweat. "Mister Larry? Where are we going?"

The man got down on one knee to be at her level, and Adrian was surprised to see affection in his eyes. "I said we're all going outside. Remember?"

"Outside?" The child's brow creased and she looked to the floor.

Larry took her small hand and squeezed it. "It'll be all right. Just stick with the group, okay?"

The child nodded, her eyes full of uncertainty, and Adrian's heart broke anew. These children would have to undergo years of therapy once this was all behind them. Would it be possible for them to ever be normal again?

*Maybe I don't want to know the answer to that.*

She and Larry took their places at the end of the line of children, and Randy opened the door, swept the outside corridor with his gaze, and beckoned for them all to follow.

Adrian's pulse sounded like a bass drum in her ears. Some of the children fidgeted while they spilled out of the dormitory, and the boy standing directly in front of her twisted his head around and gave Adrian an accusing stare as if demanding to know why his daily routine was changing.

Once everyone gathered in the hallway, Randy lowered his voice. "Remember to stick together, okay? We don't want to lose anyone."

How ironic. They'd already lost Vincent.

Randy and Joe started walking again, and the two lines of children followed. *It's going to be okay,* Adrian thought as hope surged in her chest. *We're all going to be okay.*

She walked straight into the back of the boy in front of her when the line gave a sudden halt after rounding a corner.

She lifted her head, and all hope died.

Jack stood in front of the entrance to the stairwell, his dishwater-blond hair in disarray and his eyes shot through with red lines. For the first time ever Adrian saw the true evil that lay behind them.

"Hello, Jack," Randy said, appearing strangely calm. "I see you're awake."

"Don't act friendly with me," Jack spat. "I'm in charge here now that Troy's dead." His gaze flicked to Joe. "What the hell are you doing?"

Without warning, Joe brought a fist back and slammed it into Randy's face. Adrian brought a hand to her mouth to stifle a cry. "No, don't!"

Randy brought his hands up to block another blow.

"They made us do this!" Joe wailed for Jack's benefit. "They threatened to kill us if we didn't leave with the children!"

"Liar!" Adrian screamed. "You're just a coward!"

Jack was already moving in to join the fray, and Adrian and Larry shoved through the dispersing lines of children to aid Randy, who wouldn't be able to fight off two assailants on his own.

Assuming Larry wouldn't turn on them as well.

Randy planted a blow on Joe's face, sending him to the floor. No sooner had Joe curled up and put his face in his hands when Jack started on Randy with as much gusto.

"What should I do?" Adrian whispered to Larry.

Ardor shined in the man's eyes. "Take as many as you can with you before the kids get hurt. There's another stairwell you can take."

Adrian grabbed the hands of the two nearest children and practically had to drag them in order to come with her. "Come on, come on," she panted, looking from the boy on her left to the girl on her right. "Let's get out of here."

She retreated the way they'd come and turned down a different corridor, then eyed the stairwell Larry had mentioned. "We're going this way."

She shoved the children through the door ahead of her and urged them upward. When they made it to the next floor, she peered out the door first, saw that the coast was clear, and dashed into the first floor hallway, through the lobby, past the lifeless Vincent, and finally through the door.

They arrived in the parking lot. "Stay *right here*," Adrian said, pointing at a random spot in the gravel that she hoped was a sufficient distance away from the building. "I'll be right back."

Adrian dashed back into the Domus and down to the basement, then drew up short when she reached the group of remaining children. Larry was busy putting the injured Joe out of commission by tying him up with strips of torn sheet. Randy and Jack, however, were still fighting. Even though Adrian's gut told her to hurry up and run with more of the children, she couldn't help but watch the two-man battle unfold.

Enraged desperation had entered Jack's bloodshot eyes. It seemed he was teetering on the edge of a breakdown. He kicked at Randy's shins, dodged Randy's fist that came flying at his head, and managed to plant a blow on Randy's already-swollen cheek, but neither man gained the upper hand.

"Stand down," Randy hissed through clenched teeth as he tried to grab Jack's arm. Blood glistened at the corner of his mouth. "A smart man would realize he's outnumbered."

"I'm not outnumbered!" Jack screamed. "I have friends you can't even see!"

Adrian watched, mesmerized, as the men grunted and huffed. Larry, now finished tying up his cowardly coworker, crept up behind Jack, hooked an arm around his neck, and dragged him to the floor.

His face already bruising, Randy pinned Jack's legs in place. Jack continued to flail like a beached fish that needed to be put out of its misery. "I hate you!" he moaned. "I hate all of you! You were supposed to *help* me!"

*He's raving mad.* Who did Jack think he was talking to?

Shaking her head, Adrian got the attention of two more children and herded them toward the other stairwell.

"I wonder why Giselle hasn't come to see what's up," she heard Larry say behind her.

"Giselle's dead!" Jack screamed from the floor. "I crushed her stupid throat!"

Bile worked its way up into Adrian's mouth as she pictured the blonde sitting behind the counter chewing her gum, but she forced it back down. *You reap what you sow.*

She brought the third and fourth children outside into the light. The first two stood where she'd left them, looking frightened. "I should stay here with them," she murmured to herself, realizing that like the children she'd birthed, the four she'd taken from the basement consisted of two girls and two boys. She may not have shown love to her flesh and blood, but she could show love to these so they'd know they weren't alone.

"Come on, let's sit over here," she said, gesturing for them to follow her to the front edge of the lot. They sat down in the shade of the evergreens, and the children obediently arranged themselves beside her. "What are your names?"

"Ashlynn," said one.

"Ellie," said another.

The boys were Jacob and Eric.

"And I'm Adrian," she said when they finished introducing themselves.

"What's happening?" asked the black-haired boy named Eric.

"Good things." *I hope.*

Eventually Randy and Larry emerged from around the side of the building with the rest of the children.

"That's all of them?" Adrian asked, rising from the ground.

Randy nodded. "We passed a few guests in the upstairs hallway."

"They didn't try to stop you?"

"Nope. Oddly enough, I think they were afraid of me. It must have been my face. Those two downstairs got me good."

Adrian found she wasn't surprised. "So what now?

Randy prodded a tentative finger at his swollen cheek. "We wait."

So wait, they did. Adrian leaned against the side of a Toyota and closed her eyes, relishing the sensation of sunlight on her skin. She didn't know how many days it had been since she'd been outside in the open air to see the trees and birds and sky above. It felt like a century.

After a while—an hour, perhaps, though Adrian wasn't sure— a distant wail rose through the trees, causing a flock of birds to scatter into the air. *Sirens.*

Her face broke into a grin.

"Bobby Roland," Randy said to the sky, "I think I could kiss you."

# 38

BOBBY RODE shotgun in a police cruiser as he gave directions to the stern-faced officer sitting behind the wheel, adrenaline surging through him like a tide.

Upon law enforcement's arrival at the Kwik Stop, Bobby had informed them that a metal gate guarded the lane leading to the Domus. In the present, Bobby kept his eyes peeled as he sought a glimpse of white through the trees. "It should be coming up soon," Bobby said. "On the right."

The officer, who had introduced himself only as Madsen, radioed this information to the other vehicles in their entourage.

Bobby's heart leapt into his throat as the next bend in the road straightened out. "There it is."

Madsen jerked the cruiser onto the shoulder and silenced the siren. "You're going to have to sit tight," he said.

"I understand."

The armored rescue vehicle that had been traveling behind them parked in front of the gate. Half a dozen men dressed in armored gear spilled out, ran to the gate, and shoved their full weight against it, forcing it open.

Bobby watched as the men shouted something to each other and piled back into their vehicle. "I didn't know getting in would be that easy."

Madsen gave a hollow laugh as the armored vehicle proceeded up the gravel lane, followed by another cruiser. Two ambulances brought up the rear. "Nothing about this is going to be easy, kid. If everything you've said is true, we've got quite a big problem on our hands."

After forty minutes came and went, the radio crackled to life. "10-78 and 10-79."

"Is it safe to proceed?" Madsen responded.

"Ten-four. And we're going to need more transport."

"What?"

"We don't have enough room for all of them, sir."

Madsen muttered something under his breath and threw the cruiser into gear before turning down the lane. After several minutes it opened out into the parking lot, where uniformed men were shoving Jack into the back of the other cruiser. Several other handcuffed individuals under close supervision sulked close by as they waited their turns to be hauled away.

Randy and Adrian stood off to one side speaking to another officer who was jotting down notes. Paramedics were checking each of the children, who appeared to be unharmed.

The Spirit spoke loud and clear into Bobby's heart. *Well done.*

Bobby grinned.

"Stay here," Madsen ordered, then climbed out of the cruiser. Bobby watched him stride over to the officer who drove the other cruiser.

"Okay," Bobby whispered. "So if my premonitions are really gone, how do I get them back?"

One word floated into his thoughts: *Kevin.*

Of course. Kevin was a healer. He'd be able to restore Bobby's and Randy's respective abilities with nothing more than the touch of a finger, and all would be well.

Bobby looked out the window once more to observe the small crowd amassed in front of the Domus. To think that all of those children were free because Jack enlisted someone to kidnap Adrian. *Talk about silver linings.*

As he started counting the number of children and young adults, he realized someone was missing. Vincent and his black aura did not appear among the throng.

Bobby was out of the car and running before common sense told him to stay put.

"Where's Vincent?" he panted as he came up to Randy's side, effectively interrupting his conversation with the officer. Rivulets of blood had dried on Randy's left arm and his cheek was swollen, but since Randy didn't have any apparent open wounds, Bobby guessed the blood belonged to someone else.

The look of sorrow that entered Randy's hazel eyes told him all he needed to know.

Bobby felt as though he'd been punched in the gut. Vincent couldn't be dead. He needed help, and Bobby was going to give it to him. "What happened?" he asked, his voice cracking.

"As I was just telling Officer Ortega here," Randy said in a solemn tone, "I'd pretended that I was going to shoot Vincent if the receptionist didn't let us pass. She picked up a gun from behind the counter and started firing at me but the gun must have jerked in her hands because she shot Vincent instead. He didn't even have a chance."

"Where's the receptionist now?" Bobby asked, turning back to the group of handcuffed people.

"Dead. Jack killed her for killing Vincent."

Bobby blinked back tears. He couldn't feel bad for the woman—not after what she'd done to the possessed healer. He could only pray that death had granted Vincent release from demonic bondage and that he would find peace in the arms of his Maker.

His gaze traveled to the shattered windows in the front of the building. Vincent was in there—he just knew it. He wished he could go inside and apologize to Vincent for what had happened, but corpses could not listen to the lamentations of the living.

*I'm so sorry,* Bobby thought. *And may God have mercy on your soul.*

---

THE WHOLE gang, including Adrian Pollard, Allison Mason, and little Ashley, gathered at the Jovingos' house late that night. While Ashley dozed in an armchair with a teddy bear tucked under her arm, Carly and Phil recounted their discovery of Thane's true nature and his seemingly invincible powers, and it gave Bobby the chills. The thought that the apparition that had appeared in his house and car was a flesh-and-blood human with a demonic gift was almost too much for him to handle. How could they ever defeat someone who could be listening in to their thoughts at any moment?

Unfortunately, that thought could wait.

"Bobby and I have a problem," Randy said to dispel the long silence that followed Carly and Phil's announcement. "We were healed by someone who was possessed, and it robbed us of our abilities."

Phil's face went white. He looked to Bobby. "Your premonitions?"

"Are gone. When we were trapped in that building I should have been having them left and right." Bobby paused to clear his throat and looked across the room toward Kevin, who appeared to be his usual glum self. "Kevin? I wondered if you could heal me again."

"What?" Kevin jerked out of a reverie. "Yeah, yeah, I can do that. Come here."

Bobby crossed the room, trying not to feel uncomfortable from the many sets of eyes watching him, and reached out his hand. Kevin twined his fingers around Bobby's and squeezed tight.

Bobby could feel the warmth enter him, and Kevin released his grip. "All fixed?" Kevin asked with a small smile.

"I think so, but I won't know for sure until I need to be warned about imminent danger."

"Thank the Lord you're not having one now," Phil sighed. "We've had enough 'danger' this week to last us several lifetimes."

"Can I get an amen?" Randy asked as Bobby returned to his seat.

"Amen," Carly and Lupe chorused, the latter of whom had heavy bags under her eyes.

"I guess it's my turn now." Randy stood and went to Kevin. "Thanks again for being here."

Kevin smiled. "No problem." The washed-out healer grabbed Randy's hand and released it seconds later.

Randy turned to Lupe, who occupied one end of the loveseat he'd just vacated. He opened his mouth to speak but faltered.

Lupe said something to him in Spanish, her brown eyes hopeful.

Randy's face paled.

"What is it?" Phil asked sharply.

Randy's gaze darted between Lupe and Kevin. "It didn't work."

Kevin's objection was immediate. "What do you mean, it didn't work? It's always worked!"

"Maybe you weren't touching me long enough." Randy grasped Kevin's hand tight and held on for a full minute.

Lupe spoke to Randy again, more desperately this time, in words Bobby couldn't understand.

Randy uttered a soft curse. "I don't know what's happening to me."

"To you?" Kevin goggled at him. "I don't know what's happening to *me*!"

Frankie, who had been silent for the past several minutes, spoke up. "How are we to know that Bobby is healed if Randy isn't? Could it be possible that Kevin's abilities don't heal spiritual wounds?"

Adrian, who sat quietly in a chair close to Bobby, held a dazed look in her eyes. "I've entered a madhouse," she murmured, gazing down at the carpet.

Frankie cleared his throat. "Well? How *are* we to know if Bobby is healed?"

"Easy," Bobby said, unable to look away from Kevin and Randy. "We wait and see if I have another premonition." Something fluttered in his gut. What if his premonitions really were gone for good? He would no longer be plagued with terror at inopportune moments. He would no longer panic at the thought of being unable to save people.

But how many would perish as a result?

"That could take weeks," Frankie said.

Bobby shifted uncomfortably in his chair. "I don't think that would be so bad."

A long silence fell over the group. Carly's forehead was creased, her mother sat close by in a kitchen chair looking anxious, Roger Stilgoe tapped his fingers nervously on his knees, and Frank the First was frowning in concentration.

Then Frankie stood up brusquely and went to the kitchen. "What are you doing?" Janet called after him.

"Conducting an experiment."

"Oh, God help us," Carly said, shaking her head.

Frankie reappeared with a knife the approximate length of Bobby's forearm. "Not that again!" Janet said with wide eyes. "Frankie, you put that back before you hurt yourself."

Frankie ignored her. Bobby watched in fascination as Frankie slid the blade across the palm of his hand. It drew a bead of blood that was laughably small in comparison to the size of the knife.

"Now let's see what happens," Frankie said as he stepped up to Kevin, who dutifully touched Frankie's hand. Frankie withdrew it after ten seconds and held it close to his face for examination.

The slump of Frankie's wide shoulders indicated the worst. "It didn't work."

Kevin let out a moan. "How can this even happen? What am I going to do?"

"We're going to try to be calm and figure this all out," Randy said, though his face remained pale. "Kevin, do you feel like you're under any kind of attack?"

"No. I don't think so."

Randy put a hand on his chin, deep in thought.

"It's a sacrifice," a thin voice said from the other side of the room.

Many heads turned as one. Frank the First was sitting up straight in his chair. "What did you say?" Frankie asked.

Frank the First spoke up louder this time. "It's a sacrifice. Bobby and Randy were physically healed by someone whose ability came from one of the fallen. Since this Vincent's ability was Satanic, it robbed the two of you of your spiritual gifts. It was the price you paid for being healed."

Bobby's skin prickled. "So the only way Kevin could restore my premonitions was if he gave up his gift of healing?" *That's not fair at all.*

"That's precisely what I'm saying." The elderly Frank cast a sorrowful gaze across the room. "Kevin, I'm so sorry. You wouldn't have known."

Kevin made a strangled noise in his throat.

"So this means that Bobby's gift is definitely restored?" A hopeful glint shined in Phil's eyes.

"It would seem that way," Frank said. "But only time will tell."

———◆———

EVEN THOUGH his emotions toward the woman who had birthed him were still too complicated for Bobby to describe, he allowed her to come home with him that night since she had nowhere else to go.

The short ride to the tiny rental house was fraught with awkwardness.

"You've certainly fallen in with an interesting lot," Adrian said as Bobby pulled into his driveway.

"You promise you won't tell anyone about them?"

"Of course I promise. That isn't something you just proclaim to everyone you meet."

*Boy, have you got that right.*

"You can sleep in my bed," Bobby said as he unlocked the front door a minute later. "I'll take the couch."

Tears welled up in Adrian's eyes when they crossed over the threshold into the living room. "Oh, honey, you don't have to do that."

"Yeah," he said. "I do."

Adrian turned in a full circle, taking in the modest dwelling. "It's a nice little place you've got here."

"I've only been here a few days. I like it."

"I like it, too." She gave a humorless laugh. "This whole place would fit inside the kitchen in the house I shared with Yuri."

Adrian had told him about the husband she'd left behind in Michigan. "It must have been a mansion."

"It was. But you know what? It was just a building. Now this little house here? It could be a home."

# 39

THE NEXT day Bobby helped Adrian track down her disintegrating Ford Escort, which had been towed away from the parking lot in which she'd left it prior to her being abducted.

"You drove that here all the way from Michigan?" Bobby asked as he stared at the giant patches of rust overtaking the flaking teal paint.

"It got me to where I needed to go." Adrian smiled.

They arranged for the Escort to be taken to a garage for repair and then returned to Bobby's house, and Bobby set about preparing lunch for the two of them. "I hope you like bagels," Bobby said while Adrian sat at the card table, her brow furrowed in thought.

She jerked her head up. "Honey, you make whatever you like."

So Bobby got out two bagels, divided them in half, and spread mayonnaise inside each one before stacking ham, turkey, roast beef, tomato, onion, and lettuce into them.

He set one in front of Adrian and sat down across from her.

"So what now?" he asked.

"I'm not sure."

"Are you going back to Michigan?"

She pursed her lips. "There's nothing for me there other than your two youngest siblings. I'm sure Yuri has already taken steps to divorce me."

"Why did you marry him in the first place?"

Adrian took a bite of her bagel sandwich, chewed, and swallowed. "Because I thought he cared. And he did care, but not in the way I thought. I don't think he loved me at all. He only wanted someone to control and to give him pleasure."

Bobby's face heated up in embarrassment.

"I shouldn't have said that," Adrian said as she cast her gaze down at the table.

"No, no, that's okay. You're just being honest."

"Boy, am I." Adrian regarded him again with a tilted head. "I'm proud of you, Bobby. For helping set those people at the lodge free. And for not rejecting me even though I deserve it."

Bobby nodded, unsure of what to say, so he just said, "Thanks."

They consumed the remainder of their lunch in silence. Bobby opened his mouth to ask Adrian if she had anything in mind for the rest of the day but a surge of anxiety chased the words away.

The image of Adrian lying dead on the ground flashed through his mind.

His chest tightened.

His premonitions had indeed returned.

Adrian pushed back her plate and sighed. "Oh, what am I going to do? I can't just leave now that I've found you."

"You left the other ones." Bobby's voice sounded far away as if it belonged to someone else.

Her cheeks flushed pink. "They didn't accept me."

"Maybe they will when they're older."

"Oh, I hope you're right."

The sense of impending doom pulsed stronger in Bobby's veins. *Give me clarity*, he prayed. *I can't save anyone if I don't know what I'm supposed to do.*

The image of a park strewn with colorful banners, amusement rides, and booths of food flashed through his mind.

*What's that supposed to mean?*

"I have an idea," Adrian said.

"What's that?"

"I'll settle down for a while. Maybe a year or two. I'll get a job and get my life in order. Then you and I can make the long trip back east to visit your siblings and see if..." A shadow passed over her face. "You know."

Bobby's stomach clenched into knots at the thought of a road trip of which the sole purpose was to befriend three unhappy teen-agers he happened to be related to. "Is that a good idea?"

"I can't just forget they exist. I owe them more than that."

Bobby had to ask the one question he dreaded asking. "How could you have ever thought that abandoning four kids would be a good idea?"

Her jaw stiffened. "I don't know."

Even though he hated himself for it, tears burned in his eyes. "Do you know what it feels like to have been abandoned? To won-der if I was the one who drove you away? To be left out by my stepfamily and teased by people at school? It...it hurts." *More than words can ever describe.*

"No," Adrian said softly. "I don't."

There came a light rap on the door. Without another word, Bobby rose and pulled it open to find Phil and Carly waiting for him. "For you two to not like each other, you hang out with each other an awful lot," Bobby said in a halfhearted attempt at a joke. "Where's Allison?"

"At home praying for our safety," Phil said as he stepped past Bobby, "and Randy and Lupe have gone on a day trip to the beach in an attempt to recover from all the garbage that's been happening lately. Afternoon, Adrian."

"Safety?" Bobby's mouth felt dry.

"You know that the issue hasn't been resolved with Thane," Carly said, crossing her arms.

"I know."

"Allison, Mom, and Roger's wife think that the best thing to do right now in regard to him is to pray about it." Carly paused. "And Phil and I think you need to go see him."

"See Thane? In *person*?" The thought of confronting him made Bobby's stomach turn.

"It's to see if he can be helped. We don't have the ability to sense if he has an aura. You do."

"I don't want to do it," Bobby said, but the Spirit within whispered, *You must.*

"Is there anything you do want to do?" Phil asked, his tone sour.

"I want to sleep for about a week."

"You can do that when you're retired." Phil looked to Adrian. "Will you be okay staying here alone for a while?"

"If you don't mind, I'd prefer staying with your wife. She was too kind to me, lending me some of her clothes last night."

Phil smiled. "That's Allison for you. You remember how to get there?"

Adrian tapped on her temple. "I've got a knack for directions. I visit a place once, it's permanently recorded in here."

Bobby didn't mention that it had always been the same with him because he was instantly filled with alarm. "What, were you going to take my car? You'll stay with them until we get back, right?"

"With Allison and the others? Of course."

"You promise not to go anywhere else?"

"Sure. What's the problem?"

Bobby looked her right in the eye. It would be pointless to sugarcoat something so serious. "Because my gut is telling me that if you break that promise, you'll die."

Adrian's face paled. "I should just stay here, then?"

"You could."

Phil's eyes grew round. "This is definitely a premonition?"

Bobby nodded.

Carly bit her lip. "They say there's safety in numbers."

Adrian suddenly looked resolute. "Very well. I'll stay with Allison until you get back from visiting this...person."

"Thank you," Bobby said, but he felt little relief.

———————◆———————

BOBBY EXPECTED a defensive Thane to materialize inside Phil's car as they rode over to Arbor Villa Nursing Home, but he remained conspicuously absent.

Dread gnawed at him when the sandy brick building where Thane lived came into view. A stone fountain spilled water into a pool out front, most likely attempting to create an inviting atmosphere for those arriving to visit their loved ones.

Bobby didn't want to go in.

He went in anyway, Carly sticking close to his side. Phil brought up the rear.

The woman sitting at the front desk gave them a cheery smile. "You must be Bobby, Phil, and Carly. Nate's been expecting you."

Bobby exchanged a glance with Carly, whose face went white at the woman's words.

This wasn't good at all.

"Can we go on back, then?" Bobby asked, hoping his voice wouldn't betray his fear.

"You go right ahead! Room 39 is just down that way." She pointed, smiling. "I'm so glad to see he's getting some visitors. The poor dear doesn't seem to get them very often."

Bobby swallowed, set his shoulders straight, and strode down the hallway, his shoes making a hollow-sounding *clomp-clomp* on the tile.

"You might start seeing things," Carly whispered as they passed Room 21.

Bobby nodded, keeping his gaze fixed ahead of him. The door to Thane's room seemed to draw toward him as if it and the hallway were moving and he was standing still.

The door was closed.

As he placed a hand upon the knob, a shadow reached out and touched his mind with an icy finger.

*Be vigilant.*

The moment before Bobby pushed the door open, Phil said, "I'll go in first."

Nodding, Bobby stepped aside. Carly grabbed his hand, squeezed it, and they entered the room together behind Phil.

The gray shadows danced thicker in Bobby's mind than they ever had before.

The room appeared to be a single-person unit, judging from the sole bed occupying the space, and soothing paintings hung on the walls. Like the Domus bedroom in which he'd found Lily, the floor was tile.

It must have made for easier cleanup.

Phil planted his hands on his hips and let out an irritated sigh. "He's probably hanging out with the other residents right now," he said, eyeing the empty area by the room's only window.

Carly's expression tightened. "I guess we should wait for him. Not that I want to."

"I don't want to, either, but we have to find out if Bobby can help him or not."

The shadows pulsed, thickened...

The window provided a view of a courtyard full of shrubs and blooming flowers. While Bobby watched, red letters appeared on the glass as if written by an invisible hand.

*You don't scare me, Servant.*

Carly must have sensed that something wasn't right. "What's the matter?"

Bobby pointed at the window. "I think he's here now."

Carly and Phil turned. "Oh, crap."

Phil reached for his gun.

"Don't," Bobby said, keeping his eyes on the window. "Are we all seeing the same thing?"

"You don't scare me, Servant," Carly said.

Bobby only felt marginal relief. "Good. Phil?"

"Same."

The words vanished.

The shadows in Bobby's head didn't.

"So Thane," Bobby said, wondering precisely where the man was sitting that very moment. "I thought you wanted to be my friend."

No response.

"But now I know you just wanted to get me killed. It seems odd, though. You hoped Jack would kill me, but if you want the Servant to die so badly, why don't you do it yourself?"

A man with bloodshot eyes materialized sitting in a motorized wheelchair three feet in front of Bobby, only Bobby knew he'd been there all along. Thane had simply used his ability to alter their perceptions, hiding him from view.

It jarred Bobby to see him in this condition when Thane had appeared to him as an able-bodied man. Thane's hands were clenched into fists, not from anger but from the inability to move them. His arms were motionless like a pair of white twigs.

Bobby sensed a storm brewing inside of Thane. It was best to tread carefully.

"Do you see this?" Thane asked, his voice much thinner than that of his apparition. "I'm not even forty and have to live with the old and senile because of what happened to me."

"Then why didn't you have Graham bring Phil by to help you any of the times he visited?"

Thane's eyes stared past Bobby at Phil. "I tried to plant the idea in Graham's mind."

"But you failed?"

"*Graham* failed. He didn't want to bring anyone with him." Thane's voice grew colder with every word. "I was offered another way. My injury will be healed when the time is right."

"When I'm dead without a replacement, presumably."

"Bobby, don't!" Carly hissed.

But Bobby felt emboldened. He was onto something here, if only he could put a finger on it. "Why make other people do your dirty work, though? When Randy was the Servant, you managed to fiddle around in Graham's head and turned him into some kind of killing machine, and this time it seems like you nearly had Jack kill me. If you want to walk again and can only do that once you've killed the Servant, why haven't you done it?"

The answer blossomed in Bobby's mind like the light of a supernova. The remainder of his fear melted away from him. "If you can," he said, "kill me now."

Phil opened his mouth to object but Carly's voice drowned out anything he might have said. "Bobby, stop! You know what will happen if you—"

"You don't need to remind me." He drilled Thane with a stare so intense it was sure to cut the man open. "You can't do it, can you? If you could, I'd already be dead."

"He hurt Graham," Phil reminded him. He held his gun with the barrel aimed at the floor. Bobby hadn't seen him remove it from its holster.

"Graham wasn't under Caleb's protection." A grin spread across Bobby's face. "I am."

The terror in Carly's eyes shined even brighter. "But if Graham wasn't, we aren't, either!"

"He's not going to risk killing someone here. He can't just wish a body out of existence, and I don't think he wants cops crawling all over the place, either."

Thane's face had turned a shade of crimson.

Bobby wasn't finished. "Maybe you can't really kill anyone. After all, Graham's still alive. You just try to convince people that you can so they're afraid of you."

"Shut. Your. *Mouth.*"

"Kill me, Thane. Right now. Unless you're too chicken to do it."

"You'll regret talking to me this way." Yet despite Thane's rage, Bobby did not drop dead.

"I knew it," Bobby said, feeling so lighthearted he thought he might fly away. Carly and Phil were both gaping at him as if he had lost his mind. "Come on, guys. I've learned all I need to know."

Carly clasped her hands together. "But Bobby..."

"It was nice knowing you, Thane. It's too bad you weren't able to do what you wanted with me."

Bobby strode out of the room with his head held high, Phil and Carly at his heels.

"So we've learned that Thane has at least one weakness," Phil said once they were outside. "To be honest, I'm surprised."

"We're not going to let the creep bother us anymore," Bobby said. Right now keeping Adrian safe was the more pressing issue. The sooner he was reunited with her, the better he'd feel—now wasn't that ironic?

Phil's mouth tightened into a straight line. "He can still influence others to harm us. The man needs to be stopped before that happens."

"I know." But for as long as Bobby thought about it, he could think of no way short of ending Thane's life to stop him.

# 40

WHEN THEY reached Phil's Taurus, terror slammed into Bobby so unexpectedly that he doubled over gripping his stomach.

"Oh, no," Carly whispered as she came to his side to help. "Bobby, what is it?"

"Adrian." Fresh images of what may come tumbled through his head. "She's leaving Phil's house."

"What? Why? She promised she wouldn't go anywhere!"

"I don't know. Phil, let me take the wheel."

Phil handed Bobby the key without objection.

As Bobby pulled out onto the street, he sensed that Adrian was on the road somewhere but didn't know if she'd taken Bobby's car or if she rode with someone else.

Bobby could feel the Spirit nudging at his thoughts, guiding him on his way. He wasn't even sure where they were going until he caught sight of a crowd up ahead on the left-hand side of the road.

Colorful banners fluttered in the wind and row after row of food booths and carnival games were attended by more people than Bobby could count.

It was the Autumn Ridge Summerpalooza.

If he was too slow, it was here where Adrian Pollard would meet her end.

---

BOBBY RAN onto the festival grounds, panting like he'd run a marathon. There were so many people here already. Where could Adrian be?

He raced past a row of carnival games, nearly tripped over a little kid who'd toddled away from his parents, rounded a corner, and caught sight of Allison Mason sitting with her daughter and Janet Jovingo at a picnic table. Beverly Stilgoe ambled toward a drink booth, her back to Bobby, and Adrian strode up to a pair of unfamiliar men and started screaming at them.

"Adrian, stop!" he shouted, knowing that those to whom she spoke were the very ones who would bring about the disaster he foresaw. "Get away from them!"

---

ADRIAN HAD gotten out of the car, followed by Janet Jovingo, Beverly Stilgoe, and Allison and Ashley Mason. After the prayer session concluded, Allison had suggested they all go out somewhere, and Adrian had immediately objected based on Bobby's supposed premonition.

Beverly, a round black woman a few years older than Adrian who couldn't stop smiling, had actually frowned. "Maybe we should stay here then," she'd said. She had a slight accent. Jamaican, maybe.

Janet had nodded in agreement.

Allison had then appeared agitated. "But how do we know where you'll be in danger? Something could happen here instead of somewhere else."

That had given Adrian pause. Allison was right. How could they know for certain that the Masons' roof wasn't going to cave in? What if leaving the house actually saved Adrian's life?

Her heart raced, and she wished she hadn't left Bobby's side. She knew so little about her son. How could she even know that Bobby's "gift" was accurate? For all she knew, the man called Thane could have made Bobby imagine his premonition. Would Bobby be able to know the difference?

In the end they'd decided that they would all stick together and not leave each other's sides no matter where they went. Adrian had considered staying behind at the Masons' house but didn't want to be left alone.

"Let's go to the Summerpalooza," Beverly suggested once they settled in Allison's car. "I think we could use a little levity."

But once they strode onto the festival grounds, Adrian felt anything but cheer. Families with young children stood in lines in front of different games where the kids could win cheap prizes, teenagers walked around in groups texting and taking pictures of themselves, gray-haired citizens sat at picnic tables in the shade, and loud music broadcast from speakers filled the air.

Adrian's senses were on overload, and maybe part of that was because she had been shut away from the world for far too many days.

Allison put a gentle hand on Adrian's arm. "Adrian? Are you okay?"

Adrian shook her head. "It's too much. I shouldn't have come here. I should have just stayed behind."

Allison brushed a strand of hair out of her eyes and frowned. "Janet? Beverly? Come back here a minute."

The other two women had been standing off to one side speaking in low tones. The skinny one named Janet looked worried. "What is it?"

"I'm feeling a little overwhelmed," Adrian said, casting her gaze across the sea of people. "I'm going to find a place to sit."

She eyed an empty picnic table near a booth selling funnel cakes and planted herself on it, trying to still the shakes that had taken hold of her.

If a man named Thane had caused Bobby and his friends to see things that weren't truly there, how could Adrian know she was here at the Summerpalooza? What if she was still at Bobby's house? What if she was still locked away in a concrete hell?

*No. I'm here. I know it.*

Allison, Ashley, Janet, and Beverly took seats at the table with her. "Do you need me to get you anything?" Beverly asked. "You're looking pale."

Adrian started to object but changed her mind. "Maybe a lemonade? I have a few dollars."

Beverly waved a hand in dismissal. "Oh, don't you worry about that! I'll get drinks for everyone." The woman heaved her bulk off the picnic table seat and headed toward a drink booth across the way.

Adrian watched Beverly's receding figure. She strode past two men wearing polo shirts, khaki shorts, and sandals who lingered by another picnic table, eating hotdogs. They seemed out of place from the rest of the crowd. Maybe it was the Ray Bans they each wore, or the fact that neither appeared to be speaking. There was something strangely familiar about the two of them. One had frizzy red hair and too many freckles. She had seen him and his buddy somewhere quite recently.

Then it hit her. This was the pair that had come to the basement cell and took little Monique away.

A wave of heat washed over her as the world around her grew quieter. Her vision narrowed. All she could see was those two men, who lived in the daylight eating, drinking, and being merry while the children they bought languished in dark hells.

A hand touched her shoulder. "Adrian? What's going on?"

Her feet were moving forward as if they'd taken on lives of their own—she didn't even remember standing up. The red-haired man caught sight of her and stepped aside, thinking she was trying to pass him by.

But she wasn't about to do that. She grabbed onto the collar of his shirt and jerked him closer to her face. "You took Monique!" she screamed. "You took her, and you're going to tell me where she is!"

His face became impassive. "You've got the wrong guy, ma'am. I don't know any Monique. Now if you'll kindly let me go..."

"Oh, you don't know her? Allow me to remind you, then. She was the little brown-skinned girl stuck with me in a concrete cell, and you *bought* her!"

Someone screamed behind Adrian, but she didn't know what they were saying. All she knew was that people needed to know the truth about these two men. "These men are criminals!" she shouted. "They buy little girls so freaks can have sex with them!"

Pain shot through her side, and she looked down at herself. Crimson was spreading across her shirt. Even as she watched, a second place below her breastbone bloomed with red.

*Maybe I'm imagining it. Maybe I'm...*

---

BOBBY WATCHED, horrified, as one of the men drew a weapon out from under his shirt and fired it.

The gunshots, muffled by a silencer, quietly punched into Adrian's gut.

Stunned, she staggered back half a step, grimaced, and crumpled onto her side.

"Stop those men!" Bobby's voice sounded raw as he pointed. "They've just shot a woman!"

A man wearing a National Guard t-shirt dropped his fountain Coke to the ground and ran toward the men, who were already making a beeline toward the exit. He tackled the one who'd fired the gun while others followed suit, nabbing the shooter's accomplice.

*Too bad nobody's going to shoot* them, he thought bitterly.

Bobby rushed to Adrian's side and rolled her onto her back. Bright crimson seeped through her shirt as she trembled. Her face twisted in agony. *No. No. This can't happen. This can't happen.*

But it was happening. Bobby grabbed Adrian's hand and held it tight. "Mom?"

---

ADRIAN FORCED her eyes open. Bobby leaned over her with tears in his eyes.

The pain in her midsection was eating her alive. She couldn't bring herself to look at it now. The damage might not be so bad, but would her son really look so stricken if that were so?

"Bobby?" she managed to whisper.

"I'm here."

Her mind conjured an image of him as a newborn baby, when the doctor first placed him into her arms. He'd had a patch of black hair atop his head and rosy cheeks that made her think of a doll baby she'd had as a little girl.

Another wave of agony drove the image away. "Find Monique," she gasped. "They took her."

"I don't—"

"Just do it!"

Bobby looked bewildered. She was vaguely aware of frantic people running past him. "Okay?"

"Thank you," she whispered. "For saving me."

She drifted away on a cloud of relief.

Everything would be okay after all.

———◆———

ADRIAN STOPPED moving.

"No," Bobby breathed. A high-pitched whine hummed in his ears. "Wake up. Wake up!"

The festival grounds erupted into chaos as more onlookers caught sight of what had happened. Security rushed over to help detain the pair that had killed his mother.

*His mother.* Bobby's heart was tearing itself into pieces. It wasn't supposed to happen like this. Adrian was going to get her act together and over time they would form a bond like parents were supposed to have with their children.

"Why?" he whispered.

*She is at peace now. No harm will come to her again.*

He imagined Adrian and his father walking toward each other on the sandy shore in his mind, embracing each other like long-lost friends.

He sat back on his heels and broke down into tears.

# 41

SIX DAYS later, Bobby found himself dressed in a suit standing beneath a sweltering July sun in the Holy Trinity cemetery in Eleanor, Ohio: a town he had not set foot in for two years. He'd forgotten how oppressive the humidity could be, and he certainly didn't miss it.

Upon his arrival in town, he'd found that many things had changed during his absence. Buildings that had sat empty for years following the recession contained new businesses. The old truck stop had been revamped under new ownership. New houses went up while older ones had been torn down. Several streets had been widened, the ubiquitous potholes filled in.

The village of Iron Springs, Kentucky sat across the river, as silent and seemingly as distant as always.

Even though Adrian had been away from Eleanor for so long, her funeral service in church drew quite the crowd because apparently she'd been related to about half the people in town—something Bobby's father and stepmother had failed to tell him. After the service let out, a large chunk of the crowd dispersed to go about their own business, leaving only a handful to attend the burial.

Carly, Randy, Lupe, Phil, Allison, and Ashley had flown out to Ohio with Bobby to keep him company. Even though it made him feel awkward, Carly stood at Bobby's side holding his hand as Adrian's casket was lowered into the ground.

If someone had asked him days ago how he would feel if his birth mother died, he would have told them he'd feel nothing since she meant nothing to him.

Boy, how things had changed.

*She shouldn't have come looking for me. She'd still be alive if she'd stayed put.*

The Spirit wrapped him in a warm embrace. He hadn't quite thought about it before, but knowing that the maker of the entire universe and everything in it could touch him so personally and know him so well gave him the chills. Bobby was less than a speck of sand, but as a child of God, that speck was cherished and loved.

He started crying again. "Why did this have to happen?" he choked.

"We could all ask the same thing," Randy said.

"You might feel alone in your pain," Carly said, "but you're not. We're here for you if you ever want to talk about it, because we've all lost someone close to us."

"But that's the thing," Bobby said. "Thanks to what she did, we weren't close at all."

"She was still your mother." Randy sighed, and his eyes took on a faraway look. "My own parents were cruel, but it still tore me to pieces when they died because they were still my parents. I mourned the people they could have been, not the people they were."

Randy's words contained a note of truth. Nodding, Bobby swallowed an enormous lump in his throat and blinked back tears.

"I wasn't ready for this," Bobby murmured again, staring at the box that held the woman who had given him life.

Tears glistened in Carly's eyes. "We're never ready for the things that change us the most."

Bobby gave a wordless nod. As it turned out, Adrian's death had not been in vain. The men who killed her had been arrested and interrogated, and the illegal brothel they'd run had been found, its occupants freed. Though names had not been released to the media, Bobby knew in his heart that the Monique with whom Adrian had been imprisoned was one of them.

Another silver lining.

When the funeral concluded, Bobby and his new "family" drifted off to one side to talk amongst themselves.

"So what now?" Phil asked, looking stoic in contrast to Randy, who had quietly wept with Bobby throughout the whole service.

Bobby looked Phil right in the eye. "I'm going to get in shape. If I'd been faster, Adrian might still be alive."

"Remember what I said about not thinking about the things that might have been," Randy warned, dabbing a Kleenex at his face.

"I know. But I'll need to save other people. I can't fail them, too." *Like Vincent.*

Phil cleared his throat. "I can help you come up with an exercise regimen as soon as we get back to Autumn Ridge."

"Thanks."

"Bobby?"

Charlotte and Jonas were walking toward them. Charlotte had her thick brown hair brushed out and partly fastened back with a silver barrette, and she wore a blue skirt and white blouse, unlike the black garb of many of the other funeral-goers.

Jonas wore a suit and tie and looked as though he had no idea what to say.

"Do you all want to go out for lunch?" Charlotte asked. "Or you can all come back to our place and eat there instead."

Everyone looked to Bobby. He supposed it made sense that the decision would fall solely on him. "I guess we can go out," he said. "I thought I saw a new bagel shop when we came into town."

Charlotte smiled. "Bagels it is, then."

Carly took Bobby's hand again as they walked toward the parked rental car. She gave him a sidelong glance. "You know," she

364 | J.S. BAILEY

said, "things may be hard for you now. But they get better in time. I promise."

---

NATHANIEL BAGDASARIAN sat by the window in his room at Arbor Villa glaring at a butterfly flexing its wings on one of the flowers in the courtyard.

Something needed to change.

Soon.

But he had no way of changing it on his own.

"Did you wish to speak to me?"

Thane moved his tongue so the sensor in his piercing would turn the chair a few degrees to the right. An emaciated, yellow-eyed man dressed in rags stood just feet away from him.

Though his companion had never appeared in such a way before, Thane knew exactly who it was without asking. "They found me out."

"And then you sang like a bird. It's your own foolishness that let them know you exist. If you'd stayed under the radar, they would know nothing about you."

Thane tightened his jaw.

His plan to use Jack Willard to kill Bobby Roland had failed, just as the plan involving Graham Willard and Randy Bellison had failed. He could find some other fool to bring about the young Servant's end, but how great would be his chances of success? Based on what had happened twice now, very little.

*Bobby Roland, if you only knew how much I hate you.*

Bobby was the one who'd saved Randy from Graham. Thane had been too busy watching through Graham's eyes to realize that Bobby had come onto the scene and called the cops.

Another weakness on Thane's part. He'd been so close to fulfilling his work, only to have it snatched away like leaves in the wind.

"I'd like to make a new deal with you," Thane said.

"A new deal?" His companion let out a soft chuckle. "Let's hear it, then."

"Restore my body. Now."

The yellow-eyed man clucked his tongue. "Getting impatient, are we?"

"My gift can only do so much. I can't keep relying on fools to do my work for me." *I'd much rather do it myself.*

A grin spread across his companion's face. "What would I get in return?"

"If I fail to complete my task? My life."

"Go on."

"If I don't do it by the end of the year, take me away from all this."

"You wish to forfeit your life?"

"This *is* no life."

His companion pondered this. "I'll consider it."

With that, he was gone.

Thane looked down at his left hand, which like the right was clenched tightly in his lap. He stared long and hard at white fingers that rarely saw the sun. His old life—when he'd been as normal as the next person—was so far gone it felt like a half-remembered dream.

He kept staring at his fingers—the ones that used to grasp and flex and point. While he watched, his index finger twitched.

Thane's pulse quickened. Was it possible?

It twitched again. A long-forgotten sensation traveled from the nail up to the knuckle: the sense of touch.

One by one, the other fingers on that hand regained feeling. Barely believing what he saw, Thane's eyes filled with tears as he spread his fingers wide.

"Thank you for this," Thane said as the sensation of life crept up his arm and into his shoulder.

Then his face twisted into a sardonic grin.

He had a mission to complete.

It was best he got started.

Bobby's story continues in

# SURRENDER

# DEAR READER

Thank you for taking the time to read *Sacrifice: The Chronicles of Servitude Book 2.*

If you enjoyed Bobby Roland's second full-length adventure, would you consider sharing your thoughts with other readers by leaving a short review on the retailer site or sites of your choice? Reviews can make or break a novel's success by helping other readers choose what to read next. They also increase a novel's visibility and credibility. The more positive reviews a novel has, the more likely the newbie reader will take a chance on it.

Remember, a review doesn't have to be long. "I really enjoyed this book," will work, for example, or "This wasn't the book for me."

Be sure to stop by *www.jsbaileywrites.com* for news about events and upcoming releases, and catch up with my antics on Twitter *@jsbailey_author* or Facebook at *www.facebook.com/jsbaileywrites*. I look forward to hearing from you!

~ J. S. Bailey

## ACKNOWLEDGMENTS

To those who helped turn a mess of a manuscript into a novel—Kelsey Keating, Katie Cross, Catherine Jones Payne, Christabel Barry, and Stephanie Karfelt—thank you.

# ABOUT THE AUTHOR

As a child, J.S. Bailey escaped to fantastic worlds through the magic of books and began to write as soon as she could pick up a pen. She dabbled in writing science fiction until she discovered supernatural suspense novels and decided to write her own. Today, her stories focus on unassuming characters who are thrown into terrifying situations, which may or may not involve ghosts, demons, and evil old men. She believes that good should always triumph in the end. She lives with her husband in Cincinnati, Ohio.